D0973923

THE POWER OF CAI

The hair on her nape prickled; it was the only tip-off she had before a beefy arm went around her neck. Training took over. Cai squatted and leaned forward, sliding her hand between her throat and the arm as she stepped sideways. Almost in the same motion, she brought her elbow back into her attacker's midsection, using the full force of her body to add all the power she could. She heard an *oomph,* but didn't hesitate.

Turning, she hooked her foot behind his leg and pushed. Since he was already off-balance, the man went down like a polar bear on wet ice. Cai was about to take him out of the equation indefinitely when she was wrapped in a hug. Though she had no clue how she knew, she was sure it was Jake. His arms were around her.

The man she'd put on the floor began to stand, and she tried to get free. "Down, killer," her *recep* said, mouth near her ear. She thought he might be laughing.

Patti O'Shea

THE POWER OF TWO

LOVE SPELL   NEW YORK CITY

LOVE SPELL®

November 2004

Published by

Dorchester Publishing Co., Inc.
200 Madison Avenue
New York, NY 10016

ISBN 0-505-52593-3

Visit us on the web at www.dorchesterpub.com.

For Theresa Monsey and Melissa Lynn Copeland who both went above and beyond. Thank you.

To Maria Hammon for her unfailing support and willingness to help.

To Jenny Low, Jennifer Minnick, Arianna, and the gang at TDD and PTN. Every now and then we're lucky and find a group of people who offer us friendship and encouragement. I've been fortunate enough to be part of two groups like this. Y'all are the best!

And finally, thanks to Susan Grant, Kathleen Nance, and Liz Maverick. It was fun sharing the ride with you.

THE POWER OF TWO

Chapter One

Cai wished this mission would hurry up and end. Normally, she wasn't so impatient—well, at least not when it came to her job—but today was different. Her gaze slid over to the notes at her elbow. Squinting a little, she tried to decipher the words. It didn't help. Her handwriting was abysmal.

She forced her eyes back to her console. Just because Jake blocked her out right now didn't mean she could stop monitoring the systems. Besides, she didn't need to read her notes to know what they said. The info was seared into her brain. Her heel tapped against the footrest of the chair, an outward sign of how antsy she felt. She was lucky to work from her rooms in the Bachelor Officers' Quarters because if anyone saw her jitters, she'd be facing questions.

A holounit on the corner of her station played a newscast from the area closest to where the team had inserted. Most of the time these holocasts didn't provide any useful data, but now and then Cai struck gold. So far, nothing they'd aired had any bearing on the mission, and she swiveled away.

Thanks to her nanoprobes, it took only a fraction of a second to run through the 153 systems to which she had access. Nothing seemed out of the ordinary. This was just a standard mission, similar to dozens of others Jake and his Special Forces team had been assigned. Of course, nothing was routine in their line of work, but this operation came about as close as it could: go in, destroy something, get out. Piece of cake.

She marked Jake's position, decided his team wasn't done setting the destabilizers yet, and sighed. Putting her hand on her knee, she pressed downward, trying to stop the drumming of her foot. She needed to relax; the team was well within the normal time frame for this phase of the assignment.

Easier said than done. She wanted it over and the guys safely extracted so she could return her attention to what she'd found this morning. Time was short, and while she'd already set plans in motion, there was more she wanted to do. This had to be as airtight as she could make it; she couldn't lose this chance to get some questions answered about her missing parents.

Her gaze traveled around the room and she frowned. What would her mom and dad say if they saw this place? She scanned her quarters with fresh eyes and realized her parents would be appalled that she'd done nothing to personalize it except hang her favorite family holo. She stared at the image, her heart twisting.

Her father looked so strong and handsome. His ash-blond hair was pulled back in a queue, and for once he wasn't wearing a ratty T-shirt. Her mom's happy smile beamed from the picture. She was gorgeous enough to turn heads, but she'd always rolled her eyes at male attention. Her dark hair was cropped to shoulder length, and although she was only half Vietnamese, there was little sign of her European heritage.

Then there was her, Cai, their Martian child. She looked

like an alien between these two beautiful people. If she didn't clearly share traits with both of them, she'd wonder if they'd somehow gotten the wrong baby. Her parents, though, hadn't cared about her gawkiness. It didn't show in the holo, but they both had a hand resting on her back, offering her their unconditional love and support. Too bad she'd been too young and spoiled at the time to appreciate it.

A change in light drew her attention to her station, and with a sigh, Cai blinked to clear her vision. She had to keep her mind on the job.

It would be easier to focus, though, if Jake weren't shutting her out. She understood why. Attaching those destabs was tricky work, and he couldn't concentrate on something so intricate while his implant was linked to hers. Unfortunately, there was no way to stop their minds from brushing without completely closing the connection.

When she realized her eyes had drifted to her family's holo again, she turned so that she couldn't see it. The chair moved with her, its function to keep her body in an ergonomically correct position. Sometimes she found it more of an irritation than a help. Her fingers tapped on her knee and she sighed again. Although it seemed like ages had passed, a glance at the clock said otherwise.

"Come on, come on," she whispered.

She started another scan—more for something to do than anything else. Her leg stopped shaking midbounce and she swung the chair closer to the console. It couldn't be. No way.

Where the hell had *they* come from? *Wreckers.*

Immediately, she called up her hover displays. She didn't like to use them because they gave her a headache, but she needed every available tool. The three streams of data floated in midair about a foot in front of her, giving additional visual info. She instructed one of her assets to scan deeper, to verify the findings, but she wasn't wrong. This was no longer a nice, routine mission.

Jake. No response. She tried again, putting more energy behind the mental call, but still nothing. *Damn.* Sometimes she could break through the barrier, and sometimes she couldn't. This would be one of the times he had the wall solid.

Because their nanoprobes were in sync, Cai could track him on a dozen different systems even if no one else could; the rest of the team was impossible for her to locate. She hoped they were in close proximity, because they were going to have to move fast. Quickly, carefully, she began plotting escape routes. There were many possibilities, but she narrowed them down to the top three, ready to pass the information along when Jake reopened the link.

"Come on," she urged again, but her mood was different. From the time their neural implants had been inserted five years ago, she and Jake had used them to talk even when there was no mission. They'd become friends.

Despite the fact that he didn't know she was human.

Cai leaned forward, every muscle in her body tense as she monitored the situation. The wreckers kept getting closer. She identified ten of them moving in a pincer formation. If Jake didn't hurry and contact her, his team would be surrounded. And no one, not even Special Forces, wanted to fight wreckers.

To refresh her memory, she tapped into a system for info. Cybernetic body armor was a United Colonies of Earth military invention. No surprise there. But the UCE had abandoned experiments with it about twenty years ago. Not only did the stuff cost a fortune, but it permanently damaged the person using it. The segments had to be surgically attached, and they were so heavy that if not for the nanocomputers imbedded in the composite material, whoever wore it would be unable to move. It had been ruled too unnatural for UCE purposes.

Use of the armor hadn't ended, though. About ten years ago, some mercenaries had begun sporting it. The wreckers. Cai frowned. The armor was a tremendous advantage. Those with the shielding were stronger, faster, and harder to kill than men who were without. Like Jake's team.

This wasn't the only bad news. The personality type willing to be physically altered didn't ever concede fights. These hard-core badasses wanted to be nearly indestructible no matter the cost, and they were downright nasty.

As the distance between them and Jake narrowed, Cai adjusted the routes she'd chosen to get the men out. She bit her lip and reminded herself to breathe. She'd lived through tougher jams than this with the team, even if it was only through her connection with Jake.

By the time she felt a slight glimmer in her head, she was completely calm—although the situation was worse. *Jake?*

The barrier crumbled and the neural pathway opened. The nanoprobes were meant to help their two brains process incredible amounts of data in microseconds, so his knowledge of the situation was equal to hers almost immediately. He now had all the possible ways out of the trap.

You sure there are ten of them?

Confidence level is about 90 percent. There could be more. You know if there are several bunched together I'd only get one hit.

Jake sent her the info on which route he'd chosen. Communicating, with or without words, was automatic for them now. Cai began to plan contingencies from the new course just in case. *Never, ever underestimate a wrecker.* This might be her first encounter with one, but the lesson had been drilled into her during training.

Cai moved the systems that weren't a help into the background so she could concentrate fully on those providing useful data. Now that their link was completely open, it was almost as if she and Jake shared a mind. He knew the wreckers were moving faster the moment she did.

His men picked up their pace and the mercenaries began to lag behind. Which puzzled her. When it came to speed, strength, and night vision, the Special Forces team finished second best. But Frankenstein's army wasn't catching up. Why? These weren't mindless automatons; they were men or women with cybernetic enhancements. Even if they'd been hired more for their willingness to convert than for brain power, she doubted that all ten together had the IQ of a slab of granite.

She ordered deeper scans on all systems. There had to be a reason for their actions, but nothing she received gave her answers. *Hmm.* One of the resources was busy. She used some technical finesse to get bumped to the top of the priority list.

When she still didn't find anything, she wondered if the wreckers were simply unaware they were chasing a Special Forces unit that could vanish at a moment's notice. That was feasible. The other possibility was that they knew, but had been ordered to remove the intruders from only a certain zone. That was a bit more likely—but only if the wreckers' employers didn't know why the team had made this foray halfway across the world.

Though Cai continued to have a sense that something was off, she finally had to admit it looked like Jake's team was going to escape. Since the next step would be getting them home, she began to plot paths from their current location to the extraction point. The window for pickup was good, but they were going to have to hurry to get there.

Cai, I need you.

Why aren't you moving?

Force field.

I'm not picking up a force field on any system.

It's here.

Methodically, she checked her data sources to look specifically for power output, but she didn't see anything. Without being able to find it, she couldn't tell him how far the field extended or give Jake a course around it. No wonder the robowarriors hadn't chased very hard.

Is there any way you can send me an energy signature? she asked. Without that, she'd never be able to locate the field.

Hang on.

She didn't realize he'd meant it literally until her body jerked. *Idiot.* He'd deliberately pushed himself into the power field, shocking them both. Bumping into the barrier meant a quick zap and light pain, but immersion in the field long enough for her to read it was another story. For her to feel pain as strongly as she had, he must be hurting like hell.

Got it? He sounded tight.

I'm processing. It took a couple more seconds before she had the systems scanning the new sig. Cai groaned. This was bad. The thing was enormous. *Do you see?*

Yeah. Shit. Give me some alternatives.

She did, but none of the routes was great.

There's nothing better?

I'll keep trying, but get moving, cowboy.

He was mentally sluggish from the shock, she realized, and that wouldn't help the situation. She had no way to judge his physical condition, but she was suddenly concerned about how badly he was hurt. Though she wanted to, she didn't ask how he was—he'd deny or downplay the extent of his injuries, and neither of them had the time to spare. Besides, discussing it wouldn't change the facts. He could hand off command if he needed to, but there was no one else linked to her.

Cai did a sweep. Help wouldn't be coming any time soon from the extraction unit. The transport wasn't yet showing up on her short-range scans. Where the hell were they?

The wreckers narrowed the distance between them and Jake's squad, but it was like they were playing a game. They hung back enough to let her guys think they were getting clear, but then they'd increase the pace again. It was strange: wreckers loved to kick ass, not do a cat-and-mouse routine. She factored this odd behavior into all the different probabilities she was running.

All her explanations were shot to hell in a heartbeat.

Jake, another energy wall is up at an angle to the first. They're trying to hem you in.

Got it. Give me some options besides a shoot 'em up.

Avoiding that doesn't look likely right now.

Yeah. His grimness came through loud and clear.

There had to be something she could do. Still no transport. She wanted to alert the missing crew to fly in and provide support, but she couldn't contact them. She passed the news along to Jake and was rewarded with a brief but colorful opinion on the absence of the extraction squad.

She understood his frustration. Jake was responsible for bringing all these men home, and he took his duty very seriously. Where was his ride?

For an endless moment, she lost sight of the wreckers. When she picked them up again, they'd changed position. It wasn't any kind of attack formation she'd ever seen, but . . .

Yeah, if another wall is coming, it makes sense, Jake said, confirming her thought. *Can you see anything?*

No, nothing. Someone has a good tech on payroll, and my equipment isn't up to the task.

Find some equipment that can handle it, ASAP.

She was out of resources. Short of causing an international incident by using the Global Defense Network to blast these wreckers to hell, there wasn't much she could do. Except—

The third wall appeared.

Now her guys were trapped.

Cai reached out with her probe and gave a command. The 154th system in her arsenal came online. She'd had it for only two days and hadn't used it with the other computers, but she felt confident it would fall into line for her. She *was* the queen of the tech-geeks, after all.

For once, it was a good thing.

The system was incredibly powerful; she'd nicknamed it the Monster because that sounded cooler than ADOK, its real acronym.

As she began to sync with it, the nanoprobes in her brain seemed to rattle. Which wasn't possible. Each implant was the size of a single virus, hardly something she'd feel shaking in her head.

What's wrong?

Oh, crap. He'd felt it? *I'm fine. Don't worry about me.* He had other things to be concerned about. Like the fact that wreckers were closing in on him.

If you're okay, get your circuits smoking. We're in deep shit here, sweetheart, he complained.

She winced slightly at his reference to her circuits, but she'd been ignoring similar comments for years. The endearment, however, she cherished—it was a sign of their friendship. He'd started calling her sweetheart after they'd been linked for only a few months and that was when she'd known they really were a team, that he really did value her help.

Shaking off the memory, Cai turned her attention back to ADOK. This time she disregarded the rumble in her head. The guys needed her to get them out of this mess, and she could tolerate the discomfort. Gripping her chair arms tightly, she forced her mind into alignment. A sharp pain stabbed through her, then disappeared.

Hello, Monster, she thought with satisfaction.

The joy faded quickly. She'd hoped this system would be able to come up with a better alternative than a firefight, but it didn't. It did, however, project to the second how long the team had before they were within range of the mercenaries' armaments.

She felt helpless. All the technology, all the information at her fingertips, and it might come down to which squad could outshoot the other. And even though the Special

Forces team outnumbered its foes fourteen to ten, the wreckers always had the advantage.

Cai, we have a situation here.

She knew time had run out. Jake's men were taking fire. And that damn third force field was pinning them in, making them easy targets. There were going to be casualties—she knew that intellectually, even if her heart rebelled at the knowledge. But it was the idea of losing Jake, her only friend, that cut deepest.

Okay, so there wasn't a path that would waltz the team out of there; she had to come up with another way to get them clear. There had to be *something*. It was a matter of ingenuity. No way was she going to give up this easily.

Shoving her preconceived notions out of the way, Cai expanded her probe's link to the Monster. There came another roaring in her head, but she tuned it out. Maybe if she were open to other possibilities than direct escape routes, she could discover a solution. For an endless moment, there was nothing. Then something brushed her mind.

Not good, not bad. Not Jake—it was . . . alien.

Holding on to her chair more firmly, Cai beat back the fear. There wasn't a system built that she couldn't master. ADOK wasn't any different. She wouldn't let it be.

The alien presence whispered to her.

Ignoring it, she looked for something else. How could she allow the complete merging that it suggested? How could she then mesh with a force field on the other side of the world and lower it long enough for her team to escape? She couldn't. There had to be another way.

Cai!

Jake's voice seemed a long way off. She realized then that she wasn't monitoring any of the other systems, essentially leaving him blind. Mentally, she reached for them, and as she did, her connection to him went blank.

Crap. He'd overloaded his probe in the past, but this

timing was disastrous. Still, at least it wasn't her. As serious as it was when a recep like Jake fried an implant—and in this case it was deadly serious—it was worse if it happened to an anchor like Cai. Much worse.

Maybe it was because the male receps had only one probe and the female anchors had two, but the receps recovered after a few hours. It wasn't as easy for the women.

Brain damage. Cai's skin crawled.

The doctors and scientists had tested her over and over because she was the only subject who hadn't overloaded, the only one who hadn't ended up mentally incapacitated to some degree. In fact, if she thought—

The Monster whispered again, and Cai realized she'd been drifting. Even if Jake couldn't connect with her any longer, she had to help him. From the way he'd said her name, she knew things were bad. Really bad. Merging with the energy field to put it down for a few minutes might not be such a crazy idea after all. Certainly it was better than doing nothing.

Cai closed her eyes and let her consciousness sink farther into the computer system. Her body trembled, her cells humming from the power that surged through her. *Deeper.* As she began to comply with the urge, she felt a presence that made her hesitate. It had been two years since she'd last sensed another anchor inside a computer, but she had no doubt what it was.

Except . . . she was supposed to be the last one functioning.

For a moment, she held off the Monster and sought out this person, but the trace she'd encountered was gone and there was no time to keep searching. Not with Jake in trouble. As she resumed immersing herself in the system, a shriek began.

At first she thought the noise was in her quarters. It wasn't until white encroached on the edges of her vision that she realized it came from inside her. Jake hadn't been the one who'd overloaded his implant; it had been her. Now she was frying her second nanoprobe.

Brain damage.

It was too late to stop it, but she wasn't going out for nothing. She threw herself into the Monster's embrace, took its strength inside her. Her head felt as if it were going to explode as the screech became louder. Cai reached across the Earth and found the force field. As she blended herself with the energy, the white filled her view until there was nothing else.

There wasn't going to be enough time before the probe crashed and burned.

No! Desperation and determination warred with pain for dominance. Cai gritted her teeth. Just a few more seconds. That was all she needed. Just a few more seconds.

She tried to muscle the field down even as she felt her awareness begin to fade. Too late. She'd failed.

Sorry, Jake.

It was her last coherent thought before the white swallowed her.

Chapter Two

Someone was speaking.

Cai frowned and tried to focus, but while the soothing, almost hypnotic tone registered, she couldn't make out the words or tell if the person was male or female. She shifted, turning her head toward the voice, and her chair moved with her, molded to her body. That helped her figure out where she was, and things made a bit more sense. She'd fallen asleep at her station.

Who was talking though? She struggled harder to break through the fog engulfing her mind.

"'We hold these truths to be self-evident: that all men are created equal; that they are endowed, by their Creator, with certain inalienable rights; that among these are life, liberty, and the pursuit of happiness.'"

If she weren't positive of her location, she'd wonder if she'd traveled back in time to Mr. Agassi's Advanced Placement History class. Now that would be a nightmare. She'd been a seven-year-old in with kids nine years older than she was. They'd hated her for screwing up the grading curve and had never spared a kind word for her. What had they called her? Though Cai had thought she would never forget, she was unable to come up with the name.

With great effort, she opened her eyes—and found herself staring at a three-dimensional rendering of what had to be a painting. It sat atop her console, flickering slightly. The image was of a group of men gathered around a table strewn with paper and dressed in old-fashioned clothing. Some wore white powdered wigs.

The American Revolution. Sometimes being an A student paid off. As the voice continued speaking, she tried to identify what was being quoted. It was familiar, but not quite nameable. Was this some kind of holo history class? She couldn't arrive at another reason why anyone would read a document like this aloud. Her dark hair fell into her eyes, hampering her view, and impatiently she pushed it off her face.

"'That whenever any form of government becomes destructive of these ends, it is the right of the people to alter or to abolish it, and to institute new government—'"

The Voice of Freedom!

Why had it taken her so long to figure it out? This wasn't a professor conducting an educational show, but one of the UCE's most wanted traitors trying to incite rebellion. She'd believed this Shadow Voice to be silenced, though. Cai thought about it some more, but she couldn't come up with a different answer.

"Banzai Maguire is here to lead the revolution and bring democracy to the world," the broadcast voice said. That enigmatic statement triggered something inside Cai, something that had her pulse hammering.

The holoimage changed from old men in old clothes to scenes from her time. Displays now showed men and women raising their fists in the air and chanting, people waving a colorful flag. Cai took note of this, but it didn't quiet the pounding of her heart. Why did hearing the name Banzai make her so anxious?

And why did her usually flawless memory have holes in it?

After a brief pause, the holo disappeared and was replaced by a foreign newscast. Cai listened with interest as the news team discussed the reappearance of the Voice of Freedom with barely disguised excitement. Next, the so-called experts were trotted out to speculate about what this meant for the world's powers—the UCE, the Euro-African Consortium, and the secretive Kingdom of Asia.

They cut to one of their reporters in the field with breaking news, and Cai shifted, easing muscles that were cramped from too many hours in the same position. She froze midstretch.

Quickly, she scooted forward and raised the volume on the holounit. The journalist was shouting to be heard over the event behind her. Cai was unsure what to call it. A riot? A mob scene? Whatever the label, the UCE military was using extreme force to put it down.

Sickened, Cai turned the unit off. She knew the rationale behind using such brutality, but she couldn't condone what she'd seen. It was wrong to attack civilians like that. God, she was glad Jake was in an antiterrorist unit and didn't have to deal with *this* kind of situation.

She pursed her lips. There was something she needed to recall about her recep, but it hovered out of reach. He'd been on an op; she'd been helping him. Then what? She thought harder.

She'd flamed out. He'd been in trouble. Jake!

A frantic glance at the time showed that about nine hours had passed since she'd fried her probes. Whatever had happened was long over. Taking a deep breath, Cai tried to calm down. She had to think, had to be methodical, but she couldn't relax.

She reached out with her connector probe, hoping it worked, trying to communicate with Jake along their pathway. Nothing. Her hands shook and she folded them in her

lap. Unlike the systems probe, the connector implant usually rebounded in a matter of hours after going down. She
knew he wasn't blocking her, so that meant either she
needed more recovery time, she'd burned it out, or Jake
was dead.

As much as she wanted to shake off the last thought, she
couldn't. Biting her lower lip, Cai sat up straighter. She
hesitated for a moment, but the only way to find out the
status of the team was to hack into the UCE system.

The process was frustrating and slow. Without her
nanoprobes, she was forced to do everything the hard way.
What scared her, though, was how often she had to stop
and think. What should have been almost instinctual,
wasn't. Not anymore. She'd been riding systems long before receiving her implants, but she was discovering more
and more gaps in her memory.

Finally, after an eternity, she was in. At first she couldn't
remember the name of the mission. She slowed her racing
thoughts, took another deep breath, and focused. A word
popped into her head and she did a search. Of the eleven
hits, only one seemed familiar. She selected it.

The date was correct. She checked the men's names, but
no status was listed. Cai moved to the bottom of the file
and read the final entry. Eight of fourteen had been extracted alive. The survivors had all required medical treatment, and one remained in danger of becoming death
number seven. The others had been treated and released.

There was no mention of how they'd escaped.

She returned to the names. Except for Jake, she knew
them only by their handles, and she couldn't recall who
had drawn today's assignment. After copying the list into a
separate file on her system, she went in search of each
man's personnel record. She found Jake's.

*Jacob Tucker. Captain, United Colonies of Earth Army Spe-
cial Forces.*

Although she knew the info, she read everything; it made her feel closer to him. Next, she stared at his image.

Dark, coffee-colored hair was cut short on the sides but left defiantly long on top. He'd tamed it for the picture, but there was no doubt that wasn't its usual state. His eyes were ice blue and framed by thick, long lashes. Cai trailed her gaze across his high cheekbones, over the patrician nose, before settling on his full lips. His demeanor was serious, but the corners of his mouth quirked up, and she knew him well enough to guess that he thought this picture thing was bullshit.

Even after all this time, she continued to be awed by how gorgeous he was. The only thing that saved him from being pretty was the look in his eyes. This man had seen too much, done too much, ever to be referred to in soft terms.

She realized she was stalling, not wanting to discover that he'd died. Cai made herself continue, but she found nothing. His record hadn't been updated.

Frowning, she raised a hand to rub her temple. It didn't play. This database was continually revised, never lagging more than fifteen minutes behind current events. She checked the other names, but found the same thing.

This wasn't right.

A feeling of unease crawled through her as she thought of the glitches in her memory, but she shook it off and studied her work. Maybe she'd accessed the wrong directory. The path she'd taken seemed fine, but she had no way to verify it. Hacking was illegal. Hacking into a government military database . . . Well, only a fool implicated herself by making notes.

With painstaking care, Cai backed out of the system. She'd try again later, but the wait to find out what had happened to Jake would be nearly unbearable.

Slumping back in her chair, she gave thanks for budget

cuts. The project doctors had never been able to read the implants—brain activity interfered with any kind of observation or tracking equipment—but they had once monitored the vital signs of all the anchors working missions. Then a reduction in funding about four years ago had forced them to reallocate resources. If not for that, and for the fact that anchors had always worked out of their quarters, she'd be in a med facility right now.

She'd never discovered why the scientists had opted to set her and the others up in their homes, but she had a few guesses. Her chief theory was that Special Forces crews often had to deploy fast. This way the anchors were available to their partners almost instantly at nearly any hour. There was the secrecy thing, too. The project was housed in a research building. If she and the others were seen traipsing constantly to those facilities, it would raise questions, call attention to them.

And she certainly hadn't gotten any attention here. Even if she had, the console in her living space would have been easy to explain. She was supposed to be a systems specialist, and techs all had equipment in their quarters. But she'd never had to worry about fooling anyone. In the five years she'd lived here, she'd never had a guest. The bland barrenness of her rooms reflected the emptiness of her life.

With a frown, Cai put the thought aside and decided to reread the info on the overloads, as well as the speculation by the project scientists. Maybe she'd find something in the files about her memory issues.

The Quantum Brain Tandem Project—the Quandem Project—had been the latest in a string of top-secret experiments in gestalt mind nanotechnology. The previous studies had left all research subjects dead, but instead of giving up, the scientists had kept tinkering. Cai wondered if her stage of the project was deemed a failure yet. After all, she and Jake were the final anchor-receptor pair.

She was faster at hacking into the documents this time,

and she scanned carefully, looking for some hint about her situation. None of the receps had been adversely affected by strain on their nanoprobes. Each of them had suffered multiple blowouts, but had recovered in short order. The longest time a connector implant had been off-line was six hours.

She moved on to the anchors.

A-4 had overloaded her probes at the three-month mark. When she'd regained consciousness in the med facility, the doctors discovered that she had suffered brain damage severe enough to leave her with the mental capacity of a five-year-old.

A-5 had made it eleven months. The harm to her mind had been considerably less, although she was now unable to function without assistance.

A-1 . . . She gritted her teeth. Being numbered seemed so cold. They had names, damn it. This wasn't her first excursion into these files, or the only time she'd been angered by the way they'd been dehumanized. But maybe it was easier not to care what an experiment wrought if its subjects were simply numbers.

A-1 had lost her partner in the nineteenth month of the study. He'd been KIA. Killed in action.

She blinked hard to clear her eyes. The woman had lived with the guilt for four months before committing suicide. Though it wasn't a choice Cai would make, she understood the devastation—now more than ever. A-1 had not overloaded her probes before she died.

A-3 had light brain damage. She'd flamed out about three years after the start of the experiment. Her connector probe worked, although the data implant was lost. The doctors hadn't replaced it. They hadn't been able to come up with the funds.

Cai read her own info. A-2. She didn't find anything that was helpful. There were dozens of theories why she'd never overloaded—well, at least before today—but none had a majority of support. With a humorless laugh, she exited the system. When the docs found out what had happened, they'd haul her butt down for more tests.

"A-2," she whispered, "suffers from slight memory loss. No other signs of damage to the brain are apparent. Both nanoprobes were fried. No plans to replace."

Jake. Instinct had her mentally reaching for him, but she found only that desolate nothingness again. Yet he had to be alive. Had to be. She refused to believe anything else. A few more minutes and she'd hack into the system again and find out for sure.

As she waited, it struck her how quiet it was inside her head without him. How lonely. It didn't matter if he blocked her or she blocked him; there was always a sense of his presence. But no probe meant no connection.

Even if he were alive, Cai realized with devastating suddenness, she might still have lost her only friend.

She called in reinforcements.

When she couldn't find anything about Jake or the team in the government system, she turned to some of her fellow tech-geeks. She'd never met them, had no idea what they looked like, and the names by which she knew them probably weren't real. She couldn't refer to them as friends, not exactly, but she'd communicated with them over the Interweb long enough for a level of trust to develop. And when it came to hacking, she knew they were her equals.

But even with all their skill combing the files, no one turned up any info. Only two more techs were left to check in, and Cai didn't know what to do next if they came up empty-handed.

Her stomach tied in knots, she paced restlessly around her quarters. Yes, she and Jake had worked together for five years, but would anyone think to contact her if he'd died? Special Forces definitely had the names of the mission casualties, but she didn't know any of the men in the units—at least not well enough to ask.

There was always the general. Cai thought about him, but her aversion to the idea was strong. It definitely fell into the last-resort category.

Added to her concerns was her memory. It had taken hours for her to recall running into that other anchor. Every time she thought about blanking out something so important, a shiver ran down her spine. What else had she lost? She didn't feel as if there were any big gaps in her recollections, but the tiny things were adding up.

Investigation hadn't given her any answers as to the identity of the other anchor. Her first guess—that the doctors had replaced the systems implant in the woman who'd burned out two years earlier—hadn't checked out. Cai had found no evidence on her second theory either. As far as she could tell, there were no new experiments in Quantum Brain nanotechnology. She should be the only anchor. So who the hell had she bumped into?

A soft chime had her hurrying to her station. As she neared, she instinctively reached out with her nanoprobe. The sense of losing something vital hit her again when she found nothing except emptiness. Shaking it off, she dropped into her chair and brought up the comm unit. And received her next disappointment. Maria hadn't found anything.

After thanking her, Cai slouched back. The lack of info was strange. Even the short paragraph she'd read about the number of survivors had disappeared, and if she hadn't saved it to her system, she'd wonder if her mind was playing tricks on her.

Only one more person to hear from, and it appeared unlikely that Mel would turn up anything. Cai swung the chair to the left and started to put her feet on the edge of the console when something caught her eye. Leaning forward, she grabbed the quire and dragged it closer. It was her writing—she recognized it immediately—but she didn't remember making the notes. Deciphering the words dealt her a third blow. This wasn't some small thing she'd blanked on; this was critical.

For six long years, she'd searched endlessly for some clue about her missing parents, and now that she had something, she'd forgotten it. The realization made her sick. Absently, she brushed a stray tear off her cheek as she continued reading. Of all the things in the world to be affected by her flame-out, why did this have to be one?

Cai kept scanning the notes. The further she read, the more came back to her. By the time she reached the midpoint of the document, she recalled everything. At least, she thought she did. Now she knew why the name Banzai sounded familiar. Her whole plan hinged on the woman.

When she finished, she slid the quire onto the console, reclined her chair, and stared at the ceiling. She was scared now. Really scared. To forget this . . .

One by one, she replayed what she remembered of her mom and dad, each memory even more precious. She thought back to her twelfth birthday and the laser scalpel they'd given her. How her mom had taught her to dissect a rat, and how her dad had kept the hair off her face while she threw up.

In retrospect, the earnest assurances by her parents that she didn't have to be a doctor were amusing. At the time, she'd been heartbroken that she wouldn't follow in their footsteps; though, to be honest, it had been the idea of working with them more than medicine that had been tempting. Her interest had always been in machines and inteltronics. She'd taken apart computer systems before she'd been old enough to go to school. Neither of her parents was a bit surprised when she'd decided to become a tech.

She rubbed the stone of her ring—a star garnet, her

thirteenth-birthday gift and the only piece of jewelry she never removed. Her mom had told her the gem's energy would promote success in whatever she chose to do, but Cai wore it because it was a gift from her folks and she felt closer to them with it on.

That birthday had come weeks after—

Cai, can you hear me?

She sat up so fast, she nearly catapulted to the floor. *Jake!* No other words formed in her mind. The connector implant was working!

Thank God. I was beginning to wonder if my probe would ever come up again. His tone changed. *I'm glad it's back.*

What's wrong? She was familiar with his moods, and when he seemed to balk at her question, she knew what had happened. Only one thing ever made him act like this. *You had a nightmare.*

His silence was all the confirmation she needed. The dreams came sporadically. He might have none for months, then be hit with one every night for a week. Somehow she wasn't surprised that this last op had triggered a nightmare. She couldn't imagine the horrors he'd lived through.

I'm sorry. The assignment. It's my fault. If I—

No, he interrupted, *you're not to blame. This mission was screwed up from the minute we were briefed. Half-assed intel, a moron colonel who didn't know shit about Special Forces, and a damn extraction unit that was late because they fell asleep.*

They what? Cai's hands knotted into fists. They'd fallen asleep? That didn't seem possible.

They claim they were drugged.

You don't believe that?

I was ripping off their heads at the time, so I figured they were covering their asses.

Cai's lips twitched, but she didn't smile. At the beginning of their link, he'd had difficulties shutting out their connection. Because of this, she'd been fully present while he'd berated a junior officer who'd ignored advice from the unit's warrant officer and put the team at risk. So she knew that when it came to men's lives being endangered, her recep had zero tolerance. If the extraction crew faced even a quarter of what Jake had leveled at the lieutenant, she didn't blame them for making excuses.

But after considering it, I do believe them, he added. *These are some of the most elite pilots in the army—no way would they be careless enough to fall asleep. I had to hunt the crew down and apologize for doubting them.*

He apologized?

He didn't say anything more. After a moment, Cai asked, *Jake? You're okay, right?*

There was a long pause. *I'm fine.*

She knew better. The man was hyperresponsible. Losing anyone on a mission would hurt, but to have so many killed at once had to be tearing him up. Cai wanted to ask who'd died, who was the injured man, but she didn't. Not yet. He'd tell her in his own time, in his own way. *I'm glad I didn't lose you.*

Yeah. I was beginning to wonder, though, when the probe stayed down for so long. Thought I might be on my own again.

I was wondering the same thing.

Another long silence, but she didn't try to fill it. She could feel him in her head once more and she wrapped his presence around her. God, she'd missed him.

We got the target, he said at last. *That much of the mission was a success.*

Good.

He was quiet again, and she knew his nightmare was weighing on him. It would help if he'd share with her what haunted his sleep—would share it with anyone—but he refused. Instead, he just mentally reached for her after each, and Cai guessed he didn't want to be alone when he woke up—at least not until the immediacy was gone. Mostly, he'd talk about his men. Funny stories. Nothing that involved battle or anything serious. And never about himself unless the joke had been on him.

There were other times, though, when he wanted to sit without speaking much, and that was when she knew the nightmare had been really bad. Tonight fell into that category.

You'd think I'd get over these stupid things.

The declarative sentence astounded her. Usually, he didn't say even that much. *Some things we just have to endure,* she responded. She didn't push; it had to be his decision whether or not to talk about the dreams. She did remind him that she was willing to listen, however, just in case. *You know I'm here for you whenever you want to talk, right?*

There was no reply, but she hadn't expected one. Damn, the man was stubborn. If she could erase the horrors from his head, she'd do it in a . . . Cai stopped. No, she wouldn't take his memories. His past made him who he was—a compassionate, caring man. Besides, she knew firsthand now what it was like to be missing pieces of her mind. She wouldn't wish that on him.

He was full of tension, so she let the quiet spread once more—gentle, soft, and calming. There wasn't supposed to be an empathic channel between the nanoprobes, but she and Jake read each other's emotions at times. They hadn't told the doctors in charge of the Quandem Project about this surprise.

Well, Jake was such a guy he probably had no clue that he had perceived her emotions. Of course, the fact that he thought she wasn't human might play a role in that. And Cai hadn't confessed the rapport because she knew it would mean more damn tests. No way would she voluntarily put herself through those again.

It was some time later when she felt his tension segue into resignation, and part of her relaxed. The worst was over for tonight. When he spoke again, his voice held no emotion, but she knew him better than that.

Those wreckers were vicious bastards. Nothing seemed to stop them. It was like sharks scenting blood in the water. PK went down first; then all hell broke loose.

PK. Plane Killer. Cai swallowed hard. The soldier hadn't earned his name by destroying enemy aircraft. No, he'd accidentally driven a loader into the side of a UCE fighter during a bet with a munitions sergeant over whose job was harder. PK had set out to prove that anyone could load ordnance. He'd lost—and had put a huge hole in the fuselage that cost a fortune to repair. They were probably still deducting it from his pay. She laughed even as she blinked back tears. That was typical PK.

It took her a moment to realize Jake had gone silent once more. *Who else did we lose?* she asked quietly.

He was subdued when he answered, giving her small details about the firefight and the men. Not how they died—that, he didn't share—but little things he remembered from the battle. Again he went quiet, no doubt thinking of his buddies, the men he'd fought and drunk with. The men who'd followed his orders. She knew the team only through his stories, but she was going to miss those who'd died. Cai couldn't imagine how terrible it was for him.

I thought we were done. All of us. Then the weirdest damn thing happened. Part of the force field collapsed.

What? She froze. Had she done that?

I had my back against a section and nearly fell through when it failed. It's the only thing that saved our asses. Too bad it didn't happen earlier. We barely got out of there. It was so fu— He stopped short. There were some words Jake wouldn't use with her, and this was one of them. It was actually kind of sweet. *It was so damn close, and if that wall had come back up too soon, it would have been over.*

Did you bring everyone home? she asked softly. She knew Special Forces didn't leave their men behind, whether they were dead or alive, but with wreckers . . .

We got them. And Jake's tone told her not to ask any more questions. *The extraction team showed up in the nick of time. There'll be an investigation into the drugging and the rest of this debacle, and I'll damn well make sure it gets to the truth.*

And he would. His sense of responsibility, of honor, wouldn't let him do less. *You're a good man, Jake Tucker.* Her words would make him uncomfortable, but he needed to hear them.

No, I'm not. I'm simply doing what I need to do. There was a short pause. *Hang on, sweetheart. Someone's at the door.*

He didn't block her long. *Hey, we're heading out to celebrate. Spud's going to make a full recovery. I'll talk to you later.*

Without waiting for her to respond, he severed the link, and Cai's lips twisted ruefully over how quickly she'd been abandoned. She couldn't blame him, not really, and she felt sure his discomfort over her compliment had a role in his fast escape—but they needed to talk.

Her eyes traveled to the notes about her parents. She'd need his cooperation to find them, and that meant she'd have to confess that she wasn't a computer. She knew how Jake would react. He'd be absolutely livid.

Part of his anger would be because she'd concealed the truth from him. Another part would stem from embarrassment. Not only had she heard him chew out subordinates that first year when their command over their connection hadn't been absolute; she'd also been linked to him at other moments of high emotion. She'd known when he was afraid, when he was sad, when he was envious, and she'd been privy to his sexual encounters. That would be hard enough for Jake to deal with, but when he found out she'd been only sixteen at the time and that he was responsible for most of her education on the subject, he'd be totally mortified.

She sighed. There wasn't time to procrastinate, but she didn't have to talk to him immediately either. By the time the data she'd flagged on Banzai Maguire's location was spotted, analyzed, and the decision made, days would have gone by. She could wait till he wasn't so raw from the deaths of his men. Wait for him to be more receptive, more forgiving, about her omission.

Damn, she wished she'd told him the truth long ago and faced his reaction then. She needed to talk to someone about overloading both her neural implants and her fear over the memory loss. Who else except another Quandem member would understand?

Then there was the mystery anchor. She wanted Jake's take on that too. Right now she remained undecided on how to approach this. He dealt more with the UCE and army bureaucracy than she did, and he'd give her a different perspective. Once she had more facts it would be easier to make the choice.

It had been one hell of a day, Cai thought, closing her eyes. She took time to remember the six men who'd died and to bid them a quiet farewell. Then she expressed her gratitude for Jake's safe return and Spud's good prognosis.

For the first time, she wondered why such a large group had been assigned this mission. That was another piece of the puzzle that didn't fit. Setting the destabs hadn't required fourteen men. Historically, the teams had been comprised of twelve soldiers, but it had been years since the brass pared it down to seven. Positions had been eliminated and duties combined. It had been a smart move, so why send such a large group now?

When her comm unit chimed, Cai tried to access her nanoprobe. The reminder that it was unusable jarred her, but she shook her head and sat up. She didn't rush this time. Now that she'd spoken with Jake, the urgency was gone. She brought the comm online to talk to the last remaining tech.

"Captain, why isn't your visual mode working?"

Now Cai scrambled. She turned the viewer on and jumped from her seat. Awkward in her haste, she got her feet tangled up with each other and would have ended up on the floor if she hadn't caught herself on the console. By the time she managed to stand at attention, she was mortified.

Then she realized her long hair was not only loose, but falling wildly around her. Crap. "General Yardley, sir, I apologize for my display."

"At ease, Randolph. I know you're off duty. I don't expect you to be spit-shined at this hour of the night."

"Yes, sir. Thank you, sir." Cai barely shifted from attention despite the general's permission. Unobtrusively, she tried to shake her hair behind her shoulders. General Yardley was the ranking officer over Army Special Forces. The Quandem Project had been funded with his approval, and the man had become her commander the day she'd been linked with Jake.

"However, when you report to my office at oh-eight-hundred tomorrow, I will demand a professional appearance."

"Yes, sir," she responded crisply before the words sank in. "Your office, General?" Had they found out about the overload of her nanoprobes? She didn't think so, but she'd learned never to underestimate the military.

"Relax, Captain. You're not in any trouble."

"Yes, sir." The man's tone seemed almost kindly, but Cai knew that wasn't possible. She'd read in the files that he hadn't wanted her to be partnered with Jake, that he'd thought she was too young and not up to the job. The project doctors had needed to convince him that her brainwave patterns were the only ones that could be matched with Tucker's. After she'd read that, her nerves around the general had gone up exponentially.

"Aren't you curious about the meeting?"

"Yes, General, I am." Her vocal cords seemed to constrict, and she wondered if someone was sucking the oxygen from her quarters. Either that, or maybe she was forgetting to breathe. This was why she hadn't wanted to contact Yardley about the mission unless there was no other choice. She always reverted to the age of thirteen around this man.

"Provided Captain Tucker agrees, we're going to send you on a mission to the Raft Cities with his team."

Cai lost her voice. Her plan had worked! She struggled to hide her euphoria, but the general misread her silence.

"Do you have an issue with going on an operation?"

"No, sir." She bit her lip to prevent herself from saying any more. The timing was incredible. It wasn't even twenty-four hours since she'd found the piece of intelligence buried deep within one of the systems she monitored. Though it hadn't been difficult to make the data more noticeable to army intel, she honestly hadn't expected it to be picked up so quickly.

"Good. Aren't you going to ask why we're sending you?"

She knew why they were sending her. Hell, she probably had more information about this than Yardley did. "I thought it must have something to do with a system somewhere, sir."

"We need you to access a computer that rivals ADOK, and to transmit any important information home to the UCE."

"ADOK's equal?" She barely squeaked the words out, and Cai hoped he bought the surprised act.

He nodded, then said, "I can see you have questions, but I have no intention of having a briefing tonight. You'll get answers in the morning if you're okayed for the operation."

"By Jake?" The general looked at her oddly, and Cai realized she'd slipped. "I mean by Captain Tucker, General, sir." He still stared at her, and she worried she'd gone overboard trying to correct her mistake. She swallowed hard and wished whoever was stealing her air would quit.

"Yes," Yardley said at last, and his voice sounded funny. "By Tucker. He has the final word on who goes."

"Yes, sir."

The general considered her silently until she fought the urge to squirm. Clearly he didn't want her on this mission and hoped she'd admit she couldn't handle it. Cai lifted her chin. Like hell. She could do this. The fact that she hadn't been in the field before would be a difficulty, she knew that, but she had been trained. She wouldn't cave under his stare. No way.

And no way was she losing the opportunity to get to the Raft Cities. Not when she'd done everything possible to set this assignment up. She fought to keep her eyes forward, but she could see the notes on her parents in her peripheral vision. Her one lead was there. All she had to do was convince Jake to give the okay, and the UCE would order her to go exactly where she wanted to be.

Jake. *Crap.* If she surprised him in Yardley's office tomorrow, she wouldn't stand a chance; he'd automatically say no. She had to find him tonight and talk him into taking her along.

"Captain!" She snapped her focus back to General Yardley. "My office. Oh-eight-hundred tomorrow. Do you have it?"

"Yes, sir."

He signed off, and Cai immediately disengaged the unit and sagged onto her chair. She could feel sweat running between her shoulder blades. It was silly to be nervous around Yardley, even though this operation was no doubt a new way to demonstrate how ill-equipped she was for anything outside the tech world. Well, the hell with that. Cai Randolph aced tests.

Then her bravado left her. She'd lost a nanoprobe. That was a big problem—and not something she could, or would, hide from Jake. Not when it involved his life and the lives of his men. She had to find him tonight, explain who she was, tell him about her flame-out, and somehow convince him to bring her with him. Convince him that she could access that computer even without the implant.

It wouldn't be easy. He'd be beyond furious, but friends didn't hold grudges, right? He'd help her. He had to.

She slid forward till she could lounge in the chair and started running through arguments in her mind. If she could find the right words, she felt certain he'd take her along. Too bad she hadn't inherited her father's glib tongue.

She had rejected her seventh method of broaching the subject when the chime came. Absently, Cai reached for her implant so she could connect with the comm, then promptly forgot the summons in her shock.

Her data probe was back up and functional.

Chapter Three

Cai walked into Hell, pausing just inside the entrance before spotting an empty space along a nearby wall. She moved, putting her back against it, not wanting to leave herself vulnerable as she waited for her eyes to adjust to the dimness. While her presence attracted a few sidelong glances, nobody seemed too interested. In a bar as notoriously dangerous as this, being ignored was a good thing.

The pounding beat of some neo-techsynth song made her grimace, but the volume wasn't overwhelming. Probably because that would interfere with the interchange of stolen goods, illicit substances, and illegal services. She looked around, locating a stage about halfway across the room with a holographic simulcast of a Mythica Malone concert. Good equipment. If she hadn't known that the superstar would never perform here, Cai would have sworn it was real. At least until the lighting changed and the transparency of the images was revealed.

Now that her vision had adapted, she took a good look around. Small holoflats hovered in each booth, allowing the occupants their choice of entertainment. There weren't many booths, though; the bar was mostly filled with tables, and the rest of the patrons made do with holovid screens. Each of the displays Cai spotted featured a different sporting event. The one nearest to her showed horses parading to the starting gate at a racetrack, and she gazed at the almost extinct animals with fascination.

Voices became raised in a dispute over the odds for one of the horses, and Cai tore her gaze from the screen. She couldn't lose her focus because she found Thoroughbreds fascinating; it was the people here she needed to watch. She studied the arguing men first, then swept her gaze farther around the room.

Hell's reputation wasn't exaggerated. The authorities could make quite a dent in their One Hundred Most-Wanted Fugitives list if they came here with identity scanners. How the heck had this bar become a favorite hangout for Special Forces commandos? It hardly seemed as if they'd be welcome, yet everyone here peacefully coexisted.

Since the soldiers were the only clean-cut men in the bar, it was easy to identify them despite their lack of uniforms. From a distance, they looked like muscular choirboys who were ridiculously out of place. Cai knew better. She'd trained with these men. Each was hard, formidable, and dangerous in his own right.

A bellow of rage jerked her attention back to the guys arguing over the horse race, and she saw them square off against each other. Conversation ceased as everyone turned to watch the brawl. It didn't last long. Four bouncers converged on the combatants, and a couple of zaps put both fighters down for the count, their bodies convulsing. Then they were picked up and carted away.

The customers returned to their business as soon as the show was over, but talk seemed more animated than it had been. When Cai intercepted a few calculating glances, she knew she'd delayed long enough. It was time to do what she'd come here for, then get out before she attracted more unwelcome attention. How hard could it be, anyway?

Inhaling deeply to calm her nerves was a mistake. The stench of stale beer, body odor, urine, and vomit nearly made her choke. Really, there was no reason to worry; she knew Jake better than anyone. Okay, so she never would have guessed he'd come to a bar like *this,* but it had been an unusually rough day.

Cai bit her lip. Ignoring the tension building between her shoulders, she perused the crowd. She found Jake easily. He sat at a round table in the corner with two other soldiers. Her hands clenched at her sides as she studied his profile. Though deep shadows concealed his handsome face, she could see he was watchful, his eyes never still.

She took a step forward. Stopped. Squared her shoulders and walked toward him. She could do this.

Though he didn't react as she came up, Jake was aware of her presence. He had to be. Even if he hadn't sensed her approach, which she doubted, his friends were staring at her. Cai stared right back until Jake turned.

His expression said, *Get lost,* but it quickly became neutral. She knew he was waiting for her to explain why she'd come over, but she took a moment to study him anyway. The first thing she noticed was that he was coiled, ready to spring if she posed a danger. And he was even betterlooking in person.

His glacier-blue eyes were striking with his dark hair and tanned face, but it wasn't the color that she got lost in. She was looking, trying to find the man she knew. The man who was always tender and thoughtful with her, the man she talked with and comforted in the aftermath of his nightmares. Cai's stomach twisted when she couldn't find anything familiar in this stranger's hard face.

Part of her wanted to excuse herself, but she couldn't.

She needed to talk with him. Tonight. There was no other option.

"Hello, Jake."

He lifted an eyebrow. "No one calls me Jake." His voice sounded different from his thoughts. Deeper, harsher than she'd expected.

A shiver began inside her, but she fought it off before it became noticeable. "I do. I always have."

She held her breath as he pushed slowly to his feet. In her peripheral vision, she saw him slide his chair out of the way with his foot. This had been the wrong approach, she decided, exhaling in a silent sigh. Perhaps she'd have been wiser to wait till he'd left Hell to talk to him. If she'd thought it through longer and not let impatience get in the way, she would have realized he'd be on his guard here.

"Always?" he asked menacingly. "I don't know who you are."

When the other men stood, flanking Jake on either side, Cai realized they'd heard the warning in his tone as well. Great, just what she needed. The Three Musketeers. As she met their hard gazes, Cai tried to decide the best tack to take.

Before she picked an option, the hair on her nape prickled. It was the only tip-off she had before a beefy arm went around her neck. Training took over. She squatted and leaned forward, sliding her hand between her throat and the arm as she stepped sideways. Almost in the same motion, she brought her elbow back into his midsection, using the full force of her body to add all the power she could. She heard an "oomph," but didn't hesitate.

Turning, she hooked her foot behind his leg and pushed the man. Since he was already off balance, he went down like a polar bear on wet ice. Cai was about to take him out of the equation indefinitely when she was wrapped in a hug. Though she had no clue how she knew, she was sure it was Jake.

When the man she'd put on the floor began to stand, she tried to get free. "Down, killer," her recep said, mouth near her ear, and she thought he might be laughing.

That was when she realized her attacker hadn't been one of the lowlifes from the bar, but a commando. A big, huge, enormous commando. When he was upright, she saw he was at least six and a half feet tall, with muscles that strained the seams of his T-shirt. *Holy crap.* All that practice really had paid off. She could react—and succeed—outside of a controlled situation.

"Didn't your mama ever tell you not to grab a woman without an invitation?" she snarled. She heard the snickers from the men behind her a split second before Jake let go and stepped away.

"I won't make that mistake again," the giant grumbled, sidling past her to join his buddies.

She moved with him, keeping him in front of her. He wouldn't be easy to take down a second time. It surprised her that he kept her in his line of sight too. As if someone his size would be leery of a woman who was five-foot eight, and about half his weight. *Yeah, right.*

When he stood with his buddies, the stare-down resumed. None of the men was laughing now, and she bit her lip as her nerves returned. She'd been damn lucky that the bouncers hadn't swooped in and zapped her. Since she needed to keep her mind on the situation, she put that thought aside.

"Who the hell are you?" Jake demanded.

Well, as her great-grandma Nguyen used to say, in for a penny, in for a pound. "I'm Cai."

"Nice try," he drawled sarcastically. "I don't know where you heard the name, but you made a mistake. Cai isn't human."

"Not before I've had my first cup of coffee, no, but after that, I'm as human as anyone else."

"She's not bad, Tuck," the commando she'd put on the

floor said. "Quick-witted enough to keep up with you. Maybe you should play nice for a while. You could use some fun."

Cai looked past Jake and frowned at the grinning man. She knew what he meant by *fun*. "Let me guess—you're Gnat, right?"

That wiped the mirth off his face. Unfortunately, it also brought her closer scrutiny than before. She should have kept her mouth shut. Now the cross-examination would begin. Unless . . . *Hmm*. Her idea would either preempt the questioning or they would want to haul her into headquarters.

"Yes, I know who you are and that you were nicknamed after an insect because you're a pest. They picked Gnat because of your size." The man really was a damn mountain. She shifted her focus to the guy beside him, one with a book in his hand. "You're always reading something, the more obscure the better, so they call you Professor. Not too original, but it could be worse."

Cai switched to the man on Jake's left and bit the inside of her lip when she couldn't identify him. Then she realized why. "You're not on the same team with these guys. I don't think Jake's worked with you before. Not recently, anyway."

"You sure you don't know her, Tuck?" the man she didn't recognize asked quietly.

"Do you think I'd forget?" Jake didn't take his attention from her. "How do you know this stuff?"

Cai shrugged. "You told me."

"No. I didn't."

She fought the need to back up a step at his tone. This wasn't going well. There was only one way to salvage this mess. Cai sighed. She'd hoped he'd believe her without it, but clearly that wasn't going to happen. Mentally, she reached for the neural implant and opened the pathway that connected them.

Jake, I couldn't know these things if you hadn't told me.

For a split second he stared at her; then it sank in. She saw it happen. "Son of a bitch," he muttered. He took her by the elbow and hauled her toward the exit.

"I think he remembered her," Cai heard Gnat say with a short laugh before Jake had her out of earshot.

It was a good thing her legs were long, because he wasn't making any concessions for their height difference. As it was, she had to half run to keep up. Cai didn't protest. She couldn't see the expression on Jake's face, but she did notice how the worst dregs in Hell cleared out of his way. If *they* took one look and decided to give him a wide berth, she sure wasn't going to say anything that might exacerbate the situation.

He pulled her out through the entrance, and the men and women standing in front stepped out of the way as quickly as the people in the bar had. Jake didn't release her until they'd rounded the corner and stood in the narrow space between the bar and the crumbling structure adjacent. Despite their being outdoors, it didn't smell any better here than inside.

To avoid his eyes, Cai surveyed her surroundings. The only illumination came from the moonlight seeping between the buildings, but it was enough for her to pick out two dark shapes lying on the ground. They were twitching, so she figured they were the men who'd fought inside Hell. She could also see debris scattered around the alley. Some of it had been pushed to the sides, indicating an attempt had been made to clean up, but it had been a careless effort.

The weight of Jake's stare became too much for her to ignore any longer, and Cai forced herself to look at him. His face was blank, but what she read in his eyes explained why everyone got out of his way. Ice-cold fury. Rage was normally a hot emotion, one that would burn itself out, but this . . . How would she deal with cold anger?

He crossed his arms over his broad chest and waited. She'd known he'd be pissed off, but she was his friend. He'd come around. She hoped. Cai ran her damp palms down the front of her trousers and took a deep breath. "Jake—"

"Tucker. You don't get to call me Jake anymore."

His words, spoken so coldly, hurt her more deeply than she'd been hurt in years. "Jake, please. We're friends."

"Friends don't lie to each other."

"I never lied!"

"Oh, really? Then why have I been under the impression that Cai was a computer programmed with a female personality?"

"*I* didn't tell you that," she denied.

"No, you didn't, but you knew what I thought and you didn't correct me, did you? A lie of omission."

This was going worse than she'd imagined, and she'd pictured some pretty negative scenarios. She rubbed the underside of the ring on her right hand with her thumb, trying to find reassurance. The warm metal reminded her of what was at stake. She *had* to get past his anger.

"They gave me a briefing prior to inserting the nano-probes, so I thought you'd been filled in too." She paused to swallow the lump clogging her throat. "I didn't know differently until later, almost seven months later."

"You could have said something then."

"I should have. Except it took me by surprise, and by the time I recovered, you'd closed the connection between the probes. For weeks after that I tried to find a way to tell you I was a person, but there never seemed to be a good way to mention it."

"So you decided not to say anything."

Cai couldn't meet his piercing blue eyes any longer and dropped her gaze. "I'm sorry," she apologized softly. "I should have found some way to straighten you out."

He didn't reply, and she realized he wasn't ready to forgive her. It was her own fault. She'd known Jake had trouble trusting others; that he had buddies but no close friends. Somehow she'd thought it would be different between them, that the last few years would count for something. She lifted her head again, but he continued to frown stonily at her.

How hard had she tried to tell him the truth? It had seemed easier at the time to let him go on thinking she wasn't real. Much easier. She knew Jake; he'd have been curious. He would have wanted to meet her. No way could she have agreed to that. Even if he hadn't told her so many personal things about himself, even if he hadn't slipped time after time that first year while trying to block her, it still would have been awkward.

He hadn't gotten a good look at her yet, not in the bar and not out here because of the poor lighting, but when he did, she'd be dealing with his reaction to her age. The man would be absolutely furious. Then when he calmed down, he'd do the math, figure out how young she'd been when they'd been linked, and go off again. She sighed quietly. There was no help for it now, and she had more important worries.

Hesitantly she reached for him, but he stepped back and Cai dropped her arm. His unexpected retreat was like a hard jab to the midsection, but this wasn't about her. "I *never* meant to hurt you," she said fiercely.

Again, no response. The silence felt heavy, oppressive. One of the brawlers moaned, but it sounded muted and distant. Cai's reality centered on one man and nothing else. Even if she couldn't convince him to help, she didn't want to lose his regard. Jake meant too much to her.

"If it would change anything," she said, voice barely above a whisper, "I'd apologize again. But we both know it won't make a difference. I've damaged the trust between us, I know that. Just like I know only time can start to heal the breach."

He laughed, but it was sarcastic and cutting. "Sweetheart," he said scornfully, "I want nothing to do with you."

After giving her a hard look, he turned and began to walk away. Cai couldn't let him go. She took a couple of running steps to catch up with him and grabbed his biceps. The glare she got this time did hold heat, enough fire to make her flinch. "No matter how you feel about me, we're going to be expected to work together, Jake."

"Tucker," he growled, leaning over to scowl into her face. "And I'll be damned if I'm going out on another mission with you in my head. I did fine before you, and I'll do fine again once the implant is removed. Let go of me."

She didn't. In fact, she tightened her grip. "We're too successful. They'll never let either one of us have the probes removed." Cai realized her voice was too loud and she took a deep breath before saying more quietly, "There were only ten people in the experiment; did you know that?"

He shook his head, but at least it was a response.

"They couldn't afford a bigger sampling; the Quantum Brain nanotechnology was too expensive. It still is. No matter how many years and how many scientists have worked on the problem, nobody has solved the replication issues for these probes. No one is even close. They picked the commandos—the receptors—first based on your field evaluations, your ages, and whether or not you were lifers."

Now he appeared interested.

"Once they had the five of you set, they went looking for us. The anchors. My brain-wave patterns matched yours more closely than anyone else's, so I was approached to be the other half of your team. That's how every anchor was chosen."

For a moment, Jake looked thoughtful; then Cai felt the muscles tense beneath her hand. "Does this have a point?"

"Yes, it has a point." She must have been blind to miss his sarcasm all these years. "Of the ten of us, two are dead.

One from Spec Ops on a mission, and his partner a few months later. The other three Quandems are nonfunctional. You and I are the only pair left that can be used. Get it?"

"I've got it. I'm stuck with you until one of us dies or the experiment ends." He muttered a curse; then his expression changed, became speculative. "How do you know this? And don't try to tell me you were briefed; I know better."

Involuntarily, she squeezed his arm, then pulled her hand back and retreated a couple of steps. If Jake weren't so mad at her, if he were more like the man she thought she knew, she wouldn't hesitate. But she couldn't begin to guess what this hard-edged, pissed-off stranger would do with the information.

Biting her bottom lip, she considered her options. She could try to evade, but his stubborn expression told her clearer than words that she'd be facing a huge argument if she chose that path. Deception was out of the question. She'd never lied to him, at least not outright, and she wouldn't start now. But if she told him the truth, he could use it against her.

What it boiled down to was trust. Cai studied him, tried to predict what he'd do, but his face gave her no answers. In the end, one idea swayed her: maybe if she showed her faith in him, it would be the beginning of rebuilding their friendship.

"I have security clearance into more than a hundred different systems. It's how I get the information that I pass along to you when you're out on a mission." She took a deep breath. "I merely extended my authorizations a bit."

Jake didn't show even an iota of surprise. Of course, the man was damn good at hiding his thoughts, but she suspected he'd already figured it out and was testing her. She rubbed her forehead, trying to ease the headache she hadn't been able to shake. Her emotions had been all over the map today, and it wasn't over yet. She lowered her hand and wrapped her arms around her waist. The hardest part was yet to come.

"Don't pretty it up. You hacked into restricted files."

Cai blew out a loud breath. "Are we going to argue about this now? Do you really care that much about it?"

"No, I don't. Let's get to the main issue." Jake closed the distance between them. "Why did you come looking for me?"

She'd wondered how long it would take him to calm down enough to ask. Hugging herself harder, she tried to find the perfect way to broach the subject. Though she'd rehearsed what she planned to say, nothing she'd come up with was going to work now. Not when he was so unreceptive. Maybe she should lay it out there and hope for the best.

"I need your help." There. She'd said it.

He cocked an eyebrow and looked at her as if she'd lost her mind. Maybe she had.

"So that's why you revealed yourself." His voice was even harsher, but now there was an edge of cynicism as well. "You want something from me. I should have guessed."

Cai grabbed him before he could walk away again. "No! I know you hate me right now, but please. It's important."

For a moment, she feared he'd simply break her grip and leave, but he surprised her. "Okay, let's hear it."

It wasn't "*Whatever you need, Cai,*" but it was a damn sight better than what she'd expected. "Thank you."

"Don't thank me. Talk," he ordered.

"I need you to help me find my parents." She waited, but he said nothing. The only reaction she received was the flex of his forearm beneath her fingers. She hesitated, then hurried to fill the silence. "They disappeared six years ago. The authorities declared them dead, but there wasn't any evidence to support that conclusion. After years of scanning different databases, I think I came across something that will lead me to them."

She took a breath when she finished blurting her summary. Once again, when it counted, glibness had deserted her. But then, she'd always been better with machines than people.

"You can't take this up proper channels because you'd be in hot water once they found out you got the information by hacking." Jake's eyes seemed to grow even icier as he spoke.

"You think I'm protecting myself by coming to you instead of the authorities, but I'm not. If it brought my mom and dad back, I wouldn't care if I wound up court-martialed." Cai rubbed her ring again, looking for strength. Jake made no effort to hide his disbelief, and that hurt too. She gave a shrug, trying to use a physical action to rid herself of emotional pain.

"After my parents were declared dead, I appealed the decision. I took it up the ladder of every agency that might have some jurisdiction. I presented my theories and what evidence I had, but I may as well have saved my breath. I generally got one of two reactions. Either they humored me, then patted me on the head and told me to get on with my life, or they laughed and told me grief had made me delusional. I'll get the same reaction now."

"You can't know that," Jake said, and for the first time Cai thought she detected a hint of compassion.

She looked away, blinked hard a few times, and then met his eyes again. "I *do* know. Since they didn't believe me six years ago, they sure as hell aren't going to believe me now."

He touched her, covering the hand she had on his forearm with his own. The calloused warmth of his fingers soothed her, and she took the comfort he offered without hesitation. Even if the kindness lasted only a moment, she was grateful for it.

"Have you thought maybe you're grasping at straws?"

"Yeah, maybe I am," she said quietly, "but if there's the slightest chance this could lead to some answers, I have to take it. Wouldn't you if it were your parents?"

"No." The tone didn't encourage questions.

Jake withdrew, taking his hand from hers and shaking free of her hold. Every time he spoke, the illusion that she knew him disintegrated further, but there was something in the way he retreated that made her ache on his behalf. She wrapped her arms around her waist again before she did something stupid.

"Give me the short version," he said.

Nodding to show she heard him, Cai quickly tried to organize her thoughts. She knew her plan was going to be a hard sell, but the fact that he was willing to listen after everything she'd done wrong tonight gave her a slim chance. "My parents are doctors who've been doing research in bionanotechnology. To be precise, they've been working on advanced nanites."

"What's a nanite? Is that like the implants we have?"

"No, nanites repair genetic problems, perform minute surgery, and continually remove dead cells. And that's only the beginning of the possibilities. Life spans can be lengthened indefinitely and more. The Quantum Brain thing is different."

Jake crossed his arms over his chest and leaned back against the side of Hell. "Do you understand this nano shit?"

"Some of it. I'm in no danger of being recruited for lab work, though." Cai used both hands to rub her temples. Her headache was getting worse. "My mom and dad were on the cutting edge in their field and frequently received offers to work for some megacorporation or other. They turned them all down because of ethical questions on the end use of their research, but despite the heavy recruitment, there was only one time they worried over the reaction to their refusal."

"You think this company is behind their disappearance?"

"Not a company. A man. Marchand Elliot."

When Jake straightened away from the wall, she knew he'd recognized the name. "That explains why no one wanted to reopen the investigation. Are you sure?"

Reluctantly, she shook her head. "It's circumstantial at best. I know he approached my folks at least twice. Once when I was fourteen, and the second time less than a month before they vanished. I know they were anxious after his final visit, but they wouldn't tell me why or share any details."

"So of course you concluded he'd kidnapped them."

She ignored the caustic tone. "I know it's a leap, but I find it suspicious that Elliot dropped out of sight at about the same time, and that no one knew where he went. I don't believe in coincidence, and he wanted the research badly."

"For what? The money he could make with it? He's already so damn rich that he'd never notice a few hundred billion more."

"No, not the money. What if you could decide who did and didn't get the nanites? In essence, you'd be controlling life and death. And what my mom and dad were trying to perfect was light-years ahead of anything out there now. That's not all. There are destructive nanites that, instead of healing, consume everything they come in contact with. What if you could convert a good nanite to a bad one with a command?" Cai did reach for him then, grabbing both his arms. "Think of what kind of power you'd wield and what you could do with it."

He didn't reply. She knew how wild it sounded, how impossible it was to believe. There were days when she wondered if it were some elaborate form of denial. Cai released

Jake and stepped back. She'd made a promise. If it took the rest of her life, she'd never quit looking for answers. She couldn't.

The last comm conversation she'd had with her mom and dad was seared into her brain. She'd been so devastated that her parents had exiled her, so hurt by it, that she'd lashed out. She'd told them she hated them, told them she didn't care if she ever saw them again. They'd tried to contact her the day they'd gone missing, but she'd known it was them and hadn't answered.

And then it was too late. Too late for apologies, too late to assure them that she understood that they'd sent her away to protect her from Elliot. Too late to tell them she loved them. She needed another chance; she had to set things right.

Squaring her shoulders, she continued on despite her recep's skepticism. "One of the files I was scanning through today suggested that Elliot might be on the Raft Cities."

He shook his head, looking disgusted. "Let me guess—you want to go there and question him." She nodded. "Do you know anything about the Raft Cities?" He didn't wait for an answer. "We call the people there pirates, but that's bullshit. They're terrorists, pure and simple. We sent Navy SEALs in because they'd grown too dangerous, too powerful. And now, not that many years after those Pirate Wars, they're already regrouping—that's obvious from the increase in attacks."

"I know the Raft Cities are lawless. I researched—"

"Research? God." He muttered something she couldn't hear. "Reading about a place is different from seeing it firsthand." Jake shook his head, cutting her off again. "Never mind. Do you honestly believe Elliot kidnapped your parents? With his wealth, he could hire someone who was doing the same kind of research easily enough without risking anything but money. And if for some odd reason he did have your parents abducted, do you think he'll admit to it if you walk up and ask?"

"Probably not," she conceded, answering his last question and leaving the rest of it alone. "But I have to try."

He closed his eyes for a moment and exhaled sharply. "You want me to go with you, right? To track Elliot down, get you past his security, and help interrogate him."

Cai winced at the bitterness in his voice. "Kind of, but not exactly."

He ran a hand over his chin, then asked, "What, exactly, do you want then?"

"General Yardley contacted me tonight," she told him. "I'm supposed to report to his office tomorrow morning. With you. If you approve the idea, I'll be accompanying your team on an assignment to the Raft Cities. I don't expect you to do everything for me. I'm only asking that you okay my presence."

There was a long moment of silence. Then he said, "Even if you're right about Elliot and there is something worth looking at, I don't believe you'll be an asset to the mission. Not when your head is more on your personal aims than what the op involves."

She barely stopped herself from flinching. She knew he was thinking of the men who'd died today and wondering if she would jeopardize the lives of his surviving teammates. "I'd never put anyone else at risk," she said.

Jake stared, clearly not believing her. Didn't he know her well enough to realize his team was hers too? That she would live and die by the same code Special Forces followed? And when his expression didn't change, she had to accept that he didn't know her at all. It hurt.

"Go home." His tone wasn't unkind. "If you need to find proof of your parents' deaths, keep looking. I won't say anything about the hacking. But I won't agree to your presence on the operation."

So that was that. Cai offered him a weak smile. "Thank you for listening to me. I appreciate the consideration."

"No problem." He hesitated. "You are going home, right? It's not safe out here."

"Sure." She was going home and attending the meeting with General Yardley in the morning as ordered. Then, after Jake left the office, she'd request leave and head for the Raft Cities on her own. So she wasn't lying. She just wasn't filling him in on what she planned on doing after she went home.

He looked at her suspiciously, but she must have kept her thoughts off her face, because he shrugged and walked away. When he turned the corner, leaving her in the alleyway, it sank in how truly alone she was. Any connection to him had been in her head, not his. She'd thought of him as her best friend, but to him she was nothing more than a tool to be used in the field. Maybe he didn't mind talking with her to pass the time, but look how fast he'd cut the link tonight when his buddies had shown up.

She replayed the years since her parents had disappeared, but aside from her mind-talk with Jake, there hadn't been anyone who was more than a passing acquaintance in her life. That was her fault. Yeah, she was socially inept, but she'd have to make an effort to meet people and form real friendships. After she returned from the Raft Cities.

"Lookee what I found." She whirled at the voice. "You and I are going to have some fun, little girl. At least I will."

The man swayed unsteadily, and she pegged him as one of the two who'd been stunned by the bouncers. Cai moved, balancing her weight more evenly. If she could take down Gnat, she'd be able to deal with one creep who barely managed to stand up.

"I'm after you," another voice said from behind her.

Two. She'd learned how to repel multiple attackers; she could handle this. Carefully, she shifted, wanting both men in view. *Oh, crap.*

There wasn't only one man at the mouth of the alley; there were six. That made seven against one. Cai lifted her chin.

She wasn't going down without a fight.

Chapter Four

She put two men on the ground fast. Both were out cold, and she didn't expect them to recover in time to rejoin the fray. The other five wouldn't be as easy to handle, not with the element of surprise gone. Despite the momentary confusion, the gang never gave her an escape route out of the alley. One of the men grinned, and Cai swallowed hard. He looked excited by the prospect of violence, and that worried her.

What was that old saying—the best defense is a good offense? She struck out at the nearest man, hitting his nose with the heel of her hand. He howled in outrage. Blood flowed copiously. *Good.* She had a split second to prepare.

They came at her.

She put an elbow into one man's throat, then whirled and kicked another's knee. Cai jumped away from a fist aimed at her solar plexus, but took a blow to the side of her head. Although she couldn't see straight, she didn't stop moving. She pushed one of her assailants hard, hoping he'd fall into the others.

Another whirl, but no one was fighting her.

Unsure why, she paused to find out—and saw Jake. He'd come back! There were only three men standing now, and they were after her recep. *Like hell.* She kicked hard at the back of one's knee. His leg buckled, but he didn't go down.

When he turned, she realized that she'd picked the leader of the crew. There wasn't time to worry about it.

"You're going to pay for that, bitch," he snarled.

It was the smile following the threat that made her blood go icy. But Cai pushed her fear aside and assumed a basic stance that balanced her weight evenly and gave her a wide range of possible movements. She raised her arms to guard her face, her back hand near her jaw, her front hand at eye level.

The creep pulled a knife.

Well, whoever said street thugs played fair?

One point in her favor, however, was that he'd shown the blade early and hadn't surprised her with it. His other hand was in plain view, so if he had another weapon, like a neuron fryer or dazer, he wasn't planning on drawing it. Yet. She couldn't assume he didn't have something deadlier to use if she were winning. She needed to take him out pronto.

The sleaze made the first move. He closed the distance, thrusting his knife toward her belly. Since she'd practiced this hundreds of times, she didn't have to think. She parried his arm downward and without hesitating belted him in the eye.

Quickly she moved toward him and used her elbow under his chin. She tensed when she heard a man's pained cursing farther up the alley, but relaxed when she realized it wasn't her recep. He was facing two attackers, though, and might need help.

Her worry about Jake allowed her opponent to recover. *Crap.* She should have finished him off while she'd had the advantage.

The lowlife was angry—she read it in his eyes—and he didn't use any finesse when he came at her. She delivered a blow to his arm, and the knife clattered to the ground. This time she didn't stop. With the full force of her body, she kicked him in the groin.

His scream sounded too high-pitched to have come from a human being. When he hit the ground, grabbed his crotch, and curled into the fetal position, Cai smirked. It served him right.

She turned to see if Jake needed assistance and found he'd taken care of his two attackers and was surveying the scene. "Thanks for the help," she said.

"No problem. Someone had to bail you out."

Tossing her braid over her shoulder, she stiffened. "You're insufferable," she muttered and walked away, leaving him in the alley.

He caught up to her quickly, and she shot him a glare. It didn't deter him for a microsecond.

Since he was accompanying her, she didn't struggle to pay attention to her surroundings. He'd watch out for both of them. And for some reason, she couldn't focus on anything for more than a few seconds at a time. Adrenaline, she realized belatedly; in the aftermath of the fight, she was dealing with an excess of it in her body. No wonder she felt jittery.

They crossed out of New Washington's dead zone and into an area being reclaimed from urban blight. There wasn't any graffiti here, and the buildings didn't resemble bombed-out shells. Which didn't mean all threat was gone, though it did reduce the risk. Cai breathed a sigh of relief, but couldn't manage to clear her thoughts.

"Where do you live?" Jake asked after a few more blocks.

"Why?"

"Because I'm walking you home."

"Go back to your buddies." She picked up her pace. As if that would do any good. Since he was half a foot taller, he easily kept up with her. She pretended he didn't exist. He didn't try to break the silence, and that suited her fine.

Despite the things he'd done tonight that were nothing like the Jake she knew, Cai felt sure of his reason for returning to the alley. He hadn't changed his mind about taking her on the op. Nope, her recep had reappeared because his sense of responsibility demanded he escort her safely home. It didn't matter that she'd absolved him of the duty. She gave him another scowl.

"I know you're dealing with the adrenaline," he said quietly, "but could you manage to wipe that expression off your face before we run into other people?"

She turned, ready to tear into him, but she breathed deeply and stopped herself. He'd done nothing to warrant her going off, and she wouldn't let some stupid hormone surge rule her behavior. "How much longer does this last?"

He shrugged. "Depends on the person. Half an hour maybe."

"Why aren't you having a problem?" She couldn't keep the accusation from her tone.

"I have experience channeling it," he explained blandly.

Her eyes narrowed as she considered him; then Cai forced her face to smooth out and she resumed walking. Just in time, too. They shortly passed their first group of people, but no one did more than glance at them.

They were approaching civilization again; she could see the glow from the holoboards, hear the sounds of the ads. Then they entered the main drag, and she felt Jake's gaze. She tried to disregard it—at least until he drew her to a halt and tipped her face up toward his. For close to an eternity, he only stared. "I can't believe this," he said at last. "You're a kid."

It was the agreeable, almost conversational tone that made her suspect he was livid. "I'm twenty-one, a legal adult in every corner of the UCE." She freed her chin from his fingers.

"You're twenty-one?" he asked with some skepticism.

She ground her teeth, but nodded sharply.

"Shit, you *are* just a kid."

A snarl tried to escape, but she swallowed it. "You're only five years older than me." Her hands bunched into fists and she realized she felt defensive. Before she could say something that she'd regret, Cai pivoted crisply and resumed walking.

"It's not the years, sweetheart; it's the miles," he growled as he caught up with her. She went back to ignoring him, and he finally looked away. Her feeling of relief was short-lived.

"How the hell do you know how old I am?"

For an instant she was nonplussed; then she realized what he was asking and her face went pale. *Crap.* He'd figured out that she'd hacked into his personnel file.

From where he sat, Jake had a perfect view of Cai and plenty of time to study her. Yardley had left them waiting in his anteroom. Her posture was rigid, almost as if she were sitting at attention, and her gaze remained fastened on the wall across from her. He didn't know what had her so tense.

Reluctantly, he asked, *Are you okay?*

She started slightly. *Fine, thank you.*

Jake frowned. The excruciating politeness had begun at the end of their second argument. He hadn't meant to get riled up for another go-round, but when he'd figured out how old she was at the start of their Quandem, he'd seen red. It wasn't her fault, but he'd been so hot over the UCE's using a teenager that he hadn't been able to keep quiet. She'd given it right back to him.

Why the hell had he ever believed she was a computer? Looking back over their conversations, he realized she'd never come across as reserved or emotionless. Maybe he'd jumped to conclusions when they'd informed him that she could process information from a hundred-plus systems simultaneously and pass the data on to him in the field. He hadn't thought any person could handle that kind of volume for one thing, and for another, "Cai" had sounded so much like one of the military's many acronyms.

When he thought about what he'd shared with her, his gut twisted. He never would have told her about his nightmares if he'd known she was human. He hated that she was aware of how vulnerable they left him, that she'd seen his weakness. And he wondered how he was going to handle it the next time he had one of those dreams and couldn't let himself reach for her.

He'd stewed over that for a while last night, until he recalled something worse: in the beginning, he'd had difficulty closing her out and had slipped a lot. Especially when emotions were running high. She'd heard him ream out a few subordinates, seen him lose control.

And it had taken him even longer to perfect blocking her when he was having sex. More than a year. He'd never been indiscriminate, like some of the men, but he'd been active enough. And his little voyeur hadn't made any effort to shut him out. He'd known that. When he'd thought she was a computer, he hadn't cared, but now he knew better. At the time she'd been *sixteen* years old. *Shit*.

He shifted in his seat and decided not to think about that. It was too damn humiliating. Instead, he remembered Cai going toe-to-toe with him last night when she'd heard enough. The thought lightened his mood. He liked that she wasn't intimidated by him.

They'd had another brief quarrel after he'd shaken her awake this morning. He'd gotten her home safely last night, but she'd crashed from the adrenaline and fallen asleep on him, so he'd pulled off her boots, put her to bed, and crawled in beside her. He'd spent the night only to keep her out of trouble. Jake was positive she'd take off on some poorly thought-out personal mission the minute she recovered, and if she didn't show up for the meeting with Yardley, the general wouldn't hesitate to declare her AWOL.

She hadn't appreciated it. In fact, she'd wasted no time telling him he was wrong, that she had no plans to go off and miss the appointment. He couldn't believe he'd misread her so badly. She was consumed by the need to find her parents, so why wasn't she planning to look on her own?

Wait a second. Jake replayed her exact words. She hadn't said she had no plans to go off on her own. She'd said she had no plans to go off on her own and miss the meeting with Yardley. He should have picked up on that sooner. *I'm on to you.*

He'd startled her again, and this time she looked at him. *I beg your pardon?*

You heard me. And if you think you're going to the Raft Cities by yourself, you'd better think again.

Her chin went up, and he had to hide another smile. He'd quickly learned what that gesture meant. Damn, this woman was stubborn. Too bad he appreciated that particular trait.

That place is a pirate stronghold. Do you think I'd be stupid enough to go there alone?

She was good. Another question instead of a denial. *In an instant, sweetheart. Just because I thought you were a computer doesn't mean I don't know you. You'd risk anything to find your parents.*

With a short sniff, she faced forward again, but she didn't tell him he was full of shit—which meant he had her dead to rights. How the hell was he supposed to keep her safe when there was no way he could watch her every minute?

Not that she wanted his protection. Cai had already pointed out that she'd taken care of herself for a lot of years without his help, and he knew she'd fight him if he tried to look after her. Even if it *was* for her own good.

Jake wasn't sure what it was about her that made him feel so protective. Maybe it was her delicate frame, although delicate women sure didn't take down three thugs the way she had last night. Then there was Gnat. Jake's lips twitched as he recalled the look on his warrant officer's face as the man had gone down. No doubt the others were still giving him shit about how easily she'd handled him.

As he studied Cai's clean profile, Jake crossed his arms over his chest. Maybe he wanted to watch out for her because she was so pretty. Her obvious Asian heritage made her far too exotic to be classically beautiful, but he found her looks much more appealing than the usual bland societal ideals. In fact, *too* damned appealing. He'd taken a one-two punch when he'd gotten his first look at her in good light and gazed into her soft brown eyes. Hell, he still felt half-dazed when he realized this was *his* Cai.

He'd yet to see her hair loose, but he guessed that it would fall about halfway down her back. Taking a deep breath, he pushed aside thoughts of her dark mane spread over a pillow while he . . . *Hell*. He shifted again in his seat. She glanced his way, and Jake wasn't sure what she read on his face, but she stiffened further and quickly returned her attention to the wall.

Good going, Tucker. He couldn't believe he was ogling her. Not only was she too young for him; she'd been his partner and friend for years. She'd saved his ass more times than he could count. She deserved better.

It was a relief when the general's aide entered. "Captain Tucker, the general will see you now." They both stood. "Sorry, Captain Randolph—General Yardley asked that you wait."

Jake sensed Cai's confusion as she returned to her seat. Since he didn't know what to tell her, he could only shrug when he met her eyes. She looked even more nervous. He hesitated, but when the aide cleared his throat, he had no choice but to leave Cai and follow the man.

"General Yardley." Jake snapped off a salute as he entered the man's office.

Of his superiors, Yardley was the one Jake most respected. The man's office was austere, and while there were some evident perks of rank, the man didn't brazenly flaunt his position the way other high-placed officers did. His desk was plain, utilitarian, and the holos on the walls weren't art. One showed Yardley shaking hands with President Beauchamp; another was of him with General Aaron Armstrong, the supreme military commander. Maybe the splashiest item in the room was the white-and-blue UCE flag in the corner behind the desk. For Jake, though, the important thing was that the general had genuine concern for the men under him. There was nothing he admired more.

"Tucker. Have a seat."

"Thank you, sir."

"How is Captain Randolph holding up?" the general asked once Jake was settled in the chair across from him.

"She's fine. Why do you ask?" Since Yardley had come up through Special Forces, he didn't stand on ceremony like a lot of the brass. As long as the tone remained respectful, Jake knew he didn't have to *sir* and *general* him to death.

Yardley smiled slightly. "I'm afraid I make her nervous. My guess is that one of the doctors on the Quandem team told her I did my damnedest to have her disqualified from the program, and since then I've disconcerted her."

"Her age should have exempted her from the project," Jake agreed. He nearly added an off-color adjective. The general leaned back, folding his hands on the top of his desk and studying him. Jake met his commander's scrutiny without flinching.

He didn't know what the older man was looking for, but whatever it was, he must have found it. With a nod Yardley said, "Her age, of course, was a major source of concern, but I had other objections. Of the women in the project, your anchor was the only one not originally in the military."

"Where did the army find her?"

"A government-run academy for gifted students."

Jake hid a grimace. They'd pulled her from school, and with her folks missing, she'd had no one to run interference for her.

"I felt her youth and her complete ignorance of the military would be detriments," Yardley continued after a short pause. "The project leaders, however, were insistent that she was the sole choice if we wanted to keep you part of the experiment. I made a deal with the doctors. If Randolph could pass the training I put her through, then I'd sign off on her. If she didn't, they would try to match you with someone else."

"And if they couldn't do that?"

"Then you'd be scrubbed and an alternate chosen."

"Obviously Cai passed." Jake didn't comment on the fact that he'd had no desire to be part of the study. It had quickly been made clear to him at the time that if he wanted to continue his military career, he had no choice except to agree. If Cai had dogged it and not done well, he would have been off the hook.

"She did more than pass. Randolph finished in the top five in everything I put her through. That's when I decided to send her to Special Forces school."

Jake raised his brows, and Yardley smiled at his reaction.

"Yes, I know. Major Donlin was in charge of the instructors when she happened to be scheduled."

"The Crypt Keeper?"

"I see you're acquainted."

"No, sir, but his reputation is well-known." There wasn't a man in Special Forces who hadn't heard of the Crypt Keeper. Donlin considered it a crusade to make as many candidates as possible go DOR—Dropped on Request. His belief was that it was better to wash them out in training than to have them endanger lives during an op. "Cai *happened* to be scheduled with Donlin?"

The general's smile widened, but he didn't comment directly. "I told him to push her hard."

Jake's whole body went stiff. "Let me get this straight, you told *the Crypt Keeper* to push a sixteen-year-old girl?"

"Watch yourself, Tucker."

"Yes, sir," he said tightly. The idea of Donlin riding Cai pissed Jake off. The training would have been hard enough for her as it stood. Shit, adult men twice her size routinely washed out because they couldn't hack it. The major would have been after her anyway, but with the general's order, God only knew what kind of harassment she'd endured.

"Before you get bent out of shape any further than you are already, you should know that your anchor finished fourth in that class. Donlin came out and issued his report to me in person. Said the harder he pushed her, the deeper she dug in her heels. Men all around her were ringing out, but she would just raise her chin and keep going no matter what he did. He also told me that he would take Randolph on his team any day."

Jake stopped seething and started thinking. Yardley was telling him this for a reason, and it wasn't to anger him. "You want me to okay Cai for this mission, don't you, sir?"

"Yes, I do."

"What can she do on the Raft Cities that she can't do from here? We've always worked remotely."

"Intel identified a computer that's far more advanced than anything the pirates should have. We haven't been able to pinpoint its location, though, and she can't tap into it from a distance without that. Part of the mission will be to find the system and retrieve any data the UCE would be interested in."

The explanation raised more questions than it answered. "Despite her training, she has no field experience."

"I'm aware of that. But I also believe she'll more than hold her own. You won't be babysitting her."

"Sir," he said, "are you ordering me to take her?"

"No, I'm not. If you choose not to include her, you'll be tasked with destroying the computer in addition to your other objectives. The decision is yours—but I do want her on the op."

"Why, General?"

Yardley took his hands from the desk, studied his fingers for a moment, then raised his gaze and changed the subject. "I read your report on the last assignment."

The non sequitur made Jake blink, but he moved to the new topic effortlessly. "And your opinion?"

"I agree with your conclusion. In fact, my investigation has already found some evidence to support the fact that it was a setup. Not enough for me to act, not yet, but definitely enough to warrant further examination."

Jake felt sick. It was one thing to think someone had set his team up to die; it was another to find out it was true. None of his men deserved that. They'd been good people, just doing their jobs. Yeah, they'd known the risk when they'd enlisted, but this was something else. They'd been sold out by officers within their own military, gutless traitors who'd deliberately sent them to their deaths. Jake's hands fisted.

What had these traitors wanted? Did they have some secret agenda—were they part of some enormous company, or were they just trying to thwart a government they distrusted? Hell, Jake himself didn't always agree with the UCE. But he wasn't fighting for the men and women in New Washington. He was in the army to defend innocents, to try to prevent the world from being mobbed by terrorists. The alternative to the UCE was worse than its bureaucrats; worldwide instability, unrest, and poverty. He'd worked it out in his mind, reached an internal peace. His loyalty was to the men he fought with, and to Cai, now that he knew she was a person. No matter how much he disapproved of some of his government's actions, he'd never double-cross his men.

"The colonel who briefed us?"

"Is a fool and apparently a dupe. He's still answering questions, but it doesn't appear that he was a knowing part of anything. By the way, your extraction team *was* drugged. The residual of a narcotic was found in each person's bloodstream when the medics ran tests after your return to Fort Powell."

That indicated a more widespread conspiracy, not only a few rogue officers. How far did it reach? "They wanted to wipe us out."

"Yes, that's what it seems. Losing fourteen of the UCE's top Special Forces soldiers would be quite a blow."

"Losing six *is* a blow, General," Jake corrected him.

"I'm not downplaying the loss of your men." Yardley leaned forward. "What I am saying is that it was supposed to be worse. I've implemented safeguards to ensure that this doesn't recur, but I'll be meeting with my officers to apprise them of the situation and to warn them to be extra alert."

Jake nodded. He should have pinned down that colonel during the mission briefing, demanded more answers. It had been obvious the man was a fool, but there were plenty of incompetent officers, and Jake had been given orders by them before. His team prided themselves on always performing despite the stupidity of the brass. Shit, they'd even laughed about it as they'd gotten ready for the op.

"Tucker, you had no way of knowing that was a trap. Stop censuring yourself. What's important now is preventing a repeat. Do you understand me?"

"Yes, sir," he agreed, but his heart wasn't in it. He *should* have realized something was up. It was his duty to keep his men as safe as possible, and he'd failed.

"There's evidence to suggest that someone unauthorized gained access to the records from the Quandem Project," the general said, and Jake stopped berating himself and listened. "I believe you're a primary target of whoever arranged the setup yesterday."

Someone unauthorized? Cai? Maybe. But Jake had the feeling she was too damn slick to leave a trail when she hacked. So if it wasn't her, and he was a target, that meant. . . . His head jerked up and he studied Yardley's face.

Son of a bitch. The man hadn't changed the subject. They were still discussing bringing Cai on the mission. "You think she's in danger here, don't you?"

The general shrugged. "You're a good officer, but without Randolph, you wouldn't have the advantage you do now."

Jake leaned forward, hands gripping the arms of his chair, and asked sharply, "General, is Cai in danger?"

Yardley settled back in his seat and scrutinized him carefully. Jake had to tighten his hold on the chair to keep from launching himself to his feet and pacing around the room. The general wouldn't appreciate such lack of control.

At last his commander said, "I believe they'll take her out if an opportunity arises. Not only is your effectiveness lessened without her, but so is your whole team's. And her loss would be big for the army. The woman has an affinity for computer systems that is truly amazing."

They'll take her out if an opportunity arises. And he'd be off on some mission, unable to protect her. "You think she'd be safer on the Raft Cities with me than alone on base?" It seemed impossible.

Soberly, Yardley nodded. "I trust you, Captain, but there are very few others I can unequivocally vouch for at this point. You pick your team, choose men *you* can trust, because your life depends on it. And Randolph's life, if you take her along."

Slowly, Jake released his grip on the chair and sat up straight. "She's definitely coming with me."

"I'd hoped you would feel that way."

The general stopped, but Jake had the sense he wasn't finished. With the news he'd heard already, this couldn't be good. Jake braced himself when Yardley met his eyes again.

"What I'm about to tell you stays between us. You are not to say one word about this to Captain Randolph. Understood?"

"Yes, sir," Jake agreed. Cai had access to systems he probably hadn't even heard of, which meant her security clearance was higher than his own. So what the hell was the general going to tell him that she couldn't know about?

His commander tapped his fingers lightly against the top of his desk for a moment, then went still. "I've told you about her age, and that I felt she'd be a liability to you. There's another reason I tried to disqualify her from the Quandem Project."

There was a long pause, but Jake knew he wasn't expected to answer. He felt a chill slither down his spine. Yardley looked reluctant, as if he didn't want to continue but felt he had no choice. How bad could this other reason possibly be?

"Randolph wasn't recruited only because her brain waves were a match for yours. The army wanted her mind," the general said, and Jake had the sense the man had decided to come at this from another direction. "Quite simply, she's brilliant."

"That doesn't surprise me." That earned him a nod and another long silence. Jake's hands went clammy and his stomach rolled. He wasn't sure he wanted to hear what came next.

"She's the only anchor left that's functional."

It wasn't a complete shock. Cai had told him the other Quandems were unusable, but he'd been too angry to ask questions. This was official, though, and Yardley hadn't been smooth when he said it. For a man of his rank, that was strange. "What does that mean, 'the only anchor that's functional'?"

"The probes can overload."

"I'm aware of that. It's happened to me a few times."

"Yes, I know." The general tapped his fingers again before saying slowly, "It's different for an anchor. When they overload, there are repercussions that receptors don't face."

"Like what, sir?" Jake didn't want to hear this.

"Brain damage."

"What?" He barely managed to choke out the word.

"That's the third reason why I didn't want Randolph in the program. Her mind is too valuable to risk, but everyone was confident the flaw in the nanoprobes had been fixed. At least until the first overload happened three months into the study."

"Was she told this before the implants were inserted?" Yardley looked apologetic, but Jake didn't give a rat's ass. He had his answer. They'd put something in Cai's head that they knew could hurt her, and they'd never given her any warning.

He came out of his chair, put both hands on the general's desk, and leaned forward. He knew he was damn close to crossing the line. "With all due respect, General," he said, "I consider it immoral that this fact was withheld from Cai and the other anchors. They should have been told about the gamble you and those doctors were taking with their lives. With their *minds*."

"Captain, you're skating on thin ice."

"Yes, sir, I'm aware of that," he said tightly.

"Then I suggest you resume your seat. Now."

There was no mistaking the direct order, but with fury running riot, Jake didn't want to obey. *Cai.*

What's wrong?

He hadn't realized he'd reached for her until he heard

her soft voice in his head. *Shit.* If he ended up in the stockade, who the hell would protect her? Jake reluctantly sat.

Jake! Are you okay? What's going on?

I'm fine. Sorry. I can't talk right now; I'm about to get my ass chewed. He blocked her. Oh, yeah, he was in deep shit. Yardley's face glowed with anger. Jake knew he should be more concerned than he was, but his temper continued to run hot. She'd been a kid! How could any man with a conscience agree to what his commander had allowed?

"Captain, in all the years of our acquaintance, I've never seen such an inappropriate display from you. Would you care to explain yourself?" The man was definitely pissed.

Jake ground his teeth. "I apologize, sir." It almost hurt to say those words. "Chalk it up to my disillusionment with an officer I used to admire."

The general's face became even redder. "Tucker, I suggest you keep your mouth shut. The only reason I've let you get away with this much is that I agree with your sentiments. The anchors should have been informed. However, if you say one more word I find disrespectful, my tolerance will be at an end."

"Yes, sir."

They glared at each other. It was Yardley who looked away first. "I had direct orders not to tell those women about the possibility of brain damage. This came from very high up. I might have disregarded that directive, but the doctors assured me the probes were fixed and there would be no problems."

Although Yardley hadn't said the name, Jake was sure it had been "Ax" Armstrong, the good old supreme military commander himself, who had given the order. The man was one cold son of a bitch, and Jake could almost understand why the general had caved. "And when the first anchor proved them wrong, sir?"

"It was too late then. The implants can't be removed, so what good would it do to tell anyone?"

"What? Are you sure?" That shook the anger out of him. They'd lied. He'd been told by the chief researcher that the probes would be extracted when the experiment came to an end.

Or maybe they'd lied to the general. When he'd mentioned having the probe pulled during his argument with Cai, she'd told him it wouldn't be taken out because they were too successful. She hadn't said they were impossible to remove.

"Very sure."

Jake had to digest that; he didn't want to believe that Yardley might be dishonest with him. He had to be able to trust someone besides Cai. "Why are the anchors affected and not the receps? Why weren't they told to be careful? It seems to me, sir, if they knew, they could take steps to avoid the situation."

The general rubbed his eyes and sighed. He sounded tired when he spoke. "The doctors haven't figured out what causes the probes to overload. This is one of the reasons Randolph has been tested so extensively; they want to know why she's been able to avoid the situation. As for why the anchors are the only ones affected, the favored theory is that it's the data implant overloading that causes the damage. Since the receps have only the connector implant, that's feasible."

Jake wondered if Cai agreed with the hypothesis. She might not have known about the danger before the implants, but he was damn sure she knew now. How did she live with it, knowing that anytime she used her probes she could find herself in trouble?

"I told you this for a reason."

He gave the general his full attention.

"This possibility is so slim, it's almost nonexistent, but I felt you should be aware that there is a chance. Someone could try to push Randolph into a situation where she would overload. They don't have to kill her to take her out of the equation."

Jake dropped his head into his hands and stared at the floor between his feet. There was no way he could defend her from the kind of attack Yardley mentioned. Not when the danger was inside her mind. Thank God it was his probe that had—

Hell. Jake closed his eyes and tried to remember that moment. The battle, the deaths, the escape, the reports, the nightmare, the news on Spud, finding out Cai was a person. It had been an overwhelming twenty-four hours with one thing after another since they'd encountered the wreckers. He simply hadn't taken time to consider it. But he had the opportunity now.

It had felt different yesterday when the implant had gone down. He tried to label how it had deviated, but it was hard to explain. The closest he could come was that when his probe had overloaded before, there had been a silence. He hadn't felt that this go-round. No, this time it had been more like it was turned on but not connected to anything.

There were a few other things that struck him. Like the fact that Cai had seemed shocked to hear from him. Why would she be that stunned? He always came back up quickly. Which led him to another point. Their pathway had been down for thirteen hours or so. When he'd had an overload in the past, he'd always been up within three hours. It had never taken longer than that, and most of the time it was considerably less.

He pressed his fingers into his forehead. It had to be . . .

"Tucker." The general's voice pierced his thoughts. "There's no cause to believe this is high on anyone's plan of action. Randolph hasn't had a problem in five years, and there's no reason for the subversives to think that could change. It's more likely they'll go after her in a conventional manner."

Jake lifted his head and looked at the general. He had to trust the man. Yardley had always been aboveboard with him in the past. "Sir, I think they already tried to get her through the implants. I definitely think the setup the team got caught in had the secondary goal of causing her to overload."

And Jake was pretty sure they'd succeeded. It wasn't his probe that had gone down yesterday.

Chapter Five

If the aide didn't walk faster, Cai was going to push him out of the way. Waiting to be summoned had been difficult enough, but now that she'd finally been called, she didn't want to dawdle. She'd never felt Jake so furious before, not even when she'd shown up in Hell. What had the general said to upset him? Her recep usually had great command over his emotions.

At last they reached the office, and she brushed past the aide before he could finish announcing her. Jake stood, and her gaze flew to him. He appeared grim, but he was back in control. Only then did she look at Yardley and salute. She'd done that backward, and undoubtedly she'd get another demerit next to her name, but her friend was more important than protocol.

"Have a seat, Captain."

"Yes, sir. Thank you, sir."

Jake sat when she did. He was to her right, within touching distance, and she took another moment to consider him. It didn't make anything clearer.

"Randolph." The snap in Yardley's voice demanded her

attention. "Why didn't you report that your implant overloaded?"

For an instant she gawked at him, dumbfounded. He couldn't know that. Then she started thinking. There was one person who might have been able to figure it out. The feeling of betrayal was so strong, anger nearly overwhelmed her. "Jake!" She scowled at him. "You ratted me out!"

"Sorry, sweetheart. It was germane to the discussion."

"What happened to loyalty?"

"I wouldn't have said a word if it weren't critical. You know that." He leaned toward her, face intent. "But there's a situation. I had no choice."

Cai opened her mouth to rebut, but the general cleared his throat and she blanched. She'd forgotten about Yardley.

"As illuminating as this display is, I have a full schedule today and we have a lot of ground to cover. The two of you will have to save this discussion for later. Understood?"

"Yes, sir," she said. Nervously she reached for her hair, making sure the strands were pulled securely into the knot at her nape. Confident the twist remained tidy, she ran her hands down her olive slacks, smoothing the fabric.

"Good. Now, why didn't you report the overload?"

"General, it was minor, not worth mentioning."

"That wasn't your call to make, Captain."

"No, sir." She dug her nails into her palms. Jake had ruined everything. Now instead of going after Marchand Elliot, she would be locked up with the doctors for weeks while they tested her over and over. How could he have done this to her?

"In this instance, however, it may be to our advantage that you kept it quiet."

"Huh? I mean—"

"Never mind, Randolph," the general interrupted.

Was Yardley laughing at her? Cai tilted her head to try to get a better view, but there was no hint of amusement on his face.

"Until I say otherwise, you're not to report anything out of the ordinary about the nanoprobes to anyone."

"Yes, sir." Now she was really confused. The man had always been such a stickler with her about rules and regs, but he was telling her now to disregard procedure. It didn't make sense.

Jake, what's going on? She shifted slightly toward him as she asked the question.

Did you leave a trail when you hacked into the Quandem Project files?

It's possible, but I doubt it. I'm careful. The light dawned. *Someone did gain access, though, right?*

Yeah, it looks that way. If that wasn't your footprint they found, then—

"Captains, do you think I could have your attention?"

Cai jerked forward and stiffened, not fooled by the general's agreeable tone. She always seemed to do something wrong when the man was around. Before she could think of how to apologize, Jake said simply, "Sorry, sir."

Yardley stared stonily at him, then turned to her. "This is vital. On yesterday's op, do you believe you were deliberately driven to an overload situation?"

Her instinct was to blurt out a denial, but the general's intensity told her how important this was. Biting her bottom lip, she gave the matter more thorough consideration.

"Sir, it's unlikely. There's no method to predict what will cause a probe to go down. Amount of data or systems accessed seems to have no bearing. At least that's my understanding from the testing I've been through. If the objective was to sever my connection to Ja—Captain Tucker, it was an iffy way to do it."

"What if knocking you out was a secondary goal? What about the possibility of that?" Jake asked.

With a shrug, Cai said, "If overloading me was considered only icing on the cake, then I'd say that's more likely." She thought of the other anchor she'd felt and hesitated.

"What?"

She ignored the harsh demand in Jake's voice. Instead she scooted forward on her chair and said to Yardley, "There was something odd yesterday, sir. While I was using the Monster—I mean the ADOK system—I felt another anchor. I know I'm the only one left from our experiment. Is there a new study under way? Maybe by another branch of the military?"

"I'm not aware of any more tests, Captain. I'll look into it, however, and get you an answer."

"Thank you, General."

"Could this other anchor have arranged for you to overload?" Jake wasn't going to leave it alone.

"I don't know how she could have."

"You're certain it was a she?"

"Yes, and don't ask me how I know. It's a sense I had." She met his scowl with one of her own. If he thought she was going to shrug off the fact that he'd betrayed her, he was wrong.

"You're fortunate you lost only your connector probe," the general said, and Cai ended the stare-down she'd been having with Jake. They thought only one implant had overloaded? But then why would they know differently? She'd been cut off from her recep when the second probe had gone.

"Yes, I was fortunate," she agreed with careful neutrality. Neither man knew how lucky, and she was keeping it that way.

Yardley tapped his fingers against the top of his desk. His gaze was unfocused, and he seemed to be considering something. In the lull, Cai did some thinking of her own— not only about what the general's questions meant, but about some of the things Jake had said both yesterday and today. As she put the pieces together, an image began to develop.

"Sir, was the team intentionally targeted? Is that what these questions are about?"

For a moment she didn't think she'd receive an answer. She was making plans for how to approach Jake when the general spoke. "There's evidence to support that theory, Captain."

"We have traitors in our ranks," she said sadly. "Do we know who the subversives are or why they did this, sir?"

Yardley studied her intently, weighing her, perhaps. "We haven't identified any specific individuals as yet, no. Of course, the investigation began only yesterday, and we have to be cautious. As for why—my conjecture is we have a faction within the military that supports the Shadow Voice."

Cai nodded. There had been something akin to fear in the general's voice, or maybe it was desperation. Either way, this division within the army was clearly being viewed with extreme concern. And if the UCE leaders were losing their hold on the military, they had good cause to be scared.

There was a lot wrong with the government; Cai knew that unequivocally. President Beauchamp and his top echelon liked to whip up mindless nationalism, using terrorists or other unifying enemies to keep the people from examining how much control they actually had. The media was an adjunct of the ruling elite and sounded more rah-rah than a squad of cheerleaders at a pep rally. But worst of all was the billionaire's club in New Washington. There wasn't representation by the people, for the people, but appointees who were answerable only to each other.

Despite this, however, she wasn't a fan of the self-proclaimed Voice of Freedom. The rebellion this mysterious entity was trying to foment would mean casualties, and not just among the combatants. Noncombatants, even children, could very well die if the Shadow Voice had its way.

Yeah, the UCE needed to be shaken up, but she believed in working within and around the system to bring about peaceful, lasting change. Never, not in a million years, would she betray her fellow soldiers, like those people who'd deceived Jake's team. To her, loyalty wasn't just a word; it was a code she lived by.

"These officers took an oath," she said, breaking the short silence. "How can they toss that aside? How can they think anarchy and bloodshed are good things?"

"I don't know, Captain." The general paused for a moment, then said briskly, "Now then, is there anything else you feel I should know for my investigation into what happened yesterday?" Cai shook her head. "Then we'll proceed to the mission briefing. Captain Randolph, Tucker has okayed your presence on his team."

Cai turned and stared at Jake. He'd said she could go? She never would have believed he'd agree to her participation. What *had* happened while she'd been left in the anteroom?

"Tucker, pick six men you trust." She tore her eyes from her recep as Yardley resumed speaking. "You'll be inserting covertly on the Raft Cities. I trust there's no need to fill you in on the particulars of this location, Randolph?"

"No, sir. I researched."

"Good." The general stared at Jake. "Split the men up into teams of two, each pair entering at a different point. Because of the connection, you'll stay with your anchor."

"I wouldn't have it any other way."

"Your cover story is simple. Randolph, you'll play the part of a webrider. Tucker, you'll be her broker."

"What the hell is a webrider?" Jake asked, looking at her.

"It's the same as a hacker," she said, keeping her voice bland. "Well, almost. The difference is that hackers break in for the challenge or for personal interests. Webriders illegally access systems and sell what they find. Their aim is profit."

"What are we going to the Raft Cities for?" Her partner looked relaxed, but Cai knew it wasn't true. She could feel his tension. Something was bothering him.

"The operation is multipronged. As part of your cover,

I'll provide data that you can barter if necessary, items that the pirate lords would be interested in. The story is that it was too hot for you in the UCE, so you're hiding among outlaws."

"General," Jake interrupted quietly. "It would be easier to weigh the information you're giving us on our cover if I knew exactly what the multiple objectives are on this mission."

"Are you telling me how to run my briefing, Captain?"

"No, sir."

"The success of your team is critical. Critical," General Yardley repeated, and a thread of desperation was back in his voice. Cai exchanged a quick glance with Jake, who only shrugged. "The Shadow Voice must be stopped before the situation within the UCE deteriorates further."

"The Shadow Voice is on the Raft Cities?"

No, it's not. Cai stopped herself from saying more, but it was too late. Her recep was staring at her with all kinds of suspicion on his face. *Damn it.* She was so used to sharing info with him that she'd answered without thinking.

"No," Yardley said, saving her from an inquisition. "At least, there are no indications of that at this time." Their commander squared his shoulders almost imperceptibly before continuing. "Your primary goal is the arrest of a traitor. Army intel has found indications that a compatriot of the so-called Voice of Freedom is either on the Raft Cities or soon will be there. We want her captured and brought to Fort Powell to face trial for treason. However, should the need arise, you have permission to use all necessary force."

Jake's knuckles went white as he gripped the arms of his chair. "Are you saying to bring this person in dead or alive?"

"We'd prefer her alive, but dead is acceptable."

"Just who the hell are we talking about? Sir."

"Captain Bree 'Banzai' Maguire."

"The woman the Shadow Voice has been touting as the leader of the revolution." Jake wasn't asking a question, but the general nodded anyway.

"Traveling with Maguire," Yardley continued, "is UCE Navy SEAL Tyler Armstrong, the supreme military commander's son. The second part of the op is his rescue. It's believed he's been brainwashed; approach him as a hostile. Clear?"

"That's why we drew the op and not the SEALs, isn't it?" her recep said slowly. "There's too big a chance Armstrong would recognize one of his own, and if he's tipped off, he'll run, taking Maguire with him."

Yardley jerked his head once, but otherwise ignored the comment. "The third goal of the mission involves you, Randolph. There are indications of a very powerful computer on the Raft Cities. With the majority of their resources going toward keeping themselves afloat, they shouldn't have anything like this. We want you to tap into the system and transmit any important data to the UCE. This isn't some throwaway part of the mission. Speculation is that the pirates plan to use this computer in an extensive assault against the UCE. Retribution, if you will, for the Pirate Wars."

Cai nodded, but couldn't find her voice. When she'd set this plan in motion, she hadn't yet toasted her probes. Now the thought of tapping into a computer that she knew to be the Monster's equal, or damn close to it, made her stomach sink. Maybe it wasn't ADOK that had caused the problem, but she associated her blowout with the new system. She'd managed to walk away nearly unscathed from one overload, but a second might leave her with a much worse situation than slight memory loss.

"Who knows about this assignment, sir?" her recep asked.

"Not many, but more than I feel comfortable with after discovering we have turncoats in our midst. Remember that this data was spotted by intel and traveled through channels to me."

One side of Jake's mouth quirked in a cynical smirk. "Since we don't know how deeply the faction's tentacles extend, we may as well put target beacons on our backs."

Yardley didn't miss a beat. "That's why I told you to pick men you feel you can trust. Your judgment will be the only protection you and Captain Randolph have. Tucker, one thing you'd better be clear about: The UCE wants Maguire. Everything and everyone else is expendable. That includes General Armstrong's son, you, Randolph, and any member of your team, understood?"

Cai glanced between the two men. Jake looked pissed as hell, and the general appeared resigned but resolute. "I understand the importance of the mission," her recep said, voice tight. It was a nonanswer, but their commander didn't call him on it.

"I'll forward more in-depth intel to Randolph's home system using a secured pathway; then she can transmit the data to you over the probes. Share with your men on a need-to-know basis."

Which she took to mean the general didn't think they could trust anyone, not even the men Jake would select. Her first field assignment sounded more and more like a leap into deep water. Pirates, traitors, spies, and a computer system that made her break out in a cold sweat. Okay, make that a leap into shark-infested deep water.

She touched her ring. There was no choice, and she'd risk much worse if it meant finding her parents. If the situation were reversed, she knew her mom and dad would do anything, go anywhere, to bring her home. Cai wouldn't do less. She couldn't. Her family meant the world to her.

The general was as good as his word. By the time they reached Cai's quarters, there was a list of files on her system. She sat at the console, trying to ignore Jake's pacing. It wasn't easy when the man had a way of moving that made her want to watch him. Then there was how hot he looked in uniform.

She forced her thoughts back to his state of mind. He'd been quiet since they'd left Yardley's office, and she knew he wasn't in complete agreement with the orders he'd received. But she also knew him well enough not to bring it up now.

The fasteners holding her twist in place were adding to her headache, so as she began accessing the info, she yanked them free, letting her hair tumble down her back. Jake made a choking noise and she stopped to check on him. "What's wrong?"

He shook his head as if he were coming out of a daze. "Nothing. Sorry. I was thinking of something. Tell me, is anything Yardley briefed us on in his office true?"

"You think he lied?"

"No, I think *you* arranged this whole thing, every damn piece of it. What I want to know is if there's a shred of fact or if this whole op is a big charade to get you to the Raft Cities. No bullshit, Cai, no carefully worded denials that tell me exactly nothing. I want the truth from you."

She used both hands to push her hair out of her face and sighed. It shouldn't amaze her that he'd figured it out after her slip. One of the things she enjoyed most was his quick and agile mind. "I did set it up," she admitted, "but it's all fact."

He looked skeptical.

"You want the story?" She didn't wait for a reply. "Yesterday morning, long before I was told you were going out on a mission, I was running data on associates of Marchand Elliot as a matter of routine. Megan Chance was returning from a trip."

Jake crossed his arms over his chest, raised both eyebrows, and asked, "Who the hell is that?"

"Megan Chance is the high priestess of Elliot's corporate empire. You know how hard it is to track anyone who wants to remain hidden, but I got lucky and discovered she'd come home from the Raft Cities. Why go there unless the boss ordered it?"

"You made another leap." He shook his head. "Her presence doesn't mean Elliot is there. The woman could be negotiating safe passage with the pirates for the company's ships."

"No, she'd send an underling for that. Chance is a high roller who likes the finer things in life. There's no way she'd visit the Raft Cities unless she was told to go. You're right, though; it doesn't mean Elliot is there, but I decided it was worth checking out. I found some interesting things."

"Like what?"

"The computer Yardley was talking about, for one. I doubt it belongs to the pirates. There are more important things for them to use their resources on. I also found out there's been a regular parade of high-priced aircraft and ships in and out of the Raft Cities over the last six years. Maybe it's another leap, but the timing is too coincidental."

Cai closed her eyes and rubbed her nape, trying to rid herself of some of her tension. She jerked in shock when Jake's calloused hands took over the job. "Go on," he prompted.

"Okay." Now she had to think while he was touching her. "Um, I knew the UCE would be interested in the computer because intel has been growing more concerned about the pirates over the last, oh, eight months or so. Now I needed a reason for the army to send you in, so I started scanning for something big enough to be assigned to the top antiterrorist team in Special Forces. I knew I had it when I found the snippet on Banzai Maguire. It was simple to put some tags on the data that would ensure it was discovered, flagged, and run up channels."

"Simple, huh? How'd you figure they'd send *you?*"

"I stacked the deck." Cai pulled away so she could turn and give him a grin. "Did you know that I'm pretty much the only person in the UCE who has a hope of hacking into the other computer?"

Jake shook his head as he walked across the room. "Why doesn't that surprise me? Shit." He began rubbing his neck.

"You're anxious about the mission, aren't you?"

"Only a fool wouldn't be."

"I know I'm one of your concerns. I promise I won't take any action that's stupid or precipitous."

Jake closed the distance between them again and bent over her, both his hands resting on the arms of her chair. "Somehow I think the two of us are going to disagree on the definitions of *stupid* and *precipitous.*" He crowded her, and Cai leaned back to get some space. "You'll call it a calculated risk or feel it's something you have to do. So I want a promise."

She inhaled deeply and all thought left her head. The man smelled good. Damn good. She took another full breath—and remembered waking up this morning with her face pressed against his shoulder, his arm around her waist. He'd had her pinned to the bed. How the hell had she slept through that?

"Cai."

"Hmm? Oh! What kind of promise?" He seemed unaware of why she'd been distracted.

"I want your word that you'll obey my orders. I don't want you taking off on your own or ignoring me when I tell you do to something. I'm the op leader here, which means I outrank you."

There was no doubting how strongly he felt about this, not with the firm set to his lips and the intensity burning in his eyes. She sighed. "I can't make a promise like that. I won't lose the chance to find my parents. I love them, Jake."

"I know you do, sweetheart." The gentleness in his voice astonished her. "But the military has command structure for a reason. Your disregarding orders may do more than risk your own life; it could jeopardize the lives of my men." His tone went hard. "I won't allow that. But I do understand how much this means to you, so how 'bout this? I promise to help you find some answers when it doesn't interfere with the op, okay?"

She searched his face, looking for some loophole, some half-truth, but he appeared sincere. "I have your word?"

"Absolutely. Do I have yours?"

"Yes, I promise too."

His smile made her worry what she'd agreed to, but before she could ask, he straightened and said, "I want some background. Those captain's bars indicate you have four years in, but that can't be possible. You would have been only seventeen, so did they give you a special rank or what?"

For an instant she wasn't sure what he was getting at; then she figured it out. He thought she hadn't been part of the army until she was of age, until after the Quandem Project started. "I was sixteen when I was commissioned."

His eyes went icy, and Cai was glad that frigid anger wasn't directed at her this time. "What?" he growled.

"They wouldn't put the neural implants in a civilian, so they arranged for me to go in early. I was a second lieutenant for months before we were linked." She hesitated, then added, "I appreciate that you're mad on my behalf, but trust me, there's no need. The military may not have been my first career choice, but it's worked out okay. I get to play with some of the most advanced computers in the world, and the army is an improvement over the UCE Academy for the Gifted."

She saw he had questions, but to her relief Jake changed the subject. "I want you present when I brief the men."

"Okay." It was a little staggering to be included, but it

made sense. She was part of the team now. "Have you decided who's coming with us?"

He folded his arms over his broad chest and stared at her. Cai couldn't conceal how indignant she felt. "Are you thinking I'd betray this mission?"

That startled him. "Fu—Hell, no."

"Then what's the problem?"

"It's not a problem, exactly."

This should be good. She pushed out of the chair and placed herself directly in front of him. Tipping her head back so she could continue to glare at him, she put her hands on her hips and asked, "What is it, exactly, then?"

"After last night, I'm going to need more of an explanation for the men than the fact you're our systems specialist. You can bet the Professor didn't keep quiet about how you put Gnat on his ass, or that I dragged you out of the bar and didn't come back."

So much had happened since then that she'd forgotten the scene inside Hell. His men would know nothing about the Quandem Project, since it was highly classified, and he sure couldn't say anything, especially now.

"Tell them we became friends through the Interweb, but we never met till last night. It's close to true, since the nanoprobes are microscopic computers. I came to see you because I received a heads-up on the mission and thought it best to introduce myself before we got under way. That's true too."

"I've always been completely honest with my men. I can't betray their trust."

"Really? You didn't mind betraying mine. But maybe you saw it as evening the score." The amount of rancor in her voice stunned her. She hadn't realized how deeply his disclosure to the general about her probes bothered her. Cai started to pivot away, but Jake took her by the shoulders and held fast.

"It had nothing to do with getting even." He tugged her

nearer and she had to hang on to his biceps to keep her balance. "I'd agreed to take you on the mission, and the general was warning me about anchors and what happens when they overload. You do know about that, right?"

"You mean the brain damage? Yes, I know." It amazed her how nonchalant she sounded after going through the situation.

"I figured you did. Yardley ordered me not to tell you; then he mentioned that someone could try to attack you that way. How could I not report that it might have already happened? He's in charge of investigating yesterday's mess, and you're a member of the team. Your probe going down is part of the inquiry."

When she didn't immediately say anything, Jake squeezed her arms and managed to haul her closer. She was forced to shift her hands to his shoulders and she looked at him, trying to decide how she wanted to respond. He appeared earnest.

"You've got to understand my position, sweetheart."

Cai sighed quietly. "I do, and I guess I can forgive you for telling the general about the overload. But I can't forget it." His smile stopped before it fully developed. "I guess that does make us even, because I can't trust you completely any longer, and I know you feel the same about me."

As they stared at each other, she became aware of how close they stood. Their torsos weren't touching, not quite, but there wasn't space for a laser to slide between them. The hardness of his muscles beneath her hands, the heat his skin generated, the fullness of his lips so close to hers . . . *Oh, my.* She felt her body react and had to stop herself from swaying into him.

Jake was her *friend.*

"Can you trust me to keep you physically safe?" he asked.

Without hesitation, she nodded. She knew he'd do whatever it took to prevent her from being hurt.

"Good. That's important." He gently put her aside and went to the door. "I'll be right back. Why don't you gather the data Yardley sent, and you can pass it on when I get back."

She didn't move for a long moment after he left. Had he picked up on how warm he was making her? Was that why he'd all but run from the place? That would be embarrassing. With a shaky hand she pushed her hair away from her face and returned to her station. From now on she was going to have to chant the word *friend* like her personal mantra so she didn't make a mistake again. The last thing she wanted was Jake's pity.

Leaning her chair back, she propped her feet on the edge of the console and used her nanoprobe to work the system. At first nothing felt different, but as she continued, that changed. Since she couldn't define how, she stopped to consider. After studying everything from multiple angles and coming up empty, she decided to continue. Maybe the flame-out had altered her perceptions and this *was* her first full-scale test of the implant. Once she jumped back into the groove, though, it didn't take long to breeze through the data the general had forwarded.

One fact lingered, and she paused to think about it. Maguire had been in stasis for a hundred and seventy years. Amazing. The world had changed a lot during that time; it had moved forward, and everything was different. Her friends, her family, even her acquaintances were dead. How frightening would it be to be on one's own in a place that was more strange than familiar? And how easy would it be to trust the wrong people?

Cai knew firsthand how scary it was to be alone, but at least this was her own time. She frowned. The general had said Commander Armstrong may have been brainwashed, but what about Captain Maguire? She'd been in the Kingdom of Asia too, and who knew what had been done to her. Of course, that wouldn't change how Cai and Jake approached the mission, so it had no bearing right now, and Cai had to trust that the truth would emerge at the trial.

Putting aside all speculation, she decided to broaden her search beyond what the general had prescribed. Some of the info he'd given her she'd found on her own, but some of it was new, and she searched those computers extra carefully. She was floating through the systems when she heard it.

The Shadow Voice. She punched up the volume.

"'. . . times that try men's souls. The summer soldier and the sunshine patriot will, in this crisis, shrink from the service of his country; but he that stands now deserves the love and thanks of men and woman. Tyranny, like hell, is not easily . . .'"

Jake came in then and stopped short. "Shit, turn that off."

She disengaged the transmission. He muttered something she couldn't quite hear and settled on the couch. "Where'd you go?" she asked.

"Needed this to set up the briefing and notify the team." He showed her a wafer-thin handheld. "Let me get things rolling; then you can send the data along the pathway, okay?"

"Yes, that's fine," Cai agreed. Of course he needed his own unit. If the message he sent didn't come with the correct code encrypted in it, the men would think it was bogus. She decided to do more searching until he finished working.

It was while she was checking out a file about the Raft Cities that the hair on her nape prickled. The odd sensation she'd had earlier had changed, and it almost felt like an echo now. That brought back memories of the early days of the Quandem Project. She stiffened slightly and surreptitiously did some exploring. It took a lot of discipline to remain still, both mentally and physically, but she did it.

It didn't matter. Only seconds after she felt the other anchor lurking in the system, the woman was gone. She must have realized Cai had made her. That could be the only reason—but how? Cai had been careful.

She closed her eyes and ran through her time in the systems. Testing a theory, she accessed the data again with her probe, and this time it didn't feel different from the way it had before the flame-out. Damn, she'd been afraid of that.

"Jake," she said quietly. She waited till he glanced up. "We've got a huge problem."

Now she had his full attention.

"I think the mission's been compromised."

"How?"

When words failed her, she used her implant to send her impressions to him. The odd feelings, the echo, the presence. His face became grimmer with every detail.

He rubbed a hand over his mouth, then said, "I didn't think it was possible for an anchor to trail another, yet you're saying this person, whoever she is, found you while you were in the systems and followed you while you investigated. Without your knowledge."

"I didn't think it could be done either, but she did it. And I did know something felt wrong early on, but when I couldn't explain it, I shrugged it off." Cai got to her feet and did some pacing of her own. "She knows what we're doing. She saw *everything* I saw, or almost everything. I shouldn't have written it off to the overload so easily. This is my fault."

"Send me the data now. Let me see what she has."

Once the transfer was complete, he dropped forward, his forearms resting on his thighs, and cursed quietly. "Yeah," he agreed, "you're right. The operation has been compromised."

"I'm sorry." She couldn't stop pacing.

Cai hadn't realized he'd left the couch, and when she pivoted, she plowed into his chest. His arms went around her to steady her, and she caught her breath.

"Quit blaming yourself. You didn't know it could be done. Now you do and you'll be aware in the future."

He rested his forehead against hers. With his arms wrapped around her waist, she felt protected and not as frantic as she'd been moments ago. She leaned into Jake, accepting his support.

"She knows about Maguire, Armstrong, and the Raft Cities," she said. "You're going to scrub the mission, aren't you?"

Chapter Six

Jake bit back a snarl before it could emerge. He didn't like the way Mango kept touching Cai, or how close the man sat to her. There were plenty of other seats aboard the transport, seats far away from his anchor, so why the hell didn't Mango and the others use them? The squad had practically pushed and shoved to see who would get one of the two places beside her.

"Tuck, are you listening to me?" Gnat asked.

Reluctantly, Jake looked away from the group. Gnat was the only one who'd treated Cai with the proper respect. Talk about unlikely. Nine times out of ten, if someone was going to put his foot in it, the warrant officer would be the man to do it.

"Sorry, what did you say?"

"I said communication once we split up is going to be an issue. It's not like we can take chances on the Raft Cities."

"No, I'm aware—"

Cai laughed, and Jake looked over to see Mango chuckling with her. His jaw clenched, but at least the sergeant wasn't touching her. Then Inch, who was on her right, reached out and took her hand. Instead of telling him to drop dead, she smiled at him. Jake ground his teeth. Now there were two of them.

He wasn't sure which man was worse. Inch's rep with women was more sordid than Mango's—his damn handle even came courtesy of one of his conquests—but Sergeant Mangano was pouring on the charm. Jake heard Gnat try to get his attention, but he ignored him. Inch and Mango would take advantage of any opening, and there was no way Jake would stand by and allow it. Then Cai extricated her hand, and he relaxed enough so that the muscle in his cheek stopped jumping.

"Captain!"

"What?" he growled. Couldn't Gnat see he was busy?

"I guess we'll have to discuss the comm situation later."

"Yeah, good." There was more laughter. "What the hell are they talking about over there anyhow?"

"When I walked by, the subject was fights they'd been in."

That surprised Jake enough to look at his XO. "Fights?"

"The funnier ones," Gnat said.

Movement caught Jake's eye, and he saw Kazoo and Gator giving a demonstration. As the scene unfolded, he knew the topic hadn't changed. He recognized the situation they were acting out; it was a skirmish from a recent op that had taken on farcical proportions. Jake wasn't surprised when the conclusion had everyone howling. Both the memory and the performance made him smile too. Until he noted Mango had his hand on Cai's arm again.

A low rumble escaped him when the sergeant ran his fingers up to her elbow. *That's it; he's going down.* But before Jake could gain his feet, a beefy hand settled on his shoulder, pushing him back into the seat and holding him there. Royally pissed, he stared at Gnat. "What the hell do you think you're doing?"

"Stopping a friend from looking like an ass. You can't go charging over there about nothing."

"Nothing?" he said softly. His eyes narrowed as he glared. "They're all hitting on her, and she's too nice to stop them."

Gnat appeared amused, but said soberly enough, "They're not *all* hitting on her."

"Like hell."

"It's only two of them, and to be honest, I think Inch is more interested in competing with Mango than in your captain."

Jake grunted. Gnat was wrong.

"You're underestimating her. If she can put me on the floor, she can take care of herself with that bunch." There was a note of admiration in the man's voice as he spoke of Cai's abilities, and Jake was pretty certain that meant Gnat had accepted her as part of the team. Couldn't he see how green she was?

"She's too—"

"Yeah, yeah, I know. She's too nice. Even so, she got herself free of Mango on her own."

Jake looked back, and sure enough, no one was touching her. Some of his tension drained away, and Gnat released his grip. His XO thought he was overreacting, but Gnat didn't understand. Not only was Cai young, she was a tech. She spent most of her time with systems. No way was she used to these guys. He'd seen them all on the prowl at one time or another and they were too damn slick with women. She'd never see it coming.

The close quarters of the transport didn't help. There was nothing for those idiots to focus on except Cai. Jake checked the time. At least another hour till they reached the staging facility. *Shit.* Once they landed, though, he'd damn well make sure they had more to think about than his anchor.

"Tuck," Gnat warned before he could move.

"I'm not going to interfere." *Yet.* Jake watched Mango run his thumb over the inside of Cai's wrist, and he grabbed the arms of his seat with both hands to remain stationary. Now that he'd had some time to think, he knew it would undermine her authority if he stepped in. He had to let her take care of it.

But it wasn't easy.

He wanted to pull Mango's hand off her and push him face-first into the bulkhead. Then he would explain, in words even a moron could understand, about proper conduct with an officer.

Cai dealt with Mango so smoothly that Jake nearly missed it. She simply started talking with the Professor and turned away. As she shifted, her arm slipped free. The move was artless, natural. Understated. And damned effective.

"I never thought I'd live to see this."

Now that he felt calmer about the situation, he took his eyes off the gang and turned to Gnat. "Live to see what?"

"You in a sweat over a woman." Gnat shook his head. "I've watched them come and go, and not one has made a ripple in your pond. But the captain—hell, she's caused a tsunami."

Jake frowned. Gnat had it wrong. He simply didn't want her to get hurt by one of his men. Certainly he wasn't in a sweat over her, not the way his XO meant. Of course, if he argued about it, he would hear the line about protesting too much, so he shrugged and said, "Cai's just a kid."

"So are you."

Jake grimaced, but he didn't dispute the point. Considering he was the youngest man on the mission by a good two years, and that Gnat was almost ten years older than he was, Jake knew it was a debate he wouldn't win. "And she's a friend."

His warrant officer laughed. "You keep telling yourself that, Tuck. It'll make you feel better. For a while."

The staging facility might be remote, but Jake knew it had state-of-the-art security and a few amenities. As the team entered the building they'd be using for the night, the computer greeted them by name and gave them their sleeping assignments. They trooped down the hall to stow their things. It had been a long day, but there were details to work out before anyone could rest. He followed Cai into her small room and tossed his pack on the bunk opposite hers. That earned him a frown.

"What do you think you're doing?" she demanded, voice low.

He thought about playing innocent, but decided he'd never get away with it. "What does it look like?"

"You can't stay here!"

Instead of responding, he crossed his arms over his chest and stared at her. If she wanted him out, she was going to have to remove him forcibly. For a minute it seemed as if she were considering it; then she huffed a loud sigh and picked up her bag. "Fine. I'll take the room you were given."

Now he moved, grabbing her from behind and wrapping her in a bear hug. Jake caught himself bending forward to nuzzle her neck and froze. *Shit.* What was wrong with him? This was Cai. He wouldn't scam on her, not like his men.

The feel of her body against his distracted him, and he nearly groaned aloud when she wriggled while trying to free herself. If he didn't know better, he'd swear she wanted to torture him. Although he tightened his hold, he eased far enough away so that her rear wasn't brushing his groin any longer.

She went still and said, "Jacob Tucker, back off. Now."

He hesitated a split second, then released her and took a big step away. What had come over him? It was his duty to keep her safe, not to get hot from the feel of her body against his.

Her eyes snapped with indignation when she turned to confront him. "I don't like you using your size against me."

He jammed his hands in his pockets. "Sorry," he said, embarrassment making the word sound gruffer than he'd intended. "I didn't mean to scare you."

That not only cleared the anger from her eyes, but earned him a smothered laugh. "You're not scary, Jake."

For some reason he couldn't figure out, that irritated him. "The hell you say."

"Do you want me to fake it so you can feel manly?"

He opened his mouth, but shut it before he said something suggestive. She hadn't meant it as a double entendre; it was his overactive imagination giving it that nuance. "Let's get back to the sleeping arrangements, okay?"

She switched the bag to her other hand and said, "Fine. One of us has to go to another room. If you stay here, the team is going to think we're sleeping together. You know that."

Yeah, he knew. It was the quickest, surest method to protect her from those Romeos. None of them, including Mango and Inch, would make an inappropriate advance if they believed she was his. Of course, if he mentioned this to her, she'd get mad again. She was too trusting and too damn nice.

"When we insert, I want those low-life terrorists to believe I'm more than your data broker, and if we're playing lovers, you need to get used to having me close." It was partially true. He had no plans to leave Cai unguarded on Malé, and if they slept apart, she'd be far too vulnerable.

She stiffened, and he heard the thud of her bag hitting the floor. "Lovers? Are you out of your mind?"

If he had an ego problem, that sure would have taken care of it. "Relax, sweetheart," he assured her, "I won't take advantage of you or the circumstances."

"I wasn't worried about that. I know I can trust you."

He found himself feeling even more insulted. "Since you believe me, we're going ahead with it. Get used to the idea."

"You know"—she closed the distance between them—

"you weren't nearly so arrogant and irritating through the probes."

"My feelings are hurt."

"Sure they are."

Jake sighed. Despite everything, he was having fun, but this was a mission, not a chance to verbally spar with Cai. "I'll let you pick which bunk you sleep in."

"Well, that solves everything, since my chief concern was which bed I'd get for the night."

"Has anyone ever mentioned you're sarcastic?"

"You're the first. You must bring out that side of me."

"I like the mouthiness." But he liked the idea that she saved it for him even more. She stared at him with a bemused expression, but he didn't explain.

For a moment neither of them moved or spoke, and he let the peace sink in. Quiet times had been so few and far between in his life. He knew it couldn't last—there was too much to do before they inserted tomorrow morning—but for now he savored it.

"By the way, I didn't thank you yet for not aborting the mission," she said, fleetingly running her fingers over his forearm.

"It wasn't my call; you know that."

"Don't tell me Yardley didn't ask for your opinion on whether or not to proceed. And don't try to tell me that you didn't recommend moving forward."

"Okay, yeah," he admitted reluctantly. "The general asked for my thoughts, but I didn't propose going ahead because of you. If there had been a clear risk to any member of this team, I would have advised canceling."

"I know." She took another step closer to him, and he could swear she felt her heat. "You always think of your men first."

Jake reached for her hand. Since the small room had no chairs, only the two narrow cots, he tugged her to one of them. "C'mon, let's sit and talk about a few things."

He waited till she was seated before joining her. For a moment he thought he heard some kind of soft hum, but when he turned his head to listen more closely, the sound disappeared. With a shrug, he focused on Cai.

"Here's how I see it," he said. "There's no evidence to suggest that the anchor who tracked you has any interest in Maguire or the mission. It may be simple curiosity. If you knew how to follow her, wouldn't you have found out what you could?"

"In a heartbeat," she agreed, swinging her leg onto the bed so she faced him. As he shifted to mirror her position, Jake picked up the humming again. He frowned, but ignored it.

"So although Yardley said there wasn't any new Quantum Brain testing going on anywhere in the UCE, that doesn't mean this woman is an enemy. And even if she is working against us, she doesn't know who's on the team. You didn't know who I was bringing at that point, so the men aren't exposed."

She nodded slowly. "The danger to the team remains at about the same level as it was before. Since the data went through so many people, and because we have traitors in our ranks, we have to assume that the wrong people know of the assignment anyway."

"That's my assessment. The only person who may be at an increased risk is you." He held up a hand to stop her from interrupting him. "It's true and you know it. You're the one the woman followed. However, as far as this anchor is concerned, going to the Raft Cities isn't going to endanger you any more than staying home. Your job involves computers, and whenever you access a system, she could turn up."

Her index finger ran along the inside seam of her fatigue pants. He watched her trace it up and down, up and down until he found himself damn near mesmerized. If it had been any woman but Cai, he might have suspected the motive, but he knew his partner. She was too straightforward to play games. It was one of the things he admired about her.

When she raised her eyes back to his, she said, "I'm not the only one. Because of our link, you're right there with me."

He reached out and covered her hand with his before she made him insane. "Don't worry; I'll be fine."

Her smile seemed rueful. "Jake, you worry about everyone but yourself. Since someone needs to be concerned about your safety, I guess it's up to me."

"If you want to keep me safe," he said, and gave her a practiced smile, "then you'd better sleep close to me."

She growled and yanked his hand off her thigh. "Don't you dare use your looks to try to get your way with me, cowboy. I know you too well to fall for that face."

Jake threw his head back and laughed. Cai never let him slide on anything. "It was worth a try," he said.

That got him another scowl. "I think you're very spoiled."

"Yeah, probably," he said, sobering, "but I wanted to avoid an argument. You've never been to the Raft Cities. I had a snatch-and-run there shortly after I joined the teams, so I know what I'm talking about. Trust me, that snake pit makes Hell look like a kindergarten, and sweetheart, you'll attract the vermin the minute you step foot on Malé."

"No one's going to be interested in me," she scoffed.

"Yeah? Like those men outside the bar weren't interested? I'm not handing you a bunch of bullshit. They're going to home right in on you and think they've found easy pickings."

Her brown eyes were serious as she considered. "You have a better take on this than I do, I know that," she said. "However, if these pirates are as bad as you say, why would your pretending to be my lover stop them? They lack honor."

"It isn't going to be honor that stops them. What will keep most of them clear is fear of reprisal. I can be a mean son of a bitch, and I'm going to make it clear immediately that I don't share. But if they see a weakness, like you sleeping alone, they'll take advantage of it."

He allowed her to think that over, and while he waited he let his gaze trail over her. The boots were inspection shined, not so much as a scuff mark on them. Clearly they'd never been out in the field. Her camouflage pants showed off her long legs, and that gave him a new appreciation for jungle camo. An olive T-shirt fit her closely, not only revealing how toned she was, but accentuating her breasts. He forced himself not to linger on the view, though it was worth more than a few extra seconds.

Since he was trained to note details fast, it didn't take long to reach her face. And to meet the hard stare she directed his way. Damn, she'd caught him. "Do you hear that noise?" he asked, and hoped she'd buy the diversion.

She tipped her head to the side, then held out both hands, indicating she didn't hear a thing. "What does it sound like?"

"Never mind. I'm sure it's not important." The only thing that mattered was her focus had shifted.

"Okay." She stopped, then said reluctantly, "I guess I should thank you for consulting me about our cover, huh?"

"Enjoy it. We won't be operating under a democracy once we insert."

"I know, I know. You're the op leader and you give the orders." She shrugged, and Jake had to fight to keep his attention on her face. "We'll do it your way. And I want the bunk we're not sitting on."

Her grin revealed a dimple in her left cheek that he hadn't seen before. God, she was beyond pretty when she smiled like that, and he couldn't stop staring. He took in the wisp of bangs over her forehead, the long lashes, and the stubborn chin before moving on to her mouth. Sweet. And full. He wanted to taste her lips, feel them against his.

Jake, I'm hearing a hum. Is that the noise you meant?

That shook him out of the daze, thank God, and he concentrated on the drone. He couldn't pinpoint where it was coming from or what made the sound. Cai was looking at him with an odd expression on her face. Since he didn't want to discuss why he kept gawking at her, he decided now was a good time to track down the buzz. Standing, he began to move around the room, trying to see if it was louder in some places than others.

I think it has something to do with the probes. I didn't hear anything until I unblocked our link.

To test her theory, Jake closed the pathway. The hum disappeared. And when he opened it again, the noise returned. *I don't like this,* he told her. *The implants shouldn't be affected by other computers or inteltronics.*

It has to be something that emits a signal, and probably on an obscure wavelength. She sucked in a sharp breath.

What? he demanded.

It's crazy. That stuff is so ancient that no one has used it in decades, maybe longer.

What stuff? Come on, Cai, give.

Sensors that transmit data, but in a way that's different from what we're accustomed to. Like along an ultralow frequency. Or maybe it's ultrahigh, I can't remember. That kind of equipment and technology is pretty damn old, though.

Sensors? Like listening devices?

He wasn't surprised when she nodded. With the way his luck was running, how could it be anything else? *Tell me what I'm looking for.*

Cai got off the bunk and began peering around. *It'll be small, maybe the size of a grain of rice. Color is usually a pale gray. If you see anything that makes you believe this room couldn't pass inspection, check it out closely. A collection of dust would be the perfect place to hide one of these gizmos.*

Although he kept his eyes peeled for what she'd described, he didn't ignore other possibilities. Who would use technology that old, and why? What they had now was much more advanced. He put the question to Cai as they searched.

This is only a guess, but the security on this facility is impressive. The systems scan regularly for any inteltronic equipment, but I doubt they're programmed to check for relics like these sensors.

That made a certain kind of sense. If an enemy couldn't afford to create something more advanced, then they'd use something so antiquated that no computer would be looking for it.

I think I got it, he announced.

She crowded in next to him as he plucked out one of the bugs she'd described from a tiny collection of fuzz. Before they were finished combing the room, they'd found two more. He studied each one. Then, carefully, he set all three down on the floor and ground them into oblivion with his boot.

These may not have been intended for us, she said, but he could feel her lack of conviction.

Yes, they were. The question is, who planted them and how the hell did they get onto a secure facility?

And how the hell did he keep Cai safe when it seemed like they had a million unseen foes on their ass?

Cai finished sweeping the last quadrant and put aside the makeshift detection program she'd thrown together. It hadn't taken long to scan the entire building, not with the sleeping quarters and communal room so tiny. Aside from one holovid screen, the walls were empty and the furniture sparse, which left fewer places to hide gadgets. This place actually managed to make her home look ornate, but then it was nothing but a stop along the way, not a camp for R & R.

When she turned to announce her findings, she discovered she was the center of attention for all seven men. "It's clear."

"What's our grand total?" Jake asked.

"I got us at forty-five," Gator said. He was an unexpected choice for the team, and she didn't know much about him beyond the fact that Gator was short for Navigator. Like a lot of the handles, his was sarcastic in origin; the man had gotten lost on a training exercise in boot camp.

"It must have cost a fortune to make so many of these things." Gnat picked up one of them, pinching it between his thumb and forefinger, and scrutinized it.

"Actually, no." Cai slipped her hands into her pockets. "The devices cost very little to produce; that's why they were so plentiful in their day. And since these have no additional power source, they'd be even more inexpensive. They'd work only a couple of days, but then that's all that was needed."

"Yeah," Jake said, voice grim. "Since we're only going to be here a matter hours, it's plenty of time. I don't like this."

That brought mutters of agreement from the guys. They gazed at her, then looked at each other and nodded, reaching an understanding without a word being spoken. Cai sighed. She had the sneaking suspicion she'd gained six big brothers. *Great.* As if Jake weren't overprotective enough.

Moving around the wall of men, she went to the table. The sensors had been deactivated without being destroyed, and she stared at them with fascination. At one time, these things had been everywhere, but now they were working museum pieces. She pulled her hands out of her pockets and started to reach for one.

"Here," Gnat said, extending the device he held.

She turned her palm up to accept it. If only there were a magnifier here to study it more closely. She brought her hand to her face to get the best look possible. It was utterly amazing to be holding history like this. Poking it gently with her fingernail, she turned it over to view the other side.

The absolute silence penetrated her awareness, and she raised her eyes to find the entire team watching her. Uncomfortable under the prolonged scrutiny, Cai returned the gizmo to the table and jammed her hands back in her pockets. "Sorry," she said, "occupational hazard. I'm fascinated by this kind of thing."

"If you want, sweetheart, you can bring a few with you to check out later. It's not like anyone would care."

Cai shook her head. "Can't, Jake. These may be trackers as well as eavesdropping devices. I think I disabled them totally, but I'm not sure enough to take one with us on the mission."

More glances between the men.

"Tuck," the Professor said, "I think we should lose the sensors before we even discuss the op. Just in case."

Jake looked to Cai and she nodded. She knew the ears were turned off, but she preferred to be cautious, since they hadn't been able to narrow down the suspect list of who'd planted them. They'd discussed this privately and had agreed the most likely culprit was someone within the UCE military, but her recep had insisted they couldn't rule out a confederate of the mystery anchor, either. Regardless, they'd been damn lucky it had caused a reaction in their implants, or they never would have realized they'd been monitored.

"Okay, Prof—you, Inch, and Kazoo get rid of these things."

She moved away from the table, giving the three men room to gather up the bugs. They were careful, she noted, not to drop or forget a single one. There seemed to be a flurry of activity, and Cai took another step back, wanting to stay out of the way.

"Ma'am?" She turned to see Mango standing beside her. "I'd like to say I'm sorry while I have the chance."

"Sorry for what?" She couldn't remember anything he needed to apologize for.

"My behavior on the transport." He gave a shrug. "If I'd known you were Tuck's woman, I never would have acted like that."

She began to heatedly deny she was anyone's woman, but closed her mouth without saying a word. It wasn't up to her to fill him in, and she wasn't sure how much Jake wanted the guys to know. She was certain he trusted them—he had to—but the general had said *need-to-know* about what info was passed along.

"I didn't think your conduct was out of line," she said instead. Actually, she'd found it entertaining to talk with him.

"Thank you, ma'am, but Tuck would disagree." The sergeant shook his head. "Now I understand the looks I was getting."

"What looks?"

"Kind of like the one directed my way right now."

Cai turned and found Jake glowering with obvious menace at Mango. He started toward them, but was waylaid by Gnat. For a moment she thought he'd ignore the interruption, but Jake did stop. His impatience, however, was palpable.

"When he gets here, I'd appreciate it if you would keep him from killing me. After all, I did apologize, ma'am."

"I will if you'll promise to stop calling me *ma'am*."

"Ma'am? I mean, Captain?"

"You weren't *ma'am*ing me on our way here," she pointed out.

"True," he said, giving her a smile that managed to be both extremely charming and slightly rueful. "But Tuck is about to make me pay for the lapse in protocol."

Jake freed himself then. Her recep didn't seem to rush, yet he closed the distance in no time. When he reached her, his arm slid around her waist and he tugged her against his side. It was all she could do to keep from gaping at him. He wanted to play out this ruse in front of his team?

"Sergeant Mangano." The amiable neutrality managed to sound threatening.

The sergeant stood at attention. "Yes, sir?"

"We're inserting in a matter of hours on a mission that may have been compromised, and you can't find anything more productive to do than bother Captain Randolph?"

Mango shot a pleading glance her direction. "Sir—"

"Jake," she interrupted. "The sergeant came over to apologize. He wasn't bothering me."

She met his scrutiny head-on. When he turned to Mango, his stare became harder. "I hope your apology was for coming on to the captain," her recep said, voice soft and dangerous.

Coming on to her? He'd only tried to be friendly. Hadn't he? She replayed the flight aboard the transport, but couldn't think of anything that had seemed like flirting. Jake must have it wrong. She would have noticed if Mango had a romantic interest.

"Yes, sir. I'm sorry, sir. I didn't realize the captain was yours. If I had, I never would have poached."

Cai about growled. Damn it, was her nickname going to end up being Tuck's Woman? "For heaven's sake. I don't belong to him. I'm not a pet or a possession."

"Yes, ma—er, Captain." His tone indicated he was humoring her, and that pushed her from annoyed to mad.

She took a step forward, but that was as far as she got before Jake's hold stopped her. As she turned her glare on him, she tried to pry his arm loose. Since she'd had to order him to let go in her quarters—*crap, their* quarters—she didn't expect to escape on her own, but that didn't mean she wasn't going to try.

"Mango," Jake said calmly, completely ignoring her efforts to get free. "Why don't you find Gnat and see if he needs you to do anything."

"Sure thing, Tuck." Relief was evident in the sergeant's voice, and he wasted no time leaving.

If I'm referred to as your woman one more time, someone is going to get hurt. Understand me?

When she saw Jake's lips twitch, she let her low growl emerge. That seemed to amuse him even more. He must have felt her muscles contract, because he quickly put both arms around her, restricting her ability to move.

Bending till his face was inches from hers, he asked quietly, "Why does that bother you so much?"

"Because it—" Cai cut herself off. She'd almost said, *Because it isn't true.* Good Lord, where the hell had that come from? Jake was her *friend.* "Because it just does," she substituted weakly. It was no surprise he appeared suspicious.

You're much too sure of yourself to worry that it diminishes you as a person, so what gives?

She guessed she was that confident because it had never occurred to her that it would do such a thing. So why *did* it irritate her so much? *I don't know, but I don't like it.*

When we're on the Raft Cities, I'll probably call you my woman, since it's a claim the pirates will understand. You'll need to hide your annoyance.

Jake was dead serious about this; she could plainly read that on his face. She nodded. "Okay, I can do that."

"Good."

He straightened, and she could see past him for the first time in a while. She wished he'd continued to block her view. They'd both managed to become the focus of every man in the room, and the knowing smiles on their faces made Cai self-conscious. Since she and Jake had been mind-talking, all of them probably thought they'd been standing there holding each other.

"What is it?"

"Turn around and see for yourself." Releasing her, he did just that.

"Oops," he said, but she could hear the mirth in his voice. This didn't bother him a bit.

"You ready to work now, Tuck?" Gnat asked.

"Yeah, you got the map table on?"

"Up and directed to the Raft Cities."

Cai would have hung back, but Jake snagged her hand and tugged her along in his wake. She thought about digging her heels in, but that wouldn't have stopped him, and she'd only give his men more to laugh about. And heaven knew they'd seen plenty to snicker over already.

Fortunately, they quickly forgot about her as they began to discuss where the others were going to insert. She stared down at the glowing image of the Raft Cities centered in the table and felt her stomach sink. Although it was difficult to know precise numbers, since the inhabitants tried to hide the rafts from surveillance, evidence suggested there were dozens and dozens of the metal-and-composite structures.

With so much territory to cover, how did she find someone who didn't want to be located? Elliot had hidden himself for six years. It was a sure bet that he wouldn't be standing at the landing site waving to catch her attention.

Sweetheart, give me info about Felidhu. The request was offhand, and Cai realized he'd come to terms with the probes and her risk of overload. He never even glanced away from Gator as the sergeant ran through the pros of the location in question.

She was searching a computer for the intel he wanted before she remembered the other anchor. Cai stopped and scanned, trying to sense the woman, but the system felt empty. Quickly, in case she appeared, Cai accessed the data and passed it to Jake.

He made several more requests as they discussed rafts, and each time she expected to be tracked down, but it didn't happen. Where was the other woman? It made Cai nervous. Did it mean that she wasn't there? Or did it mean she'd become so adept at hiding that Cai couldn't pick her up any longer?

When they'd narrowed down the list of choices, the talk became more centered. Cai found it interesting which points were considered pluses and which were minuses when it came to inserting into an area. Listening to the team argue probably taught her more than weeks of training would, especially when they started weighing one location against another. At last, they picked the three additional spots, paired up, and decided on when they'd arrive.

By the time they finished discussing how they were going to keep in contact with each other while remaining completely covert, Cai was amazed. They'd managed to cover a lot of ground in less than an hour, and she had a feeling they could have made the decisions a lot faster if they'd needed to.

When they started shooting the bull, she tuned them out and stared at the map again, running through the facts she had about their destination. The population wasn't huge; the UCE estimated it at around twenty-five thousand total, and Malé, where she and Jake were inserting, was the most densely occupied, with 7,500 residents.

Living there didn't offer much opportunity. No farming, no tourism, no industry. Without assets, many of the people had turned to piracy to exist. Of course, the savagery employed in their raids hadn't elicited sympathy for their circumstances, and most of the civilized world labeled them terrorists.

The bottom line, though, was that they needed resources—and that Marchand Elliot had enough money to bribe every pirate, woman, and child to remain quiet about his presence. So even if she was right and he was there, finding the man might be impossible.

"Are you okay?"

Cai looked up and found she and Jake were alone in the

communal room. She wasn't certain when the others had left. "Fine, just thinking."

"About what?" He stood with his hip leaning into the table and his thumbs hooked in the belt loops of his fatigue pants.

She turned off the map, returning the table to its normal condition, and sighed. "It won't be easy to find someone on the Raft Cities who doesn't want to be found, will it?"

"No, but Maguire will give herself away somehow. We'll get her." He paused. "But that's not who you were thinking about."

"Elliot might not be there; I could easily be grasping at straws. I know that *here*." She tapped two fingers lightly against her temple. "It's another story in here." This time she tapped her heart.

He reached for her hands and pulled her closer. "I know you're worried that you won't find anything about your parents, but I promised I'd help you, and I will, every way I can. You have to remember one thing, though. We're going to the Raft Cities to find Maguire and Armstrong. The op comes first."

Cai didn't disagree, just smiled faintly. She'd given her word to obey orders, and she would; there was no way she'd take any action that jeopardized Jake or the team. But as far as she was concerned, nothing took precedence over finding information about her mom and dad. Nothing.

Chapter Seven

No amount of research prepared Cai for Malé. The stench—*oh, my God*—the stench would stay with her the rest of her life. This place made Hell smell daisy-fresh, but then the bar hadn't put rotting, mutilated corpses on display. It had taken all her willpower to keep from gaping, or gagging, when she'd spotted the first body. The hot tropical sun beating down on the Raft Cities had increased the rate of decomposition, and she'd been unable to tell if the remains were male or female.

The bodies weren't the only surreal thing. Never before had she walked through a city and not been inundated with holographic billboards touting one product or another. The whisper-light drone from scads of inteltronic equipment was missing too. It wasn't quiet here—there were too many people jammed into too small a space for that—but it was a different kind of noise.

Signs of poverty were rife. She'd never seen anything like it. Most of the dwellings were shacks put together with whatever material had been available—metal, wood, composite; it didn't matter, not as long as it could provide shelter. Of a sort. All the houses seemed to have gaps that would let wind and rain blow in, and she doubted most residents could afford better. Piracy might have made a few wealthy, but the majority of people were barely eking out a life on the Raft Cities.

The hair on the back of her neck rose. Her hand slid down, touched the weapon holstered on her thigh, and rested atop its butt as she scanned for the threat. It came from a girl who didn't appear old enough to take care of a puppy, let alone be heavily pregnant. Her eyes were ancient, though, and bleak beneath the hostility. Despite the pity she felt, Cai met the glower with her own till the girl finally turned and resumed sweeping.

It hadn't taken long after their arrival to figure out why Jake had said she'd be considered an easy target. The women here, even the children, had a hardness that she lacked. As much as she hated to admit it, her recep's solid presence at her side made her feel much safer. Not that she'd tell him that.

Careful not to catch anyone's eye, she perused the area. Men stood around, loitering, while the women labored. But she supposed when someone was a high-seas terrorist, it was beneath them to do daily chores. Kids were put to work too, although she saw the tiniest ones playing barefoot. She suppressed a shudder. Grime and filth were everywhere, and even wearing lightweight boots, she didn't want to think about what she was stepping in.

It wasn't only the lack of technology and the abject poverty that had her off balance here; her inner ear claimed there was motion, but her eyes said no. If it weren't for the nanomeds she'd taken before leaving the staging facility, no doubt she'd be green by now. Even with the rafts anchored, the sea swells surely made them bob. She suppressed a grimace. Good thing she was army, because she never would have made it as a sailor.

Maybe it was the tone that attracted her notice. Or

maybe it was the laughter that followed the sneering voice, but either way, she became aware of the five young men standing in a cluster against the front of a building. Although she kept them in her peripheral vision, she took care not to look at them. They were spoiling for trouble, and catching their eye might be all it took to set that off. Cai hoped she and Jake were long gone before they grew bored enough to start something.

They weren't so lucky. One of the pirates put himself in front of her. Cai stopped short to prevent touching him, but the odor he emitted was strong enough to make her gasp. He was her height and slightly built, but the contempt in his gaze made him appear larger. His voice dripped with disdain, but her translation device was able to decipher only a few words. *Whore* was one. The other two were the crudest terms possible for sex.

Before she could react, Jake took over. He picked the man up, growled something in the same language, and then tossed him away like so much garbage. She could hear the thunk the jerk's head made as it met the metal plating of the raft. He didn't get up again. Her recep looked around, as if daring the others, but no one took him up on the challenge.

She didn't blame them. Her clean-cut Special Forces captain had been replaced by a man most women would cross the street to avoid. It was more than the stubble on his chin and his unkempt hair. She could sum it up in one word: attitude. Her Jake ran intense. This Jake took it to the nth degree. *Badass* didn't begin to cover it. For the first time, she actually felt young in his presence.

Are you okay, sweetheart?

The question knocked the ridiculous idea of two Jakes out of her head. Jake Tucker, no matter what guise he wore, would always have a core of honor that made him the person she knew.

Yeah, I'm fine. Thanks.

"C'mon, let's go," he ordered with a nod of his head, and she fell obediently into step beside him.

Woof, woof.

Hell, Cai, don't make me laugh.

Sorry. Badasses don't laugh. Got it.

His left hand wrapped around her nape, and a tiny thrill shot through her. He clasped her for only an instant, but it was long enough to get the message across. Honestly, she didn't question the tenuousness of their position, not after seeing those bodies decaying in the hot sun and the populace going about their business as if this were a normal deal. Her weak attempts at humor were meant to release tension more than anything else.

I could have handled that guy. But she'd been too slow to respond. That was a problem. This was hostile territory, and she didn't have the luxury of thinking things through. She needed to get her head in the game and strike out instinctively at threats.

I know you could have, but they were testing me, not you.

What do you mean?

Jake's gaze swept their surroundings as they continued forward. He carried so much hardware, both hidden and in full view, he should have rattled when he walked. But then who was she to talk? She was heavily armed herself. As a systems specialist, she usually wore weapons only when she was training. Granted, she'd had a lot more intense instruction than most techs—hell, than most soldiers, since she'd been through Special Forces school—but it seemed strange to feel this extra weight.

How much of what he said did you pick up?

Very little, Cai admitted.

He used so much patois, I'm not surprised the translator couldn't help you. When we find a place to stay, I'll have to send you the language, and the cant, through the probes.

She nodded, certain Jake caught the movement even though he didn't look at her. It would definitely be a good idea to understand everything people said to her. *My translating device was supposed to be the best. How come it can't handle what's spoken on the Raft Cities?*

His amusement at the question came through loud and clear. *What language programmer is going to voluntarily stay here and work? I'm betting you've got the words and phrases that come from other dialects, but that's it.*

Cai didn't ask how he'd come by the knowledge. He probably spoke fluently without any kind of device. Special Operations had their own way of doing things, and they didn't necessarily share their methods with the rest of the military. She knew that, historically, they sent their members through deep language immersion as a matter of routine. Maybe they still did.

So what did that guy say anyway?

He may have been looking at you, but he was talking to me. The sleaze asked how much I wanted for you to service him.

She had to bite her lip to keep from smiling. As tempting as it was to tease Jake about cleaning up what had been said, she resisted. It wasn't the time or the place for that. But she felt better now, not so tense, and that was a good thing.

He didn't tell her what he'd replied, but she could guess. He'd probably started by claiming her as his and then gone on to the not-sharing part. In any case, the line had been drawn and the next approach wouldn't be a test. Cai brushed her hand over her holster again. This time she'd be ready.

Their room wasn't the best available on Malé, but it was far from the worst. She knew that. They'd gone through at least half a dozen different places offering lodging, and that didn't count the ones they'd walked past without entering. Some they'd bypassed because they were hardly more than shacks; others Jake had deemed too nice. As if that were a possibility here.

It amazed her how many options there were. Apparently this was a hotter spot for visiting criminals than she'd realized. Or maybe a lot of the pirates didn't bother with a permanent residence, but rented space when they were in from sea. There were accommodations for every budget, but Cai was thankful most weren't as run-down as the buildings in the first area she'd seen.

Even so, it hadn't been easy to find something that met both their criteria. She wanted clean. He wanted secure. They'd managed, finally, and the room even boasted a small private bath. As far as Cai was concerned, that made it the garden spot of the Raft Cities and worth the negotiated price.

She sat on the mattress and watched Jake arm the window. They'd paid extra for that. Considering that their home away from home was barely more than a cubbyhole, the view, as ugly as it was, saved the place from feeling like a tomb.

Hell, *cubbyhole* was probably overstating it. The bed took up most of the available space, and it was only slightly larger than twin-size. They'd be sleeping nearly on top of each other, especially with her recep so broad through the shoulders. She pushed that thought aside. A small bureau was crammed in, and to reach the window he'd needed to edge through sideways. That was it. There wasn't room for anything else.

As for decor—well, the walls were a dingy gray and so was the ceiling. There wasn't so much as a cheap holo to spruce it up. The only mirror was in the even more minute bath, and it was made of a highly polished metal alloy rather than glass.

Cai sighed. It was clean. That was what counted. No rats like she'd seen scurrying in one of the inns, and no stains on the mattress or the bed linens that made her gag. The bath was mildew free and held nothing crawling. *Thank*

God. Nope, she wasn't complaining. She was more than happy with the room.

Jake continued to work, and she scooted farther back on the mattress to lean against the wall. *I'm surprised you asked for a window,* she said. *Isn't this an unnecessary security risk?*

He didn't look away from what he was doing. *No window means the only way to escape is through the door. Always make sure you have multiple exits in case the shit hits.*

Good point.

As Cai watched him continue his work, she tried to tamp down her emotions. She was really on the Raft Cities, and maybe she'd have some answers about her parents before she left! Maybe she'd even find them.

She took a deep breath, lowering her excitement a notch. Getting her hopes up would be a huge mistake. But as she toyed with her ring, she thought about the apologies she needed to make. Not just for saying she hated them, though one of the first things she'd do when they were reunited was say *I love you.* No, she had more to atone for than that final conversation.

For the last year or so before they'd sent her away, she and her mother had been at odds. She'd been a teenager, and spoiled to boot—that was reason enough for the dissension, she guessed. But for all their arguing, there had been only one issue where both of them had stubbornly dug in their heels and refused to budge.

Cai's mom had wanted her to know of her Vietnamese heritage, to hear the stories of her ancestors, including how they'd fled Saigon in the 1970s and come to America. She'd even suggested Cai learn the old, unused language. Cai could smile about it a bit now, although it made her sad. With a flip of her hair, she'd announced she lived in the UCE and had neither an interest in people long dead nor a need to be fluent in anything but English.

Cai twisted her ring faster. After her parents vanished,

she *had* learned to speak Vietnamese, and she'd studied the history of the country that was now part of the Kingdom of Asia. But there had been no one to tell her the family stories. Her brattiness had cost her something irreplaceable.

There. That should do it.

It was a relief when Jake pulled her from her thoughts, but the memories had hardened her resolve. No matter what it took or how long she had to search, she was finding her mom and dad.

Jake stepped away to stow the tools and she studied his handiwork. Or tried. She didn't see one thing that was different from before he'd started. Probably nanotech. She was still staring at the window when he joined her on the bed, but the feel of his hip against hers made the curiosity evaporate.

"We should probably go reconnoiter," she said, keeping her voice low. "Both of us need to know the area just in case, and we need to establish our cover."

Who's the op leader?

You are. She tried to keep quiet, but she didn't manage. *But we need to let it slip I'm a webrider and you're my broker. You know any stranger is going to be suspect until a legitimate—or rather an illicit—reason for their presence here becomes known. The quicker we divert attention from us the better. You know I'm right,* she added when he sighed heavily.

You are right on both counts, but do you mind letting me lay out our plan of action?

Forgive me.

With another sigh, he leaned back against the wall. Those shoulders of his were causing problems already, and he wasn't lying down yet. She scooted over, trying to put more space between them so she could sit upright, but the mattress worked against her. It sagged enough to drive her into his side.

Shifting slightly, Jake put his shoulder behind hers and

tucked her against him. "Sorry, I didn't realize," he apologized. "Is this better?"

"Yes, thanks." But it created a new problem. Now she was plastered against him, and the hand he'd rested on the bed behind her was damn close to her butt. It suddenly seemed as if the air cycler wasn't doing its job—not as hot as she felt. Cai gulped and tried to think of something to say to disguise what he was doing to her. Nothing came to mind.

Before we survey the area or announce that you're a computer genius, I want to pass along the language they use. Okay?

She ignored the sarcasm and said, "Sure."

Because he didn't have the second implant, it took quite some time to complete the transfer. They'd rarely done an exchange of personal knowledge like this, although twice she'd passed along what she knew about a particular inteltronic device to help him during a mission. This was the first time they'd operated in reverse, but she'd never needed to know something that wasn't in one of her systems before.

Once she understood the local dialect, she tested out her new proficiency, exploring different words and phrases. Because of her fascination, it took her a while after assimilating the information to notice that her head rested against his chest and his hand stroked up and down her arm.

Oh, my God. Cai stiffened and quickly sat up straight. He must have women throwing themselves at him all the time. Now he probably thought she'd joined his legion of groupies. Jake went rigid and she felt her face scald.

Before she could apologize, he held his finger to his lips in a shush signal and crept to the door. The security was lax, but there was a viewer he could use to peer into the hall. She held her breath, waiting to see what was up.

Jump up and down on the bed.

What?

Make the bed rock, Cai.

With a shrug, she raised her butt off the mattress and dropped back down again. The frame lightly banged into the wall.

Keep going. Don't stop till I tell you.

She followed the order without asking any more questions, but that didn't prevent her from wondering. Or worrying. Nothing about his stance or demeanor gave her any hint about what was going on or why he wanted her to rattle the bed.

With a silent sigh, she continued to use her arms to push up onto her heels before dropping her body back to the mattress. How much longer was he going to expect her to do this? It seemed like she'd already been shaking the bed forever, but he didn't tell her to stop.

Harder and faster. Good. Now moan, sweetheart.

What? One of them had lost their mind.

Come on, moan.

She moaned.

Not like you're a dying water buffalo. Moan like you're on the verge of the best damn orgasm of your life.

Call her slow, but she finally understood what was going on. This time when she cried out, she knew she'd given him what he'd asked for. She even improvised as she bounced on the bed and added, "Oooh, yes! Yes!"

That earned her a quick glance and a raised eyebrow. She almost laughed aloud at the look on his face, but stopped herself in time. Her humor, though, was short-lived.

She was arching and moaning as if they were having sex, and it didn't take long before her mind started imagining what it would be like if it were true. To feel Jake's hard-muscled body on top of hers. To press her hips against his as he thrust into her. To experience his bare skin sliding over hers.

The fantasy was arousing her for real, and her next groan wasn't entirely fake. Reminding herself that this was a ruse, part of their cover, didn't help. Neither did recalling that someone was in the hall listening to her performance. *He's a friend*, she told herself. *Your only one.*

But somehow she couldn't see him as just a friend anymore.

Almost desperately, she sent a question along their pathway. *Aren't you having a good time too?*

What?

She was glad not to be the only one who was confused. *If you don't grunt or groan, how do I know you're having fun?*

This time she got a smirk. *I'm the quiet type.*

No, you're not. She smiled weakly when he turned to gape at her, but she saw the blush under his tan before he looked away again. *Uh-oh.* Reminding him of how much she knew was a mistake, and not only because it embarrassed him. It also made her recall what he was like in bed, and that sent her further into the land of imagination.

Cai continued on, but not only was she growing tired, she was feeling uncomfortable with the depth she'd traveled into her delusion. How long was their spy going to stay and listen? She needed to end this before she said or did something that tipped Jake off. *Can I come now?*

His head whipped around so fast, she would have laughed if she weren't so concerned about what was going on inside her. He only looked at her for a few seconds before his attention returned to the hall, but she'd managed to surprise him.

Explain that.

I'm exhausted. Partially true. *Unless you need to prove you have incredible stamina, can I fake coming so I can stop rocking this stupid bed?*

She saw his shoulders shake and suspected he was smothering a laugh. This situation was ludicrous. And since she'd been bouncing for darn near ever and their voyeur remained, maybe he was waiting for the grand finale.

Jake?

Yeah, go ahead.

Without hesitation she went into her performance, emoting loudly and with great feeling. After all, he did say to pretend she was having the orgasm of her life, right?

When she finished, she gave the bed a few more hard shakes and then halted her jumping. As she sat looking at Jake, she rubbed her upper arm with one hand, then switched off to rub the other. This had used muscles that didn't get a workout during her daily training, but that wasn't what had her troubled. Would he still be comfortable being her friend if he knew she'd gotten hot envisioning him between her thighs?

He stood by the door for a long time after she concluded her show, his forehead resting against the wall above the viewer as he gazed out. Cai stayed quiet. Her anxiety about her reaction to him changed to worry over their eavesdropper. Who was there, and why did they linger outside the room? Clearly the fun was over, so there shouldn't be a reason to remain.

Unable to stand the waiting any longer, she asked, *Why isn't he leaving?*

Jake's body stiffened. *She's gone.*

Why are you standing there then?

Making sure she doesn't sneak back.

Common sense said that if anyone was going to return, they'd have done it by now. He'd been over there a long time, but she leaned against the wall, crossed her legs at the ankle, and waited. Besides, looking at him was no hardship, and the holster emphasized his fine backside. She tore her eyes away. *Stop it,* she ordered herself, but her gaze slipped back to him anyway.

They'd dressed for the tropical climate in light-colored, lightweight clothing. Jake's pants hugged the lower half of his body closely, giving him easier access to the myriad of arms he carried. The shirt was looser, but not too loose. He couldn't afford to be impeded by fabric in case he needed to draw. If she hadn't seen him conceal them herself, she'd never have guessed how many weapons he could hide beneath such simple clothes.

What surprised her most, however, was how easily he seemed to fit in as they'd walked through Malé. Most of the people here traced their ancestry back to the original residents of the Maldives, or to Indonesia and Malaysia. A minority could even claim ties to Vietnam. Jake should have stood out more than she did. Except being part Asian didn't help her blend in here. He had an edge. She didn't. That counted.

Attitude. Cai wondered if she could fake that too.

When he showed no signs of leaving his post, she said, *I think it's a pretty safe bet that if whoever was listening isn't back by now, they're not coming back.*

He didn't comment, but he did turn to face her.

Who was out there anyway? she asked, aware of how he kept his distance. He probably didn't want to chance her cuddling into him again; thank God he didn't know about the lascivious thoughts she'd been having about him while she'd bounced. A sick feeling rose when she realized her inadvertent lapses may have put stress on their friendship. Somehow she'd have to subtly reassure him that she didn't expect more from him than that.

For a moment, she thought he'd ignore her question, but then he shrugged. *The woman who rented us the room.*

Cai nodded and considered that. It made sense. If the pirate lords who ran the Raft Cities wanted to keep tabs on newcomers, bribing or intimidating the innkeepers into providing intelligence on their guests would be a logical move.

When Jake kept staring at her with a contemplative expression on his face, Cai felt her stomach turn over. Any second now he was going to bring up how she'd snuggled into him during the data transfer. She didn't want to talk about it and began to scramble off the bed. *We should go reconnoiter, huh?*

Not yet. He smirked and she relaxed, confident that the chance for a serious conversation had passed. *After you all but screamed, we'll need to bask in the afterglow a while longer.*

Are you implying I overplayed my role?

Did I say that? She raised her eyebrows at his sarcasm. His expression sobered. *I hope your joke doesn't backfire, though, and call our cover into question.* He shrugged and grinned at her. *But if it doesn't, I'm going to have a hell of a rep, since you got so worked up over a quick afternoon tussle.*

Joke? It was Cai's turn to blush. Sure, she'd exaggerated, but she hadn't thought she'd gone that far overboard.

"Shit," he said softly, and the look of awareness that crossed his face had her hurrying to change the subject.

Do you want me to sweep the room for bugs? After our nosy landlady and what happened at the staging area, we shouldn't take any chances. I'll have to put together another scan to search for the relics, but inteltronics won't be a problem. She touched the small pendant nestled in the pocket of her pants.

For a moment she thought he wasn't going to go along with her, but to her great relief, he finally said, *It wouldn't be a bad idea, as a precaution at least. I don't expect you'll find anything, though.* The smirk returned. *The woman had her ear against the door.* The implication was clear; the innkeeper had no tool to listen to them from a remote location.

What about our retrotech?

For a moment he looked puzzled; then his smirk changed to a smile. *Do you remember how fast she showed up when we walked in?*

She nodded. The innkeeper had appeared almost before they'd set one foot in the reception area.

I'd wager a month's pay that she watches everyone who enters or leaves this place. No spy is getting past her. Jake shrugged and hooked his thumbs in the belt of his holster. *Sometimes a nosy owner beats high-tech scans.*

If he'd realized from the start how big a snoop the

woman was and had still chosen this inn, then obviously he wasn't concerned with their movements being monitored. In fact, there had been a certain satisfaction to his words that indicated it may have been a deliberate choice. But why? It wasn't like the woman would share her observations with them.

Something on Jake's face stopped Cai from asking for an explanation. She couldn't name the expression, not for sure, but it made her think he was uneasy.

"Come here a minute," he said quietly.

Simply sliding to the edge of the bed and standing put her face-to-face with him. Cai looked up expectantly—and became anxious when he hesitated.

"Unbutton your shirt."

"What?" Her voice came out sharply, but she managed to keep the volume down despite her shock.

"Just partway."

He didn't talk any more. Didn't try to convince or cajole her. Instead he stood and waited. She studied him, gauging the order against what she saw. His blue eyes were calm, patient, and his face impassive. Although she couldn't sense any emotion from him, somehow she knew he needed her to show her faith in him.

She reached for the top button.

Short of her parents, there wasn't another human being she trusted more than Jake. She might do the best she could to conceal it if she lost her probes again, as long as it didn't endanger lives, but when it came to anything else, her confidence was unlimited.

A second button was unfastened, then a third.

"That's good enough," he said.

Lowering her hands to her sides, she stood and waited to see what happened next. He appeared to be in no hurry, and Cai felt a bit ill at ease as he watched her, but along with the self-consciousness came a return of her arousal. She bit her lower lip firmly, trying to force the feeling away.

"Lean your head back and toward the right."

This time she didn't hesitate, but she couldn't stop from becoming rigid when she felt his hands gently fold her shirt open. Only the swell of her breasts was revealed, no more than that, but she felt oddly exposed—and vulnerable—to be standing before him like this. She closed her eyes. It made it easier.

Because she couldn't see, her other senses began working double time. She heard her quickened respiration, felt the heat of his calloused fingers resting against her collarbone, and smelled the sexy scent that belonged only to Jake. She knew when he leaned closer to her, and though it was involuntary, her lips parted. His breath puffed softly against her cheek and her heart stopped for an instant, then began beating wildly.

His chin touched her throat; his stubble prickled. They both froze for a long moment; then her recep rubbed his jaw along the side of her neck.

Cai gripped his waist and gasped in surprise. He slid one hand to her nape, holding her in place until he finished. She opened her eyes when he lifted his head, and he tipped her face till she met his gaze.

"I'm sorry, sweetheart." His remorse was obvious. "But if you didn't have any whisker burn, it would raise questions."

"It's okay."

"It had to be visible, but I didn't want to mark your face. This was the best I could come up with."

"Jake, it's all right. Really."

He continued to look regretful, although he didn't apologize again. She was trying to come up with something else to say, something that would make him stop fretting, but what happened next was not conducive to clear thought. His fingers started rubbing circles on the back of her neck. Though she knew it was a means of apology, the gesture sent shivers through her.

Her hold on him tightened as she fought to remain composed. The stroking faltered, then stopped, and the silence hung heavy in the air. There was a hint of awkwardness as her recep released her, but before she could do more than take a deep breath, he surprised her again.

Jake reached over and fastened her shirt. He didn't linger after finishing the task, but jammed his hands in his pockets and edged away from her. The wall kept him from going far, and she couldn't move back either, not without falling onto the bed, but the gulf between them was far greater than the few inches of physical space. She bit her lip again, trying to figure out how to fix this, how to get things normal again.

"That's a good idea. I should have thought of it."

"What?" God, there she went again. She couldn't follow what he said at all today.

"Biting your lips to make them look swollen." His hand rose, and for a heartbeat she thought he was going to touch her face, but she'd misread him. He patted her shoulder like he would a pal. "You'll want to catch your upper lip too."

She didn't try to explain that biting her lip was a habit, one of nerves or deep thought. It was easier to let him believe what he wanted. And safer. Instead, she followed his advice, sinking her teeth in firmly enough to sting. She held it for a count of three, then ran her tongue across where it felt bruised.

Jake stared at her mouth. The intense scrutiny had her feeling fidgety, but she made herself remain motionless and let him judge whether or not she could pass for a woman who'd taken a recent tumble with a man. But when he kept examining her and not saying anything, the tension became too much.

"Um, I think I bit my lower lip twice, maybe three times. Do you need me to do the upper one again? Is that the problem?"

"No." His voice sounded a shade or two deeper than

usual. "There's no problem. Your lips look perfect." His eyes dipped down for a moment before he met her gaze once more.

Something about his actions didn't seem right. Concerned, she leaned forward. "Jake—"

"C'mon," he interrupted gruffly. "We need to get out of here."

Chapter Eight

"I can't believe I ordered you a beer," Jake grumbled as the barmaid walked away. "You don't look old enough to drink."

Cai sighed. "But you know better than that, cowboy. And even if it were true, take a look around you. Do you think anyone here cares about underage drinking?"

He grunted, and she decided that meant he didn't have a rebuttal. Besides, she didn't appear *that* young. Her recep was being difficult, that was all. Ever since they'd left their room at the inn he'd been oddly irritable, and spending hours walking every inch of Malé hadn't improved his mood.

Jake's gaze swept the bar, and Cai studied the crowd as well. Most were pirates, but she spotted a group of wreckers to the right and stiffened. It stunned her to see such a high-priced mercenary band here, but maybe the pirate lords could afford the fees. Yet the pirates didn't like them; their furtive glares and griping told her that. Since the wreckers had gotten the name after one of them had bragged on the Interweb about how much damage he could "wreck" on the human body, she didn't blame the Malé men for being wary. She glanced at her recep again, trying to judge how he was handling their presence, but his face was unreadable.

"You okay?" she asked with a short nod toward the robomen.

He turned to her, one corner of his mouth quirking. "Yeah. Don't worry; just keep your eyes open. This place is bad news."

Like she couldn't figure that out for herself. As awful as Hell had been, this joint was much worse. *Hovel* barely touched on how filthy it was. At first she'd been surprised it was so well lit, but the more she thought about it, the more sense it made. Probably the customers wanted to see any blood enemies present. Or to be able to keep a close watch on their fellow pirates to make sure no one pulled a weapon.

But in addition to revealing the people, the brightness also displayed the bar's seediness. Cai could see the dried pools of vomit on the floor, and she didn't even want to guess about the other stains. The place reeked, but she'd spent enough time on the Raft Cities now to become inured to horrible odors.

And like in the rest of Malé, there were no bells and whistles in the place. Hell hadn't been on the cutting edge when it came to technology, but this dive had nothing; no holovids, no music, no automatic servers. It was downright rustic.

As they sat, neither of them talking, Cai tried to listen to the conversations going on around them. Odds were long that she'd pick up anything about her parents, or Maguire, but it was worth a shot. Most of what she heard involved sex. Who the various pirates had had, who they wanted to have, how long they lasted, and so on. There was some bragging about their exploits at sea, told with great relish and lots of attention to the gruesome details. Jake was right: these men were more terrorists than pirates.

The phrase *orang luar* stopped her. *Outsider.*

She quit breathing for an instant, her ears focused on that discussion. Whoever was being discussed was hated, reviled. But as she continued to eavesdrop, her excitement died. The more the outlaws talked, the more it sounded as if they were bad-mouthing one of the lords. Not Elliot.

As the men caught sight of the barmaid headed in their direction, the topic switched back to sex, and Cai tuned them out. She shrugged off her discouragement. Had she honestly thought on her first night on the Raft Cities she'd find the location of a man who'd stayed hidden for six years? She was more pragmatic than that.

The server stopped in front of Jake, plunked down their beers, and announced the total. She eyed them suspiciously till she was paid; then she slid one of the bottles across the table. Quick reflexes allowed Cai to grab it before it landed in her lap. The woman served Jake differently. With a smile that was pure invitation, she moved closer and set it gently in front of him.

Cai's lips twitched. She felt certain the care was directly attributable to the fact that he was drop-dead handsome. This was too marvelous an opportunity for teasing to let pass, and she ran through various smart-aleck remarks in her mind, trying to pick the best one to zing him with when they were alone.

Her sense of humor deserted her abruptly, however, when the woman leaned over and offered Jake a view of her bare breasts. There was no way she was unaware of the way her blouse gaped open, and Cai's hold tightened on the neck of her beer as her temper started to climb. Tucker, she noted, had his eyes glued right where the barmaid wanted them. Cai scowled at him.

A demanding bellow from across the room had the

woman slowly straightening, but before she sashayed away, the barmaid gave Jake a long, sultry look and promised to be back. Soon.

Cai wanted to tell her not to rush, but forced herself to stay silent. Instead she strangled her bottle of beer and wished it were her recep's neck. *Jerk.* Okay, they weren't really involved. So what? They were pretending to be, and the idea of others thinking she meant so little to him that he would ogle another woman in front of her teed her off.

What added to her pique, however, was that the server was beautiful and curvaceous—two things she wasn't. The ridicule she'd received in school echoed in her head. *Geek, toad, ugly dogface, freak, hag.* The names hadn't stopped. She understood now that it had as much to do with her brain as her appearance, but at the time it had been devastating.

Not all the kids had made fun of her, of course, but nobody had defended her from the ones who had. And honestly, she *had* been a freak. At seven she'd still been playing with dolls while the girls she went to school with were sixteen and dating. How had anyone thought she'd fit in? But the alternative had been to stay with students her own age and be bored senseless waiting for them to grasp concepts that she found simple.

Or to be sent away from her parents.

She'd been fifteen when they'd put her in the academy. By then she'd been doing college-level work for years. The school offered a self-paced curriculum, and students were kept segregated. Of course, the lack of contact with her peer group was part of why she was so alone now, but it had been a relief not to be expected to interact with other kids anymore. Not to have to face more name-calling.

Anger was replaced by resignation. How could she blame Jake for his interest in a woman whose looks were as stunning as his own? It wasn't as though he were truly hers.

Putting down the beer, she reached for her ring. As her

thumb rubbed the stone, she thought of the times her parents had consoled her. Outward beauty faded, they'd told her; the important thing was who she was inside. Inner beauty would shine through. It hadn't been much comfort to a heartbroken thirteen-year-old—and it wasn't much solace at twenty-one either.

"What's wrong?"

She went rigid. *Damn.* If he sensed she was hurt by his actions . . . Well, she couldn't let that happen. Her brain stuttered, then jumped into hyperdrive. For what seemed like an eternity her thoughts whirled chaotically; then in a flash, the idea came. *Nothing's wrong. I'm merely taking advantage of an opportunity that's been presented.*

He looked suspicious. *What opportunity?*

We need to get the info out that I'm a webrider without it seeming contrived. I'm betting you were planning to use the old drink-too-much-and-let-it-slip ploy, but that's so predictable. I set the stage for an alternative.

This time he was the one to sigh. Loudly. *Who's the op leader on this mission?*

Oh, come on, Jake. Cai frowned at him. *I know you're in charge, but that doesn't mean I can't think, does it?*

He reached for his beer, opened it, and took a long swig before growling, "You think too damn much sometimes." He took another swallow. *Okay, I'm fortified. Hit me with it.*

Oh, for heaven's sake. It wasn't like she kept pitching harebrained schemes at him. *You and I are going to have a fight.*

You've decided that, have you, Captain Randolph?

She didn't miss the edge in his tone. He wasn't happy with her. Okay, so maybe she could have phrased it more carefully. She was used to sending info to him and having Jake use it, not argue with her about it. *Hear me out, all right?*

For a minute she didn't think he'd answer; then he gave a nod. It was grudging, but it was acquiescence.

We're supposed to be a couple, so no one will think twice if I get jealous over our barmaid coming on to you and we have a blowout. You can tell me I wouldn't have squat without you, and I can yell back that if it weren't for my webriding skills you wouldn't have squat either. Then, at some point, you grab me and haul me out the door. The beans are spilled and we leave before anyone is tempted to use our distraction against us.

Jake looked out over the room, but she was sure he was thinking about what she'd said. It gave her time to think too, and Cai realized that if he agreed, she'd be screaming at him in a crowded bar. She felt the blood drain from her face. *Crap.* Too bad she hadn't thought this through before blurting the idea.

The plan definitely has merit, he said at last. There was another pause and she held her breath. *Okay, let's do it. Here's how I think we should play it. When the barmaid comes back, I'll respond more blatantly to her flirting. You need to look angry. When she leaves, you and I will have a few short words, nothing loud, and then ignore each other. On her third visit I'll be more flagrant, and of course you'll be furious. That's when the knockdown, drag-out fight begins.*

Cai's brain started zooming again, looking for a way out. The last thing she wanted was to be the night's entertainment. *I found a hole or two in my scheme. Why would you hit on a woman right in front of me? Won't that look odd?*

No. No one here would find it unusual that I'm with one woman and trying for another.

She scanned the bar again and decided Jake was right. This group wouldn't blink an eye. She had one last shot of getting out of this; then she was stuck. *What about not wanting me to appear vulnerable? You were damn adamant about that. If we're on the outs, doesn't that undermine the reason why we're pretending to be lovers to begin with?*

He reached over, cupped her jaw, and ran his thumb over her cheekbone. *When we get back to the room and our landlady has her ear against the door, we'll finish our argu-*

ment. *I'll beg you to forgive me and swear that I'll never look at another woman again. Then we'll bounce the bed for some kiss-and-make-up sex.*

We'll sure have the Malé grapevine buzzing.

With a shrug, Jake withdrew, reached for his beer, and took a pull. *Let me get to work on this so our barmaid returns.*

She could have told him not to worry. The woman would be back, reorder or no; she wouldn't stay away from Jake long. Slowly Cai opened her own bottle, though she had no plans to drink anything. It would look odd if it remained sealed, and they didn't need any mistakes to blow their cover.

He hadn't said how to act before the barmaid returned, so she sat quietly and psyched herself up for what was coming. She noticed the noise level had gone up another notch and looked around again. The bar was packed, and there would be a standing-room-only mob for her performance as a jealous lover. She made a choking noise, and Jake glanced over.

"Don't worry; you'll do fine." His fingers settled on her leg and rubbed her thigh, and her disquiet over how easily he'd read her vanished. She knew the gesture was meant to be reassuring, but it made her go hot and shivery.

"Here we go, sweetheart. Showtime."

He pulled his hand away quickly and she blinked hard, trying to focus on the situation rather than the way her nerves were dancing at his touch. When she saw the provocative smile the server cast at Jake while swaying toward their table, Cai felt her ire rise. It spiked higher when the woman threw her a derisive smirk.

That disdainful regard reminded her of the girls in school. Usually she'd gotten the same look right before they'd said something cutting and painful. As a kid she'd stood mutely and taken it. Well, she wasn't a child any longer. She tapped into that long-stored anger and mixed it with what she felt at being dismissed now.

For an instant her temper faltered as she realized that she had issues over something that had ended years ago. But when the barmaid caressed Jake's shoulder, Cai forgot that and saw red.

"Is there anything I can do for you?" the server cooed.

Jake leaned in and gave her a sweet, phony smile. His gaze ran over her body, boldly checking her out, then returned to meet the woman's eyes. "I'm still working on my beer. When it comes to some things, I like to move slow." His voice came out husky.

Cai wasn't acting when she grimaced. No wonder she didn't flirt; there was no way she could say lame stuff like this. It surprised her that Jake wasn't smoother, but when a man looked like he did, probably all he had to do was crook his finger. She knew intimately that he hadn't been hurting for female company the first year they'd been connected.

"Slow can be very good." The woman ran her nails lightly across the side of his neck.

Jake's smile broadened, and Cai snorted. Could she have chosen a more predictable response? Both of them looked at her—her recep impassively and the barmaid with a superior air. It lasted only an instant before their attention returned to each other. Then the server moved closer and continued petting him. Jake put his hand on her waist, but things stopped there. A shout came from the bar, drowning out the snarl that Cai couldn't contain. The barmaid didn't look pleased, but she shifted away from Jake nonetheless.

"I'll be back shortly. Maybe you'll be ready for something then. Remember," she added, as she trailed her hand along his skin, "Isdu will satisfy your needs." She gave Cai another condescending sneer and left.

A few short words, nothing loud, Cai recalled. "Men can't really want someone like that." She gestured toward Isdu. "I mean, for heaven's sake, talk about feeble conversation."

"Trust me," Jake said mildly. He appeared irritated. "Men aren't thinking about *chatting* with her."

He leered at the barmaid, and Cai's frown deepened. She gave his shoulder a light smack. "Stop staring at her rear end."

Nice touch, Jake sent softly to her, even as his frown deepened. *Now turn away from me in a huff.*

She did as he ordered, but had to quash the urge to giggle. It had to be nerves. She toyed with her beer bottle, rotating it slowly as she worked on getting herself in the proper frame of mind for what was coming. It wouldn't be long. Not with the hungry looks the server had been giving Jake.

The wall she stared at was covered with graffiti. Some were marked with names and dates, but most of what she read was obscene. Isdu's name, she noted, was scrawled more than once.

Here she comes. Don't look around till you hear one of us speak; then turn and glare. I'll up the ante then.

Got it. She took a deep breath and balled her hands into fists. She had to do this. Jake was counting on her.

"You haven't finished your beer yet? You truly *are* a man who likes to take his time. Perhaps you can demonstrate such a leisurely pace later, when I get off," Isdu said.

Cai turned and frowned, though she was more tempted to laugh. But as her recep said, men didn't care if the barmaid was smart. Her hands rested on Jake's shoulders, and she stood between his splayed legs.

"It would be my pleasure to do just that," Jake replied. And then he did exactly what he'd said; he upped the ante. It wasn't a small bump either. He took hold of the woman's hips and pulled her close, his face almost resting between her breasts.

Cai waffled, trying to decide what to do, and Isdu turned a triumphant smirk her way. The barmaid said to Jake, "You'll find my company a refreshing change, I imagine. You must hunger for the feel of a real woman beneath you and not a child, my little honeybee."

Even her insult was obvious and stupid, but it didn't matter; Cai's anger soared. "Back off, *Isdu*, or I'll put you on your ass."

Her recep pulled away, but Cai barely noticed. She was facing down a smug, arrogant woman who thought she wasn't worthy of someone like Jake; she was facing down demons from her school years.

"You wouldn't dare." Isdu gave a toss of her dark hair.

Consciously mimicking what Jake had done the night she'd shown up in Hell, Cai slowly stood and pushed her chair out of her way with a foot. "Try me," she growled.

Isdu looked at Jake.

"Don't think he's going to help you. 'My little honey-bee'"—Cai almost choked saying that—"knows better than to interfere."

"You don't scare me."

Cai rolled her eyes. She didn't want to tumble around on the grungy floor, but she wouldn't back down. She sized up her opponent, not underestimating her. The woman had a hardness, and after working in this bar it was safe to assume she wouldn't be a pushover. The server met Cai's glare, but Cai saw the hint of uncertainty in her eyes and knew she had the upper hand.

The men around them had gone quiet as they watched the show. The rest of the customers kept talking, unaware anything was happening. Yet. Cai felt sure that wouldn't last much longer. She took a step toward Isdu and the bar-maid backed up.

Then Isdu's name was bellowed by the man behind the bar, and the server cast a glance over her shoulder at him. She turned back and said haughtily, "I've work to do and no time to waste on someone like you." With one last sneer, she beat a quick retreat.

"Sweetheart—" Jake started, but Cai cut him off.

"Don't you 'sweetheart' me!" She swallowed hard. Now

what did she say? She felt odd, especially with the eyes of so many people on her. None of them made an effort to hide their interest.

Jake saved the situation by pushing to his feet and shoving his chair out of the way, squaring off with her. "C'mon, you can't blame me," he said, voice raised. "You haven't been overly generous with your affection lately."

She felt her face heat, but it wasn't just embarrassment. Anger hit, and hit hard. "Yeah? Is that what you were thinking this afternoon? That I wasn't affectionate enough? You sure weren't complaining then, but maybe you didn't have enough breath left after you came."

"There you go, cutting at me again." He became even louder. "You're always getting in a dig. Well, sweetheart, I don't have to take this abuse. If it weren't for me, you'd be selling your data for pocket change—like you were when we met."

"Maybe I wouldn't be making digs if there wasn't so much room for improvement," she snarled. The entire bar was focused on them now. "And don't think I couldn't do fine on my own. You're the one who'd be in a world of hurt if I walked out. Webriders of my skill don't come along often, and you know it. Try brokering for some second-rate wannabe and see how much money you get!"

He went toe-to-toe with her. "So what? It doesn't matter how good you are if you don't know who to contact or how much the data is worth. Face it, you need me."

"Guess what, cowboy. It would be one hell of a lot easier for me to replace you than vice versa. Brokers are a dime a dozen. So *you* face it—you need me much more than I'll ever need you." She raised her chin and glowered.

"You just try it," he threatened.

"Maybe I will. Maybe I'll find someone who'll do a better job than you. After all, it's your fault that we're hiding on Malé. You had to squeeze more out of that buyer than what we agreed. You knew she had influence, but did that stop you?" Her tone became sarcastic. "Oh, no, not the great deal maker. 'Just a few thousand more, sweetheart,'" she mocked. "'She'll never balk, not for this info.' Yeah, right."

"If you think I'll stand around while you find another broker, you'd better think again. You're not pushing me aside."

"And if you think I'll stand for you playing around, *you'd* better think again. You're mine until I say otherwise, and I don't share." She leaned forward, getting in Jake's face. *Say something that will really piss me off,* he said. *We need to end this and get out of here soon or we won't be arguing alone.*

"But, hey." She didn't miss a beat. "If monogamy is boring you, maybe we should both take other lovers." Though it wasn't what she wanted, Cai ran her gaze over the men standing nearby. "Seems I've got a roomful of candidates."

He grabbed her arm and jerked her toward the door. "Like hell. I'll kill any son of a bitch who touches you." She dug her heels in for show. The last thing she expected was Jake to turn, bend down, and put his shoulder into her stomach. Her screech was one of surprise, but that changed to outrage when he gave her bottom a smack. "I'm going to prove to you who needs who," he said as he carried her out the door.

It was a heck of an exit line, Cai realized as he strode away from the tavern. She expected him to set her on her feet when they'd put the bar far enough behind them, but he didn't. He kept walking, his long legs eating up ground.

"Jake, put me down."

He slapped her butt again. Not hard, but she stiffened in shock. What was he up to?

Jacob Tucker, what the hell is this about?

Sorry, sweetheart.

He didn't sound sorry. In fact, he sounded like he was enjoying himself. Cai considered the situation and her position. She was hanging over his left shoulder, leaving his right arm free to draw a weapon if need be, and for some unknown reason, he wouldn't put her down. She didn't have leverage to escape, but she did have a very nice target right in front of her.

For a moment she watched the play of his glute muscles as he walked; then, taking a deep breath, she did it. She slapped his rear end, just as he'd done to her.

Caught off guard, the man stumbled to a halt, and Cai smiled, satisfied with the results. She couldn't help but wonder, though, what he would have done if she'd bitten him. Her face was right there; she could have done it without much strain.

"What the f—hell?"

"Didn't you like that, 'my little honeybee'?"

She wasn't certain, but she thought she heard Jake growl. He resumed walking. Now she was enjoying herself.

Why'd you do that, Cai?

Sorry, honeybee, she mimicked.

Smart-ass. There are people along the street watching us, and we have our spy at the inn. We need to keep up the act until we reach our room. It's the safest and smartest thing to do.

All you had to do was explain.

We're going to talk after we finish tonight's performance. You see, you're operating under a misconception. I'm not going to explain every action I take. You're going to have to trust me.

Cai didn't say anything. He was right. She'd never question, say, General Yardley if he threw her over his shoulder and didn't put her down. And although they were equal in rank, Jake was in charge on this mission. He didn't have to offer her any reasons. It was easy to think of him as her friend, not her op leader, but that was a mistake—one she was sure to repeat.

Laughter and some catcalls came from her left, and she turned to look. The boys weren't old enough yet to be pirates, but they weren't far off. She blushed at the advice they hollered to Jake, and buried her face against his back. Op leader or not, she'd make him pay for this.

Malé, at least this section of it, was surprisingly well lit. Part was the tropical moon, but there were artificial lights as well. She knew that made it safer, since Jake would be able to see what was coming for them, but it also meant she was in full view of anyone who cared to look. The raft seemed to be bouncing, and she closed her eyes. It had to be the position she was in, but damn, she was grateful for the nanomeds keeping her stomach calm. Her being seasick would only add to the spectacle.

She felt him turn, and she put her hands on his waist and peered around his body. They'd reached their lodgings. He paused to open the door, then carried her inside and up the stairs. Cai raised her head in time to see the innkeeper watching them, and she groaned. Yeah, this was what they wanted, but it was humiliating.

Another brief hesitation; then they were in their room. She couldn't stop a surprised squeak when he tossed her on the bed. The frame thudded loudly into the wall, and she guessed he'd been aiming for that sound. She propped herself up on her elbows and glared. "Why are you throwing me around like a damn rag doll?"

Louder, he ordered.

Oh, yeah, she could do louder. Easily. "How would you like it if someone bigger than you picked you up and carted you around?" She rose to her feet and crowded him. "You used your size against me, and I never want to see that again."

"If you don't like it, then don't provoke me." Jake shifted so he could peek out the viewer, and when he looked back, he was smiling. Their nosy landlady must be at the door and listening.

"Provoke you? I'm the one who was provoked! I thought we had an arrangement. I thought we'd decided not to cheat on each other. Tell me, has that changed? Because if it has, it's going both ways, *honeybee*. If I have to share, so do you."

"I already told you, I don't share. You're mine!"

"Yeah, well, maybe I don't want to be yours anymore. Not after what I saw from you tonight."

Jake's grin broadened, but not a single note of amusement came through when he spoke. "I'm sorry." He sounded conciliatory. "I was pissed and wanted to hurt you. I'm not interested in being with anyone else. I swear."

"So, every time we have a disagreement in the future, I can expect this from you? I'm not willing to live with that. We need to decide if we want to remain lovers or if it's better to be nothing more than business partners."

"Cai, please, I was a jerk. I know it." He checked the viewer again. "But don't throw what we have away. No one will ever love you more than I do."

"I don't know," she said, sounding torn.

"I do. I know you love me, too, even though I can be an ass. You can't throw five years away over one stupid misstep. Come on, sweetheart—give me another chance. I swear, I'll never look at another woman again. I really am sorry."

Should I forgive you now or make you crawl some more?

Forgive me. Let's get to the kiss-and-make-up sex.

Cai almost laughed. She never would have guessed that Jake liked acting so much. He'd called this a show. It was. And he was a born ham. But she saw why he'd find this entertaining, especially when she considered what his job usually entailed.

"You swear to be faithful?"

"Always." He held his finger to his lips and checked the hall. After several minutes, he signaled her to get on the bed.

With a sigh, she complied. Cai stretched her legs out and used them to push up before falling to the bed. To keep from fantasizing about Jake, she forced herself to build computer code in her head. It worked. After a dozen bed-rattling bounces, she was bored senseless and going through the motions on autopilot.

She paid attention, though, when she heard him think, *Shit!*

Before she could blink, Jake dropped on top of her and began tugging at her shirt. "Wh—" His mouth covered hers.

Oh, my God! Not only was Jake Tucker lying between her thighs, kissing her and unbuttoning her clothes, but he was hard. And since he was the one moving to rock the bed, he was rubbing himself against her. The moan that escaped Cai wasn't faked.

He took the opportunity to explore her mouth more deeply. As their tongues touched, tasted, she arched into his thrusts. Her hands found his shoulders, and she tried to pull him closer. Then her shirt came open and cool air touched her, but only for a moment. His body covered hers and she felt warm skin and hard muscle. She had no clue when he'd unfastened his own shirt, and it didn't matter. The only thing that mattered was getting more of him.

The sound of the door opening pushed at the haze of her arousal, demanded Cai's attention, but she ignored it. Jake didn't. She groaned in protest when he stopped and turned toward the noise.

"What the hell are *you* doing in here?" he demanded hoarsely.

Chapter Nine

Cai stared at his profile for a stunned instant, then followed his gaze. The innkeeper stood inside their room, eyes hard as she watched them. Awareness slammed into her. It made sense now. Why Jake had cursed, why he'd jumped on top of her. Why he'd kissed her. Desire had nothing to do with it.

He'd known the landlady had decided to enter to make sure everything appeared as it sounded. Cai's cheeks flamed. She'd been melting all over him and he'd been coolly setting the stage for their audience. How would she meet his eyes again? He must know she'd been clueless, that she'd truly wanted him. The fact that he'd had an erection didn't make her feel better. He'd been in the field nearly nonstop the past seven weeks. She didn't think he'd had enough time between ops to find a woman and take the edge off. Sheer willpower kept her from choking in mortification.

Jake got to his feet and she pulled her shirt around her, not wanting to be exposed physically. There was nothing she could do about being emotionally naked. Her blush deepened when she noticed that not only was his shirt open, but so was the top button of his pants. There was no mistaking the fact that he was excited. Of course, he didn't seem fazed by that at all.

"I asked what you were doing in here." His words were soft, but only a fool would mistake the danger.

"I came to see if you required anything before I turned in for the night." The innkeeper's voice was as hard as her gaze.

"Sure you did. Ever think of knocking?"

The woman shrugged. "I began to tap on the door; then I heard a moan and feared someone had fallen ill." She made no attempt to sound sincere, and the lie hung defiantly in the air.

Cai swung her legs off the bed and stood beside Jake, ready to back him up if he needed. It didn't seem likely that the innkeeper posed a threat, but she wasn't going to be caught on her back in case she was wrong.

"Try again. No one reaches your age without knowing the difference between a moan of pain and one of pleasure."

Although he appeared relaxed, her recep was poised to respond in an instant. She could feel him vibrating with pent-up energy. The innkeeper, though, only stared at Jake. She didn't try to explain, nor to apologize, and Cai realized she didn't care if they believed her or not.

For a moment Cai feared that Jake and the woman would continue challenging each other indefinitely, but the innkeeper folded first. "Since you don't need anything," she said blandly, "I'll leave you to the bed and your pleasures."

Without waiting for a reply, she walked from the room. Cai was struck by a sudden urge to flee herself, rather than remain here with Jake. What if he wanted to talk about how she'd reacted to him? She didn't want to clear the air, didn't want to hash it out and reach an understanding. All she wanted was to travel back in time and undo the last ten minutes.

But heaven help her, even knowing it meant nothing to him beyond solidifying their cover story, she couldn't help wishing it had gone further. He'd left her aching.

"Fasten your shirt," he ordered abruptly.

The harshness startled her, and she quickly reached for the buttons, embarrassed that she'd forgotten her state of undress. He wasn't looking at her and, coupled with his tone, she could only assume he was angered by her behavior. This was a mission, and she'd behaved as if it were a tryst. No wonder he was mad.

When she had the uppermost button done, Cai decided to do what she could to delay the unwelcome discussion. "Someone is much too interested in us. This eavesdropping is understandable given the environment of the Raft Cities, but barging into our room to verify what she heard goes far beyond that."

Jake turned from the window, his clothing secured again too, and said quietly, "I know." Frowning, he rubbed the back of his neck. "I don't like the obviousness of her lie either. Since she was so unconcerned with whether or not we believed her, I'm betting that whoever she's working for is damn powerful. If she didn't have his influence behind her, and feel confident it was unassailable, she would have at least *tried* to sound truthful." His lips quirked. "I have a feeling, though, that she wouldn't mind if we moved to another inn. Then she'd be out of it."

"Is that what we're going to do? Change lodging?"

He shook his head. "No."

She opened her mouth to ask for an explanation, but shut it without speaking. *Op leaders don't have to say why,* she repeated silently, but it made her half-crazy with curiosity.

Jake explained, "If this person has the kind of control that it appears he has, then his reach goes beyond this innkeeper." Cai barely hid her surprise. After what he'd said about needing her to trust his decisions, the last thing she expected was for him to voluntarily share his reasoning. "Since we'd be targeted anyway, we may as well remain here. I might be wrong, but I think our charming hostess doesn't like the boss."

"You think we can work that to our favor?"

He shrugged. "She'll do exactly what he tells her to do and pass on any information he wants, but maybe she won't volunteer something he hasn't specifically requested."

She thought about that. "It would have to be a small something, otherwise there would be retribution."

"Definitely. But if I'm right, and she doesn't bother to mention little things, it may give us an edge. Maybe not much of one, but hell, we need any advantage we can get."

The silence that descended then seemed oppressive. Jake was at the window, Cai was next to the door, and despite all that space between them, it was still too close.

"Cai," he said, voice serious.

Here we go, she thought. It looked like she wasn't going to avoid the embarrassment of this conversation after all. She slipped her hands in her pockets and braced herself.

"You can access non-UCE systems, right? That wasn't some bullshit to get yourself to the Raft Cities, was it?"

She stared at him until the words sank in; then relief hit. Considering how she felt about that second monster computer, it said a lot that she found this preferable to talking about what had happened on the bed. "No, it's not a lie. I can use the implant to ride other systems, but I have to know a general physical location. I can't try for the big computer until we pin it down more precisely."

Jake leaned a hip into the bureau and crossed his arms over his chest. "That's not what I had in mind. I want you to get on the local systems and find out everything you can about our innkeeper. I'd like to know who's pulling her strings."

The second wave of relief wasn't as strong as the first, but Cai had to wait for it to pass before she could speak. "The computers here are old and it's unlikely they'll have complete intel on the woman. As for who, specifically, she's tied to, there's almost no chance of discovering that. The best I might be able to come up with is who seems to be influential."

"I know that, swee—Cai." Jake looked away from her, and she felt the blood run out of her face. From the start she'd valued the endearment, considered it an indication of their closeness. Now, because of her loss of control, he wasn't comfortable using it any longer. Her hands balled into fists where they rested in her pockets. What had she done?

Somehow, some way, she had to restore normalcy to their relationship. *Friendship*. They were *friends*. She couldn't let him feel ill at ease because she'd lost her good sense. And as soon as an idea on how to do this struck her, she'd implement it.

"I'm guessing the computers are kept near the center of Malé to protect them as much as possible." Cai pulled her hands free and pressed them flat on the wall behind her. She wanted to sit down before she attempted this, but the only seat was the bed, and she was afraid that would make things worse.

"A bit off the midpoint, I think. Try this building." He sent her an image of a structure, then pulled away to show the surrounding area, then even farther back to give her the relative position between their inn and this other section of the raft.

She was pretty sure it was one of the places that he'd made note of during their reconnaissance. So many of the buildings here looked similar that it was difficult to tell for sure, but thanks to his mental map, she knew where to test. Closing her eyes, she leaned her head back and sent out a shallow scan with the implant. Jake had almost been right. The computers were stored in the structure next to the one he'd shown her.

With the location known, she sent her probe deeply

into the system. It was jury-rigged with odd patches, and the core of the computer dated back to before the Pirate Wars. Not only would the condition make the three searches she planned more challenging, but she had to wonder what state the data itself was in after feeling how banged-up it was.

She gave herself a mental shake and began. First up, she needed to identify the woman. Cai checked the records to find the owner of the inn; then she sought a visual to match the name listed. Though the picture she found was at least ten years old, there was no doubt it was their innkeeper. Amina Goma.

Now that she had a name, she began the second task: a broader hunt through the files for any line of detail about the woman. As she'd feared, there wasn't much. A lot went undocumented in a place like the Raft Cities, but there were also gaps she knew came from computer damage.

She sent what she'd found across the pathway to Jake and went looking for possibilities on whom Amina reported to. This process required inference on her part, but since the same names kept popping up again and again, she thought she'd labeled the pirate lords. Maybe. The death records didn't appear to have been updated in at least two years, so it was possible some of the men had died. It was also feasible that a lord or two preferred to keep a low profile and not call attention to themselves. After the way the UCE's SEAL teams had kicked their pirate butts during the wars, who could blame them?

Cai was taking one last run through some files when she felt something—or someone. She stayed resolute even as her heart began to pound. Carefully, she traced the path through the system and found the other anchor. Something about the woman's presence seemed different than when she'd felt it in the UCE systems, almost as if the anchor had become stronger. She wasn't aware she'd been detected.

With more caution than she'd ever exercised before

while inside a computer, Cai edged closer. It wasn't easy to do, but she tried to blend her consciousness with the circuitry as much as possible, hoping it would help keep her hidden. When she remained undetected, she drifted nearer, then nearer still.

And she saw the file.

The anchor was researching Amina Goma.

Her sense of being hunted grew, but Cai pushed aside the uneasiness. She needed to uncover as much as possible while she could, and crept closer. The woman was transmitting to her receptor, she realized with surprise. There was a pair. Cai couldn't pick up the info, but she could follow the flow.

Cai.

She quickly blocked Jake, but it was too late. The woman pulled back, disappearing in an instant. *Damn.* Just when she'd started to learn a few things about how to track an anchor/recep team. She lingered, reluctant to leave, but the systems stayed quiet and slowly Cai opened her eyes. Her own recep hovered nearby, his face concerned, but that eased when she met his gaze.

"What the hell happened?" he demanded.

Instead of answering, she considered what she'd seen. How was it possible that the link between partners was noticeable to another anchor? True, it was a connection between two nanocomputers, so it might be the data stream, but it was so fast and so minute, it should be impossible. Should be, but wasn't.

"Cai?"

With a small shake of her head, she continued thinking about what had happened. She'd found the woman before she'd started sending data, and hadn't been detected. Not until Jake had transmitted to her. She frowned and tried to puzzle through why her sense of this other anchor had changed. It was important; she could feel it.

Jake's hands gripped her shoulders and squeezed. "Talk to me, damn it. What the hell happened, sweetheart?"

At least his worry had reduced the awkwardness enough so that he could call her sweetheart again.

That was the good news. The rest . . . well, not so good.

"I hate to tell you this," she said.

"Shit." He closed his eyes and girded himself. When he looked at her again, he said, "Okay, hit me with it."

"I ran into the other anchor inside the computer." She held up a hand to stop him from commenting. "Wait, there's more. She was transmitting to her partner."

Suddenly one of the pieces fell into place. She barely heard Jake when he said, "There are two of them then?"

"Yes," she said, eager to share what she'd figured out. "And they're here. They're both on the Raft Cities."

He hoped to never have another night like last night. Yeah, Jake figured he deserved to pay for lusting after Cai, but the tortures of the damned seemed kind of steep. And the universe wasn't through exacting a price from him. Hearing her moving around in the bath had his imagination running wild, and he swore he could almost feel the slickness of her wet skin under his hands.

Taking a deep breath, he forced his fists to unclench. They had to get out of this room before he lost his mind. He reached for his holster and strapped it on. Instead of focusing on what they needed to do today, all he could remember was the feel of Cai's body beneath his. Or the way she'd fit against him once she'd fallen asleep. Her bare legs tangled with his, her hair loose and draped over both of them—shit. Jake closed his eyes and fought for control. He was damn useless in this state.

To help battle the arousal, he forced himself to recall a few other things. Like the fact that she hadn't realized how much she'd overplayed her role yesterday afternoon. He'd honestly forgotten how young she was, at least for a while, but that had driven it home with the force of a stake through the heart. And it made him wonder how much experience she had.

Whenever he worked, she worked, and he was out in the field a lot. When he factored in the hours he'd spent talking to her and how much time that stole, when did she have a chance to meet anyone? Hell, his own social life had suffered because he'd enjoyed their conversations more than going out and meeting other women; that was why Gnat had made that crack in Hell about him needing to have some fun. Jake scowled at the memory of his XO suggesting he take Cai to bed. Hadn't he corrupted her enough?

Damn, his face still heated when he recalled her comment about how he wasn't quiet when he had sex. She couldn't hear him unless he transmitted, which meant that not only had he been unable to block her those first fifteen months or so, but he'd been unconsciously sending to her as well. Talk about embarrassing.

Shaking off that thought, he forced himself to replay how she'd pressed herself against the wall after they'd gone to sleep last night, trying her best not to touch him. Or the way she'd referred to him several times as her friend. She couldn't have made it any clearer that she wasn't interested in him as a lover.

He wished his body would get the message. It didn't care that they were on a mission, or that the danger had increased considerably with the discovery that the second anchor and her recep were on the Raft Cities. Things had been dicey enough before; this made their position even shakier.

Cai had told him that while she didn't know what they looked like, she'd be able to identify both of them from their energy signatures. He had to assume it went both ways, and that he and she were every bit as vulnerable to detection. This couple could blow their cover with a few words.

But was this what he'd lain awake worrying about last night? Hell, no. Jake bent and secured the bottom of the holster around his thigh. He'd bounced back and forth between figuring out how to beat his attraction into submission and honor Cai's decision not to go beyond friendship, and how to convince her to give this fire between them a chance. He was twenty-six years old, had enjoyed his fair share of women, and he'd never before—not once—felt desire as strong as this.

He retrieved his weapon, checked the cartridge, and slid it into place. Now all he had to do was wait for his anchor. And keep his mind on the job.

He ran a hand through his hair, pushing it off his forehead, and tried to compartmentalize the op from his interest in her. No way would he allow his unprofessional thoughts to endanger her or prevent them from finding Maguire.

The progress he made was lost in an instant though when Cai came into the room. Her red shirt went to her throat, but it fit her body closely, and her light-colored pants were like a second skin. Damn, he wanted to press her into the wall and kiss her till she lost her head. His gaze drifted to her rear as she bent to tug on her boots. If he had half a brain, he'd look the other way.

As she straightened, he watched her tense then glance at him over her shoulder. Color filled her cheeks as she figured out where he'd been staring, but even being caught red-handed couldn't make him turn away.

Her movements weren't as graceful as she armed herself, and he knew he'd made her self-conscious. Jake sighed and rubbed the back of his neck. He wasn't going to be able to lock down his feelings when it came to Cai. He'd learned as a kid to stay in command of himself at all times. With his experience, this should be second nature to him. His failure grated, but he accepted it. Pretending the attraction didn't exist would be stupid, even if he did plan to pull back and work at respecting her wishes.

"Are you ready?" he asked, and winced when his voice sounded as if he'd swallowed a handful of Sartonian blades.

When she nodded, he opened the door, checked the hall and then stood aside to let her precede him. They were quiet as they descended the stairs, but the innkeeper must have heard them because she stood at the bottom, watching them with her cold eyes. Jake moved, putting himself between his anchor and the woman, and slipped his left arm around Cai's waist.

Damn. As much as he wanted to pull away, he couldn't. Not with Goma spying on them, ready to report any lapse in their cover to her boss. And it was a sure bet that they'd be observed by others wherever they went on Malé.

Once they were outside, he sent her that information. Then he added, *I'm sorry, but I can't back off.*

She nodded. *I understand.*

Part of Jake relaxed. He'd been worried she wouldn't accept this, and would view his actions as an attempt to coerce her into something she didn't want. But Cai was smart; he should have remembered that, and known she'd see the truth.

"Any preferences for breakfast?" he asked.

"What are the odds of finding someplace clean? A place where I don't have to worry about eating fried rat?"

He pulled her closer. "I'll do my best. I don't suppose you found any information in the local systems?"

She looked up and gave a mock expression of shock. "You think the Raft Cities have a health department and inspectors to check out their many fine dining establishments?"

"Smart-ass," he muttered. But it was impossible to be annoyed by her sarcasm. Not when it was delivered with a good-natured mien and a twinkle in her deep brown eyes.

Jake made himself look away and study the area. The streets were mostly empty because of the early hour. A few women went about their tasks and some children played, but that was it. Even many of the businesses were closed, since they catered to pirates and those men were sleeping off last night's revels. It looked like he and Cai would need to adjust their schedule as well.

Signs of the damage the Pirate Wars had left on the Raft Cities were everywhere. He made note of the condition of the buildings and of this raft itself. Parts seemed spliced together, and the upkeep had to be constant. But he also saw indications that confirmed that the raiders might be making a comeback. He'd have to report this to Yardley when the mission concluded.

He looked at Cai. If he'd been teamed with one of his men, he would have already shared what the plan was for the day. She deserved the same consideration. *After we eat, we'll start the search for Maguire and Armstrong at the landing sites. Malé only has two—the one where we came in, and one that's primarily pirate traffic. Since we can't flash pictures of them around, the story will be that we're checking out rides home for when the heat is off. I need you to let me do the talking, okay?*

That got him a frown, and he had to glance away to keep from smiling. Damn, he enjoyed this woman. *It's the culture of the Raft Cities,* he added before she could say anything.

I know. It's a patriarchal society. She sounded glum.

Jake nodded. It was male-dominated, not merely leaning that direction. *I'll get chummy with the men who work there and see what I can find out about other visitors from the UCE.*

They wouldn't have come in from the UCE. The last solid report of their location was the Kingdom of Asia.

Sweetheart, we didn't appear to come via the UCE either, but even if we hadn't shouted in the bar last night, do you think anyone here wouldn't know where we call home? He didn't wait for an answer. *Maguire and Armstrong won't fool them either.*

The residents would need to read people quickly to survive.

Quickly and accurately, he confirmed.

With a slow nod, she smiled up at him and her dimple peeked out again. That thing was a lethal weapon. At least, it stopped *his* heart every damn time she flashed it at him.

"Feed me, cowboy." *And let's get this show on the road.*

But finding somewhere to eat didn't prove easy. They popped into several establishments, but after the first, Jake left Cai outside as he checked out the kitchens. Although she'd remained expressionless, he'd felt her reaction. She couldn't go without food, but if she was too disgusted, she might balk at eating. He figured his best bet was to keep her from seeing anything that would make her queasy. At the same time, he was cognizant of the danger in leaving her alone.

He lost track of the number of places they stopped, but all were too dirty or dangerous, and he was beginning to lose hope. It was late in the morning, and more people were out and about. He and Cai couldn't afford to waste too much more time, though; their ultimate mission was to capture Banzai Maguire, not to find a clean restaurant.

In front of one last place, he made a sweep of the area with his eyes. There were some kids playing nearby, but the oldest was maybe five and their mothers weren't around. Lining Cai up with the restaurant window, Jake ordered, "Don't move."

She nodded, but he didn't miss the roll of her eyes. He ignored it. Since he'd told her the same thing at each stop, she was probably tired of hearing it. He simply didn't want to take any chances, not when the thought of anything happening to her ripped him up inside. Leaning forward, he kissed her hard and fast. It had nothing to do with their pint-sized audience, though if she called him on it, he'd insist it did. He walked away before she could say anything.

When he stepped inside the restaurant kitchen, Jake froze in surprise. The place appeared sanitary enough to pass UCE health codes. Not trusting his first glance, he moved deeper and checked things more thoroughly. He looked outside to reassure himself that Cai was where he'd left her, then investigated the pots on the stove.

The door opened and an older woman entered. She frowned fiercely, then came over to where he stood, slapped his hand, which was holding a lid, hard enough to sting, and demanded, "Why do you bring your dirty feet into my kitchen? Have you no sense?"

Carefully he replaced the cover and stepped back. "I needed to make sure your kitchen wouldn't make me sick."

The woman gave a sniff. "As if men bother with such things. All you concern yourself with is taste and cost."

Jake shrugged. "Perhaps. But my woman cares."

The old lady stared at him, hard, then said, "I'm to believe you cater to your woman's whims?"

"If I indulge her desires"—he gave her a smile he knew was roguish—"then she indulges mine."

That brought a chuckle. "Sounds as if you found a smart woman. And perhaps you aren't so stupid either."

It won him an abbreviated tour of the facilities, with emphasis on what the woman did to keep the food from spoiling or becoming contaminated. "This satisfies you?" she asked as she completed the circuit of the room. When Jake nodded, she said, "Then bring your woman in through the front. I'll not have anyone else traipsing through my kitchens, do you understand me?"

"Yes, ma'am," he said, responding to her authority with the respect she deserved.

He was still smiling when he walked outside, but his good humor deserted him abruptly when he didn't spot

Cai. His heart pounded so loudly, the only thing he could hear over it was the sobbing of a child. Panic swamped him and he had to force it aside to function. He drew his weapon and did a quick scan of the area, but didn't see anything to indicate what had happened.

"*Cai!*"

Nothing.

Calm down, he told himself. Since he needed to be thorough, he searched again. This time he walked more slowly, looking farther from her original position. He found her. She was crouched in an alley, in front of a crying child, trying to soothe her, and Jake felt his knees sag as relief slammed into him. His hands shook, and it took several attempts to slide his weapon back into its sheath. *Shit.* What the hell was going on with him?

He stayed where he was and took deep breaths until his heart rate returned to normal. Somehow he had to ensure that she never wandered off like this again. He didn't need explanations to know what had occurred. The little girl had started squalling, no other adult had come over to help, so Cai had hustled her ass over here to make it all better. Her caring about some stranger's kid was a weakness, one the pirate bastards would use against her. But how the hell could he scare her badly enough to keep her from trying to help the next child in distress?

He and the girl calmed down about the same time, and when Cai straightened, Jake called her name. She waved and jogged toward him. Jake ground his teeth, annoyed by her obliviousness.

"We're eating here," he announced, and reached for her elbow to escort her around the building to the entrance. He tried not to say any more, but the words slipped out anyway. "You promised to obey orders, and I told you to stay put."

"You're mad."

"No shit."

"Jake—"

"No, not one word. I can guess exactly what happened, so spare me the story." At least, until he could talk about it without his blood turning to ice.

Inside he held out a chair for her and, when she was settled, seated himself with his back to the wall. The restaurant was clean, and though the structure wasn't great, there were small touches on each table to give some ambience. That sank in as Jake studied the occupants, mostly a few old men seated in the far corner and a couple of others scattered around the room.

With no immediate threat visible, Jake was able to take it down another notch. He looked at Cai, then glanced away. Nope, he wasn't ready to talk to her yet. Not without getting her pissed off at him, and since he was still angry, they'd end up having an argument. Best to keep his mouth shut.

The menu was scrawled on a tented card placed at the center of the table. It didn't take him long to choose, and when the woman he'd met in the kitchen came to take his and Cai's orders, they were both ready. He ignored her curiosity. No doubt she was wondering what had happened to cause the tension between him and his woman, but he wasn't going to satisfy her interest.

They ate in silence, the food both good and filling. There was even real coffee, and he leaned back in his chair to enjoy it. His mood was definitely improving.

Jake!

He heard the urgency in Cai's tone and set his mug down hurriedly as he straightened. *What is it? What's wrong?*

Someone's accessed the files about my parents!

What files?

The UCE files. Since you were ignoring me, I decided this was the perfect time to do a run-through, and it's a good thing I did. Someone else has been in the data.

Part of him relaxed even as another part tensed. *How can you know something like that?*

He felt her confusion and knew she didn't have words to tell him. When that happened, she usually sent him something along their link, but she didn't do that either. *Cai?*

I'm sorry, it's nothing I can explain. She shrugged. *I just know.* She reached over and clutched his hand. *But we have to figure out who's been checking on my parents and why!*

Her concern came through clearly. *Damn.* The last thing he wanted to do was confess he'd asked Yardley to run the data. He'd been sure there were strong reasons the authorities had declared her folks dead, and he'd wanted to see them without emotion biasing the facts. What he'd found, though, was the opposite; there was no proof they'd died. Of course, there was no evidence of kidnapping either.

Reluctantly, he opened his mouth to admit what he'd done, but Cai interrupted.

Do you think it was the traitors? If they know about us from the Quandem Project, they could have decided to check into our backgrounds further. The pause was less than a second. *What if they found out I was researching Elliot? What if they tracked him to the Raft Cities? What if they decide to use my parents?*

She was scaring herself half to death, he could feel it. Now he had no choice but to tell . . . wait a second. He could work this. Of course, she'd be furious at him when she found out the truth, but if it frightened her enough to keep her close, it would be worth it. He couldn't protect her if she wandered off.

Yardley said he thought we were targeted and someone did try to monitor us at the staging facility. He wasn't lying.

Her grasp tightened. *Do you think they're on the Raft Cities right now? We have to find Elliot first or my mom and dad could be in danger.*

I think you're the one in danger. You know what a long shot it is that Elliot's even here, let alone that he kidnapped your par-

ents. But the easiest way to get to me is through you, and you're a more accessible target. Still accurate, he told himself, but it made him uncomfortable. He covered her hand where it rested atop his.

Me?

Yes, you. I want you to promise to stay close to me no matter what. And that includes crying children, okay? The hesitation worried him. *Promise me,* he pressed urgently.

Okay, I promise.

Jake closed his eyes for an instant. God, when the truth came out, he hoped she'd believe he'd done this to keep her safe. But he knew if the situation were reversed, he wouldn't be understanding at all, no matter what the reason. He'd simply have to count on Cai having a more forgiving nature.

Chapter Ten

Cai had mixed feelings about Jake's assessment of the amount of danger she was in. On one hand, she truly didn't believe that someone running the file on her parents indicated she was at any greater risk; she was much more concerned about the potential threat for her folks. On the other hand, her recep was the one who had years of field experience. She'd be foolish to discount his take on things.

However, Jake had proven himself to be overprotective, and had quickly used the situation to get a promise from her to stick close. She studied him, trying to puzzle it out, but he seemed distracted. To be honest, she wasn't sure what to think right now, but the bottom line was that she trusted him.

His absorption remained while he paid for their meal and escorted her from their table. Funny how quickly it had become natural to feel Jake's hand at her waist. Not that it left her unaffected. The man's slightest touch got her hot and bothered, but that seemed right. Reminding herself that he was her friend was beginning to take on an edge of desperation.

They stepped outside and the late-morning sun momentarily blinded her. Maybe that was why she missed the threat until it was too late. She froze at the poke of a gun barrel in her left side and squinted to check out the situation.

Wreckers.

A damn army of them.

The only place to go was back inside, but even as she had the thought, she felt someone come up behind her. A glance over her shoulder showed another pair of the mercenaries. She and Jake were completely surrounded. He may have been right about the risk.

She looked around to assess the situation more thoroughly, and that was when she noticed the audience. It wasn't just women and children either. More Malé men were out now, and they looked on, hatred in their eyes, but the antipathy wasn't for her or Jake. It was directed at the wreckers.

The Maléans didn't yell any comments or hoot and holler, and the silence was downright eerie. Cai fought off a shiver as she considered how cruel these hired soldiers must be if *pirates* were leery of them.

The wreckers took her recep more seriously than they did her. While Cai had only one muzzle against her body, Jake had two: one at his head, the second in his side. She studied what they were. Looked like neuron fryers. Depending on the setting, they could either knock someone unconscious, cause varying degrees of harm to the cerebral cortex, or outright kill.

Even the lightest blast carried repercussions, like short-term memory loss. Cai shuddered. What would happen to her mind if she took a hit so soon after overloading her probes? She forced aside her worry and concentrated on their predicament.

Right now, at least two-thirds of the robomen had their weapons trained on Jake. It wasn't that they discounted her; they'd merely labeled her the lesser threat. She couldn't fault their reasoning. Her recep was a couple inches over six feet and heavily muscled. If one of them had a chance to cause damage to their cybernetic body armor, he was the more likely candidate.

"Let me see your hands." The sun's glare made it impossible to view more than a silhouette of the man who gave the command.

Do it, Jake ordered when she didn't instantly comply.

You first. She wanted to make sure he didn't try anything stupid in some chivalrous attempt to save her. She knew him too well, knew he'd protect her till he took his last breath, but she wasn't going to stand by and watch him die.

I'm not planning anything, he said as he slowly brought his hands up to shoulder height. *The odds are lousy right now.*

Cai raised her arms as well. *Glad you realize that, cowboy.*

The mercenaries didn't waste any time. They roughly yanked the weapons free from Cai and Jake's holsters, then patted them down to find what else might be hidden.

As they frisked her, Cai got her first up-close-and-personal look at a wrecker. She'd touched pieces of the dark matte body armor in training; she'd viewed images and read reports; but that was far different from seeing in person these people who'd had this surgical enhancement. Their heads and faces were covered by some kind of plating, giving them a ghoulish look. And they were *huge*. Maybe the shielding bulked them up, but she thought it was more than that. That stuff was heavy. It had to take a very strong, muscular person to wear it, so it made sense that most of the mercenaries were at least Jake's size or bigger.

None of them spoke as they searched her, but she didn't like the way she was touched. It wasn't sexual; there was such a lack of . . . well, humanness, and that creeped her out. But then the psych profiles she'd read on the average wrecker didn't portray a personality that would inspire a case of the warm fuzzies.

None of the weapons she'd concealed were missed, and she was pretty sure all of her recep's hardware was found too. If she had been watching the proceedings and hadn't lost her sense of humor, she'd have thought it amusing how long it took to disarm her and Jake. Unfortunately, she didn't consider anything too funny right now. Maybe later, once she and Jake were safe, they could laugh about this together.

At last it was decided that there was nothing left to find, and the men who'd inspected them stood back and waited. Cai waited too, half-afraid that they'd begin a new search for something other than guns, knives, or fryers. Maybe it wasn't much of an edge, but the small gizmo she'd doctored to look like a pendant still hung on a chain around her throat. The wreckers had checked it out, but since it was round and smooth, not dangerous, it had been written off.

"Move," the leader ordered harshly.

Cai felt a hard shove in the center of her back, and she barely caught her balance in time to keep from falling down the two shallow steps in front of the restaurant.

"Watch it," Jake growled.

Crap! "I'm okay. Don't worry about it." He stared at her intently, as if trying to compel her to tell him the truth. Cai shook her head. "Really, I'm fine. I'm tough enough to take a little push."

"Little push, my ass." But he subsided enough that she didn't worry about him taking issue with her treatment. And the next prod she received was dispensed far more gently.

She went down the steps side by side with Jake, but when they reached the bottom, a hand grabbed her shoulder and pulled her to a stop. That frightened her. Up till now, everything had indicated they were being taken prisoner, but this seemed much more ominous. Cai looked to her recep, who was staring at the wreckers. His face was expressionless, but she sensed a grimness from him that reinforced her concern.

Her heart thundered in her chest. *Think.* There had to be something she could do, some way to save both of them. Not only did she have the implants, but she was a hell of a tech-geek, and wreckers were loaded with the stuff she knew best.

The first blast came before she could do more than take a deep breath. Jake fell. For a split second she was shocked; then terror rocketed through her. Depending on what setting they'd used on the neuron fryer, her partner could be dead or brain damaged.

"Jake!" She was deaf and blind to everything but getting to him, making sure he was alive, but she didn't take more than two steps before she was jerked to a halt. Cai tried to claw at the hand holding her back, but she couldn't reach it.

No matter how she twisted, she was unable to escape. Fear became fury. She was being kept from Jake! Without giving any warning, she whirled and directed a snap kick at the knee of the mercenary who held her back.

Pain filled her foot. But before she had time to think about it, she saw the leader had his weapon pointed at her. Training had her trying to drop to the ground, but the blast caught her before she could get out of the way. There was a last instant of awareness at what had happened; then consciousness left her.

Cai woke disoriented. She didn't move while she tried to recall why her body ached and where she was. Then it all came back to her. She sat up in a hurry, ignoring the way her head swam.

Jake!

There was no response.

As soon as her vision cleared, she looked around and found her recep on the bed beside her. "Jake!" Her voice emerged hoarse and weak. She scrambled to her knees, and her head hurt so badly it felt like it would explode. Biting her bottom lip, she fought off the pain and bent over him. He had a pulse. She took a deep breath. But if they'd only stunned him, he should be coming around about now. He showed no signs of regaining awareness.

"Jake," she said quietly. "Come on, you have to wake up." She ran shaking fingers over his face, trying to bring him around any way she could. He couldn't be brain damaged; she refused to consider it. But part of her was tight with fear. The wreckers had clearly been more worried about him; who knew what setting they'd used? "Come on, Jake!"

She couldn't fall apart, wouldn't fall apart, but the idea of her Jake, with his vitality and intelligence missing, broke her heart. *Like hell,* she thought, putting some steel into her spine. Things might not look good, but she refused to think negatively. With renewed purpose, she continued calling his name and stroking him, not just his face but his chest and arms too.

Yet as time passed and she received no response, Cai became terrified. *Not Jake,* she beseeched. *Please, not Jake.* When she'd fried her implants, she'd felt a kind of dismayed acceptance that there would be consequences to deal with. She wasn't so complacent when it came to him.

What she should do was check out the room and get an idea of their situation, but Cai couldn't force herself to walk away from Jake even for a few minutes. He'd be irritated when he woke up and found she'd disregarded procedure, but right now she'd welcome being reprimanded. The reminder, however, of what she should be doing had her visually inspecting the location.

Their cell was nice. A hell of a lot nicer than their room at the inn. Bigger too. If this was what prisoners received for accommodations, she had to wonder what kind of quarters the welcome guests stayed in. She noted the position of the door and moved, putting herself between Jake and the most likely point of entry. Since he was out of it, she was his only protection.

With what she hoped appeared to be a casual move, she reached for her throat and relaxed when she discovered that her device remained attached to her necklace. Using her neural implant and the tiny gadget, she gave the room a quick scan and realized it was loaded with inteltronic bugs designed to monitor everything they said and did. A second survey showed that the door and both windows were sealed, locking them in.

Okay, now, when her recep woke up and asked for a report, she'd be able to tell him something.

Jake's breathing changed, and Cai forgot about everything but him. "Can you hear me?" she asked. "You need to wake up now. Come on, Jake." Although the movement was slight, she was sure he'd turned his head toward her. Encouraged, she continued talking to him, hoping it would bring him around.

There was no warning before his eyes opened. She sucked in a sharp gasp of surprise and then grinned until she remembered that *awake* didn't mean *fine*. "Talk to me," she ordered softly. "I need to know if they did more than stun you."

"I'm . . . okay, sweetheart," he said. His voice was a rasp, even rougher than hers when she'd first come to, but as far as Cai was concerned, nothing had ever sounded better. When she saw lucidness in his gaze, she sagged with relief. He *was* okay.

He pushed himself into a sitting position without grimacing, but she was connected to him and knew he was in as much pain as she'd been at first. Maybe more, since he must have been hit with a harder blast.

Tell me what you know.

She passed everything along their pathway in microseconds.

"I'm going to check out the door. You make a circuit of the rest of the room." It wasn't a request.

Though it was tempting to tell him to stay put until he had more time to recover, she didn't argue. Cai stood and swayed unsteadily, but the vertigo passed. She stayed close, however, in case Jake had trouble. He staggered when he gained his feet, and she reached for him, but he shook his head and crossed to the door. His concentration was total as he examined it.

She began to walk through what she labeled the sitting area. The large room was effectively divided into two sections by the groupings of furniture. This side had a sofa, chairs, and a low table arranged to provide a cozy conversation area. Finding nothing of interest, she moved on.

The other half held nothing but the bed. Surprisingly, it wasn't utilitarian, but had a frame, like a bare canopy, with swags of some floaty, gauzy material draped in swoops. Pretty. But odd for a cell.

She stopped at the windows and looked outside. They were on the second floor, and that gave her a good vantage point. From what she could see, they were on a totally separate raft than before. This one appeared to be meticulously kept up; certainly in better repair than Malé, and it appeared to be filled with greenery: grass, hedges, other plants and flowers. It was only then that Cai realized how barren of nature the Raft Cities were. In the distance, a tall force field was just visible, and she suspected it totally encircled the generous grounds around their prison.

She used her implant to tap into a satellite system and pinpoint their location. It should have been done when she first woke, but she hadn't been thinking clearly. They were near the outer edges of the Raft Cities. Jake was still studying the door, but she passed the info on through their link. He grunted.

She looked through the UCE systems for images of their location, but found nothing. This raft didn't exist. That raised her curiosity. What these people used as camouflage wasn't sophisticated, and it couldn't have completely concealed a raft as large as this one appeared. The only thing that could do that was cloak shielding. Very expensive cloak shielding. Not something anyone here could afford, not even the pirate lords.

Her heart picked up speed. Marchand Elliot. He had plenty of money. It had to be him. She took a deep breath and fought to quell her excitement. There could be another reason. Maybe.

When she was calmer, she moved from the window, rounded the bed, and stopped short. "Jake, our gear is here."

That garnered his full attention. "What?" He crossed to where she stood and looked down at their knapsacks. "Shit. Check our stuff while I look at the windows. Find out if anything is missing." *And if anything has been tampered with,* he added silently as he walked away.

She knelt on the floor and opened the first bag. *Our stuff being here isn't a good sign.*

No. It means we won't be going back to the inn anytime soon. What I want to know is how long those wreckers were on our asses. I didn't spot them, and it's not like they can blend in—not with that body armor.

Cai stopped unloading the pack to look at him. She'd heard the self-reproach in Jake's tone and knew he blamed himself for their capture. *Maybe they weren't tailing us. Maybe someone in the restaurant tipped their boss off.*

Maybe. He didn't sound convinced.

She'd have to work on that later; right now she had to focus on her task. Every item she examined needed to be scanned. Some of the clothing had inteltronic trackers attached, but they had to be nanotech. She never would have discovered them without the help of her pendant, since she saw and felt nothing. When she finished with her stuff, she opened Jake's pack and found the same thing. After he was done checking out the second of their two windows, she sent the info along their link.

Figures, he said, and held out a hand to help her stand.

C'mon, let's go sit down and talk like normal humans for the monitors. We need to give them what they'd expect from two fugitives grabbed and taken prisoner.

He escorted her to the couch and waited till she sat before settling himself beside her. Cai turned, putting one leg up on the cushions so she had a good view of him, and he took the same position. "The doors and windows are sealed?" she asked.

"Tightly," he confirmed with a frown. "I can't see a way to get around it either. Was all our stuff there?"

"Everything but the handhelds. Those are gone." She waited for him to comment, but got nothing except a nod. "Why did they take us?" she asked, reaching out and laying a hand on his knee.

"I don't know. I doubt our customer was pissed enough to go to these lengths, not over what happened, so it must be something else. You didn't ride into anything about some crime lord, did you?" The in-character question came out half-joking, half-serious. A nice touch to the performance, she thought.

She shook her head. "You don't suppose we managed to step on toes in the time we were on Malé, do you?"

"Shit, we've been there less than twenty-four hours."

"I know, but what about a man jealous over Isdu?"

"Who?" He was honestly blank on the name; she felt it through the connection, and that puzzled her.

"The barmaid, remember?"

"Oh, that's right. I doubt it. This is too much for what happened last night." He shifted and she felt the play of his leg muscles. "Any other thoughts?"

Yeah, but they involved running her palm up the inside of his thigh, so she planned to keep them to herself. Hoping he wouldn't read anything on her face or in her eyes, Cai shook her head. "I'm stymied," she said, and cleared her throat to get rid of the huskiness. "I can't think of any reason for this."

"Me either," he said quietly.

She couldn't come up with anything else to say. What would she be thinking if she really were a wanted webrider taken hostage with her broker? "How long do you think they'll make us wait before we meet with whoever wants us here?"

Jake shrugged. "Could be minutes. Could be hours or even days. It depends on why they took us."

She gave his leg a squeeze and pulled her hand away. "We won't know anything till we meet with them."

"Nope." He leaned back, making himself more at ease. "Nothing to do now but wait it out."

Cai nodded. For the hell of it, she gave the door a light probe. While she couldn't be sure with such a shallow scan, she believed she could undo the seal. The windows were a bit more complex, but given time she could handle those too. She passed this along to Jake to see what he thought.

No. For a moment she thought he'd leave it at that, but after a brief pause he explained. *Two reasons. One, it's not going to be that easy. I'm sure we have wreckers outside the door and probably patrolling the grounds as well. Two, the only way we're going to find out what's going on is to meet the pirate lord who ordered our capture and see what he wants.*

I think it's Elliot.

Her recep leaned back farther and moved to put his feet up on the small table in front of the sofa. When he closed his eyes, he looked as if he were on the verge of taking a nap. It was probably good for their show. After all, it demonstrated to their captors that he was unconcerned about their imprisonment, and it gave a reason for them to be sitting silently.

I know you do, but the odds are against it.

Maybe, but my instincts say I'm right.

She knew what Jake was thinking without his saying a word. Cai sighed and shifted so she could prop her feet up beside his. It threw her off balance when, a moment later, he slung an arm around her shoulders and pulled her into his side. She stiffened in surprise, then rested her head on his shoulder and wound her arm around his middle, letting him take her weight.

We're not suffering memory loss. The realization popped into Cai's head out of the blue.

She felt Jake tense; then he relaxed and said, *No, we're not. We should be, though. I've never heard of anyone taking a hit from a neuron fryer and not having blank spots.*

Do you think it's a different kind of fryer?

Nope, those were DT-1400s. Standard UCE Special Operations–issue. He paused. *Do you think our probes protected us?*

It's a possibility. There's nothing else different about us. They both fell silent again.

The longer they sat quietly, the more at ease Cai became. There was something reassuring about the motion of Jake's chest rising and falling as he breathed. Something calming about the warmth of his body against hers. Something so right about it. He turned and put his other arm around her, wrapping her in a hug.

Even the idea that he was doing it only because of the inteltronic eyes trained on them couldn't shake the contentment from her. *Friends,* she reminded herself, but it was hard to put a great deal of conviction behind it.

Not when he felt like so much more.

Twelve hours later they were still locked in the room, and there was no sign that it was going to change anytime soon. Cai fought to keep her impatience in check—and her eyes off Jake. The man wore nothing except a pair of abbreviated shorts as he worked out. Since the place was devoid of entertainment, not even a simple holovid, they were forced to pass the time any way they could. About half an hour ago he'd started to exercise, and watching his muscles flex as he did push-ups was making her crazy.

If they'd been left to cool their heels in order to increase their anxiety, it had backfired. The fear she'd felt after being captured was long gone. All she wanted was to get this meeting over with and get out of here before she jumped her recep.

She wasn't about to pace off her annoyance and frustration in front of the monitors—it would show weakness—and that added to her irritation over the wait. Jake wouldn't let her do anything in here, but she'd blasted the bugs in the bath. No way were those staying active while she made use of the facilities. And though it hadn't been her primary objective in taking them out, she'd expected someone to make an appearance to discover why the equipment had stopped working. No one had.

Meals had arrived through an automated delivery system, so they hadn't seen a live person since regaining consciousness. It made her feel like some kind of trained animal. The thing chimed and she rushed over to the compartment door. What was sad was that this had become the high point of her time in captivity. She sighed. It made sense that they'd been left with no method to procure their own food, because some very common things, things that people consumed every day, could be made into detonation devices. Hell, she knew how to start a fire with powdered coffee creamer, though that was not included on their trays.

At least they didn't have to worry about being poisoned. As Jake had pointed out, if the boss wanted them dead, the wreckers would have done more than knock them unconscious.

Cai tapped her foot against the edge of the table. She couldn't stop herself from watching him. The motion of Jake's glutes, of his biceps and forearms as he completed each rep, was more interesting than anything else in the room.

Finally he finished the push-ups, and she took in the light sheen on his torso and chest. Heaven help her, the man's body was even more perfect than his face.

He got into position to do sit-ups. She had a front row seat and could see the play of his taut abs without obstruction. Either someone had decided to turn on the heat or she was about to spontaneously combust. Telling herself to think of something else didn't help. She didn't want to do anything but stare.

When Jake finished, he lay back, his hands behind his head, and looked at her. His ice-blue eyes seemed to smolder. She didn't glance away, and she knew she should. Instead, of their own volition, her eyes began to wander over him. His broad chest, narrow waist, his powerful legs. And that tiny scrap of material he called shorts.

She had to look away. Had to. It would be mortifying beyond belief if he caught her ogling him *there*. But once she caught a hint of movement, she was far too fascinated to tear her eyes away. Was he reacting to her? No one else was in the room, and what were the odds he was fantasizing now? As she watched him get bigger, she licked her lips. She couldn't stop herself.

Then it dawned on her what was happening. *Oh, my God*. She was transmitting her emotions to him. He was aroused because he'd picked up how turned on she was. Her face felt scalding hot. Frantically, she tried to block their pathway. It was too late—she knew it—but it seemed the only way to retain some semblance of dignity.

He made an odd, choking, groaning noise, and her startled gaze flew to his. His pupils were so dilated, she could barely see any blue. And if she thought his eyes were hot before, that was nothing compared to what she saw there now.

Despite herself, her attention returned to his groin. She thought she heard Jake mutter something, but she couldn't be sure, not with the blood roaring in her ears, inhibiting her ability to hear. When he abruptly pushed to his feet, she shook her head and tried to focus on something other than his erection. But it was right there at eye level now.

"Let's get rid of these bugs."

"What?" She blinked as she fought her way out of the daze.

"I said"—his voice was a growl—"let's debug the room." *But don't blast them, point 'em out to me.* "Maybe that will get things moving."

"Okay." She stood, forcing herself to act normally. Maybe it was stupid, since he knew too much already, but she had to save face. Trying to behave as if nothing had happened, though, taxed her acting skills. How did he do it? She had physical evidence that he wasn't calm, but apparently he was able to ignore it and think of work. "Where do you want to start?"

He pointed to a corner and she joined him. As she used her probe and the pendant to locate the monitors, Jake faked discovery and crushed them. It wasn't hard to guess that he didn't want to get too close to her, but this time she knew it was because he was struggling to stay in control. It made her feel better that it wasn't as easy for him to rein in as it appeared. At least she wasn't the only one grappling with need.

She made the circuit on autopilot, and when they finished, ran another scan to double check, but she hadn't missed any devices despite her distraction. "The room's clear," she said.

"Good. Now let's see if we get any visitors."

Cai didn't know how Jake could sleep. Yeah, he was trained to nap whenever he wanted, and with the hard zap he'd gotten today, he could use the rest. But after hours of waiting she'd given up on anyone coming and wasn't concerned about that; her body roiled with need. She couldn't believe he slept so peacefully when she was trying not to toss and turn. This bed was larger than the one they'd shared at the inn, but it didn't make a difference. Not when she was so terribly aware of every breath he took.

Again, Jake had put himself closest to the door. His protectiveness warmed her, though it shouldn't. She knew him well enough to realize deep feeling had nothing to do with it. He would stand between any woman and danger.

Moonlight streamed through the windows, illuminating the room. There were no curtains, no shields of any kind, and she already knew the glass wasn't reactive. Since it wouldn't darken as the sky grew lighter, that meant the tropical sun would be shining in bright and early tomorrow morning. She needed to get some rest. Instead, she slowly turned her head and studied his face.

Even unshaven as he was, his handsomeness was plain to see. The stubble hid the firmness of his jaw and blunted the impact of the high cheekbones, but it also added a wickedness, a bit of the rogue, to his appearance. Rather than making him seem soft, his long lashes underlined his toughness. The way his hair fell across his forehead was sexy as hell, and so was the fullness of his lips. But despite his looks, Jake was no pretty boy. When his eyes were open, the intelligence there made that fact obvious. Cai knew she was in deep water.

How could she ever believe a man who looked like this was interested in her? Yet how could she deny what had happened? She hadn't even touched him. All she'd done was stare at him. Okay, to be fair, she'd inadvertently let him know what she was feeling and devoured him with her eyes, but she'd been a good six feet away, and he'd gotten hard because of her.

She couldn't quite wrap her mind around it. For years she'd been derided about her looks. Teenagers hadn't wanted her in their classes, and she couldn't blame them. But she'd gone from being cosseted by her parents to being continually disparaged. The shock had been tremendous, like an unexpected slap, and as she'd grown older the taunting had become worse. It hadn't stopped until her mom and dad had sent her away.

Which had felt like a betrayal. The only two people in the world who'd loved her, who didn't think she was a freak, and they didn't want her around anymore either. Or at least that was how it had seemed. Cai knew better now. She'd known then too.

But the hurt had been unbearable. She sighed quietly. Really, the UCE Academy for the Gifted hadn't been that bad. Though her social skills had been neglected, she'd flourished academically, and working one-on-one with a computer meant she'd never had to wait for anyone else to catch on.

Then her parents had disappeared and the army approached her. She looked over at Jake. Even as a teenager, she'd known they were trying to sell her a line of crap, but she'd leaped at the chance to be part of the Quandem Project. Access to some of the world's most advanced systems might have lured her anyway, but it was the idea that she could maybe find a clue to help locate her parents that had sealed the deal. Except, the top-secret nature of the program had kept her sequestered from most other people, and she hadn't had a chance to develop real friendships there either.

Not face-to-face friendships.

She could have gone out and made an effort, she supposed. That was what she should have done. It had simply been easier to stay apart, to keep her relationships superficial. Besides, she hadn't felt a great need to make other friends. She'd had Jake.

Her recep had been an unexpected gift.

He hadn't known how old she was or what she'd looked like. Hell, the man had even thought she was a computer. But it hadn't mattered; somehow they'd meshed. They were both loners, though outwardly Jake seemed to have a bunch of pals, and she had her nameless, faceless, voiceless Interweb acquaintances. She and Jake shared the same core values. And they both had sarcastic senses of humor. She'd laughed more with him than anyone else.

But they were also very different. No one had ever made fun of him about his appearance or called him names. She knew she wasn't as gawky as she'd been at thirteen, but when she looked in the mirror, she didn't see any great transformation.

So why had he gotten turned on?

It wasn't because she was there and available. It didn't matter how long he'd gone without sex. She'd known him for five years, and he was all business when he was on a mission. There was no questioning his dedication.

Cai froze as he shifted, fearing that somehow her whirling thoughts had disturbed his sleep. She was sure she'd blocked him, but then she hadn't noticed she was transmitting earlier tonight either. His eyes remained shut, though, and she relaxed. At least until he moved again and she realized that he was agitated. It took her another instant to guess why.

Nightmare.

She hesitated about waking him up. He already thought of the dreams as a weakness, but before tonight he'd never had one on an op. He'd berate himself for what he would view as a huge lapse. And he'd be extremely angry—and embarrassed—if he knew she'd seen him in the throes.

His torment became more pronounced, and Cai saw no choice but to dare his wrath. She couldn't let him suffer through this, not when she could stop it so easily. Rolling onto her side, she nudged his shoulder. No response.

Then, a groan—soft, barely audible. *Crap.* His dream was getting worse. She jabbed his shoulder harder and harder, but still he didn't wake. Desperate to stop his agony, she did the only other thing she could think of: she moved on top of him, straddling his hips, took hold of both his arms, and shook him.

Their positions were reversed so fast she didn't have time to react. His hand wrapped around her throat. Cai didn't move. There was no recognition in his gaze, and the Jake looking down at her was 100 percent deadly. He could snap her neck before he realized she was his partner.

Chapter Eleven

Jake!

Please let the connection work. If he killed her, he'd never forgive himself. And she wouldn't be too happy, either. The cloud over his eyes didn't lift.

Jake, you're dreaming, she thought, as calmly as she could, deliberately using his name again.

His hand tightened around her throat.

Oh, damn. This wasn't good. *Jake, please, you have to wake up now. I'm in trouble here and need your help.*

His hold loosened a bit. Confusion entered his eyes, and she hoped that indicated he was starting to break out of his fog. She continued using the words she was sure would reach him. *It's Cai, Jake. You have to help me; there's no one else who can.*

Cai? he asked, disoriented.

Yes, Cai. Help me out here and snap out of it.

He went rigid, and she knew her Jake was back. She saw the horror at what he'd done fill his face, and he quickly released her neck. Muttering the curse he tried never to use in her presence, he shifted so that his weight no longer pinned her to the bed. He didn't move off her, however, and she reached for him, wanting to soothe him before he started flaying himself.

"Did I hurt you?"

"No, I'm fine," she hastened to assure him. Already she heard the self-contempt in his tone.

"Are you sure?" He remained propped above her while his fingers lightly caressed her throat. Tremors coursed through him, leaving him unsteady.

"I'm sure. You weren't out of it long."

She didn't think he fully believed her. Really, she was okay, though for a moment there she had been worried. His hand moved to her face and he cupped her cheek, running his thumb across her lips. There was a pause as he reached the corner of her mouth; then he bent his head and kissed her. It was gentle, slow, and careful. She sensed contrition in him, and tenderness, and some other emotions she couldn't label before he broke off and gazed down at her again. "I'm sorry, sweetheart."

"I know you are. Please don't worry over it." Cai ran her hand up and down his side, trying to reassure him, but she knew it wasn't working. "It was the nightmare. I know that."

"Don't worry about it? I could have killed you." His voice was tight, intense.

"It was my fault. I shouldn't have tried to wake you the way I did." She should have been smarter. The only reason she could come up with to explain such a stupid idea was lust. The thought of climbing on top of him had driven all intelligence from her head.

"Stop trying to make me feel better."

Instead of continuing to comfort him with words, Cai gathered him closer. Then she froze, almost as shocked as when she'd found his hand at her throat. Jake had an erection. That shook her. Since he always mentally reached for her after his nightmares, she *knew* how shattered they left him. She was amazed that he was aroused.

"Jake?" She wanted to know why, but he misunderstood.

"Sorry," he apologized gruffly, and tried to pull away. She hung on to him, not ready to let go yet, and when he quickly stilled, she knew he wanted the closeness too.

He turned so that she was on top once more. That left the blankets hopelessly tangled around them, and he kicked at them until they were free. She pushed herself up far enough to see his face, but he was unreadable, completely closed to her. With a soft sigh she reached out and smoothed the hair off his forehead. It took an awfully long time before she felt him calm, but she remained silent. When she sensed the time was right she said, *Do you want to tell me about the dream?*

He stiffened.

She waited till some of the tension left his muscles before she added, *You should discuss them with someone. It'll help.*

"Leave it alone." His words were hard, implacable.

With another, heavier sigh, she gave up. She was right—he did need to share what tormented him—but he couldn't trust anyone enough to do so. It gave her a small pang, but she shook it off. This was about Jake, not her.

When he realized she planned to honor his decision, his body lost its tautness. He stroked her, his fingers combing rhythmically through the length of her hair. The motion soothed Cai, and as the tension seeped away, she finally grasped that he wasn't the only one shaken up.

The cool air in the room brushed at the back of her bare legs. Wearing only a pair of shorts and a T-shirt, she should be cold, but she wasn't. Jake's skin emitted enough heat to keep her warm. Way too warm. Her thoughts centered on how little he wore and how much of him she was touching. She responded to him; she couldn't stop it from happening. When his hand faltered midstroke, she knew he'd felt it.

His free hand slid to her bottom, pressing her against

him, and she allowed herself to enjoy the proof that he wanted her. It didn't last long. "Shit." He pulled his hand away as if he'd been jolted. "Get off me, Cai."

Her face went red and she moved quickly to obey. Once she was off, he sat up, arranged the blanket so it fell neatly over both of them, and settled back on the bed. His arms came around her, urging her closer, and she froze in surprise. He'd ordered her to stop touching him and now he was snuggling her into his side? She didn't get it, but that didn't stop her from relaxing into him. It was stupid. While it meant nothing to him beyond contact with another human, for her it was more. Much more.

Diversion—she needed a diversion.

Why don't you have a nickname? Okay, inane topic, but it was the first thing to pop into her brain.

I have a handle. He answered, as if the non sequitur hadn't knocked him off balance, but she knew better.

No, you don't. Tuck is an abbreviated form of your last name. It's not like Gnat or Gator or Inch. Someone must have been able to come up with something for you.

Jake hesitated; then he grimaced and said, *They tried to give me several.*

Really? Like what?

The scowl deepened. *First they wanted to stick me with PC, short for Prince Charming. You know how well I liked that.*

Yeah, she knew. On a scale of one to ten, that handle would have scored negative numbers. And it didn't fit. No matter how gorgeous he was, there was much more to him than looks.

The second was Blade. If it had been because of my skill with a knife, that would have been fine, but it wasn't.

Blade as in Blade Sorenson?

Yep, New Hollywood's glamour boy. She heard the disdain, and she bet it wasn't for the actor, but because Jake's teammates couldn't come up with anything that didn't involve his looks. She began to wonder if he'd found his appearance as big an onus as hers had been, though in a different way. How many people couldn't see the man beneath the beauty? And how many hadn't cared about anything more than his looks?

How did you avoid those names? she asked slowly.

He grinned. *I just didn't respond to them. My men figured out damn quick that if they wanted me to hear them, they'd better use 'Tucker.'*

Cai returned his smile, then rested her head on his shoulder, since stretching to see his face was beginning to make her neck ache. Besides, she didn't need the visual cues to know how he felt, not with their connection. His smugness at avoiding those appellations came through loud and clear.

This felt so normal: lying in bed and mind-talking with Jake. She'd done it time after time since the nanoprobes were inserted, but this was more intimate. Now while they spoke, she was in his arms, her body cuddled into his.

What about you? Did you get called anything?

Now she paused. She knew the question was innocent, but it brought home how silly she was to lose herself in some fantasy about him. It was too easy to forget the real world existed and that they'd be part of it again once this assignment ended. Soon there would be no more conversations while he held her. If she was lucky, their relationship would return to the way it had been, but she couldn't count on that. Not when things kept happening between them, and he might feel the need to distance himself once he had time to consider. She knew Jake only let people *so* close, and she'd crossed that line. Once they were home, he might pull back. Hard.

No, no handles, just the nasty names the kids called me in school. She told him this as a reminder that she wasn't in his league. Not even close. And maybe to let Jake know that she realized this was a moment out of time.

Why would anyone call you names?

Pain shafted through her and she went still, afraid to breathe until it passed. Her first reaction, the one that came from years of being ridiculed, was that his question was sarcastic, meant to mock her. But as her head cleared, she realized he would never deliberately hurt anyone. That wasn't the kind of person Jake was. Almost afraid to find out she was wrong, Cai gently probed and discovered he was sincerely confused.

Because of my appearance, she said, although she couldn't comprehend why he needed clarification.

There was a long silence. *What about the way you look?*

If anything, he seemed even more bemused. She didn't get it. What more did she need to say? She spelled it out for him. *I know I'm kind of homely. That's what they made fun of.*

"That's bullshit!" It exploded violently out of him.

Cai raised her head again to see his face. Jake looked seriously angry. "I'm telling the truth. They made fun of me."

"Sweetheart," he said more softly, "I'm not doubting you. I meant, bullshit, you're not homely. How can you even think that?"

"I own a mirror, Jake. I know what I look like. But even if I didn't, years of being told how ugly I was and then more years of being treated as if I were invisible got the message across."

He went red. "You're *not* ugly," he growled.

"Not anymore," she said quickly. "I grew into my face."

"But you still think you're homely, don't you?"

She shrugged. He was right, but she didn't say anything. Jake was a nice guy; he'd give her compliments to make her feel better, and she didn't want that. She knew her mouth was too wide, her eyes slightly too far apart, and her forehead a bit too high. Then there were the muddy brown eyes and dirt-brown hair. Her body was okay— years of training had seen to that—but she wished her breasts were larger. Of course, she had no plans to itemize her faults for him. No way.

"You're not homely," he repeated. "I don't know what you see, but when I look at you I see a very beautiful woman."

The blood left her head in a rush and she wanted to cry. He was doing the very thing she didn't want him to do—lying to make her feel better. She didn't refute him. Her parents had taught her never to argue with someone who gave a compliment; to do so meant she was insulting the person who'd given it. So, though she didn't agree, Cai said, "Thank you."

"You don't believe me, do you? You think I'm being kind."

With a sheepish smile, she shrugged again.

He rolled her onto her back and her eyes widened in surprise. Before she recovered, he moved over her. "Do you think I'm faking this to be polite?" He pressed forward, letting her feel his arousal. "You're not ugly, you're not homely, you're not plain. Do you think I'd have a hard-on if I didn't find you damned attractive? You've been driving me out of my freaking mind since Hell. We're on an op. I should be thinking of you as a member of my team, not as a woman, and I can't."

The only thing that kept her from staring at him with her mouth agape was the censure she heard in his voice as he spoke of his inability to maintain control. She knew Jake would see that as a failure on his part, probably a big one, and she didn't know what to say. Not when her head swam with the things he'd told her. "You think I'm pretty?"

Oh, man, she was pathetic. She should be reassuring him, but instead she was all but begging for more compliments.

"You're more than pretty. Trust me."

She wanted to—he had no idea how badly—but she couldn't manage it. Not even with the evidence hard against her. No one else except her mom and dad had ever told her she was attractive, and her parents were hardly impartial judges. Cai put a hand on his shoulder and said again, "Thanks, Jake."

"You're a hard sell." He shook his head ruefully. "At least think about what I said, okay?"

"I will." She'd hardly be able to concentrate on anything else.

He shook his head and slipped to her side. "You're not going to quit until I've lost what's left of my mind, I know it. No," he said before she could interject, "don't say anything. You don't have a clue what you're doing to me."

What she was doing to him? That didn't make any sense. He didn't explain and she couldn't read him. "What do you m—"

The sound of the door opening cut her off, and both of them jumped off the bed. She was on her feet a few seconds after Jake, but then she'd had to travel from the far side. Jake put himself in front of her, but Cai moved beside him. She'd fight with him, not cower behind him.

Light flooded the room, and she struggled to adjust to the sudden brightness. There was no time to take advantage of the open door. Four wreckers were inside the room, their weapons trained on them, before she had time to blink.

"Get dressed," came the order from one of the mercenaries. That hard voice with its lack of inflection sent a shiver down her spine. How did a person become so inhuman?

We're following instructions? Cai asked, wanting to be sure the game plan hadn't changed.

Yeah, we are. But put some clothes on before I notice the way they're ogling you.

Huh? Ogling her? She studied the wreckers but saw no signs of interest. At least not *that* kind of interest. Jake must be suffering some lingering effects from the neuron fryer.

"Get dressed now."

Still no emphasis, but she knew the wreckers wouldn't calmly wait much longer. She gathered up Jake's clothes and handed them to him, then reached for her own. As he stepped into his pants, Cai started for the bath. She didn't get far.

"Halt." She stopped and looked at the man in charge. "You'll stay here," he told her.

This shouldn't bother her. Really. In the scheme of things, dressing in front of these tin men was nothing. But it bugged her. She'd have to do what Jake had done and pull on her clothes over the shorts and tee she was wearing.

She stepped back to the bed and put her things on top of it. Although she turned her back to the men, she was uncomfortably aware of their presence. A glance behind her showed they continued to watch. Jake was already dressed down to his boots, and he was standing, arms crossed over his chest, glaring at the wreckers. She didn't have time to waste.

As she picked up her trousers, Jake shifted, concealing her as best he could behind his body. *Thanks, Jake.*

C'mon, before they decide they don't like this either.

With a tiny smile, she started getting dressed. Jake could act as gruff as he wanted, but she knew how considerate he was. Did he think that, after living with him in her head day in and day out for years, she'd miss that?

Her tee bunched up under her shirt, and Cai tried to tug the fabric free, but although her outer garments were roomy, they weren't roomy enough. With a last jerk, she conceded that she'd have to put up with the irritation. She reached for her boots. When they were on, she straightened and moved to Jake's side.

The next command wasn't given verbally. Wrecker number one gestured with his weapon, signaling that they were to go. Jake and Cai were surrounded as they entered the hall. Cai counted eight mercenaries, and raised a brow. Two unarmed detainees shouldn't warrant this kind of escort.

Unless they were Special Forces.

And if these mercenaries knew about Jake, that meant Elliot—or whoever it was who had ordered their capture—

was likely tied to the other anchor. No one else on the Raft Cities could have the data, and the woman *had* been in the UCE files. Cai passed the info along to Jake.

Not necessarily, he disagreed. *If we're considered important prisoners, we would still pull this kind of detail.*

As they walked, Cai studied the path they took through the house. *Mansion* was probably a more accurate term, since the place appeared to be enormous, with very wide, elegant halls. She couldn't be sure, but she thought the flooring was real wood in a mosaic pattern. *Why would we be important?*

A good webrider is hard to find.

Now that was true. Jake had obviously done some research since their briefing in Yardley's office. Very few high-level talents chose this path, what with all the UCE laws and penalties in place, and someone who belonged to that top rung could command a hell of a price. She'd been subtly questioned herself through anonymous contacts on the Interweb. If she ever decided to walk on the dark side, it wouldn't take five minutes before she had more work than she could handle.

The mansion, though beautiful and ornate, was a fortress, its halls a maze. It wouldn't be easy to escape even with the route memorized. When mercenaries were thrown into the mix, the odds became worse. The advantage from her implants would be slight with so much stacked against them.

The group finally stopped in front of a door, and the head wrecker—she smirked at the name—opened it without waiting for permission. He gestured for them to enter behind a trio of his men. When Cai hesitated, a large hand settled between her shoulder blades and pushed. Not as hard as she'd been pushed outside the restaurant, but firmly enough to make her stumble across the threshold. She heard Jake snarl and glanced over. When she saw the look on his face, she grabbed his arm.

Her recep was a smart man. He knew he couldn't win this fight, but he was so damned protective that she wasn't sure he wouldn't say to hell with it and confront them anyway.

I'm not a hothead, Cai. No matter how much I dislike their behavior, I'm not going to fight a bunch of wreckers over a push. But you need to understand that they're not going to kill me if I take issue with how you're treated. Trust me, I know the line.

She felt someone staring at her, but Cai ignored it and said, *I know, you're right. I'm sorry. I just don't want anything to happen to you.* Only when she was finished talking did she turn to face her captor.

It took all her strength to keep from visibly reacting. There was nothing she could do about her interior response. It didn't matter how much she'd prepared herself or how much she'd believed, it felt like being sucker punched.

She'd been right! Though seven years had passed since she'd last seen him in person, she would recognize this man anywhere.

Marchand Elliot.

He didn't introduce himself. She didn't know why not. Maybe he thought he needed no introduction. Though he'd always kept a low profile, the man was a multibillionaire and had been pursued by the media relentlessly. Or maybe he felt two ciphers like a webrider and her broker didn't need to be clued in. It sure wasn't because he was worried about being identified.

Apart from the tabloid holoshows, no one in the UCE had cared when Elliot dropped out of sight six years ago. No one had listened to Cai when she'd told them about the connection between the man and her mom and dad. No one had thought he was guilty of any crime. No one but her.

Even Jake hadn't believed her.

Although maybe he'd think twice now that one of her

other guesses had been accurate. She knew this didn't prove her folks had been kidnapped, or that they were here on the Raft Cities, but she couldn't stop excitement from surging through her. Her mom and dad could be mere feet away! Cai tucked her arms behind her back and locked a hand around her wrist to control the shaking.

She wanted to charge across the room, grab Elliot by the throat, and force the bastard to tell the truth about her parents. And she wanted to make him pay. Not only did she blame him for her mom and dad disappearing, but she knew it was his fault she'd been exiled from her home. Because of him, her folks had felt they needed the UCE to protect her. He was the reason she'd been sent to the academy. And while her emotions seethed, Elliot silently studied her.

Cai, ice it, Jake warned. She knew he'd picked up on her fury and was warning her to keep it in check. He was right. The wreckers remained in the room, and she wouldn't make it three steps toward the snake before they were on her. She struggled harder to rein it in. As much as she hated Elliot, she couldn't do anything stupid. Not now, not when she was this close.

Their host didn't offer them a seat, though the office had more than enough chairs. Instead he reached out with hands that appeared to be soft and pampered, manicured, and freshened the cup of tea on the desk in front of him. She wasn't a bit surprised that he didn't ask if they cared for any. One of the strongest memories she had from meeting him at fourteen was of his self-centeredness.

She wouldn't have guessed it was possible to disregard a roomful of people for such a long period of time, but Elliot managed. This was the kind of crap that Jake usually had little patience for, but he'd gone into battle mode the instant their door had opened, and she knew he'd stand here mutely for the rest of the night if that was what it took.

To pass the time, and to keep herself from doing something rash, she studied the changes in their captor's appearance since the last time she'd seen him. There weren't many. He had to be fifty, but he looked younger than her. His blond hair was thick, with no touch of gray, and there wasn't a wrinkle on his skin. The nanites available to the very rich right now weren't capable of entirely reversing the aging process, but surgery—and a lot of money— could guarantee nearly perpetual youth anyway.

She scrutinized the room next. Cai didn't think she'd ever seen so much wood, not used so abundantly. The stuff cost the moon, and the walls were covered with it. Leaning forward slightly, she squinted, trying to examine the globe behind the man. It was in a high gold stand, and was made with inlaid gemstones. She identified lapis for the oceans and maybe nacre for some of the land, but she couldn't name the rest.

Elliot finished his tea and set the cup back on its saucer before pushing it away. He stood, nodded toward the wrecker who was in charge, then walked to the darkened window. One of the mercenaries quietly left the room, but their host kept staring at the inky glass. Cai wasn't sure what he could see outside with the interior light on, but maybe he wasn't looking out. He could be watching their reflections.

Neither she nor Jake gave him a reaction. Her recep had a mask of boredom firmly in place, and she'd choked off her feelings, burying them deep. Instead she coolly made note of Elliot's white shirt and black trousers. No matter how many images she'd scanned through in her research, she'd never seen the man wear any other colors.

At last, he deigned to acknowledge them. He turned from the window and asked, "May I call you Cai and Jake?" Her blood ran cold with fear, but he didn't wait for a response. "Good." He acted as if they'd graciously agreed.

"How do you know our names?" Jake asked.

Cai held her breath. Her recep was posing the question

uppermost in her mind. What if Elliot knew everything about who they were? God, if he was aware of who she really was, who her parents were, he could use her against them, use her to make them cooperate if they hadn't cooperated already. She was certain that was what they had been afraid of when they'd sent her away to the academy all those years ago.

"The Raft Cities are much like a small town, and I'm an influential man. I knew your names almost as soon as you set foot on Malé." Cai took a deep breath; Elliot didn't know the truth. The man rested both hands on his hips and smiled coldly. "Many try to curry my favor by passing along news. I'm aware of everything that happens here. There are no secrets."

So much for her sense of relief. His voice made a shiver go down her spine. He was telling them something, but the question was what. Did he know who they were, or didn't he? Before she had time to analyze it, he extended his hand toward the chairs directly in front of his desk and returned to his own.

This was pure gamesmanship, Cai decided. His seat was positioned much higher than theirs. Cai almost laughed aloud over how silly it was, but she knew it wasn't a good idea to infuriate Elliot. Not when he had command of an army of wreckers. Not when she was his prisoner.

"Now," he said, lacing his fingers before him on the desk. "I'm in need of a webrider, and I've heard you're good, Cai."

She inclined her head even though her stomach turned at the sound of her name coming from his lips. "I'm the best."

"That's what my sources tell me. I also heard that you may be looking for a new broker to handle your sales."

"You heard wrong," she said with an edge in her voice that was barely discernible. The implied threat to Jake inspired her own version of warrior mode. She'd fight to the death before she'd let Elliot take another person that she cared about. "I'm attached to this one, and I intend to keep him no matter what I may have said in the heat of an argument."

"Pity that." He studied her recep with disapproval. "Ah, well, there's no accounting for a woman's taste in men."

She stiffened at the slur. Her recep was worth a thousand—no, a million—men like Marchand Elliot. She wanted to say that, but knew better. His ego couldn't take the jab, not without striking back, and maybe Jake would take the blow. So instead of speaking, she gazed at him blandly and waited.

Their captor seemed disappointed not to get a reaction, but it might have been Cai's own bias coloring her perceptions. Elliot stared at her. She stared back—and fought to keep her emotions under wraps. From the corner of her eye, she saw the wrecker return and move forward. Elliot looked at him. She turned her head and saw the wrecker nod. The smug satisfaction she felt pouring from the billionaire made her worry. Something was up.

"How long will you require to retrieve some data?"

"That depends on what you want and where I have to look for it," she said, forcing herself to sound unconcerned.

"And if you don't succeed? Will I receive a refund?"

"I don't fail."

"There's a first time for everything."

His tone was reasonable, agreeable, but she had a bad feeling about this. "I don't fail," she repeated, not caring if she sounded obstinate. If this was some kind of test, she was passing it. Hell, she was going to ace it.

"That's a bit arrogant."

She smiled, but there was no warmth in it. "I prefer to call it confident."

Why was Jake so quiet? It was all she could do to stop herself from looking at him. He'd taken charge since this mission was assigned, and had reminded her he was the op leader every time she tried to suggest anything, but now he seemed content to sit back and let her work. It confused her enough to ask, *You're letting me handle this?*

He's responding better to you.

What—

"Do you honestly believe you're the best?" Elliot asked conversationally, and Cai jerked her attention back to him.

Uh-oh. There was danger ahead somewhere; she had to be careful and hope she saw the trap before she stumbled into it. "I've never met anyone better," she said cautiously.

"I see." Elliot raised a hand and pointed two fingers at one of the wreckers. "In that case, there's someone I'd like to introduce. I think you'll find you have much in common."

Cai heard the door open and braced herself. A woman crossed in front of her and stood beside his desk. Cai felt a pang as she looked at this newcomer. She was everything Cai wasn't—poised, elegant, willowy, blond, and stunningly beautiful. And she knew it. Her confidence was ingrained, not faked. She reminded Cai a bit too much of the popular girls who'd taken such pleasure in tormenting her while she'd been in school, but that wasn't what was teasing at her brain.

There was something she should be seeing; she knew it.

"Jake, Cai, I'd like you to meet Nicole. She's one of my employees and quite good with systems herself."

Nicole smiled at them, but her gaze lingered on Jake longer than on Cai. Much longer. "I'm pleased to meet you," she said, addressing Jake alone. Cai sighed silently. The woman's voice was as perfect as her looks.

"Have a seat, my dear," Elliot invited.

Nicole sat on the front edge of the desk, near Jake. She wore a sarong-style skirt, and when she crossed her legs it fell open, displaying most of her right thigh. Cai sighed again. Her recep had another woman panting after him.

Cai looked at him, but he appeared unimpressed. A tension inside her eased, but the sense that she was missing something became more pronounced. Cai tuned out what was going on around her and focused only on Nicole. What was it about her? As soon as she stopped looking at the woman's appearance and started seeing her, she knew. *Oh, my God!*

Nicole was the other anchor.

Chapter Twelve

Cai hoped she didn't appear as shocked as she felt. Elliot *had* been playing games with them. This anchor must know who she and Jake were, and since she worked for their captor, he must know too. This talk about needing a webrider was so much crap. He was the cat and they were the mice.

What's wrong, sweetheart?

Nicole is our mystery anchor.

His surprise lasted only an instant. *Shit. Did she make us?*

Cai didn't turn to look at him, though she wanted to. *I made her. It took me a few minutes, but not that long, and I knew something was different as soon as I saw her.*

Okay, we have to assume she knows we're the other Quandem—it would be stupid not to. But we keep playing webrider and broker as long as she acts like she believes our cover, got it?

Yeah, got it. She had a good idea why her partner wanted to keep up the charade. If Elliot or Nicole slipped, it could give them valuable information. She and Jake just had to be careful that they weren't the ones who made a mistake.

It took her a beat to realize he'd referred only to Nicole's

NAME: _____

ADDRESS: _____

_____

_____

TELEPHONE: _____

E-MAIL: _____

_____ I want to pay by credit card.

__ Visa   __ MasterCard   __ Discover

Account Number: _____

Expiration date: _____

SIGNATURE: _____

Send this form, along with $2.00 shipping and handling for your FREE books, to:

Love Spell Romance Book Club
20 Academy Street
Norwalk, CT 06850-4032

Or fax (must include credit card information!) to: 610.995.9274.
You can also sign up on the Web at <u>www.dorchesterpub.com</u>.

Offer open to residents of the U.S. and Canada only. Canadian residents, please call 1.800.481.9191 for pricing information.

knowing who they were. Didn't he think Elliot knew too? Then it occurred to her that maybe he didn't. Not yet. If this was the first time the other anchor had seen them, she'd just discovered their identities herself. And Elliot wasn't Nicole's recep; unless she was telepathic, they would have heard her tell him about them. Of course, there was no doubt their delightful host would be informed soon, but maybe he hadn't been playing with them as much as she'd assumed.

Nicole tore her attention from Jake and looked Cai's way. As the woman studied her, Cai became uncomfortably aware of the wad of bunched fabric under her shirt and the way her shorts rode up beneath her pants. It made it difficult to hold her gaze, but Cai did. When the woman looked away, Cai knew she'd been measured, judged, and deemed lacking.

As a kid, her defense had been to try to make herself invisible, but as she began to draw inside herself, Cai stopped. *Like hell.* Elliot was watching her, looking for weakness. She wouldn't give him—or Nicole—the satisfaction of finding one so easily. Besides, Jake was relying on her, trusting her to do her job, and she'd never let him down—not if she could help it. Cai lifted her chin and stared hard at the other anchor.

The woman turned back to her and cocked one perfect blond eyebrow. Cai ignored the silent question. It was an attempt to fluster her, and she wasn't falling for it. Instead she conducted her own perusal. Nicole was older than she was, maybe early thirties, and the poise she possessed was extraordinary. But was she as composed as she appeared?

Something deep within the anchor's eyes made Cai wonder.

"Nicole," Elliot said.

That one word, though softly spoken, seemed to reverberate through the room. The woman moved from her place on the desk to the arm of Elliot's chair without needing instruction. His hand came out, stroking her thigh, and Cai barely kept from gaping.

Where was Nicole's partner? And what did he think of the closeness between her and the boss?

While the relationship between anchor and recep wasn't necessarily romantic, it was always emotionally intimate. It had to be. Case in point, her and Jake. He'd believed her to be a computer, but the rapport had been there. From what she'd seen in the UCE reports, there was a distinct pattern of Quandems protecting their pairings against outsiders. Other friendships and affairs were tolerated, to a degree, but there was a line that simply wasn't crossed. Usually it was the involved person who pulled back, but she'd seen incidents cited where the other half of the team had interceded and returned things to the status quo.

Granted, the size of the group studied made any conclusions questionable. It would require a much bigger sampling before it could be definitively stated that teammates protected the Quandem above all else, but the indications were there. Even the first anchor to overload, the one that was severely brain damaged, recognized and responded to her recep in a way she didn't with anyone else. That said something, as far as Cai was concerned.

The silence hung expectantly in the room, but no one broke it. She decided it was up to Elliot to lead the conversation, and waited, but he seemed more interested in gauging their response to his behavior. Why did he think they would react unless he knew about the implants and her connection with Jake?

She vacillated on what their captor was aware of, but he was up to something. So if he was in the dark about what she and Jake really were, what was his game? He wanted something or he wouldn't have had them kidnapped.

"Shall we get down to business?" Elliot said at last.

Cai inclined her head, more than ready for things to progress. This sitting in a dead-quiet room had been uncomfortable, but that had undoubtedly been the point. Easy to start talking to fill the gulf and say too much. Good thing she was reserved by nature and became even more reticent when she felt ill at ease.

"I'd like to hire you to retrieve some information from a UCE computer for me. You can do that?"

"Of course." Why would he even ask?

"No matter what system it is?"

"Yes. Which one are you thinking of?"

Elliot watched her closely. "ADOK."

No explanation. Cai pushed her unease over the Monster aside and stared back at him, trying to guess what he was up to. She'd first run into Nicole on ADOK, so he didn't need her to get into the computer for him. "That's a new system. I don't believe it's been up and running a month yet."

"That doesn't answer my question. Can you access it?"

"I can." Cai lifted her chin. "But it'll cost you extra."

A small smile tipped the corners of his mouth at the words. "I will, of course, compensate you adequately for the job."

"Define adequate."

He named a figure that made Cai's eyes widen. It was at least triple what the best webriders earned in a month.

"That's satisfactory," she said, as if she received such outrageous offers daily. Elliot appeared honestly amused.

"However," he began, and Cai braced herself. Here it came. No one paid that well unless there were strings attached. "For my money I want more than data."

"What else do you want?" Jake asked, voice hard.

"Not what you're thinking," Elliot said.

The derision in his words made Cai aware of her appearance again. She stopped herself from squirming in the chair, but barely. Jake thought this man, who was clearly sleeping with the gorgeous Nicole, would be interested in her? If it weren't so embarrassing, it would have been laughable.

"No?" Jake prodded.

"No. I don't have to pay for sex."

The look that Cai saw flit through Nicole's eyes made her wonder what the other woman was thinking. Was she sharing Elliot's bed because she wanted to, or because she was an employee? The answer to that question might explain a lot.

"What do you want me to do in addition to webriding?" she asked to deflect the man's ire from Jake.

"I want you to train Nicole, one-on-one, to gain entry to ADOK and continue the lessons until she's proficient." Elliot gave the woman's thigh a pat. "Is that agreeable?"

"Yes," Cai said at the same time Jake said, "No."

Elliot looked pleased over the division. "Ah, a difference of opinion. Which of you calls the shots? The broker or the webrider? I await the outcome with bated breath."

Cai turned in her chair and played her role. "Why would you want to turn down such a lucrative deal?"

"Because I don't trust it. Or the man who made it." Jake stared pointedly at Elliot as he spoke.

"Why wouldn't you trust me?" Elliot sounded curious, not offended, and Cai had the sense he was vastly entertained.

"A couple of reasons. First, the middle-of-the-night meeting. Having us rousted out of bed for this? It's pure bullshit. Nothing you've brought up couldn't have waited for daylight. I don't like power plays. Second, why bother to have us kidnapped? If you wanted my woman to web-ride, you could have approached us. Grabbing us off the street and holding us prisoner because you wanted to hire her? I don't believe it."

There was an expectant pause, as if everyone in the room were holding their breath, waiting for Elliot's response. That didn't bode well, Cai thought. She wasn't familiar enough with the man to predict his reaction to being challenged, but if the wreckers and Nicole were wary, there had to be a reason.

"A cynic," Elliot said lightly, and there was a collective sigh in the room. Maybe it was her imagination, but she had the impression they'd yanked a tiger's tail and had lived to tell the story. What was Jake thinking, to confront the man outright?

"A realist," her recep countered.

Their captor shrugged. "Perhaps this hour of the night was meant to catch you off guard; a man looks for advantages in negotiations. However, inviting you to my home was no ploy."

Inviting them? Cai bit her lip to keep from refuting him. The wreckers had used neuron fryers. She'd feared Jake had been killed or brain damaged. And Elliot had the nerve to refer to this as an invitation? She looked at her partner, waiting for his response. And worrying over it. Jake raised both eyebrows in clear disbelief, but he didn't say anything.

Silence fell in the room again, but Cai was too relieved that he hadn't forced the issue to fret over this. Jake had gotten away with questioning Elliot once; she didn't think the man would stand for it twice. Not in front of his employees. Maybe not even if they were alone. When she looked at him, she got the sense that he felt he had the divine right kings used to have back in ancient history. The divine right to rule. To take the life of any subject who annoyed him. To do whatever he pleased, whenever he pleased, with whomever he pleased.

"My offer remains on the table," Elliot said.

"At the completion of the contract, once you have your data and Nicole learns how to access the ADOK system, do I have your word that Jake and I will be returned to Malé?" Cai asked.

Cai, what the hell are you doing?

What I have to do, she replied, and blocked him. For heaven's sake, they were prisoners here. Did he think that Elliot would let them refuse him anything? In her opinion, it would be smart to play along and not infuriate the man. That would only lead to trouble and make it harder for them to get out of here in the long run. If Jake weren't so damned overprotective, he'd see this for himself.

"Of course, my dear," Elliot agreed smoothly.

Cai repressed a shudder at the endearment and said, "Then we have a deal. I'll need access to a computer, of course."

"Of course. I'll send an escort to accompany you to Nicole after lunch. That should give you time to rest after having an interrupted night. It was inconsiderate of me."

He was all solicitousness now that he'd gotten his way. "Thank you," she said, as if she believed he cared about her lack of sleep. "I appreciate your thoughtfulness."

"You don't need a broker," Elliot continued as he looked at Jake. "You do quite well on your own. That might be something to consider in the future."

Ass, Cai thought, but she smiled politely and said, "Thank you for the compliment, but Jake is much more than a broker to me, and I have no desire to change things."

She expected him to get in another dig about her taste in men, but Elliot merely shrugged and said, "Gentlemen, please escort our honored guests back to their room so they may rest."

The meeting was adjourned, but Cai didn't mind. She wanted to get out of this study and away from Elliot. The man was a snake.

He didn't wish them good night, as she half expected him to do in his role of benevolent host. As they reached the door, Cai looked over her shoulder and saw the man return to stroking Nicole. Her eyes met the woman's for an instant, and she read resignation there. Then the mercenaries closed in behind her and blocked her view.

There wasn't time to contemplate what the look meant. The wreckers used a completely different route on the return trip to their cell, and Cai was busy memorizing—and attempting to keep Jake blocked. He was angry and trying to mind-talk with her. As insistent as he was, it was hard to hold the wall between them. Maybe she didn't want to go back to the room. She was going to get a mission-leader speech; she knew it.

As soon as the door was sealed behind them, Jake rounded on her. "What the hell were you thinking in there?"

"Now, Jake," she began, trying to calm his temper, but he backed her against the wall and glowered down at her. As his body pressed into hers, Cai lost her train of thought.

With care, his hand cupped her jaw, turning her face up to his. "Open for me," he ordered before kissing her.

For a moment confusion reigned; then she opened her mouth to him. His tongue met hers, but she also felt him brush her mind barrier. *Crap.* He'd meant mentally, but even though she felt embarrassed, she didn't stop kissing him. Reluctantly, she lowered the wall between them.

Why the hell did you agree to meet with Nicole alone? You promised you'd stick close to me.

Computer access. She was proud she'd managed two words.

You can connect remotely with the implant.

It bothered her that he could hold a coherent conversation while kissing her senseless. Cai reached for his shoulders and leaned into him. If she was going to lose her head, he was going with her. *I can do more with an actual unit in front of me.*

I know better than that. His hands found her hips, pulling her away from the wall and more tightly against him. *You might feel more comfortable, but you can do everything without one.*

Think of it as an opportunity. I can see more of the building and pass the info on to you.

And you can look for your parents. He began moving against her. *Damn, Cai, you're going to get in trouble.*

It was too late; she was already in trouble. She knew what she felt for Jake was creeping way beyond friendship, and that wasn't smart. It was too easy to forget this was an op, to lose herself in him and the feelings he raised in her. To go to bed with him and damn the consequences and repercussions. To risk ruining their Quandem. Oh, yeah, she was in deep, deep trouble.

We need . . . He stopped short as he ground his erection against her. *We need to scan again for monitors.*

Something inside Cai went cold. She hadn't thought about the room being bugged a second time, but clearly Jake had. Abruptly she pulled away and sagged against the wall. Her knees were weak, damn him. Closing her eyes, she scanned and found that he was right: they were being watched.

She sent him the locations and he released her to start removing them. He didn't appear nearly as affected by their embrace as she was. His hands were steady as he reached for the devices, and he didn't seem to be breathing hard. Cai frowned. Her whole body shook, and she panted as if she'd run a klick full-out. In gear.

When she felt steadier, she went to the bath and scanned. It was loaded with inteltronics too, and she quickly disabled them. She didn't know why Jake wanted to pull the things by hand when she could blow them all out at once, but she let him do it his way. When it was safe, she contemplated stripping out of her pants and shirt. But while the bunched-up tee and shorts were uncomfortable, she decided to stay dressed; she needed every barrier possible to keep herself from doing something stupid.

She sat in one of the chairs and waited till he finished. When he looked at her, she ran another scan and nodded. Yes, the room was clean. He sat on the sofa across from her. For a minute he closed his eyes; then he pinned her with his gaze. *Here it comes,* she thought.

"Would you like to explain to me why you overrode my

decision tonight?" His moderate, almost conversational tone didn't fool her. He was still angry.

She sighed quietly. "Your decision was more emotional than logical. I appreciate that you want to keep me safe, but Elliot isn't going to let us say no to his requests. It's safer for both of us if he thinks he's getting his way."

"Emotional?"

Ooh, he didn't like that, Cai thought. The quiet way he said the word told her she'd driven him from mad back to furious. Perhaps she should have stated it differently.

"My decision was not emotional."

"I'm sorry," she apologized, without indicating what she was talking about. It was a good way to quickly defuse anger. If that didn't work, her next step would be to agree with him. She didn't want to fight, not over this.

"Damn it, you don't know what you're going to be facing tomorrow, and I won't be there to help you." It worked; the ire in his eyes had dwindled, but she wasn't sure she liked the weariness any better.

"I know I have no experience in the field, but I have been trained. And it wasn't just a one-time deal; I've kept it up. You have to trust that I can handle this." She leaned forward, resting her arms on her knees. "And you know that if I need to, I can ask for your advice over our link."

"And you know that sometimes things happen so fast there isn't time to ask a question, let alone hear the answer."

For a moment she stared down at her hands, then back at Jake. He looked tired. It had been a rough day and night for him, and she felt bad for adding to it. "I know," she said quietly, "but we can't stay locked in this room forever."

"Yeah, we've got Maguire to find, and I doubt she's in the room next door. Shit." He rubbed his forehead for a moment. "Come here, sweetheart," he said, and held out a hand.

She hesitated. The last thing she needed was to be that close to him, but he didn't look away or lower his arm.

Torn between reluctance and eagerness, Cai stood and took his hand. She wasn't prepared for the tug he gave, and she fell onto his lap. Apologizing, she tried to move off of him, but he wrapped his arms around her and settled her against his chest. She went rigid. Her hip was right against his groin, and while he wasn't hard, he hadn't calmed down completely either.

"Relax," he said easily, and then began talking strategy as if this were completely normal.

Cai lost track of how many scenarios they ran through, how many cautions he gave her, but she paid attention. And the surreal experience of receiving what was in essence a military briefing while sitting on the op leader's lap started to feel comfortable. He wasn't happy about what she'd done—she could feel that—but he was resigned and determined that she be able to handle anything that arose with Nicole.

After he finished, they sat quietly together, her head resting on his shoulder and their arms around each other. "We need to get some sleep," she said softly. Already hints of dawn crept into the room.

"Yeah." She felt him take a deep breath. "First, though, we need to contact the team and let them know the deal."

She nodded and enjoyed the feel of her cheek rubbing against him. "I can do that when I get near the computer."

"You can do it now. I don't want you trying to hide a message to Gnat while you've got that anchor hanging off your side." He didn't wait for her to agree or disagree. "Tell him we've been captured, our weapons and handhelds confiscated, and pass along the coordinates of our location. Apprise him of the wreckers and that we've seen approximately twenty of them, but there may be more. And tell him and the team that they are not to attempt to free us; they will continue the mission. Since we're out of the picture for now, it's gonna be up to them to locate Maguire and Armstrong. Make sure they know that's an order and not a suggestion."

He used their pathway to give her the proper codes, and reluctantly Cai tapped into a UCE system to send the info he wanted Gnat to have. She was careful because of Nicole, but she couldn't be as quick as she wanted to be, since she needed to wait for Jake's second-in-command to give the response code.

When it didn't immediately come, she worried whether the message had gone through. Then she received the reply. And the start of an argument. She cut it off and pulled out of the system. Now that they'd been identified, Cai felt sure Nicole would be watching, waiting for her to access the computers. She couldn't linger or debate Jake's instructions with Gnat.

"He's not happy about your orders," she told her recep.

"Tough shit." Jake stood, still holding her, and Cai gasped. "Now, sweetheart, let's go to bed."

Nicole looked every bit as good in sunlight as she had in artificial light. Then there were her clothes. Cai sighed. She not only felt young and plain in comparison; she felt dowdy as well.

She tried to imagine Jake's reaction if she'd attempted to pack a pair of abbreviated shorts and a skimpy top. The thought made her smile. He would have questioned her brains, her training, and her suitability for the mission. And he'd have been right to do so. The way she was dressed—long pants, a gauzy white shirt, and boots—was more appropriate for the Raft Cities.

Despite the midday heat, the other woman had wanted to walk the grounds of Elliot's compound. The four wreckers who'd escorted Cai from the room remained a discreet distance away, but they were close enough to react if she tried anything stupid. With Jake locked up, they didn't have to worry. She'd do nothing to chance endangering him.

"I'm supposed to be showing you how to webride," Cai said.

"You will." But Nicole continued to stroll.

The grounds were beautiful. This was the only grass she'd seen on the Raft Cities, and there were plants and bushes everywhere. No trees, but then she doubted that the dirt Elliot had imported went deep enough to support such root structures. Of course, the barrier around the estate kept out the people who lived here, and that was a shame. Cai bet that the children, maybe even many adults, had never seen anything like this.

"Here, this is where I wanted to bring you," Nicole said, gesturing toward a large white gazebo.

This may have been worth the walk, Cai decided as they climbed the few steps into the shaded interior. It was cooler here, and refreshments were set out on the table. Iced bowls had kept the sorbet from melting, and her mouth watered.

More wood, she noted, looking around the interior. Elliot had spared no expense for his raft home. A fan hung from the ceiling, swirling idly, but it seemed aesthetic more than utile.

She waited for the mercenaries to join them, but Nicole stunned her further by ordering them away from the structure and then by playing hostess. Cai became suspicious. She wasn't a guest and hadn't been treated like one until now. Still, she went along with the conversation about the weather—it was fine—and about the condition of the Raft Cities—they weren't fine—until they'd finished the treat.

After putting her sorbet bowl aside, Cai leaned back in the chair and waited. It wouldn't be long now; she was sure of it. The other woman didn't seem quite so poised at this moment; in fact, she seemed downright nervous, and that set Cai on edge.

"I know who you are," Nicole said abruptly.

Cai stayed cool and merely lifted one brow while she did a quick scan for monitors. There were none, and that was another surprise. She would have thought Elliot would want to listen and watch this conversation unfold.

"Or maybe I should say I know what you are," the other woman continued. "You and your receptor."

So much for their cover. Time to wing it. "I know who you are too."

Nicole nodded. "I decided you must. To be honest, I didn't expect it to be so easy to detect."

"I didn't either."

"But you've been around other anchors. You had to know."

Cai wasn't sure why they were talking about this. Did the woman want to discuss the experience? Granted, there weren't many like them, but Nicole had access to the same data in the UCE systems that she did. "No, I've never been around another anchor. The research team discouraged our meeting."

"Tainted test results," the other woman realized with a nod.

Cai decided to confront Nicole head-on. "Why are we out here? Is it to discuss what it's like to be an anchor?"

"No," the woman replied tersely. "I know more than what you are—I know why you're here. But you're already aware of that. You spotted me watching you while you gathered the data for the mission. Elliot knows you're with the UCE military and what your assignment is, but that's it. He doesn't know you and Jake are a Quandem, and he doesn't know whose daughter you are. I haven't told him. And maybe I won't share it with him."

Cai fought hard to stay calm, at least outwardly. She'd been doing well until Nicole had brought up her mom and dad. Her hands were concealed beneath the table, and she reached for her ring, turning the stone to her palm and closing her hand around it. She clutched it like a talisman and lifted her chin.

"And your point is?" She felt out of her element here, as inexperienced as Jake kept insisting she was, but she managed to sound calm as she spoke.

Nicole smiled with a superiority that put Cai's back up. "Your parents are here. They've been in the compound the entire time I've been on the Raft Cities."

Cai tried to keep from reacting, tried hard, but the gasp escaped anyway. *God, oh God.* Her mom and dad *were* here. They were alive. Tears welled up, and Cai had to blink hard to keep from crying. She wanted to see them, wanted to hug them so badly. Wanted to say she was sorry, that she hadn't meant the things she'd said. Impatience, relief, anger, joy—all rolled through her along with about a gazillion other feelings.

Cai, what's wrong?

Damn. Jake must have picked up on her emotional state, and now he was even more worried. *Nothing. I'll explain later.*

"Where?" she demanded thickly, and blocked her recep.

"They're in the east wing, but you won't be able to free them, not easily or quickly, even with your implants." Nicole shrugged. "I can get them out for you, though. For a price."

Battle calm. It settled over her with such suddenness, it was as if she'd flipped a switch inside herself. "Why should I believe you're telling the truth? If you know I'm looking for my parents; you could be making this whole thing up."

"I knew you'd want proof," Nicole said, looking satisfied. She pulled a holounit out of her pocket. The thing was small, no bigger than her thumbnail, and she set it on the table. "I was able to smuggle one of these in to your parents. Once I chime them, you'll have less than two minutes before the power source runs out to assure yourself that they're here and well."

Two minutes wasn't very long. Cai wanted to organize her questions beforehand or the clock would run out before she verified Nicole's claims. At last she nodded, and the anchor activated the device.

When her mom and dad appeared, about three inches high and standing on the table in front of her, Cai lost her voice—at least until she heard her mom gasp her name. "Mom, Dad, are you okay?" She sounded hoarse and shaky.

"We're fine," her dad answered. Although the image wasn't crisp, her mom seemed to be crying. She *never* cried.

"We won't have much time. Can you give me the date and time?"

Nicole laughed softly to her right, and Cai stiffened. Her dad, though, gave the day's date and time, and she knew then that he understood why she was asking these questions.

"Do you know where you are?"

"Not for certain, but we suspect we're on the Raft Cities. The motion of the building and things we've heard support this supposition." Her dad barely paused. "Are you here too, baby?"

"Yes."

He nodded, but it was her mom who spoke. "I knew that was you walking across the grounds. I told your dad it was you."

"You saw me?" Cai brushed at her cheek, getting rid of the tear she hadn't been able to contain. The holounit beeped softly, and she stiffened. Time was almost up. "The power is running out and I'm going to lose you. I love you," she said quickly. "I'm going to bring you home." The image flickered, then disappeared. "I promise," she finished, but knew her parents couldn't hear her any longer.

She tipped her head back and closed her eyes. It was instinct, need, that had her reaching for Jake. He didn't ask any questions, but wrapped her in the mental equivalent of a hug. She wanted to go to him, have him hold her for real, and tell him what had happened. This wasn't something she could share over their link. It had to be in person. Had to be.

"Satisfied?" Nicole asked, long before Cai was ready.

Resigned, she opened her eyes and squared her shoulders. She'd handle this. The holounit was gone, and the other woman was watching her, measuring her. Cai grimaced. She'd given far too much away, but she hadn't been able to contain her emotions.

"What are you offering, exactly, and what do you want in return?" she asked.

"I'm offering to free your parents from some impressive security and bring them to you. I'm also willing to give you the location of Banzai Maguire and Ty Armstrong. Yes, I know where they are, and I can save you a lot of search time."

"And in exchange?"

"That's simple. In return I want your agreement, and the promise of your captain, that you'll take me and my recep back to the UCE when you leave the Raft Cities."

Chapter Thirteen

For a minute Cai said nothing. So many questions were ricocheting through her mind that she couldn't focus on which one to ask first. "That's it? That's all you want?"

"That's all. Once we're back in the UCE, I know Tony can keep us hidden from Elliot."

The sneer in Nicole's voice as she said her boss's name was slight, but Cai picked it up. "He's your lover," she said.

Nicole snorted softly. There was a bleakness in her eyes that touched Cai, but she knew better than to take anything at face value. This whole thing could be an elaborate ruse.

"You think I *want* to sleep with him?" She sounded appalled. "He threatened Tony if I didn't cooperate, and I'd do anything to protect him. Even prostitute myself." The woman pinned Cai with a defiant look. "You should understand. I've seen you with your recep; you'd keep him safe at any cost."

"How long have you and Tony been a Quandem?" Cai asked instead of agreeing or disagreeing.

"A little over four years."

Cai considered that. The timing would be about right if

Elliot had been tipped off early to the Quantum Brain Tandem Project and decided to emulate it. He would have needed months to get his hands on the nanoprobes and to find a neurosurgeon capable of performing the procedure.

"You haven't told Tony that Elliot's coercing you?"

"I couldn't. He would have confronted him and gotten killed. What do you think Jake would do if you shared something like this?" she asked defensively. Her posture was rigid.

"His first reaction might be to confront and maim," Cai agreed, "but I would calm him down enough to think things through more clearly; then we'd work together to find a solution. You've read the UCE files on the experiment, I'm sure of that, and you know why the implants involve pairs. The doctors discovered that teams of two are more powerful than one alone."

The woman gave her hair a toss. "So you think I should have told Tony? You don't know him."

"No, but I do know that if you'd worked together you'd be better off than trying to deal with Elliot on your own." And it was a damn good thing Jake wasn't here to hear this. After last night and the way she'd agreed to meet with Nicole by herself, he wouldn't be able to resist a pointed comment or two.

"Don't judge me," Nicole said, voice low and tight. "You don't have the right."

Cai met the woman's gaze until she saw some of the anger seep out of her eyes. "I'm sorry," she said. "I didn't mean to sound judgmental."

There was a long pause, but she didn't break it. Instead she listened to the wind brush against the bushes. She'd never been a nature girl, but Cai had missed that sound since arriving here. How could the people of the Raft Cities live without anything green and beautiful?

"Maybe I didn't make the correct decision." Nicole sounded resigned when she spoke. "At the time it seemed like the best choice, but what I've done has caused a chasm between Tony and me, one I'm not sure we'll be able to bridge." She looked down at her hands, studied her nails, then lifted her head again.

"But that's neither here nor there," she said briskly, apparently pushing aside regrets about what had occurred. "The past is done and I can only move forward. Let's discuss the bargain I've proposed. Is it something you're interested in, or do I tell Elliot the truth about you and Jake? If I'm going to remain trapped, it wouldn't hurt to please the boss and he'd be thrilled to have another Quandem under his control. And perhaps he'd be so fascinated with his new anchor, that it would lift some of my burden."

The tough veneer was back in place, and Cai knew the woman regretted letting it drop for even a few moments. "You know I'm interested without throwing out threats," she said mildly. "Tell me, though—how do you know where Maguire and Armstrong are? Elliot can't be holding them hostage as well."

That brought a smirk. "No, he has nothing to do with their presence on the Raft Cities. I was listening when he told you there are no secrets from him, and that's true. The pirate lords loathe him and would kill him if they had the opportunity. He's invaded their territory and usurped their power, but he has the wreckers on his side, so they do their best to gain his favor." A breeze caught a lock of Nicole's hair, and she pushed it behind her ear. "There's a regular parade waiting to share information with Elliot. Maybe they believe they can enlist his aid in an attempt to overthrow another pirate lord, or maybe they want to ensure that he doesn't attack them." She shrugged.

"So you're saying one of the pirate lords told Elliot about their whereabouts?" That seemed incredible to Cai.

"No, the second-in-command to the pirate lord who's helping them passed along the news that they were coming here."

"And you're aware of this how? Because you were in the room when the info was shared?"

"You sound skeptical, but that's exactly what happened. He was trying to gain Elliot's goodwill—do you think the pirate would risk offense by asking that I leave?"

"I'll need proof that you know where they are."

"No." Nicole shifted and crossed one leg over the other. "I showed my good faith by letting you talk to your parents. You don't get more until I have some promises."

Cai rubbed her ring and scrutinized the anchor. She *had* talked to her parents. There were tricks that could be done with holos, but she knew what to watch for and hadn't spotted any signs of a forgery. The fact that her dad had mentioned the time also helped authenticate what she'd seen. Nicole might have been able to fake the date, but there would be no way to predict what time it would be played. It had to be genuine.

And Nicole didn't like Elliot. Cai had seen the look in her eyes last night as they'd left the room, and there had been several other times when she'd caught an expression on the woman's face that suggested she wasn't happy with her present circumstances. If she was pretending to be averse to her boss, she'd started the act immediately.

A soft breeze blew into the gazebo, and Cai turned her face toward it. Nicole had no need to offer Maguire and Armstrong. Her parents would have been enough incentive for her to agree to help the other anchor and her recep off the Raft Cities. When she added everything up, she believed the woman did know where the couple was and that she was legitimately holding the info back until she felt confident that an agreement had been struck and would be honored. She'd do the same in this situation.

Looking over at Nicole, Cai said, "Okay, I agree. You have my word that we'll take you and Tony with us when we leave."

"No offense," the blonde said, leaning back and resting

both arms along the rail of her chair, "but that's not good enough. I know who's in charge of this mission, and it isn't you. I'll want your recep's promise that we leave when you do."

It was impossible to be offended by the truth. Jake was in charge. "I'll talk to him," Cai assured her.

"Good. You can give me his answer at my next lesson."

Which brought to mind another question. "Why does Elliot want me to teach you to webride? You can access ADOK anytime you'd like. It doesn't make sense."

"He wants me to gain your trust."

"For what purpose?"

The woman shrugged. "He hasn't shared his plan with me, but I have pieced a few things together. Once we're friends, I offer you the site of the fugitives and, since I like you, I help you escape. He wants you to finish your assignment quickly."

Cai had more questions, a lot more, but she wasn't sure Nicole had the answers. "Why kidnap us? Why not let us complete our mission without interference?"

"I have no idea." Nicole sounded impatient. "I could guess, but what good does that do either of us?"

"Why—" But Cai didn't get to finish.

"We don't have time for this." Nicole looked out at the wreckers. "I convinced Elliot that you and I could start becoming friends more easily in a relaxed setting than at the computer, but he can't listen to our conversation here, and the security team is out of earshot. If we stay away from the house too long, he'll become suspicious."

"I'm surprised he didn't bug the gazebo."

Nicole's smile held smug satisfaction. "Monitors are incompatible with the nanoprobes—didn't you know they blow the 'tronics? There's no way to prevent it."

Cai returned the smile. Maybe she could become friends with Nicole for real. She liked the way the woman handled things. "So you want to be a webrider? I guess we should get started with the first lesson."

"Yes," Nicole agreed, and rose to her feet. "Let's begin. The computer is in the secondary office."

As she followed the other anchor across the grounds and back toward the house, Cai felt like dancing a little jig. Thanks to Nicole, she was going to rescue her parents, the team would complete their assignment, and they would return to the UCE in a matter of days. Things were definitely looking up.

"You bought that bullshit?" Jake looked as incredulous as he sounded. "Sweetheart, I thought you were savvier than that."

Cai sighed silently. Maybe she should have waited until he'd calmed down before springing this on him. He worried far too much about her, and she'd seen how tense he'd become in her absence as soon as she walked in the door. She'd just been so excited by what had happened, she hadn't been able to hold back.

"Yes, I believed her," she said calmly.

He shook his head, then pivoted. She could hear him muttering under his breath as he walked away, but was thankful she wasn't able to make out the words. Smart money said either he was cursing or questioning her intelligence. Not quite the reaction she'd been hoping for when she told him of the bargain.

This time she forced herself to be patient, to let this settle in his mind before she pushed ahead. He couldn't seem to stand still, not for long. Whenever she'd thought he was starting to absorb it, he'd look at her, mutter, and begin pacing again. Cai sat cross-legged on one of the chairs and watched him move. Even with her thoughts whirling, she couldn't help but appreciate his gracefulness and the play of his muscles.

Finally he dropped down on the low table in front of her and leaned forward, resting his hands on the arms of her chair. "Okay, tell me again exactly what happened. Give me her words."

They were practically nose-to-nose, close enough for her to see the tautness of his jaw. Close enough to see the navy flecks in his light blue eyes. Close enough to be totally distracted by his scent. Her body went hot and achy. Damn, but Jake Tucker affected her more strongly than anyone she'd ever met.

"C'mon, Cai, don't clam up on me. Talk."

She had to clear her throat first, but she succinctly ran through the conversation with Nicole, trying to remember the precise phrasing the anchor had used.

As she repeated it, she began to get excited again, but it was clear that Jake didn't share her enthusiasm. When she finished, he didn't say anything. Although she could see a sort of grimness on his features, Cai found herself holding her breath as she waited for his reaction.

He didn't break eye contact as he straightened and rubbed a hand across the back of his neck. She leaned forward, narrowing the gap between them. "Well?"

"It smells like a setup to me."

"Why do you say that?" The euphoria began to seep from her.

"How about the fact that I don't like coincidence? What are the odds of having this one woman hold the key to everything we're here for?" He took his hand from his nape and laced their fingers. "I'm sorry," he said gently. "I know how badly you want to find your parents, but I doubt you talked to them today. I think Nicole was playing you."

"No." She dropped her feet to the floor, her knees sliding between Jake's thighs. "I know that holo was real."

"She gave you almost no time to talk. You didn't get a chance to verify their identities by asking any personal questions. You didn't have a chance to curb your emotions and observe it dispassionately."

"It wasn't faked," she insisted. "I watched carefully for that. I know a thousand ways to doctor the things so they're seamless, and I promise you none of those techniques were used."

She could see and feel his compassion, but he believed the image had been fabricated. He didn't think she'd spoken to her parents or that they were here.

"Jake," she said, edging forward a fraction more and resting her free hand on his thigh, "Dad told me the date and the time."

"*Someone* told you the date and the time." The sympathy in his eyes increased. "If the holo was real, that doesn't mean those two were your mom and dad. You haven't seen them in six years. How hard would it be to find a couple who resembled them, splice together the dialogue from speeches they've given at various research symposiums, and then play it back to convince you?"

Cai wasn't sure how he knew about her parents' lectures, but she shrugged that off. "She couldn't know what I'd ask."

"No? She—or Elliot—couldn't guess that you'd be concerned about their well-being? They couldn't guess that you'd ask some kind of question that would prove they were still alive, for example, what today's date is?" Cai flushed. "The holo was only three inches high. There's not a lot of detail in something that small. Sweetheart, I doubt they were your parents."

Could he be right? Could it be a deception? She knew how easy it was to remix audio. Hell, any ten-year-old could do it. She looked down at her hand where it rested against his leg and studied the ring her mom and dad had given her. The stone seemed to glow in the sunlight, casting prisms of color across Jake's pants. "It truly was them." She raised her eyes and met his gaze again. "I know it in my heart."

He kissed her, undoubtedly trying to make her feel better, and her lips clung to his as she sought assurance, comfort. For a moment he rested his forehead to hers; then he opened his eyes and pulled away. "Okay," he said quietly, "for now, let's say you're right. That doesn't mean she wasn't using them as bait."

"Bait for what? Elliot already has us."

"To capture the team." Cai opened her mouth to interject that the guys knew nothing about her mom and dad, but Jake squeezed her fingers. "They use your parents to keep us off balance. Let's face it, this op was a means to an end for you from the get-go. Nicole is part of a Quandem, so she knows how tied we are. She'd be able to tell Elliot that if you're obsessed, I'd have difficulty focusing on anything but that."

She nodded, finally seeing where he was going with this. "So while we're distracted with my parents, we're given the location of Maguire and Commander Armstrong. We pass it along to the team to carry out the mission, and it's a trap. The wreckers are there instead and they take the guys captive."

"Or kill them," Jake said, voice hard.

Now it was her turn to offer solace. She knew the death of his men was fresh in his mind, and she ran her hand up and down the outside of his thigh, hoping her touch reached him. It was tempting to lean forward and give him the same kind of sweet kiss he'd given her, but she couldn't work up the courage for that. "Why? What does Elliot care about us or the team?"

"I doubt he cares about the team; that's why he'd consider the men expendable. You and I, however, are a different matter. Aside from Nicole and her recep, we're the only two people in the world with working neural implants. Elliot would double his forces instantly. And since we've had the probes for years, there's no learning curve for us. We're ready from the start."

"He'd have to get us to follow his orders," she said slowly, then guessed in the next breath, "but he could do that by using us against each other. Holding you in line by threatening me, and threatening you to keep me from disobeying."

Jake nodded. "Exactly."

He'd done it, she realized. He'd ruined her good mood. Resolutely, she held on to the hope she had spoken with her parents. He *had* admitted that was possible, though unlikely. "I was so sure. My instincts said she was on the level." She raised her eyes from her lap. "Are you certain it's a trap?"

"I'm sorry, but believe me, coincidence is rare in the field. Convenient coincidence is unheard-of. There's an old saying about if something sounds too good to be true, it is. Keep that in mind."

She waffled for a few more seconds before she said, "You're the one with the experience. I have to trust you're right."

"Thanks. Now here's how I think we should play it. When you meet with Nicole, tell her I've agreed to the deal and you want the location of Maguire. Promise whatever you have to in order to get it. Then we pass the data on to the team, warning them that it's a trap and that there'll be wreckers. They'll go, do a sneak-and-peek, and if Armstrong and Maguire aren't there, we have them blow the building. That should take out the mercenaries, body armor or not."

"What if they are there?"

"Then the team pulls back and we work out another plan."

Cai stared at Jake. "You want *me* to lie to Nicole? I know," she said quickly, "what you think of me, but a lie of omission is different from looking someone in the eye and deceiving them."

She sat tensely, waiting for some scathing remark about her ability to prevaricate, but it didn't come. Instead he toyed with her fingers and stayed silent. Her nerves became more and more strained, and she decided maybe his reticence was worse than a dig or two about her honesty. "Jake?" she prompted.

He looked up from their joined hands. "I know you're not a liar. I don't understand why you kept quiet about being human, but I've watched you. If you have a choice between being wily or being straightforward, you always choose the direct route. I'm not asking you to lie to Nicole because I think you're dishonest. I'm asking because you're the one who'll be meeting with her."

"Then if I tell you I'm bad at lying, you'd believe me?"

One side of his mouth quirked up. "Yeah, I'd believe it. Are you that terrible? Really?"

"Definitely." She leaned forward a little more. "I never got away with anything as a kid."

He nodded. She could tell he was thinking things through and hoped that meant he'd come up with an alternate plan. He stood, paced back and forth a few times, then stopped short.

"You've done a good job playing your part on this op."

"That's different," she said. "It's like acting in a way."

"So think of it as acting when you talk to Nicole."

"I don't know." She could hear the doubt in her voice. "It's not the same thing."

"We'll do some rehearsals till you're comfortable with your lines," he said, then shot her that killer smile of his.

Before she could think better of it, Cai nodded, then shook her head ruefully as she realized what she'd done. Too bad Jake wasn't meeting with the other anchor. With his looks and that grin, he wouldn't have to lie. And the woman would be confessing her secrets in no time.

Cai glanced over her shoulder at Nicole, but the blonde continued to ignore her. She had a bad feeling this meant her lie hadn't been successful. Jake had helped her practice last night and this morning, making her repeat what she'd say over and over, but though that had helped, her delivery had never become smooth. She really was a horrible liar. Despite pressing hard, she hadn't gotten the whereabouts of Maguire and Armstrong either, another indication she hadn't pulled it off.

Jake had trusted her and she'd failed.

The computer in front of her tempted her to explore, but she resisted. She'd already done as much as she dared, and any more would be asking for trouble. Everything this system did was being logged, she knew that, and it was important that she not give anything away with her impatience. She'd circumvented the security once already, and since the dropout had been so brief, it could be written off. A second lapse would be suspect.

Slouching in her chair, she stretched her legs in front of her and crossed them at the ankles. She could almost hear Jake lecturing her, telling her not to put her back to the other woman, telling her to sit up straight and be ready to react. Cai ignored the voice. Nicole wasn't going to attack her from behind. Not physically.

No, if the other anchor wanted her taken care of, she'd simply have Elliot order his wreckers to do it.

This whole situation left her stymied. Why had the man grabbed her and Jake? What was the point? To gain another Quandem? This scheme seemed too involved for just that.

Jake seemed to think Elliot was using them to lure in the rest of the team, but that didn't make sense. The man was rich enough to be above the law, but he wasn't stupid. Special Forces took care of their own, and he had to know that if he wiped out a team, they'd never stop gunning for him no matter how many wreckers he put on payroll.

A noise came from Nicole's direction, and Cai abandoned her relaxed pose. She swiveled in her seat and watched the blonde come toward her. Damn, she wished she were that graceful, that confident, when she walked.

"I think we've dawdled enough this afternoon," she said. "Let's call it a day, shall we?"

There was a brittleness to her words that worried Cai, but she nodded her head in agreement. She wanted to get back to Jake. Although he'd been pretending to be fine, he hadn't slept since he'd had the nightmare. She hoped he'd taken the opportunity to get some rest while she was gone, but knowing him like she did, Cai doubted it.

When the wreckers arrived, Nicole gave her a smile that seemed friendly enough, but Cai saw the coolness in her eyes. She returned the gesture and fell into place with the mercenaries. They'd done this often enough that their formations—and what they wanted from her—had become routine.

She wished they'd move faster, though. Jake was probably ready to climb the walls by now. He was such a worrier, but at least he'd respected her enough to not use their link to constantly check up on her.

As they walked, Cai took the opportunity to study the shielding of the man in front of her. There were nanocomputers filling every inch of the plates, and this was the only reason they could move. Not only was the composite material heavy, but it covered their joints. It allowed them to run faster, take hits from most weapons without being injured, and put more strength behind their blows—but it had its minuses too. There had to be a way to use those to their advantage.

Before she had time to dwell on what this transformation had cost them, they arrived at the room. Even with her view blocked, Cai zeroed in on Jake. He stayed motionless until the wreckers withdrew and the door closed behind them; then he moved, pulling Cai into his arms and hugging her close.

With a sigh, she put her hands at his waist and relaxed against him. She hadn't missed the way he'd checked her out from head to toe, making sure she was uninjured, and while part of her was insulted that he didn't believe she could take care of herself, another part of her was warmed by his concern.

"Are you okay?" he asked.

"I'm fine." And she was, now that she was with him.

His hand settled at her nape and began massaging the

tension away. Tingles went through her at his touch, but she pushed them aside and relaxed, letting Jake take more of her weight. No doubt it was foolish, but she enjoyed the way he fussed over her. It made her feel as if he honestly cared. More than as friends, more than as partners.

They didn't say another word till they were settled on the couch. He tugged her against his side, and Cai hesitated only a moment before snuggling against him. *Oh, man.* She was in such trouble here.

"How'd it go, sweetheart?"

She hesitated, then said quietly, "I don't know. I don't think she believed me, but she didn't call for the guards or go running to Elliot."

"Why do you think she doubted you then?"

Cai shrugged. "It was something in her eyes; they seemed to harden. And she wouldn't tell me where Maguire was despite my efforts, and believe me, I pushed her."

And she had. Jake had asked her to get the location no matter what she had to do, and she'd tried. She'd tried until it became obvious she had to give up.

He slouched down and leaned his head against the back of the couch. "We'll play it as it comes, then."

"I'm sorry," she said, resting her hand on his abs.

"It's not your fault. You did the best you could." She felt his tension begin to ease.

Neither one of them said anything, not for a while. She let herself sink into the pleasure of touching him and lightly traced the hard muscles of his stomach. Although they were locked up, she realized that right now she was content just to be. And maybe Jake felt the same. He was as relaxed as she'd seen him since they'd started this assignment.

Too bad she was going to have to ruin it. She sighed; it was better to tell him straight-out.

"I found that computer I'm supposed to ride."

Chapter Fourteen

Although Jake knew Cai felt him stiffen, she continued as if he hadn't reacted. "It's in this building. I couldn't sense it before because of the shielding around it."

"How did you find it now?" he asked with careful neutrality. He doubted he would like her answer.

"While I was working with Nicole, I tapped into the security system and noticed a few unusual areas. I took them down for a split second and did a shallow probe." He tensed further and she started to circle her fingers lightly on his stomach. It was distracting as hell. "Once I saw Elliot, I considered this raft the most likely location for that computer, but my searches came up empty. This was too good an opportunity to pass up."

"Where was the other anchor?" His voice was harsh, but he couldn't help it. Did she have any idea what kind of risk she'd taken? Probably, he conceded, but she'd done it anyway.

"She was near the windows," Cai said, completely unruffled.

"You're telling me you hacked into Elliot's system while his lover was standing several feet away from you?"

"Yes." She bit her lip, then added, "I made sure she wasn't paying attention to me or what I was doing."

He snorted. Cai pulled away from him and sat up straight. She looked angry. Too bad; he was royally pissed. "What the hell did you think you were doing?"

"What I had to do."

"No. What you had to do was lie to Nicole. Everything else was optional and better left alone." Some of his control slipped. "Even if it didn't appear as if she were watching you, that doesn't that she wasn't."

"Oh, for heaven's sake, give me some credit, will you? Maybe you don't believe I can handle myself in the field, but for damn sure I can take care of anything system-related and do it covertly. When it comes to computers and inteltronics, I'm the expert, not you."

A muscle began to tic in his jaw, and Jake surged to his feet. He paced, going from sitting to sleeping area and back again, trying to work off some of his fury before he spoke. Did she have a clue what she was doing to him? He doubted it, but it didn't help cool his temper.

Finally he faced off with her. "I'm the op leader."

"I know that." Her voice sounded strangled, and he figured she was approaching his level of anger. *Tough.* He was the one who had the right to be irate.

"You jeopardized the assignment with your actions." He took a step toward her and stopped. When he was near her his thoughts became muddled, and he needed a clear head.

Cai closed the distance, going toe-to-toe with him. For a moment she did nothing but glare at him; then she reined in her irritation and said crisply, "First, I didn't jeopardize anything and you know it. We're already being held prisoner and our captor is aware of exactly why we're on the Raft Cities." She didn't sound quite so professional on her next point. "Second—and you tell me the truth—if Gnat or Mango or one of the other men did this would you be pissed off, or would you be slapping him on the back and congratulating him for a job well done?"

"That's different."

"The hell it is." It came out as a growl. "I'm better at this stuff than your whole team combined, and you've worked with me long enough to know it. If one of the guys had tried this, they probably would have been caught before they ever located the security system. But because you think I'm so young—"

"It has nothing to do with your age," he denied heatedly. "Damn it, I know you're capable. I never would have let you out of this room if I didn't believe it, and I sure wouldn't have let you do the talking that night in Elliot's office if I were concerned about your abilities."

"Then you tell me what it is."

With a grimace, Jake jammed his hands into his pockets and put some space between them. He was reluctant to explain, not when he didn't understand it himself. All he knew was that it would damn near kill him if anything happened to her. He'd recover from losing his men; he'd never get over Cai's death. "I don't want you to take any stupid risks, that's all."

"I told you I was careful, so it wasn't a stupid risk. We both know I need to access that computer, and before I could do that I had to locate it. Stupid would have been trying to enter it as soon as I found it, but I didn't do that. I was in, out, and had the security back up in a flash."

He clenched his hands inside his pockets. She was far too cavalier. "You don't think," he said harshly, "that the systems are monitored and that the flash was recorded?"

"I know it was, but these things fluctuate constantly. If I'd kept the system off-line for three seconds, that would have caused an investigation into why, but for a fraction of a second, nobody will even pause as they glance over the data."

"Elliot is a security freak; why else would he surround

himself with wreckers? Don't you think that his men are told to ignore nothing, no matter how inconsequential it might seem?"

She tossed her braid over her shoulder. "The energy doesn't maintain a constant stream, and there are always ups and downs. And yes, sometimes the power will be gone altogether for a nanosecond. It happens every day, every hour. No matter how paranoid Elliot is, it wouldn't take long for his men to tire of checking out normal flickers in the levels."

"You can't be sure of that." He struggled to keep his temper from soaring at her patronizing tone. So he wasn't a tech like she was; that didn't mean he had no knowledge of systems. And he'd picked up more in the years they'd been connected.

"About his security team? No, I can't be one hundred percent sure, but it's an educated guess. About the energy grids, it's my business to know info like that."

He took a deep breath, then another. Somehow she'd totally missed what he was trying to say. "I don't want you hurt." He saw some of the anger leach out of her. "When you do things like this, I want to be there to protect you."

"I can take care of myself. I proved that outside Hell."

"You were going to lose!"

"It was seven against one! You would have had a problem too, and you know it, cowboy." The fire was back in her eyes.

He did know it, but no way on earth would he admit it.

"You have to start trusting me! I can handle myself."

"It's not about trust," he insisted.

"It is." She was so furious her voice shook. "After my implants went down, you managed to trust me to use the nanoprobes again. After seeing me fight in the alley, you should be able to trust my self-defense skills too."

"Whoa, whoa, whoa!" He was in front of her again in about half a second. "What the f—hell do you mean your implants, *plural*, went down? I thought it was only the connector probe."

That knocked the temper right out of her. If he hadn't been so pissed off, he might have laughed over the way her eyes widened as she realized what she'd said. "Now, Jake—," she began, clearly trying to pacify him.

"No, I don't want to hear it. All I want to know is if you lost both probes."

Cai bit her lip again, a sign of nervousness. He waited quietly, sure the silence would get her talking. There was no way in hell he was letting her off the hook on this.

"Yes." She admitted it so softly he barely heard her.

He closed his eyes and fought back the terror rising inside him at her confirmation. God, he could have lost her mentally the same day he'd lost his men. The idea made his blood turn to ice, and then fear became anger. He scowled and said harshly, "Every other anchor that's overloaded has some amount of brain damage. Do you have any idea how lucky you are?"

Her voice was even as she said, "Yes, I do know."

"Son of a bitch," he muttered, and took her shoulders. She was trying to hide it, but her tone tipped him off. She hadn't escaped scot-free. Gently, he asked, "How bad, sweetheart?"

"Really, it's nothing."

His hold firmed. "Don't you dare try to brush me off or downplay it. Now, damn it, how bad?"

Reaching up, she curled her hands around his forearms. "Just a little light memory loss."

"Shit." He tugged her against him and wrapped her in a tight hug. His body was trembling, but he ignored it and hung on to her. Although he had questions about what kinds of things she'd forgotten, he didn't ask. Honestly, he wasn't sure he wanted to know. He should, because it might affect their operation, but the thought of finding out that it was worse than he imagined might be more than he could take.

All he could think was what would happen if she over-loaded again. The idea of Cai looking at him blankly, as if he were a stranger, was bad enough, but it could be even more serious than that. She could end up completely inca-pacitated, like the first anchor whose probes had gone down. The idea made his knees sag.

"Jake—," she began, but he cut her off.

"No, don't say anything, not yet."

Somehow he needed to come to terms with this. He'd known from the time Yardley told him about the problem with the implants that there was nothing he could do to protect her from an overload. That, in essence, she had a bomb in her brain waiting to go off. But it had been easier to accept before he'd discovered she'd had a detonation.

Her hands were running up and down his back, and he found it ironic that she was trying to comfort him. Then he remembered that night. He'd had a damn nightmare, one of the worst in his collection of bad dreams, and he'd reached for Cai. It had been about him and what he'd been through. She'd needed him, but he hadn't known it. Hadn't sensed anything was wrong. And then, after she'd soothed him, he'd run off to the bar with his buddies and had left her alone again. What an ass. Even if he wasn't aware yet that she was human, he should have known his anchor well enough to realize something had happened.

And she'd overloaded trying to help him while he was on a mission. Oh, yeah, what a great guy he was.

"I'm sorry, sweetheart."

For a moment she stopped moving, then resumed her stroking. "I'm okay," she assured him.

Her voice was muffled against his chest, and he noticed then how tightly he held her. He loosened his grip and eased her back so he could see her face. She was a little flushed, but considering she probably hadn't been getting enough oxygen, she looked okay. "I'm sorry," he apologized again, although he wasn't sure himself if it was for crushing her or for his blindness.

She smiled at him and that was it. He kissed her. Though he wanted to take her mouth fast and furious, he refused to lose control. No, he kept it sweet, gentle, reverent, and savored the way she returned his kisses. He wanted her, and he was through pulling away whenever things became heated between them.

Jake walked backward, easing Cai along with him. He didn't take his lips from hers. When he hit the couch he sat, lifting her so she was on his lap. He took the kiss deeper, exploring her mouth thoroughly and enjoying the taste of her, the way she responded to him.

His body trembled again, but it had nothing to do with fear. As hot as their embrace was, as close as he held her, it wasn't enough. He shifted, laying her down on the cushions and covering her. When she parted her legs for him, he gave a short groan of appreciation. "Oh, yeah, sweetheart," he murmured against her lips before diving in once more.

He meant to keep going slowly, to inch her toward becoming lovers, but when he settled between her thighs, he lost his self-command. Cai met him kiss for kiss, arching into him as he rocked against her. Jake tugged her shirt from her pants and worked the buttons free. He wanted her naked and he wanted it now. It felt like forever before he cupped her bare breast.

"Stop," she said, breaking the kiss. Her muscles were rigid.

Shit. He froze and lifted his head. The arousal in her eyes told him he could convince her to continue with a little persuasion, but he wouldn't do that to Cai. Even if stopping damn near killed him. It was her decision, and she'd made the call. Reluctantly, he moved his hand to safer territory.

"Why?" he asked, barely able to get the word out.

"I'm not sure about this." She was panting and it didn't help him rein it in when he saw she was as affected as he.

"Sorry. I forgot how young you are."

"Damn it, Jake, I am so sick of hearing about this. It isn't about my age; it's about our friendship and how it will change if . . . if we do this. And for the last time, you are not that much older than I am." She gave him a shove, but he was expecting it and she didn't budge him.

"It's not the gap. When I was your age I'd been on the team a year and in the army for three. I was leading a squad and I'd already killed. Do you understand, Cai? You were linked with me when I was twenty-one; you know what I was like."

"I know," she said, and bit her lower lip. As far as habits went, it was innocuous, but it made him want to do some biting of his own. With fingers that weren't steady, he began to redo the clothes he'd opened. As he fastened, he saw there was a hint of insecurity in her eyes. It wasn't easy to spot because it was hidden behind so many other layers, but he realized she couldn't trust his attraction to her. And he was willing to bet it came down to those damn kids she'd grown up with and the way they'd made fun of her. She honest-to-God believed she was homely.

Homely. *Shit.* She was freaking gorgeous.

From things that she'd said, he gathered she'd been a late bloomer. That would color her perspective, but come on. He didn't care what she'd heard from those brats; she should be able to see past childhood taunting. No, she wasn't conventionally beautiful, and some people wouldn't look beyond that, but lots of men had to be making it clear to her how spectacular she was now.

Except she didn't send out signals. None at all. Maybe other men weren't letting her know. When a woman looked like her, a lot of guys were intimidated and hung back unless there was some indication of interest. Cai didn't flirt. Not even a bit. Jake smiled. It looked like it was up to him to convince her.

When he finished buttoning her shirt, he rested his hand

over her collarbone and said simply, "You're beautiful."

She blushed and looked discomfited. He didn't think she believed it, not yet, but she didn't argue with him. One step at a time, he reminded himself. He knew how to be patient; he could wait. He was so busy worrying about her doubts, her next words hit him from the blind side.

"You keep raising the disparity in our levels of experience—is that why you won't talk about your nightmares with me? You think I'm too green to handle them or to understand what you've lived through, what you've done?"

His body jerked. Jake pushed to his feet, putting distance between them. He might have to discuss the dreams. He couldn't risk hurting Cai. It had scared the shit out of him to wake up and find his hand around her throat. Since then he hadn't dared to doze, let alone sleep. And although he'd caught a twenty-minute nap while she'd been with Nicole, it hadn't been enough.

"Or what about your life before you joined the army? That's been another thing you've kept secret from me," she continued.

Closing his eyes for a moment, he ran his hand over his mouth and looked over at her. She sat up now, knees primly together. Her hair was braided but wonderfully messy, and her lips were red, moist. He felt that kick again. Before he got lost in it, he met her gaze. What he saw there made him sigh. He wasn't sharing the nightmares, not unless there was no other option, but he could give her the story of his childhood. It wasn't that big a deal; he simply didn't like to remember it.

"I grew up with the Sartonians," he said quietly.

Surprise filled her face. "But that's a—"

"A cult. Yeah, I know. Both my parents were—and as far as I know still are—believers."

"I didn't think anyone ever got out of there."

Jake smiled grimly. "There are damn few of us, and if

you're born into it, it's harder to escape. They start the brainwashing from the time you're in the cradle, and it doesn't stop." He could recite the chants as if he'd left yesterday, not eight years ago. And despite his best efforts to forget, he bet he'd be able to repeat the words at ninety.

"How did you resist the training? How did you get out?"

There was so much compassion, so much understanding in her eyes, that he had to look away for a minute. When he felt calm again, he shrugged and said, "I'm not sure. Stubbornness, maybe. I didn't like to be told what to think, and I was smart enough to keep my opinions quiet. Wariness. I knew not to trust anyone, that if I were to voice any idea that deviated from the Pioneers' beliefs I would be betrayed. And patience. I had to wait till I was of age to leave or I'd be dragged back and there wouldn't be another chance to get free."

"Your parents?"

"What about them?"

She winced at the hardness in his voice, but she didn't stay away. Instead she came toward him. He had to fight the urge to retreat. When she stood in front of him, she reached for his hands. "Don't you miss your parents?" she asked softly.

Damn. She was going to dig into things he'd rather not recall. It wasn't that they bothered him, not really. He'd come to terms with his past, but it was hard for him to admit the truth to someone who'd been so obviously adored by her mom and dad. "No." He knew she wouldn't let him leave it at that, and reluctantly he kept talking. "They never loved me. My conception was their duty to the leaders. The Sartonian Pioneers were the only people they had feeling for."

Her hands squeezed his and her head tilted as she studied him. "They didn't protect you, did they?"

Jake laughed, a bitter sound. Protect him? Hell, they'd been harsher with him than anyone else in the cult, and that included the Pioneers' enforcers. The beatings they'd given him were the one thing he had trouble putting behind him. There hadn't been that many—he'd learned young not to reveal anything—but he would never forget the sense of betrayal he'd felt. "Believe me, there was no leniency from them."

"It's their loss," she said fiercely. "Not knowing you, I mean. Not seeing what a good man you are."

Amazed, he watched tears well in her eyes. For him. No one had ever cried for him. Freeing one hand, he rubbed his thumb over the droplet rolling down her cheek. Her empathy reached a dark place inside him and brought light. It felt easier to breathe somehow, as if he'd been constricted and she'd cut the bonds.

"Don't cry; it wasn't all bad. I swear."

"Tell me something good."

"Thanks to the weapons master I'm probably better at knife fighting than anyone else in the UCE Army."

"What?" It was half laugh, half question, and he smiled.

"Maybe you aren't aware of this, but the Sartonians are known for the perfection of their blades. All children are assigned to a weapons master for training when they're old enough to begin school. Our extracurricular activities involved knives—learning to forge them, to use them, to care for them. I knew how to attack with a dagger and how to throw it with deadly accuracy before I reached puberty."

"This is a good thing?"

He smiled. "It's saved my ass more than once."

"Then it is good," she said. And going up on her toes, she pressed her lips against his in a fleeting kiss.

Jake pulled her against him, wrapped his arms gently around her, and closed his eyes. Oh, yeah, he'd definitely lost his mind, but what the hell. Cai was worth the cost.

The invitation for dinner—or summons, rather—arrived with appropriate formal wear and orders to be ready in an hour. Cai found it slightly unnerving that Marchand Elliot managed to produce garments and shoes in their exact sizes. More than exact—the gown fit as if tailored for her.

She scrutinized her image in the bathroom mirror. The floor-length dress was sleeveless and the neckline veed, displaying her cleavage—what she had of it, anyway. The slit went from the hem to nearly the top of her thigh and revealed her left leg with every step she took. It was the color, however, that had her staring. Red. Bright red. Come-and-get-me-boys red.

Come-and-get-me-Jake red.

Cai nearly groaned aloud at that silly thought. Just because he'd kissed her senseless didn't mean she'd suddenly become some siren. She stepped into the matching red satin pumps and ran a comb through her hair. Elliot hadn't provided jewelry, but she couldn't imagine herself decked out in diamonds or rubies anyway. She touched the small disk at her neck. Her ring and pendant were more important than precious gems.

There was a tap at the door. "The hour's nearly up."

"I know. I'm almost ready."

Almost. All she needed to do was find the courage to open the door and see Jake's reaction. The dress, the shoes, the makeup—this was as good as she got. What if it wasn't good enough?

She raised her chin. To hell with it. It wasn't like she was getting ready for a date with her recep; this was a mission. Shoulders squared, she stepped out of the bathroom. He turned from his prowling at the sound.

She forgot to breathe. A clean-shaven Jacob Tucker in a tuxedo. *Oh, my.* Reflex finally kicked in and she inhaled. With those broad shoulders and dark good looks, the man was enough to inspire more than a few fantasies. When she realized she was gawking, Cai hurriedly raised her eyes to his. And was shocked by what she saw there. He was looking at *her* the same way?

Before she had time to absorb it, the door opened and the wrecking crew appeared. Jake moved to Cai's side, and, hand at her back, escorted her into place in the formation.

Sweetheart, he said as they left the room, *you look amazing.*

Amazing could mean anything, but the tone that went with the words was admiring. And when she remembered the look on his face as he'd caught sight of her . . . Maybe she was okay.

Thank you, she said belatedly.

His fingers curled around her hip, squeezing for an instant, but then he loosened his hold. She knew why. If he needed to react, he couldn't have her plastered against his side. Heaven knew she wouldn't be much help, not in two-inch heels and a form-fitting evening gown. Cai smothered a smile at the mental picture of trying to fight in formal wear.

Instead of checking out the area as they made their way through the maze of hallways, she found herself drinking in the sight of Jake again. *We match,* she said, astonished.

He gave her a quick, puzzled glance before he resumed scanning their surroundings.

Your tie and cummerbund match my dress. It was such an odd detail that Elliot, or one of his employees, must have done it deliberately. And the peculiarity jarred her, reminded her that this wasn't a social event but a mission.

Before she had time to work through why anyone would take the time to attend to such a minor point, they reached their destination. The dining room was elaborate. More than elaborate. She searched for the word she wanted. Ostentatious. That was it. And it brought to mind her earlier thought about Elliot and his attitude. This was without doubt a room fit for a king. Or a despot.

She was taking in the appointments, all gilt and shining wood, when she felt Jake's hold tighten. Cai followed his gaze and saw Elliot staring at her with a predatory expression.

It was probably a ruse to leave her recep unsettled, but

she couldn't quite convince herself of that. If he'd coldly leered at her, she would have been confident it was meant to needle Jake, but the heat in Elliot's eyes said different.

Male attention, at least of this sort, was unusual for her. Since Jake was her friend, she couldn't quite believe his admiration, but their captor wouldn't bother trying to make her feel good about herself. She didn't think he was staging this, and that made her wonder: had her self-image been skewed by the kids she'd grown up with? Was she always seeing herself through their eyes?

"My dear, you look lovely."

Cai's skin crawled, and as Elliot approached, she was tempted to step nearer to Jake. She wouldn't, though; she was tougher than that. But when the older man took her hand then pressed his lips to her palm, she had to grit her teeth to remain stationary. Especially when he used his tongue to tickle her. She battled the urge to yank free of his grip and let fly with a right cross to his mouth. Or to wipe her hand on her dress.

She heard Jake's soft growl, and she worked herself loose and stepped closer to him. "Is it just us for dinner?" she asked quickly, trying to divert both men.

"No," Elliot answered with a note of impatience. He checked the time. "Nicole is running late."

As if the woman were waiting for her cue, she rushed into the room, all apologies, which their host waved aside as he moved to a sideboard. He selected a bottle of wine and put on a show as he opened it. He then sniffed the cork and talked knowledgeably about the wine's nose.

After deeming what he'd sampled satisfactory, Elliot poured a glass for each of them. "This is a charmingly complex cabernet-sauvignon-and-merlot blend," he said as he handed out the crystal goblets. "It has a wonderful intensity and depth of flavor. I'm sure you'll enjoy it."

Cai was less than enthusiastic. She'd never been much of a wine drinker, and reds gave her a headache, but Elliot was watching her intently, so she took a sip. It was clear he was waiting for some kind of comment, and she said, "Very nice."

He laughed, and her hackles rose because she knew it was *at* her. Jake's arm went around her waist once more, and he tugged her against his side. She liked his support.

"I should have known better," Elliot said with mock disappointment. "You can dress up the webrider, but clothes don't translate into sophistication."

Webrider? *Jake, do you think Nicole is keeping her end of the bargain? She hasn't told him.*

I don't know, but play along.

Something made her turn to Nicole. The woman's simple black gown and intricate coiffure gave her a sophisticated, elegant look, but it was her unshakeable poise that made Cai feel like a kid playing dress-up. The other anchor was standing quietly, observing, but what Cai saw in her eyes made her lean more firmly into Jake. The cold calculation was only visible for an instant, but it was long enough to know that Nicole had some plan in mind.

"Shall we sit?" Elliot offered Nicole his arm.

Cai looked at Jake. He shrugged, and with as much style as their host, escorted her to the table. As they neared, she saw there were place cards at each setting. Jake seated her where she was assigned and then took his own chair. Cai's nerves were taut, and it relieved her that he was at her side. To give herself something to do, she reached for her napkin and painstakingly smoothed it across her lap.

"The vast array of utensils must have you at a loss," Elliot said with a smile. "Start at the outside and work your way in. I trust you can manage."

Cai began to stiffen, but her brain kicked in before she could be truly offended. What *was* the man's game? Why was he acting so insulting, and assuming they were uncultured idiots?

"So, my darling Nicole, how are your lessons progressing?"

"Quite well," the blonde said, sipping her wine with obvious appreciation before setting the glass on the table. "Did I mention that Cai seems to have an uncanny instinct for computers? Why if I didn't know better, I'd swear . . . But that's silly."

"What's silly? Share your thoughts."

Cai forced herself to relax the death grip she had on her napkin. This was some kind of ploy, she assured herself. It wasn't like anything new was going to be revealed.

"No, I'd feel far too foolish to say it aloud."

Elliot placed his glass on the table and straightened in his seat. He turned to the blond anchor, and the tension in the room suddenly seemed palpable. Cai became very aware of the dozen or so wreckers standing at attention along every wall.

"Share your thoughts," their host repeated, but this time the demand was unmistakable.

"Very well, but you'll laugh at my nonsense," Nicole said, seemingly unfazed by the implied threat in her boss's tone. "For a moment I wondered if Cai's ability with computers came from a set of neural implants. I know how unlikely that is, however."

The expression on Elliot's face made it clear that this was the first he'd heard of such a possibility. Jake's hand came down on Cai's thigh, and he gave her leg a squeeze. Although he didn't say anything, she knew he was warning her to stay calm, not to react. She concentrated on the rough heat of his fingers to distract herself from the sense of impending doom and took a deep breath.

"Check it out," Elliot commanded, voice tight.

Nicole didn't demur again. She shot Cai a look that held veiled triumph and an edge of satisfaction, then closed her eyes. When she opened them again moments later, Cai braced herself.

"Oh! I was right, there are implants. These two"—she gestured to across the table—"they're a Quandem."

Chapter Fifteen

Elliot gaped at Nicole, his mouth opening and closing, but no sound emerged. He looked like a landed fish. It didn't take long before he regained his composure, but that momentary lapse clearly showed how shocked he was.

It made one thing plain. Jake had been wrong when he'd told her Nicole's deal was a setup. She'd been offering them everything they were on the Raft Cities for, and had asked for little in exchange. If only Jake had believed her when she'd told him the other anchor was on the level.

It wasn't his fault. She understood why he'd doubted Nicole's sincerity, and his reasoning had been sound. But she'd been the one to talk with the woman. She'd been the one who'd received the proposal. The blame rested on her shoulders. If she'd argued more skillfully, had persisted longer, or had presented it more clearly, maybe he would have made a different decision. Maybe they'd be on their way back to the UCE already, Maguire and Armstrong in tow and her parents rescued.

True, Jake hadn't trusted Cai's instincts, but why should he when she hadn't trusted them either? At least not enough. She'd capitulated far too easily. Now they were going to pay the price for his lack of faith and her lack of confidence.

"Are you certain?" Elliot asked, breaking the silence that had fallen over the table.

"Quite certain," the blonde said firmly. "I ran through the UCE files. Their names aren't attached to the Quandem Project, but there are images." She paused, then added, "I realized something was different from the moment I met them, but I didn't recognize what. It's so obvious now that I can't believe I didn't notice at once."

The woman was a hell of an actress. If she didn't know better, Cai would buy the story—hook, line, and sinker. Elliot showed no sign of doubting her, and it wasn't like Cai could point out that this was a charade, that Nicole had been aware for a while of who they were. Not only would the man think Cai was lying, but it served no purpose to implicate the other anchor in subterfuge. It wouldn't get them out of the situation and would only antagonize Nicole.

And Cai didn't want to make her angry. So far the woman hadn't revealed the truth about Cai's parents and she'd do anything to keep that information secret.

"Why didn't you mention that something felt odd that first night?" Elliot asked, continuing his questioning.

"I should have, but it never occurred to me that they might be a UCE Quandem." Nicole looked chagrined.

"I imagine it wouldn't. At least you discovered it before the plan could be set in motion."

"Plan?" The question slipped out of Cai's mouth.

For the first time since the show started, Elliot turned to her, and Cai wished she'd kept quiet. The table was long, and, of course, their host sat at its head. Nicole sat directly to his right and Cai on his left. Now that his attention was aimed at her, the position seemed far too close.

"I should have surmised that the UCE would send their

last remaining Quandem after the traitor. They've been quite fixated on quelling the Voice of Freedom. Shortsighted on my part, particularly when it involved Armstrong's son."

"Quandem?" Jake asked. "What's that?"

Though he sounded convincing, it was a lost cause; Elliot wouldn't believe anything they said. If Nicole proclaimed them to be from Neptune, the man would nod and try to negotiate a deal for the mineral rights.

Their host barely spared Jake a glance. "Do you honestly believe that playing dumb will work?"

He didn't wait for a response before Cai was back in his sights. With a predatory gleam in his eye, he studied her. This time the coldness was there, the calculation, and it concerned her. All she could think of was the way he'd threatened Nicole's recep to get her into bed with him—and surrounded by wreckers, it became easier for Cai to understand why the woman had agreed.

"I could use the help of another anchor," Nicole said, and if Cai didn't know better, she'd swear the woman had spoken to deflect Elliot's attention.

The man broke off his scrutiny and addressed her. "Yes, I have kept you busy. This should not only help your workload, but increase your efficiency. I imagine Cai has been well trained on the UCE's systems and she'll be faster at navigating them.

"Of course, you *will* share what you know with Nicole," he said to Cai. Though snakes didn't smile, his smug look made her think of a reptile spotting an injured mouse.

He ran his fingers over a control panel on his chair arm, and a woman entered the room. She appeared to be a native of the Raft Cities and was dressed in what had to be a uniform.

"Yes, sir?"

"Set another place for dinner. I think to Nicole's right. We'll have one more at the table tonight."

With a deferential bow of her head, the woman went to the sideboard. Quickly, quietly, she laid out dishes and silverware. No one spoke while she worked, and Cai glanced at Jake. He appeared relaxed, and she forced her hands to smooth out the napkin she'd been twisting.

Don't worry, sweetheart. His hand covered hers where she'd folded them in her lap. *We'll get out of this; we'll bide our time until the right opportunity.*

Cai pulled one of her hands free and ran her thumb over the inside of his wrist. She craved the contact, needed the feel of his skin. Jake was here, and the rest of the team was somewhere nearby. She could contact them if there was no other option. *You gave up pretty fast on convincing Elliot that we're not linked.*

He wasn't buying it, but I knew it was a long shot before I started. There was no point in continuing. Jake hesitated, then said, *I'm going to let you do most of the talking again. Elliot responds to you, and he barely tolerates me. I'll back you up if I have to, but you've got the lead on this, okay?*

Yeah, I can do it.

I know you can. His fingers squeezed her hand. *Be careful what you agree to, though; he's ruthless.*

Like she needed to be told. *I'll stay on guard,* she promised. Jake was trusting her to take care of this volatile situation, and that meant a lot to her. It was understandable, however, that he would be a bit anxious.

All eyes were on the woman setting the table. If it had been her, Cai knew the audience would have made her nervous enough to drop something, but the server flawlessly completed her job and asked, "Will there be anything else, sir?"

"Yes, have a message sent to De Luca requesting his presence for dinner. In formal attire."

"Yes, sir." She bowed her head again and backed out of the room. Royalty, Cai recalled, didn't allow servants to turn their backs. Elliot was definitely king of his little domain.

"You're going to hold dinner?" Nicole asked. A note in her voice had Cai gripping Jake's wrist. On the surface, the blonde sounded idly curious, yet something both hopeful and reluctant seeped into her tone. And into her eyes.

"Do you have a problem with that, my dear?" The words were silky, charming, and it felt as if the anchor had baited a cobra.

"Of course not," she replied smoothly. "It's merely that I skipped lunch today and I'm starved."

"How inconsiderate of me," Elliot said after the smallest of pauses. "I'll have appetizers served to tide you, and our guests, over until our last guest arrives."

It took no time before they each had a small plate in front of them filled with a selection of hors d'oeuvres. Cai didn't want to eat. Her stomach was tied in knots, and the thought of adding food made those coils pull tighter. She should have realized, though, that Elliot would comment.

"Perhaps you'll release Cai's hands so that she can eat."

For an instant she clutched Jake more tightly, then reluctantly let go. Their captor didn't like her recep, that was clear, and Cai was afraid of what the man would do if Jake disregarded his orders. The same reasoning made her pick up a small canapé and nibble on it despite her roiling stomach.

She'd barely finished the last bite when Elliot addressed her. "You're no doubt wondering what will be expected of you and your partner while working for me. It's quite simple. You'll function much like Nicole and her receptor do."

Her nausea increased, and Cai wished she hadn't eaten anything. "How do they function?" she managed to ask.

"Your receptor will be assigned to my security force. He'll be sent out to retrieve items for me, handle problems, that type of thing. You, of course, will assist him when he's out on assignment. The remainder of your time will be spent on my personal projects."

Cai didn't like the sound of *personal projects*. Data retrieval was one thing, but what if he expected more? Something intimate, like he required of Nicole?

"You seem very confident that we'll do your bidding." It made her nervous, challenging the man this way, but she had to do it. He surely expected it.

The smile was slimy. "Of course you will. Both of you will. If one balks, I'll have the other hurt; it's that simple. I know how it works between Quandems. You'll do whatever you must to protect each other." His smile broadened. "It will also be interesting to see where the line is. When will self-interest overcome your unity?"

He popped a pastry into his mouth, and Cai wished he'd choke. Threats against loved ones were the easiest method to command obedience, and she wasn't surprised by his tack. Her eyes went to Nicole. If the other anchor passed on the information about her parents, Elliot would have another weapon to use against her. And a weapon to use against her mom and dad. But the woman didn't say anything. Not yet. The risk of exposure hung like a guillotine, and Cai waited for the blade to drop.

"Come, my dear, it won't be so terrible. You'll have the run of the grounds, and I pay much better than the UCE Army."

"The army won't stand idly by and let us be held prisoner. They'll send others in to recover us."

"No," Elliot disagreed easily, "they won't. The pirates here have this nasty habit of killing people they believe betrayed them, and hanging out their corpses to rot in the sun. It won't be difficult to associate your names with a pair of bodies. And do you honestly believe the UCE will risk more soldiers to verify whether you and your receptor are dead?"

"Maybe not," she said grudgingly. But it was different with Jake's crew. With Special Forces. They didn't leave their men behind, dead or alive. End of story.

The door opened, stopping the conversation. De Luca,

she guessed, and immediately she knew he was the other half of Nicole's Quandem. Unobtrusively, she studied the blonde. The woman's longing was evident, but so were her efforts to conceal the response. Elliot watched both her and the newcomer with avid interest, and Cai bet he was waiting for some kind of slip, anticipated it with glee.

Tony was close to Jake's height—maybe an inch shorter—but that was where the similarities ended. The man's looks were average, nondescript. Perfect for blending in on a covert job, but hardly a match for his anchor's blond beauty. But that didn't seem to matter. Cai had seen, had sensed, the depth of feeling Nicole had for him. She loved Tony.

So why did Cai have trouble accepting that Jake might honestly find her attractive? She knew he wasn't shallow, and that he hated when people judged him by his appearance. Not only was she being unfair to him, but she was underestimating herself as well. It was time to quit that, time to let go of the past and the hurt of her childhood.

Tony ignored his anchor and addressed the boss. "You requested my presence at dinner, sir?"

"I did. Take your seat." Elliot indicated the chair next to Nicole. The hesitation before De Luca followed orders was brief, but the older man noticed and smirked.

Nicole hadn't been exaggerating when she'd said there was a division between her and her recep. It was perceptible, and Cai wondered how they worked together when things were so tense. Sure, they could block each other, but it took a lot of energy to do that. She and Jake didn't always transmit, but it was also rare that they walled each other out. It had become ordinary, normal to feel his mind brush against hers at odd moments, and she missed that closeness when they were shut off. How did this couple stand it?

Jake, that's Nicole's recep. Tony De Luca.

That makes sense. I don't think he likes the situation between his partner and his boss.

Tony's jaw dropped when Elliot introduced them as another Quandem, and that reinforced Cai's feeling that he was blocking Nicole. If not, the woman would have told him who they were, the same way she'd kept Jake informed.

Cai met the man's gaze evenly as he scrutinized her. He seemed steady, levelheaded, and she couldn't help but wonder how he'd ended up in Elliot's web. Something else occurred to her as she looked at him: he didn't trust Nicole. But then she didn't trust him either. If they had that bond, she would have told him about the boss's threat, and even if she hadn't, Tony would have realized his anchor wasn't interested in Elliot.

Jake, if you were in De Luca's shoes, would you know that I wasn't sleeping with Elliot because I wanted to?

He started to turn toward her, but stopped himself at the last second. *Where the hell did that question come from?*

These two don't trust each other. If they did, the situation wouldn't have deteriorated to this point between them. Look how careful they are to not let their shoulders brush—and I'm sure there's blocking going on.

So you're asking if I have enough confidence in you to realize you'd never cheat on me? Yeah, sweetheart, I know that. And I know how much you hate Elliot. Let me turn this around. If this guy blackmailed you for sex, would you trust me enough to tell me about it?

I'd worry about what you'd try, especially with the wreckers at his command . . . but yes, I'd tell you. And hope I could calm you down quickly enough to keep you from doing something rash.

Really? Jake had a slight note of disbelief in his tone.

In what she hoped was a stealthy move, Cai put her hand on Jake's thigh and squeezed. *I understand why Nicole made the choice she did. I'd be scared to death if it happened to me. Scared of what you'd do and how the sleaze would respond, but in the end, I'd let you know what was going on. I swear.*

His hand covered hers, and she turned it so they were

palm-to-palm. She remembered Elliot's carefully manicured nails and smooth skin and preferred Jake's calloused
touch. Her recep was always gentle with her, always considerate. It demonstrated more clearly than words how un-
selfish he was. Elliot, she had no doubt, wouldn't care if he
were rough, wouldn't care about anything but his own
gratification.

I'm holding you to that promise, Cai.

Okay, she agreed, but it worried her. Didn't Jake believe
they were going to get out of here soon? She'd assumed it
would be a matter of a day or two before they started planning an escape, but maybe she was wrong. Now wasn't the
time to ask, though—not with Elliot and his employees
around.

The meal arrived, and Cai reluctantly released her recep.
She felt cold without his heat against her hand, but she didn't
want Elliot commenting again on her being unable to eat.

Course after course was served with elegant precision.
She was sure the food was good, but she couldn't taste it,
not as anxious as she felt. Elliot kept the conversation
flowing, all small talk, but he primarily addressed Cai or
Nicole. The two men were ignored almost entirely, though
from time to time he'd deliver a verbal jab. From Tony's
lack of reaction, she guessed this was standard operating
procedure for the snake, but it added to her discomfort.

When dessert and coffee were served, Cai knew she
couldn't keep following Elliot's lead. She wanted some answers, so why not ask for them? As long as she didn't push
too hard, it wouldn't make their situation any worse, and if
she were wrong, Jake would straighten her out in a hurry.

"I have a few questions," she said. Her recep tensed beside her, but he didn't tell her to stop.

Their host paused, his cup partway to his lips, and said,
"Very well." He sipped his coffee and returned the cup to
its saucer. He seemed amiable enough, but she had to be
careful.

"I don't understand why you had us brought to your house as your guests"—she almost choked on that word—"when you didn't know what Jake and I were. Does that tie in with the plan you mentioned earlier? And why was I supposed to teach Nicole to webride when she already can access any system she wants with her probe?"

Her questions brought a soft chuckle, but it was mocking, not amused. Tony and Nicole stopped eating to stare at her as well, and she had the feeling they thought she was stupid to ask. That put her back up. She knew what she was doing.

Elliot didn't immediately respond. Instead he dug his fork into a slice of lemon pie and savored a bite. "You realize," he said, "that I don't have to satisfy your curiosity."

"I know." She kept her voice even.

"But I will, and since I'm showing my goodwill, I'll expect the same in return when I ask something of you."

Cai nodded, since she couldn't speak around the lump of fear in her throat. What the hell was he going to want from her?

"When Nicole informed me that the UCE was launching a mission to the Raft Cities to capture a traitor and rescue their supreme military commander's son, I knew they wouldn't stop until the assignment was successfully accomplished. Unfortunately, it's difficult to find anyone here, particularly when one of the most powerful pirate lords is assisting them. Quite simply, I wanted this finished as quickly as possible so that I could be left in peace to continue my own projects."

He had some more coffee and looked at her over the rim of the cup. It took all her control to sit still for his perusal.

"It was very uncomplicated," he continued at last. "You stay as my guests, and in exchange teach Nicole. This provides the opportunity for the two of you to become friendly, and she offers to help you escape. She likes you and feels bad. And since she knows you can't leave until you've completed your task, she provides you the where-abouts of your targets. You break out, grab Maguire and Armstrong, and depart the Raft Cities."

So Nicole had been right about Elliot's scheme. Cai didn't glance at the blonde, but went on to another question. "Why do you care if the UCE knows you're here?" He hadn't said he did, not exactly, but it was obvious that it was a concern. "In fact, why *are* you here? The Raft Cities are pretty seedy for someone of your refinement."

The benevolence left his face. "Let's say that I was re-ceiving some unwelcome scrutiny from our illustrious President Beauchamp and his minions and leave it at that, shall we?"

Though he'd phrased it as a question, Cai knew it was a command. If she persisted, it was at her own peril. To be honest, she wasn't sure why he'd bothered to respond, but it was a very telling reply. "One last question, if I may?"

Cai, Jake said, the warning clear in his tone.

Elliot only stared at her, so she went ahead. "Without us to return Maguire and Armstrong to the UCE, how do you plan to get them off the Raft Cities?"

He set his cup down and said, "Please don't take me for a fool. A team is more than two people; I'm well aware that you have more men here. You were simply the first I identified."

Lucky us, Cai thought, but what she said was, "I apolo-gize. I certainly know you're no fool." *A self-centered ass, yes. A fool, no.* He was sly and ruthless, two traits that had gotten him much of what he wanted. She didn't underestimate him, not after the years she'd spent researching the man.

Don't ask him another question, and that's an order.

She could tell Jake was dead serious, but she hesitated. In the end, though, she obeyed. He was the op leader, and protocol demanded she follow his commands. If he'd been a bit less resolved, she might have gone ahead anyway, but he'd been adamant. Then there was the fact that both Tony and Nicole were looking at her as if she'd lost her mind, and Elliot's demeanor was cold. Definitely time to back off.

Dessert was eaten in an atmosphere of icy silence. Elliot stood when he finished and walked to the door. Cai started to breathe a sigh of relief, but at the last instant, he turned to her. "I'll see you tomorrow evening, my dear Cai, and we'll discuss your demonstration of goodwill then. Nicole. De Luca." He jerked his head toward the door.

Without waiting for a response, he exited. The other Quandem, after only a brief hesitation, followed.

Cai didn't know what time it was, only that it was very late. Both she and Jake had been lying in bed staring at the ceiling, but he'd finally drifted off about an hour ago. Maybe it helped that she'd kept transmitting serene energy to him through their link. She knew he'd been fighting his need to rest, although he'd been clearly exhausted.

Sleep continued to elude her, however. Elliot's parting words kept echoing in her mind. Maybe he wanted nothing except for her to access data for him. Or maybe he simply wanted her to sweat; that was another possibility. But she feared it was more.

She and Jake had talked about it when they'd been returned to their room, but he hadn't known anything more than she. His opinion was that Elliot was deliberately enigmatic, that he'd hoped they would worry. And reluctantly, he'd conceded that the fact that the man wanted her uneasy didn't mean he didn't have more on his mind than what Cai could do with her neural implants. He'd tried to hide it from her, but she knew her recep was concerned, and that put her further on edge.

Jake shifted and Cai turned her head, hoping her thoughts hadn't disturbed him but wanting to talk if he was awake. He wasn't, and the grimace on his face told her he was having another nightmare. *Ah, damn.* Cautiously, she shook his shoulder, but again it had no effect.

His scowl deepened and he mumbled something unintelligible. This time she knew better than to restrict his movements, but she couldn't let him suffer through this either. She shook him harder and called his name more loudly. She continued until he sat upright, his head swiveling as he scanned for danger.

"Jake," she said quietly, "you had one of your dreams. You're safe. I'm safe. Nothing is going on."

He went still; then after a long moment he cursed and lay back down, his arm going over his eyes. Cai reached for him, resting her hand on his chest. His heart raced beneath her fingers, his lungs strained for air, and she started stroking him, trying to bring him calmness. Thank God she'd blown out the spy devices in the room after dinner. If Elliot knew about Jake's dreams, he'd use them against him.

When his respiration and heart rate returned to normal, she said softly, "You have to discuss those nightmares with someone."

"Yeah, I know."

Cai had been expecting his usual response and was marshaling her arguments when she realized he'd agreed with her. "What? I'm sure I must be hearing things."

"Smart-ass." It sounded like an endearment. He lowered his arm and pulled her against his side. "I don't want to talk about it. You know that. But I can't go without sleep indefinitely, and it looks like I'm on one of my streaks. I won't take a chance on hurting you again." He turned so she could see the resolve in his eyes. But she also saw the ghosts. Though he sounded relatively normal, she suspected he'd had the worst dream tonight.

"Your reaction last time was my fault. I should never have pinned you with my weight."

"Doesn't matter, sweetheart. If talking about it will make them stop while we're on this op, then I'll talk. I won't risk you, period." His hand covered hers on his belly, forcing her to stop caressing him. "Give me a minute."

He was quiet, and she suspected he was working up his nerve. These nightmares tortured him, embarrassed him, and he saw them as a weakness, but she didn't view them that way.

Tonight's dream . . . it was a real event. It happened not too long after the probes were inserted. Almost five years—you'd think I'd be over it by now.

Some things we never get over. Although she'd told him this before, she didn't think it had registered.

It's her eyes. I don't think I'll ever forget the look in them. He stopped long enough to curb his emotion. *It was the mission when intel thought they'd located the leader of the Red Star. You remember it, right?*

I remember. She'd never forget. In fact, she should have realized this was one of the things haunting him.

Silence again; then grudgingly he admitted, *The dream started out same as always. He's running. Gotta stop him. Mostly we let them run, you know? It isn't worth hunting down one terrorist when we've got a dozen others. But I recognized this one. We couldn't let him get away.*

No, you couldn't. Not the second-in-command of a huge network of terrorist cells. They'd had to capture him no matter the cost. Unfortunately, it had been an innocent child and a man with too much conscience who had paid the price.

We lost him. The group was well-funded, and he had a fu— Jake stopped short. Even as riled as he was, he still wouldn't use the word in front of her. She could count on one hand the number of times he'd slipped and actually said it. *Anyway, he had a scrambler, so we had to split up and hunt him the hard way. It was slow going, and the terrain left him lots of crevices and depressions to hide in. I might have walked right by him.*

And been shot in the back for the mistake. Terrorists

didn't fight fair, and even the vests the teams wore couldn't stop everything. She gave him a small nudge to keep him talking. *But something spooked the man enough to run.*

Yeah. Not only did he run, but he wasn't quiet about it.

There was another pause. She knew they were getting to the part he hated to think about.

When I saw him, he was darting up an incline. I ordered him to stop, and that's when he turned. There was no choice then; I know that.

No, there wasn't, she told him. The coward had been carrying a weapon powerful enough to destroy the entire village. Hundreds of innocents, people whose only crime had been living in a community that had strategic value to the terrorists, would have died if Jake hadn't taken the jerk down.

She came out of nowhere. Stepped right into my line of fire at the same moment I pulled the trigger. There wasn't a damn thing I could do. I know that in my head. But I can't forget. He wasn't able to conceal his anguish any longer. *God, she was so tiny. Maybe four. Just a baby.*

Cai crooned soothingly over their link and pulled her hand free so she could stroke him again. There were no words to ease his pain. She was certain he'd carry this wound on his soul till the day he died. Despite his claim that he realized there was nothing he could have done to save the girl, she knew he didn't believe it. He blamed himself for not spotting the child sooner.

I had to shoot again to get the bastard. By the time I reached the girl . . . it was too late. I could see that.

He'd reined back. She could discern how much control he was exerting to keep his emotions in check.

She looked up at me with these peaceful eyes, and her gaze held forgiveness. Like she was reassuring me.

"Maybe she was," Cai said aloud, but he ignored her.

I was holding her in my arms when she died.

His lack of inflection told her a lot. This still hit him

hard. She remembered the aftermath, the four days he'd gone without sleep. The way he'd beaten himself up over his mistake. She'd stayed with him the whole way, not even dozing in case he'd needed her. And he had. He'd reached for her again and again during those bleak days, but he'd never shared what this had done to him. She'd been sixteen, too inexperienced to know how to get him to talk, and for the first time it dawned on her how young Jake himself had been when it happened.

It's good she wasn't alone, Jake. That means a lot.

She should have been with her mother, not her killer.

Sorrow, for both the child and Jake, filled her. *Yes, it should have been her family, but she did have someone who cared about her when she passed.*

"Cai." He met her eyes again for the first time since he'd begun talking, and she saw how it tortured him, heard it in the thick rasp of his voice. "I killed a baby."

"It was an accident. A tragic case of bad timing." She blinked rapidly to hold back her tears. "I know you never would have fired if you'd seen the girl, and I'm sure she knew it too. I think that's why she looked at you like she did before she died."

He shook his head. "I'm not asking for absolution. I don't deserve forgiveness for this."

"Oh, Jake." Now she *was* crying. Damn him and his overdeveloped sense of responsibility. It wasn't his fault, but there was nothing she could say to convince him differently. He needed to see someone who counseled professionally, and he'd need to see them for a long time before he came to terms with this.

He held her tightly and she clung to him. And though her heart was breaking, the past few minutes had made a couple of things clear to her. Jake trusted her. If he didn't, he never would have talked about this no matter how concerned he was about what he did while in the throes of dreams. Not when this conversation had required him to lay his soul bare.

The other realization wasn't a comfortable one. She'd been lying to herself. Over and over, she'd been forcing herself to believe that what she felt for her recep was simply sexual attraction and friendship, but it was more. So much more. Earlier that day she'd been afraid, sure that if they became lovers she'd lose the closeness they currently shared, but her awareness changed everything. Now she knew she had to take the risk, had to experience it all.

She was in love with Jake and probably had been for years.

If he hurt, she hurt; and there was nothing she could do to ease the pain he felt right now. There were no words she could say, no action that would lift this from him. So instead she pressed her lips to his chin. He froze and she kissed him again and again, moving up his jawline.

"Cai?" He shifted so he was looking down into her eyes. She heard the question in her name. It didn't require any thought; she'd made her decision. Her answer was simple.

"Yes, Jake."

She saw his eyes flare, and then he took her mouth.

Chapter Sixteen

Jake forced himself to slow down, to stop being so greedy. Just because he was hotter than a sun about to go supernova didn't mean he had to give Cai a *wham, bam* experience. She meant more to him than that. For her, he dug deep and found control.

He lightened the pressure, sipping from her mouth rather than devouring it. She returned his kisses, but there was a hesitancy that made him pull away. He studied her face, trying to read what bothered her. There was no uncertainty in her eyes, and that left him puzzled. "Are you sure, sweetheart?"

"Yes."

He continued to hold back. Then it occurred to him what might be troubling her. "This has nothing to do with forgetting the nightmares or because you're handy. This is about us. I've wanted you since you walked up in Hell."

Her smile was amused. "I know you're not using me. So, now that we have that clear, are you going to keep talking or are you going to kiss me some more?"

"I plan to do a hell of a lot more than kiss you," he said

thickly, lowering his head. But again he stopped short. "The door. Can you access the seal and jam it to keep everyone else out?"

"Hmm, I think so." She closed her eyes and he felt her extend her nanoprobe. While he waited, he pushed the blanket off and ran his palm from her calf up her leg to the back of her thigh. "Jake, I can't concentrate," she complained.

"Good," he said, but withdrew his hand. No way did he want the wreckers—or anyone else, for that matter—bursting into the room while they were making love. If she couldn't block the door, it wasn't going to stop him, but they'd both be more at ease if they didn't have to worry about interruptions.

"Got it," Cai said.

"Good," Jake repeated, his voice rougher than it had been minutes earlier. But still he hesitated. Something about this felt bigger than anything he'd experienced. Almost as if it were a pivotal moment in his life. Then Cai wiggled, and he forgot about everything but tasting her.

He nipped at her lower lip, then ran the tip of his tongue over it to soothe the sting. With a soft gasp she opened her mouth, but he teased her upper lip instead. At least until she growled and rolled to straddle him. Jake laughed quietly, pleased with her impatience. It matched his, but he was going to take his time, even if it drove them both crazy.

She paused, staring down at him, and he forgot to breathe. The tropical moon was full, or near enough to fill the room with a soft glow. With the moonbeams dancing over her body she appeared more delicate than usual, almost ethereal, and he was afraid to move, afraid to shatter the moment.

Hesitantly, he put his hands on her thighs and ran his thumbs over the sensitive inner skin. A shiver went through her, and she shifted her hips, rubbing against his erection. He drew in a sharp breath and gritted his teeth as he fought for command.

I haven't told you how sexy your long legs are. He used their link because he didn't think his voice was working after that shimmy of hers. *I'm dying to have them wrapped around me.*

Cai blinked a couple of times, as if trying to clear her head. *You like my legs?*

Oh, yeah, sweetheart. More than like them. I had a hell of a time tonight keeping my eyes off the slit in your dress.

He kept moving up her body until his fingers were below her breasts. She stiffened and he found the strength, somehow, to wait till she relaxed again. Lazily he slipped his hands under her shirt and traced her ribs with the pads of his fingers. With a sigh she leaned over him, seeking another kiss.

Her hair cascaded wildly around them, and he smiled against her lips; he loved it free of the braid. Not a man to pass up an opportunity when it presented itself, he cupped the back of her head, letting his fingers tangle in her dark tresses.

Soft. Her hair was so soft and smooth. He broke the kiss, turning his head so he could nuzzle her neck and breathe in her spicy scent. Holding her tighter, he groaned as her breasts pressed into him. He stopped himself for a moment, having to savor the feel of her, then turned them so he was on top again.

Propping himself on his elbows, he gazed down at Cai. Moonlight bathed her features, and he was so dazzled by the way she looked that all he could do was stare.

"Beautiful," he murmured.

She shook her head.

"Yes," he insisted. *Beautiful.*

If he couldn't convince her with words, he'd have to show her. This kiss had less control, but he couldn't pull it back. Not this time. Cai did something to him, left him with an inexplicable ache that undermined all his plans. He allowed his desire free rein, explored her mouth thoroughly and let her explore him.

She brought one knee up, her thigh against his hip, and he couldn't keep from grinding against her. They both groaned. That one movement nearly undid him, and he eased to the side before he forgot about taking things slowly. But damn, she wasn't helping him. Her hands were on him, teasing him, sweeping over his shoulders. Headed downward. He withstood the grazing of his bare chest, his belly, but when her fingers slid beneath the waistband of his shorts, he had to grab her hands.

"Jake." Her protest was breathless.

Sweetheart, I'm set on hair-trigger right now. He pressed a kiss onto one palm, then the other, before pinning her wrists beside her head. If she touched him again, his control would be in shreds. And it was already pretty damn tattered.

He moved faster. Had to. No way could he continue this leisurely pace. With shaking hands he skimmed down her arms, over her torso, brushing the sides of her breasts on the way. When he reached the hem of her shirt, he touched the warm skin of her stomach. She shifted to her knees and he tugged the tee off.

Moonlight gilded her body. Beautiful. But he didn't say it this time; Jake let his eyes talk—and his touch.

They knelt on the bed, only inches apart, but he didn't close the gap between them. Instead he trailed a fingertip across the underside of one breast. She watched him for a moment, then raised her deep brown eyes to his. Her gaze hit him with the impact of a rifle butt to his gut.

He froze, denying the needs of his body, and tried to figure out what it was that struck him so hard. A short growl escaped her, and she took his hands, raising them so he cupped her. He remained still, relishing the sweet weight.

"Jake. For heaven's sake. Move!"

"Yes, ma'am." He grinned at her demand and put all introspection behind him. Later. He'd think later. Now he had Cai in his arms, right where he wanted her. He moved.

His touch remained light, worshipful. The contrast between her pale skin and his tanned, calloused hands captivated him. She pressed herself more firmly against his palms, but he continued with his adoration. Her snarl made him lift his gaze.

"Okay, cowboy, that's it. You've had your chance." She pushed his shoulders. "I've been patient." Cai leaned forward, plastering her body against his. "I've kept my hands off you." She rubbed against him. "But all bets are off now."

"Cai—" Her name was the only thing he got out before her mouth covered his and demanded total compliance. He was used to being the one in charge during sex, but for her he acquiesced.

Everything was different with Cai. Everything. But before he could get beyond that realization, her hand slipped under his shorts and kneaded one cheek. His groan was torn from his soul. As if that were the signal she was waiting for, Cai trailed her lips to his throat, teased his pulse point with her tongue, and then moved to his chest. He forced himself to remain motionless, to let her have the reins; but it wasn't easy, and his hands bunched into fists at his sides as he struggled with the need to take the lead.

He lasted until she started running her fingers up and down his shaft; then Jake shot a hand out and stopped her. Although she could no longer stroke him, she squeezed rhythmically. *Keep it up,* he warned, *and I'll be finished in thirty seconds. Maybe less.*

She froze and raised her head. Jake sucked in a sharp breath. Her dark eyes were nearly black with arousal, her lips red and slightly swollen. His control was gone and he knew it.

I wanted to go slow.

Another time, she told him, smiling as he stripped her out of her shorts and panties. Once he had her naked, he shucked his own shorts and bore her onto the bed. Moving between her thighs, he covered her with his body. Eyes locked with hers, he rubbed against her experimentally. She gasped, and he too sucked in a sharp breath at the intimate contact.

Perfect. She fit against him so damn perfectly.

Jake wanted it all. Now. He couldn't wait. He slid a hand down to make sure she was ready for him. She was wet, but not enough. *Shit.* Closing his eyes, he girded himself. Finesse wasn't an option. He needed her as hot as he was, as fast as possible.

He teased her with his fingers and thumb, brushing circles around the heart of her pleasure, and gauged her response. She needed more. He kissed her lips, her chin, lower. When he reached the valley between her breasts, he nuzzled her before turning to lavish attention on one nipple. She writhed against him, her hands fisted in his hair, and he shifted to the other side.

Her soft sounds, the way she arched into his hand, into his body, drove him closer to the edge, and he had to put some space between them so he could hang on.

I can't wait to get inside you, Cai, he said as he kissed his way down to her navel. *As deep as I can go. I'm in a sweat thinking about how damn good it'll be.* Her hands stayed in his hair, more loosely now, as his tongue rimmed her belly button. *I can almost feel you around my—* Jake paused, rephrased—*around me.* He continued on, nibbling her taut abdomen. *The slide of my body in yours.*

She whimpered and he smiled against her skin. He'd have to remember that she liked this. Maybe next time he'd talk dirtier.

He replaced his hand with his mouth.

Jake!

Since he wasn't sure whether or not she was protesting, he waited to see if she had more to add. When she opened her legs to allow him more space, he knew she was giving him the okay. He went back to work, using his tongue and lips to push her higher. She tasted sweet. Perfect. He drank deeper, wanting more.

As he focused his attention on the center of her pleasure, he had to hold her hips to keep her still. His whole body shook as he fought to retain control, but he concentrated on Cai and put his own needs out of mind. He didn't quit, not until he felt her on the verge of orgasm.

Reluctantly, he stopped. He ignored her moan of objection and covered her body with his. *Open your eyes.*

She did, blinking hard to focus. *Jake . . . need you.*

He suspected his grin was feral, but it didn't scare her. She reached for him, and he jerked at her touch. Her smile was fiercely satisfied; she liked having that kind of power over him. Jake put his hand over hers, helping guide himself, and began pushing into her body.

As wet as she was, he expected to slide home with one long stroke, but that wasn't what happened. She was tight. So damn tight. If he didn't need every ounce of strength to hold on, he would have cursed. The last thing he wanted was another delay.

Keeping his gaze on her, he watched intently as he edged forward. She stayed relaxed, trusting him, and it made him more determined to do this right. Sweat practically dripped off him as he struggled to move carefully. It seemed to take forever before he was fully sheathed, but his caution had been rewarded. She hadn't winced, not even once.

For a long moment he stayed stationary, letting her become accustomed to him; then he pulled out a fraction and thrust back in. When her hips rose to meet his second stroke, he began moving freely, confident now that she was okay.

He wasn't going to last long, though, and he wanted Cai with him. He shifted position, making sure he rubbed against her with every inward motion. She teetered on the edge; he could feel it. Though he couldn't manage words, he sent images, sensations along their pathway. It worked. On his next stroke, she arched urgently and went rigid.

As soon as she was coming, he dropped the restraint he'd been clinging to with both hands. He pushed into her hard and fast, looking for his own release. It arrived with an intensity that he'd never experienced.

At last it ended, and he collapsed on top of her, his arms unable to hold his weight. Tremors continued to shake his body long afterward, and they became stronger as her hands ran along his sides. If she was trying to calm him, she was failing miserably. He hadn't gone completely soft yet, and at her touch he twitched and pushed more deeply into her.

Shit. He couldn't be ready for more. Not this quickly.

Her fingers found some interesting places and his body proved him wrong. Jake lifted his head, kissing her long and slow. *I hope you know what you're doing.*

She tilted her pelvis, seating him more firmly, and brought her legs up. That was answer enough, since he'd told her earlier that he wanted her wrapped around him.

He broke the kiss, looking into her eyes. *Mine,* he thought, but he didn't send the word, afraid she wouldn't appreciate his possessiveness. Instead he began to move, claiming her again in the most elemental way possible.

Cai opened her eyelids a fraction. Bright sunshine filled the room, and she closed them. Turning on her side, she snuggled the blanket to her chin and let herself drift. She'd hardly gotten settled when she felt Jake. He spooned his body against hers and his arm went around her waist.

Neither of them had bothered to put on any clothes, and the feel of his nakedness perked her up. She cuddled into him, finding his embrace warmer and cozier than any blanket. Of course, there was that little zing as well, but that was what made it special. He brushed her hair off her neck and kissed her throat before resting his chin on her shoulder.

"Morning, sweetheart." His voice was husky with sleep.

"Hmm, morning." She brought her hand up, linking her fingers with his. "What time is it?"

"I'm not sure. Ten, maybe eleven."

She stiffened and he kissed her again. "No one's come?" Only when she felt his chest shake, did she realize how she'd phrased the question. Men. "You know what I meant, sex fiend."

"You weren't complaining last night."

"I'm not complaining now either." She rolled her hips against him and smiled with satisfaction as he pressed more firmly into her bottom. Thanks to his slips that first year they'd been connected, she'd known for a long time what he liked in bed. The hours spent making love last night had not only given her hands-on experience, but she'd also learned what she could do to him. Then there were their implants. It had been an incredibly intimate way to communicate what they wanted.

"No one's tried to get in. Don't worry about it yet, okay?" He sounded sober, serious, and it jarred her until she remembered what she'd been worried over before they'd started playing.

She decided to try to lighten the mood, since he'd probably done enough brooding for both of them. "Ten or eleven, you said? Wow. We're a pair of sloths today."

"Considering it was dawn when we finished the shower, we only got about five hours of sleep. Hardly slothlike behavior."

Mission accomplished, she thought when she heard the teasing note in his voice. She opened her eyes again and shifted so she could see him. The stubble was back, shadowing his face, but the man looked incredible. Cupping his cheek in her palm, Cai lifted her lips so she could kiss him. She liked this, the freedom to touch him at will and the casual way he touched her. Even the possessive gleam in his light blue eyes thrilled her.

The kiss started out sweet and deepened into an intense tenderness. Heat bubbled beneath the surface, but it remained restrained. Jake meant so much to her. So much. She slid her hand to the back of his neck and caressed his nape. His fingers flexed at her waist, but he didn't move, letting her set the pace. She began easing back, her lips clinging to his as she slowly broke away.

Things had turned serious again, and she didn't want that. Not this morning. "I'm starving," she said, and gave him a big grin. "Do we have some breakfast?"

For a moment she thought he wouldn't go along; then he said, "Never let it be said that I didn't take care of my woman."

This time being referred to as his woman didn't bother her. In fact, she liked it—liked the sense of belonging it brought. He tossed back the blanket, and she had a great view of his bare butt as he crossed the room to retrieve a tray. The view when he returned was even better. Cai fought the urge to squirm, but she couldn't stop herself from responding.

He placed the tray on the far end of the bed, then sat facing her. Taking in enough oxygen became a problem, but she didn't care. She'd die a happy woman if she could stare at a naked Jake Tucker as she went.

"Sweetheart, I thought you said you were hungry. For food."

There was laughter in his voice, and she yanked her gaze up. Yep, he was amused by her ogling. Damned if she was going to be the only one heated up, though. She let the blanket drop, exposing her breasts, and leaned toward the tray. Her self-consciousness had disappeared during their night together. There wasn't an inch of her body that he hadn't touched, hadn't kissed, and it would be silly to feel modest now. The food was far enough away that it gave her the perfect excuse to move out from under the covers and crawl across the bed. She just hoped her attempt at slinking looked sexy and not silly.

When she heard his soft choking, she knew she'd hit the target. She turned her head and looked at him from under her lashes. He was most definitely affected by her.

"Fresh fruit," she said, trying to sound like she had nothing else on her mind. "Yum."

She lay down on her tummy and reached for a piece of pineapple. Her body was diagonal on the bed, her shoulder brushing Jake's knee. Propped on her elbows, she took a bite. The slice dripped and she caught the drops with her hand. "Oops, I'm getting juice on the bed." She managed to say that with innocence, but his groan told her he'd understood.

She rolled on her back and held the fruit over her mouth. It was fun to tempt him. Her lips were moist with pineapple juice. She ate messily and watched Jake watch her take each bite. "Aren't you hungry?"

"I know what you're doing," he said, and reclined beside her, his weight on one elbow. His free hand rested below her right breast. "And I like it." He gave her a killer grin.

It was her turn to groan, when he bent over her and licked the sticky, sweet juice from her lips. She should have known better than to play with fire. Jake was the big leagues, and she was strictly an amateur. By the time he lifted his head, she was hanging on to him, trying to keep him from pulling away.

Her protest was met with a smug smile. "You said you were hungry, and I would never put my needs before yours."

When she opened her mouth to complain, he popped in a grape. Papaya came next, and he traced her lips with it, pulling the soft fruit away when she tried to take a bite. "I thought you were feeding me," she complained.

"I am. My way." As he bent to lick the juice from her lips again, she began to understand the game. And why he'd said earlier that he'd liked what she was doing. There was an edge of frustration, but the teasing also aroused her.

Finally he broke a piece off. "Open," he said And when she obeyed, he slipped it into her mouth, along with a couple of fingers. She ran her tongue around, tasting the sweetness. He withdrew his hand, and as she chewed she saw how dark his eyes had become.

The second chunk of papaya dripped over her chin and neck, but he happily put his all into cleaning her up, using his mouth, his tongue, and even his teeth to suck the juice from her skin. By the time he lifted his head, she felt his erection pressing firmly against her. Oh, yeah, this attraction definitely went two ways.

She took the remainder of the fruit and fed it to him. Since he continued to lean over her, each bite sprayed more drops of moisture onto her body, this time on her chest. He swallowed and gave her a wicked smile, then bent down and put his mouth on her breasts. And though she hadn't felt anything fall on her nipples, Jake spent an inordinate amount of time ensuring both were completely juice-free.

Cai shifted impatiently as she waited to see what he'd choose next from the tray. A wedge of orange. He made no attempt to even bring it near her mouth. Instead he squeezed it over each breast, then trailed it over her skin to her navel and wrung out the remaining liquid. Tossing the pulpy remains back on the plate, he brought his fingers to her lips for her to clean. She held his hand with both of hers, licking her way down, then running her tongue over his palm until she felt him rubbing against her hip. She smiled as he pulled away.

Her satisfaction didn't last long. It was Jake's turn to drive her crazy, and he did it so well. He started with the orange juice pooled in her belly button and worked his way north. Her nipples were still peaked from his earlier attention, but he ignored them, licking all around instead. She shifted, trying to encourage him that direction, but he didn't take the hint.

"My turn," Cai said, pushing him onto his back. That he went so easily told her he was willing to let her play too. She mimicked what he'd done almost exactly, but added her own twists based on what she knew he liked. For a moment she lost track of what she was doing. She loved the hardness of his body so much that she could happily touch and kiss him indefinitely. But she had a goal. Something she wanted to try.

Waiting till she had one last chunk of juicy pineapple, she knelt between his legs and ran it slowly up the length of his shaft. When she saw him jerk, she felt it in the pit of her stomach. With one sticky hand, she held his sex away from his belly and ran the fruit around the crown. By the time she popped the pineapple in her mouth, she'd managed to drench him. Cai raised her head then and smiled at Jake. His eyes were hot, his body rigid, and his hands were fisted in the blanket.

She swallowed and licked her lips.

He jerked in her grasp and she knew she'd teased him long enough. Putting her mouth at the base of his shaft, she lazily ran her tongue over him. Despite his groans and occasional pleas, she didn't hurry as she laved to its tip. His hips came off the bed, but she disregarded his wordless request and tickled just below the head.

She'd never heard a noise like that from Jake before, and she looked up to make sure he was okay. The expression on his face made her grin and go back to what she was doing. After all, he'd been thorough in his efforts to clean her; how could she do less for him?

Her elbow gave his thigh a nudge, and he widened his legs for her. Cai liked a man who could take orders. When she reached the point she'd started from, she brought her other hand up to cup him and licked lower. She didn't quit until she heard him begin cursing under his breath; then she finally moved to take him in her mouth. He began to thrust, but quickly stopped himself. No wonder she'd fallen in love with him. How many men would be considerate enough to go still at this point?

It wasn't long before she knew he was close to release. She was willing to take him all the way, but he told her to stop. Reluctantly, she did. "Are you sure?"

Hell, no, but stop anyway.

He had the tray safely on the floor and her on her back in seconds. Even though he was obviously at the end of his tether, he took the time to kiss her long and deep. She felt him slide two fingers inside her but she was more than ready.

"Are you too sore for me?" he asked as he pulled back.

"No." And she felt herself fall a little deeper in love.

Good.

He began to enter her, but he moved at glacier speed. Since he had her hips pinned to the bed, she couldn't hurry him along. *Jake, you're dawdling.*

You promised me I could go slow later, remember?

She did, but obviously she'd been out of her mind. He laughed when she passed the thought along to him, but he didn't go any faster. It was her turn to fist her hands in the sheets as she fought for control.

I want to have sloth sex, he told her.

Cai's eyes widened. *What?* He moved the smallest increment farther and she gritted her teeth.

You said we were a pair of sloths, so let's mate like they do. It pleased her greatly to realize he wasn't calm either. But then she had taken him to the brink just moments before.

This is how they do it?

Jake slid a little farther into her and said, *I don't know, but the sloth is the slowest land mammal on earth. If it takes them all day to go up and down a tree, it must take them a long, long time to mate.* He grinned at her quiet moan.

She suspected this was payback for teasing him as she had. Probably she deserved it, but right now it was hard to be fair. She tried to wriggle, but he tightened his hold.

By the time he was completely inside her, they were

both covered in sweat, and Jake wasn't smiling any longer. It was tough to enjoy that, though, when she was about ready to scream. He wasn't moving. Cai released the sheet to grip his butt, but he didn't let her rush him.

He withdrew, prolonging it as much as he could, then eased back in with excruciating deliberation. She let him go like this a few more times; then she fought back by tightening her inner muscles around him. His groan sounded heartfelt.

It took only maybe a half dozen clasps like that before he lost his self-command. His pace went from sloth-like to furious in a single thrust. As hot as he'd had her before she'd pushed him, it didn't take her long to hit her peak. Cai pressed her mouth to his shoulder, trying to muffle the noises she made as she came. If the room wasn't soundproof, she didn't want the mercenaries to hear her.

Jake showed no such concern as he followed.

It was quite a bit later when he asked, "Damn, Cai, why do you like me out of control?" By then he'd shifted to her side and was lightly stroking her back.

"Probably the same reason you like me out of control."

He grunted, but didn't have a comeback. With a tiny smile she reached for him, but he took her hand and moved it to his chest. "Sweetheart, try to remember that I'm five years older than you. I need recovery time."

"I thought you Special Forces guys had stamina," she teased, and settled against him. That surprised a laugh out of Jake, and she grinned. He didn't do that often enough.

"Stamina? Do you want me to count how many times we—"

She kissed him, cutting him off midsentence, then snuggled into his side again. Their time of blissfully ignoring the mission and the threat Marchand Elliot posed was quickly coming to a close; Cai could feel it. Part of her was saddened to lose it, but she'd known from the start that it was a sliver out of time.

Once they were back in the real world, Jake wouldn't be making jokes about their age difference. He'd pull away then, for sure. He'd find some excuse—like she was too young to know what she wanted. Too young to commit herself to one man. Too young for him.

But that wasn't true. She'd always been older than her years. She'd related better to adults than other kids, and she'd been surrounded by classmates nine years her senior. And after her parents vanished, she'd lost her remaining immaturity. By the time she'd been linked with her recep, she'd been an adult in every way but chronological.

Still, she knew that argument wouldn't sway him. He'd say he was protecting her, watching out for her best interests. No, she wouldn't be able to keep him as a lover; she knew that. But she'd fight for their friendship. She wouldn't lose that no matter what.

Chapter Seventeen

Elliot's office seemed different in the light of day, less welcoming somehow. Window screens blocked the bright tropical sun and helped keep the heat out, but they dimmed the room, giving it an almost sinister feel. Of course, that might be her imagination working overtime. Waiting for the boss to make an appearance was starting to wear on Cai's nerves.

They'd garnered a full dozen wreckers as an escort this time, and more had been waiting at the foot of the stairs. The extra manpower negated Cai's relief that Jake was with her. She'd originally assumed his presence meant that she wouldn't have to worry about Elliot coercing her into sex, but now she wondered. If he wanted to ensure her cooperation, all he had to do was force her to watch them hurt Jake. She wouldn't hold out long.

As they'd discussed last night, maybe it was a ploy on Elliot's part. Maybe he wanted her thinking these things. Maybe he'd deliberately put her on edge. Maybe.

But she'd seen him at dinner, how he'd subtly taunted Tony, and she knew Elliot had taken a perverse satisfaction in dividing anchor and recep. He would undoubtedly enjoy coming between her and Jake even more. After all, they weren't his creation; they were UCE officers. That must add to the appeal.

It didn't matter how much more beautiful Nicole was than her; this wasn't about appearance. It was about power. Cai had finally worked that one out, although her self-image had blocked her from seeing the truth at first.

She was tense, but didn't fidget in her seat. And she kept herself from transmitting any of her emotions to her recep. He was wound tighter than she was, and the last thing she wanted was add to his concerns. She'd picked up one of his worries. He hadn't meant to send it, she knew that, but he may as well have spoken aloud, she'd gotten it so clearly.

Jake not only thought Elliot might try to make her sleep with him, but he feared that the man wanted him to watch. She hadn't thought of that, but it would be the ultimate power trip. To have the mercenaries hold Jake so he couldn't do anything while she sacrificed herself. It would demonstrate who was in charge. And the snake had to know it would eat at Jake. The feeling of helplessness would be overwhelming.

Hell, it was nearly overwhelming right now.

Cai counted eighteen wreckers. Even with their link, even with her access to all those computers, she and Jake couldn't hope to defeat so many. Unless . . . Well, that idea was far-fetched.

As apprehensive as she was about her own predicament, it was Jake she was truly anxious about. He knew she didn't want Elliot to touch her, that she hated the man. And she knew how protective he was of her. Her heart began to pound whenever she considered what Jake might do. She couldn't let him die for her. No matter what action she had to take.

The door opened and Cai stiffened. She knew it was Elliot; she could feel it by the way the hair on her nape stood on end. He made her skin crawl, plain and simple. She couldn't hear him cross the floor, but she knew where he was by the intensity of the knot between her shoulders.

He walked behind his desk with a casual disregard for their presence and took his chair. For a long moment he silently stared at her. It was uncomfortable looking into those cold eyes of his. Reptile eyes. Predator eyes.

Something was up. He always had a smugness, but it seemed more pronounced than usual this afternoon. Cai's stomach turned over. She had a bad feeling. Her toes curled in her boots, the only outward sign of stress she allowed herself.

"How nice of you to join me on such short notice," Elliot said smoothly.

She inclined her head graciously; at least, she hoped that was how it looked. The summons had been a surprise, earlier than he'd said last night, no doubt about that. She and Jake were only half-dressed when the wreckers had tried to open the door. If they hadn't showered together and become distracted, they might have been clothed and had the seal unjammed, but as it stood, they'd been left scrambling.

Even now, she felt a bit unsettled, but, man, she was glad they'd had time to wash. The idea of facing Elliot sticky with fruit juice and Jake's scent on her made her sweat. He'd use it against them somehow, she knew.

"I see I caught you at an inconvenient time."

How could he know that? The man didn't read minds. Did he?

He must have sensed her confusion. "Your hair."

Her hand went to her braid. Wet. *Crap.* She glanced at Jake. His hair was clearly damp, too. Of course, that didn't mean they'd showered together, just closely in time, but a glance at Elliot's face told her he knew. One of the wreckers had undoubtedly reported to him that her recep had been fastening his clothes and stalled so she could finish dressing.

Breathe, sweetheart. Remember, most of what he knows about Quandems comes from his own pair. Even if he's had Nicole access the UCE data, he'll put more weight on his own personal observations.

Right. With that, and the fact they'd been posing as lovers since inserting on Malé, the man would have made some assumptions about her and Jake even if they'd never taken such an intimate step last night. It was her own knowledge that was making her react, the newness of what they had.

"It's so easy to fall into pirate time," Cai offered with a weak smile, and she felt Jake's amusement at her explanation.

"Of course, my dear," Elliot said.

There was a slyness to the way he looked at her that had her fingers closing over the arms of her chair. His stare was piercing, assessing. It made her more uncomfortable, and she suspected that was his aim. She knew for sure now that he was up to something new, but couldn't guess from which direction it was coming.

When it became obvious that she wasn't going to reply, Elliot continued, "There's always been one thing that's interested me most about the Quandem Project."

"What's that?" She had to fight to get the words out.

"How two strangers who share similar brain-wave patterns can be connected via a set of neural implants and rapidly forge such trust between them. Take Nicole and her receptor. De Luca was part of my security force and the best choice for my Quandem. Nicole was merely a drone in one of my offices, but she was the most compatible. Yet they became close in almost no time."

Cai's body tensed. Elliot had started playing, but she didn't know the rules of the game yet. She had no intention of commenting on the closeness she shared with Jake, so she gave the man a noncommittal smile and nodded.

His lips curved in amusement, but there was a sneer hidden in the expression. For the first time since he'd entered, their host looked at Jake. He seemed to be scrutinizing her recep, and her eyes narrowed. She wouldn't let him hurt Jake. No way, no how. Her muscles bunched, and she braced herself for whatever he tossed at her partner.

Instead, Elliot turned to her. "Tell me, dear Cai, how long did it take you to trust your receptor once you were linked? Or have you yet to fully trust him?"

"Of course I trust him," she said stiffly.

Their captor nodded knowingly, as if he'd received the answer he'd been expecting. "Did you trust him from the start?"

Her fingers flexed on the chair arms again, but she kept herself from grasping them tightly. Cautiously she said, "Nearly the beginning."

"And does he trust you?"

Uh-oh. Shaky ground, but she wouldn't let Elliot pull a divide-and-conquer on them. "More than anyone else in the world."

She hoped the inflection she used hid the fact that she'd told the complete truth. Jake did trust her more than anyone else—after all, he had told her about the nightmares—but she didn't think he had complete faith in her.

Elliot's smile was slow, smooth. Pleased. Somehow, when she wasn't looking, she'd walked right into his snare. And even knowing she'd fallen for something, Cai couldn't identify what it was. *Jake, do you have an idea where the attack is going to come from?*

No, but watch out. He's enjoying this too much.

Like she needed him to tell her that. The man glanced between them, and she wondered if he had an inkling that she and her recep were talking. He might. Nicole had lied to her boss about some things, but she wouldn't be able to conceal everything. She wouldn't try. Then there was Tony, who had been on the security team from the very beginning. Was he loyal to Elliot above all?

"Trust is such a fragile thing," their host said with an almost philosophical air. "So easy to break. So difficult to mend. I've heard it said that the greater the faith, the harder it is to heal a breach. What do you think?"

She bit her bottom lip. Although she stopped the nervous gesture almost immediately, she knew it was too late. It had been noted and the knowledge filed for future reference. "I think it depends on the people involved and what kind of breach," Cai said, still being careful.

"How true. Perhaps we should leave the abstract behind and try a concrete example. I'd like to hear your thoughts on this." Their host unfurled his system screen. "Let's see, what might be a good discussion point?"

He pretended to be perusing the data, but she knew that was a bunch of crap. The creep knew exactly what he wanted to spring on her. She wasn't going to react, no matter what he hit her with. Besides, what could he know that she didn't? Jake had shared a lot with her, particularly over the past few days. She doubted there was anything left that Elliot could throw at her.

"Now this is interesting. A General Clinton Yardley at the request of one Captain Jacob Tucker ran a background search for information about the parents of Captain Cai Randolph. Special emphasis was placed on verifying your actions over the past six years, my dear."

Cai couldn't breathe. She couldn't move. She couldn't do anything but stare at Elliot. Jake was talking to her over their link, but she couldn't make out the words. There was nothing but numbness filling every cell in her body, particularly her brain.

"It's quite interesting," the man continued, his voice the only sound she heard. "Nicole wouldn't have discovered who your parents were if your receptor hadn't asked his superior officer to conduct the inquiry. I suppose I owe him a thank-you for pointing us this direction, since I never would have recognized you. You've changed quite drastically from the unattractive and gangly teenager I recall meeting."

She finally managed to inhale some badly needed oxygen, but it didn't help the light-headedness. Jake had investigated what she'd told him about her parents? He thought she'd been lying? Didn't he know her at all? Didn't he realize how much her mom and dad meant to her? He thought she'd made up the story about them to go on this op? She couldn't get past the fact that he trusted her so little, that he'd thought her one small omission made her so conniving that she'd use her own missing parents to maneuver herself onto the assignment.

"I'll have to arrange a reunion. I'm certain your parents would enjoy seeing you as much as you would like to see them."

Her nod was jerky, abrupt. She inhaled again, her breathing shaky, almost a wheeze. Reluctantly, her brain was starting to come back to life, but she wasn't ready to leave the blessed detachment she felt. Not yet.

"You have to appreciate the irony," Elliot continued as if she were conversing with him. "The one person in the world you thought you could rely on, and his actions are what cost you the chance to take your parents and return home."

Jake's thoughts were more urgent, but they came through as an annoying buzz, not words. She didn't spare him a glance. Looking at him would rip the numbness from her mind.

"You . . ." The word came out strangled, so Cai cleared her throat and tried again. "You had to know I was looking for them. Surely you were getting accounts of my search attempts."

"Indeed. However, you were referred to simply as 'the

Randolphs' daughter.' My security force knows I have no interest in unnecessary details. Between your forgettable appearance and the fact that I hadn't heard your name in years, who you are would have escaped my attention entirely."

"If not for Jake."

"Correct." Elliot smiled, clearly pleased, but Cai couldn't care about that. Not with the ramifications starting to seep in.

"I'm certain that once you're reunited with your family, your parents will be inspired to work much more diligently on their project. They haven't made the amount of progress I'd expected by now."

She'd known from the start that he would use her against her folks if he discovered who she was. Now one of her biggest fears had come to pass. Family reunion? What a bunch of hooey. He was going to parade her in front of her mom and dad and make veiled threats about her well-being. And her folks would cave, would stop stalling on the nanites, in order to protect her. There wasn't a doubt in her mind.

Jake. The man she was in love with. The man she'd trusted with everything she was, everything she had. The man she'd believed was her friend, if nothing else.

But she knew better now.

He'd betrayed her.

And that betrayal had endangered her mom and dad.

Memory flooded her as her brain started to thaw, and she couldn't prevent another gasp from escaping. She'd told him someone had been in the files about her family; she'd told him, and he could have revealed the truth right then and put her mind at ease. Instead he'd lied to her. He'd deliberately fostered the idea that it was the UCE traitors creeping around the system. Her recep, the man who'd been so outraged to discover her lie of omission, had done her one better.

Pain struck then, deeper, fiercer than anything she'd

known before. She clasped the chair with all her strength, her grip the only thing keeping her from shattering into a million pieces the same way her heart was breaking.

Slowly, almost blind with agony, she turned her head to look at Jake. *How could you? How could you betray me?*

Jake felt sick. God, the look in Cai's eyes about slayed him. He'd tried to explain, tried to tell her why he'd run the search, but she hadn't heard him. She wasn't blocking him, he knew that, but it was as if she weren't receiving what he sent.

Cai, sweetheart, let—

Were you trying to even the score? Is that why you misled me in the restaurant?

He'd forgotten about that. *Shit.* He'd known at the time that this would come back to haunt him, but he hadn't expected the repercussions to be so severe. And he hadn't thought his well-intentioned lie would hurt Cai so deeply. *No, of course not. All I wanted to do was keep you from wandering off on me again. It wasn't malicious.*

The words didn't register; that was obvious. How could he get through to her? She stared at him with such disillusionment, such anguish, that he wanted to hold her and comfort her, soothe her, although he was the one who'd hurt her. Maybe *because* he'd been the one to hurt her. Her expression broke his heart.

And when she turned away from him, terror filled his soul. What if she couldn't get past this? He'd never been so scared in his life. Not when he'd waited for his father to beat him, not when he'd made his escape from the Sartonian stronghold, not during his first firefight, and not even when he'd walked out of that restaurant kitchen and found her gone. He couldn't lose Cai. It would kill something inside him.

Maybe it was panic that drove the knowledge home with enough force to make him freeze. But as it settled, as he let it fill him, he realized it explained a lot of things. He was a fool not to know it sooner.

He loved her.

God help him, he loved her and she couldn't look at him. *Cai!*

She glanced back, the first indication she'd heard anything he'd sent, but the torment remained in her gaze. He almost wished she'd become angry, that she'd glare at him and tell him to go to hell. At least that would be something he could fight, something he could meet head-on. But this kind of pain was outside his realm of experience. All he knew was he felt it almost as deeply as she did, and it left him reeling.

Damn it, Yardley was supposed to bury that freaking request so deeply that no one, especially Cai, would ever find out about it. But it must not have been hidden well enough if Nicole had stumbled across the info. And if she could discover it, heaven knew his own anchor would have found it—if she'd investigated, if he hadn't deliberately led her to jump to the wrong conclusions. Jake wished now that she had uncovered it that morning instead of hearing it from Elliot. The fact that he'd been the one to drop the bomb added to the impact.

Cai, please, listen to me.

Why? So you can lie some more?

There still wasn't any heat, more of a weary resignation in her words, and it felt as if Jake's heart were being ripped out of his chest.

No lies, I swear.

She shook her head. *It comes down to trust, doesn't it? You couldn't believe I told you the truth about my mom and dad. That's bad enough, but your lack of faith, your need to verify my story, has jeopardized my parents. That's what I can't forget.*

And what she might not forgive.

It had nothing to do with trust, damn it.

Oh, right. I'm supposed to believe that? Her eyes widened

and she leaned toward him. *You didn't tell Yardley I thought my parents were on the Raft Cities, did you?*

I didn't. I'd never do that to you.

Why should I believe that? You've sold me out before. Anger started to creep into her words, and Jake wasn't sure why he'd thought that would be easier to hear than the pain. It skewered him every bit as sharply, but in a different way.

He swallowed hard. *The only reason I told the general about your probe going down was because it was vital to his investigation and might help lead to the traitors. I've told you this already.*

So you lied to Yardley about the reason for the request?

No, I didn't. He never asked why I wanted the info, so I didn't tell him anything, okay?

Cai tossed her braid over her shoulder and shifted in her seat. *He didn't ask? I find that hard to accept.*

Now he was starting to get mad too. She wouldn't listen to him, wouldn't give him a chance to explain. Since she'd never been an unreasonable person, it had to be because of the way this was dropped on her. If Elliot hadn't—*Damn.* Jake tore his attention from Cai and found the man observing them, unmistakable delight written on his face. He might not know what they were saying, but he knew they were arguing privately.

Our warden is watching, he reminded her.

Do you think I care? Incredulity flew across their pathway.

You should. You know he'll use whatever he can against us. Do you really want to give him more ammo?

No, of course not.

Then put the emotions aside and do your job. We have an op to complete, remember? He almost winced at how that came out. They did need to put aside their personal problems till they were off the Raft Cities, but he didn't have to slide into his role as operation commander and give her an order. Since he was sure the only reason Cai had forgotten herself, and her training, was because of how deep the blow was, he could have gently reminded her of the inappropriateness of the timing.

Oh, yeah, we can't forget the mission. Nothing is more important than finding Maguire and Armstrong, right? Certainly not the safety of my mom and dad.

Her sarcasm spiked his temper, but he understood she was scared. *I'll do whatever I can to protect your parents; you have my word on it.*

You can't give me any guarantees.

No, I can't, but I will do everything in my power to help get them out of here. That's the best I can do.

I know. And with that, she faced Elliot again.

For a moment Jake continued to stare at her. He wasn't certain if she was merely agreeing with him to stop the discussion or if she honestly had at least some faith in him. With a grimace, he followed his own directive and put the personal stuff aside. They couldn't afford to be distracted now.

"Done arguing?" Elliot asked.

Jake didn't react. He hated keeping quiet and putting the whole burden on his anchor's shoulders, but Elliot ignored him whenever he could and was abrupt the rest of the time.

"Yes, I believe we are," Cai replied easily.

Jake tensed, but didn't say anything. This wasn't the way he'd handle the situation or the man, but he made it a policy not to interfere with how any member of his team did their job. Still . . . since this was Cai, it was tempting to make an exception. Not because he didn't think she could do it, but because he didn't want to risk her.

"Shall we continue our discussion on trust then?"

Damn. Elliot wasn't done with the game yet. Apparently he had more up his sleeve than what he'd shown so far. Jake didn't think there was anything left for him to lob at Cai. He'd shared his other secrets with her already, but that didn't mean there wasn't something he'd forgotten to divulge.

"What's left to say on the topic?" Cai asked. Jake had to admire her calmness. She was so smooth right now that Elliot would have no idea how successful his attack was if she hadn't been so visibly devastated at first. Unfortunately, there was no going back in time, no erasing those moments, and everyone in this room knew he'd scored a direct hit.

The man retracted his system screen and leaned back in his chair. "Do you trust your receptor?"

"I've answered that already."

Jake fought the need to intercede when he heard the thread of impatience in Cai's voice. Fortunately Elliot missed it. If he hadn't, she'd be facing the consequences for disrespecting him. *Damn it.* What the hell was she thinking?

"I'm aware of that. However, I'm curious whether your perspective has changed."

"No, it hasn't."

Elliot lifted one eyebrow, clearly amused. "No? You continue to trust this man after what he did?"

"I'd trust Jake with my life."

Emphatic. It should have pleased him, but it didn't. He knew Cai, and she was splitting hairs. There was a hell of a difference between trusting him to keep her physically safe and trusting him emotionally. And he needed it all from her.

Frustrated, Jake fought to lock down his feelings. His lapses in professionalism had been alarmingly frequent on this op and he had to do better. He'd like to blame Cai— he'd never had a problem on an assignment before—but it wasn't her fault. It was his. With his experience, he should be able to ignore the distractions and do his job. He couldn't protect anyone if he didn't keep his cool, and it was crunch time. He felt it in his gut.

As he half listened to Cai and Elliot debate, he ran

through his priorities and came up with strategies to increase the odds of meeting them. It had been easy to forget the actual mission with his anchor so focused on her parents. But it didn't matter if it was a consequence of the link or of their close relationship; either way, he needed to get himself organized.

One of the first things on the list was to acquire weapons. He felt naked without a blade, and he wanted at least a couple of neuron fryers. Next came contacting his men again—and for longer than a couple of minutes. He needed to know if they'd found anything on Maguire's whereabouts before he enlisted their help.

It was time to escape from Elliot's fortress.

He had a bad feeling, though, that Cai wouldn't leave without her parents. And when he considered what had happened in this office today, Jake wasn't certain he could talk her into doing things his way. He couldn't even be sure that she'd obey a direct order. If she believed that leaving would endanger her mom and dad, she'd stay, insubordination be damned.

Jake tuned back in to the conversation as he heard Elliot say, "Let's put our cards on the table, shall we?"

What the hell had he missed?

"Yes, why don't we."

The muscles in his jaw went taut. There was a hint of challenge in her voice, and he wanted to tell her to back off. He didn't, though. If he'd been the one talking, he'd have done the same thing. Because he wanted to keep her safe his first reaction was to cocoon her, and Jake knew he couldn't do that. Not if he wanted to keep Cai in his life as more than just his anchor.

"As I mentioned last night at dinner, I know why you're on the Raft Cities. I know you want Captain Maguire and Commander Armstrong."

Cai raised her eyebrows, her expression irritated, but

she didn't respond verbally. She was pushing Elliot, no doubt about it, and Jake had to clench his hands tightly to stay out of it when he saw Elliot's eyes go hard.

"Captain Tucker."

Jake tensed at the use of his rank. That wasn't a good sign. Not when the man hadn't addressed him as such before this. "Yes?"

"You'll be coming up for promotion shortly—less than three years now, correct?"

He said nothing. It sounded like Nicole had found his personnel file, and that made him warier.

"I wonder how you'll fare if you fail to bring the supreme military commander's son home?"

Jake shrugged. He didn't think he'd be judged by one op alone, but there was no doubt that his failure here would be a big black mark on his record. Bracing himself, he waited for Elliot to mention the last disaster of a mission. It was a sore spot and would be good for a poke or two. That wasn't the tack their captor took, however.

"Losing a promotion would be a setback to your career, one from which you might not recover. However, I can help you. I can ensure that your assignment reaches a favorable conclusion."

"Oh, really. How?" His sarcasm was deliberate.

Elliot's frown was immediate, but his face quickly smoothed out. "I can deliver these two people directly into your hands."

"You have them?" Jake asked, even though he knew better.

"No, but the second-in-command to the pirate lord who's been assisting them is an ambitious man. He and a crew of mutineers would be more than happy to hand the pair over in exchange for aid from a squad of my wreckers in a fight against their captain."

Jake suspected that if the rebellion weren't already afoot, Elliot would foment it himself. "Why would you do this?" he asked. "I know you don't give a damn about my career."

The man leaned forward, hands folded atop the desk. "If you fail, team after team will be sent here until someone prevails. I want the UCE off the Raft Cities, permanently."

He was sure Elliot wanted the UCE military to stay away from here, but he knew there was a hell of a lot more to it than that. Elliot could kill the fugitives and arrange for their bodies to be returned to the Central UCE; it would achieve the same results and be less complicated. Less risky. This whole scheme, starting with him and Cai being grabbed off Malé, was too elaborate. There was more here, more than he was seeing, more than the bastard was saying, but Jake couldn't begin to guess the real game.

"And to achieve this, you'll hand over Maguire and Armstrong, as well as offer protection until we're safely out of here?"

"Yes." The smile was so smarmy that Jake tensed further. "There's one thing I want in exchange, however."

Here it came. "What's that?"

"You'll leave the Raft Cities without Cai."

It took one hell of a lot of control to keep the rage he felt off his face. "You can't expect me to agree to that."

"Ah, but I do. It's a fair and equitable trade." Elliot lightly tapped his index fingers together. "You'll have what you need to ensure your promotion and safe passage off the Raft Cities for you and your men. I'll have what I want, a second anchor to further my aims. And dear Cai will have what she wants, to be reunited with her parents. Everyone wins."

"I'll never leave her," Jake said adamantly.

"Consider the alternative. You'll have to escape my estate—not an easy task with the barrier that surrounds the grounds, and with my security team. Even if you enlist the assistance of your men, they'll have to face my guards. Do you want your team to do battle with a large group of wreckers? Especially so quickly after your previous encounter. How many did you lose last time?"

Jake ground his teeth at the reference, but he refused to show a reaction.

When no response was forthcoming, Elliot continued. "Your men would lose. Six more dead. Maybe seven, since I don't need you. Your anchor can transmit information through a comm unit to a wrecker almost as easily as she does to you through the probes. And despite your team's sacrifice, Cai would remain my guest. You see, the outcome is the same for me whichever choice you make. The only part that will cause extra work is arranging to return Maguire and Armstrong to the UCE without you. So what will it be, Captain? Do you send your teammates to their deaths, or do you accept my offer?"

Images flashed through his mind of his men falling, but he pushed the memories aside. Instead, he considered the situation from a tactical perspective.

Elliot was right about one thing; seven men attacking his wreckers in a frontal assault wouldn't free Cai, but Jake wasn't leaving her behind. No freaking way.

Special Forces teams were trained for covert ops. They didn't come in the front gate while the enemy was waiting; they slipped in the back and accomplished their mission before anyone knew they were there. He had to devise a strategy that capitalized on his team's strengths and exploited the weaknesses in their captor's security.

For damn sure he needed the element of surprise. Maybe they'd guess he was coming, but no one would know when. Getting out of here and playing on his terms was smarter than obstinately arguing when he couldn't win.

Still, even knowing he wasn't really abandoning Cai, wasn't trading her freedom for Maguire and Armstrong, Jake had to force the words out. "I accept."

Chapter Eighteen

Cai gasped and swung around to gape at him. "What?"

He spared her a quick glance, but his expression was closed. "When will the handoff take place?" he asked dispassionately.

"In approximately twenty minutes." And she knew from their host's smug look that he was not only pleased by Jake's response to his deal, but that he'd been confident enough of the answer to put the arrangements into motion before walking into the room.

It didn't make sense. Regardless of where her recep was, she'd be connected to him through their probes. She could pass intel to him whenever she wanted, and if she were careful of Nicole, no one would realize what she was doing. Elliot knew this; he was familiar enough with Quandems. Was he counting on anger preventing her from contacting Jake?

That didn't add up either. His own pair worked together despite their uneasy relationship. The man was smart enough to guess that she and her recep would start talking to each other sooner or later. There had to be something she wasn't seeing.

"How do we leave the Raft Cities?" Jake asked, pulling Cai from her musings.

Elliot's smile widened. "I'm certain you have a military transport on standby. I'll let you make contact and allow them to land on my raft, although not on my grounds. I'll also permit you to contact your men so they can join you at the pickup point. An escort of wreckers will assist you in loading your prisoners, and wait until you're safely under way."

Cai read between the lines: an escort of wreckers would ensure that Jake upheld his end of the bargain. She knew better. Now that she'd had a few seconds to get over the shock, she realized her recep would never leave without her. It didn't matter what he said, what he'd agreed to; she knew unequivocally that he wouldn't quit trying to free her until he died. Cai bit her lip. She couldn't let that happen, so she'd have to free herself—and her parents—before Jake could endanger his life.

Trust. In this situation, there was no room for reservations. She either had complete faith or she didn't. It was that simple. The answer was simple too.

She trusted Jake. Despite his earlier actions, despite everything. And she knew he trusted her.

It didn't matter that he'd had the general run a search on her parents. Whatever the reason, she was certain it was a good one. It didn't matter that he'd agreed to Elliot's deal. She knew it was a ploy. She trusted him. She *loved* him.

It was liberating. Cai wanted to tell him how she felt. Not in case they didn't make it out alive, but because it filled her with joy and she needed to share that. And because she knew her confidence would bolster Jake. He thought she had lost faith in him, and he had every right to think that after seeing her reactions this afternoon.

Though she could have told him over their pathway, she didn't want to do that. First, it might distract him at a critical point, and she would do nothing that might increase his level of risk. Second, she wanted to say it aloud. Wanted to look him in the eye and state quietly, *I love you*. And she wanted both of them to be safe when she spoke so that he knew it wasn't anxiety that prompted her but true and deep emotion.

It was time to put aside her fears and, as Jake said, do her job. After all, she hadn't come here to be rescued; she'd come to do the rescuing.

Now that she knew the way in, she didn't have to worry about the security around Elliot's mega-computer. Not with her nanoprobes. She simply accessed it and found her way into the system as Jake and the sleaze hashed out the details of their agreement. Her stomach twisted as she probed deeper, but she refused to let worries of another overload stop her.

The first piece of information she searched for was the strength of the security force: sixty-two wreckers and about three hundred mercenaries without the cybernetic body armor. Since Jake wasn't blocking her, she transmitted the info to him. His shock rippled through her, but his voice didn't falter as he negotiated how large the escort to the transport would be.

She didn't waste time trying to conceal herself from Nicole. If the woman spotted her, she spotted her. At the speed with which things were coming to a head, it would be over before the anchor could divulge this foray anyway.

Cai went after the intel the UCE wanted next. Since she didn't know what would be of interest, she linked to the Global Defense Network, bounced the info off one of the satellites and into the ADOK computer. In essence, she was transferring everything using her implants as a channel. Though she'd done this before, she'd never felt comfortable with the flow of data through her brain. It was like standing still in the middle of a transport race and letting the craft zoom past.

As fast as the computers were, as fast as her nanoprobe worked, it took precious minutes to complete the process. There were so many files on the system.

The last of the information was going through her implant when her recep said to Elliot, "Okay, let me run through what you're offering so there are no misunderstandings. Eight wreckers accompany me to the far side of the estate where I meet the pirate who has Maguire and Armstrong. He turns them over to me, then your mercenaries escort the three of us to the transport where my men are waiting. Once the prisoners are secured, your men stand down and we leave. Did I miss anything?"

The snake shifted in his chair. "You omitted two important points. One, your anchor remains behind, permanently. Two, the transport lands on the far side of the raft, outside my security field. Neither your extraction unit nor your Special Forces team will be allowed on my grounds. Is that clear enough for you?"

"I've got it."

"Good. If you plan to contact your team to pass along the coordinates and still make the rendezvous with the pirates, I suggest you be on your way. I doubt Cino is a patient man."

After a slight hesitation, Jake stood and a contingent of wreckers moved to encircle him. Even though Cai knew he would never abandon her, she felt a pang and her gaze locked on him as he began to exit.

He paused, and Cai tensed. Though he was overprotective, he couldn't be planning anything now. It would be stupid.

Twisting to look at her, he said, "Sorry, sweetheart."

And then he was gone.

Slowly she turned to face Elliot. He stared at her, amused

that she'd been left behind. Or maybe the delight came because he thought he'd divided another Quandem. He did seem to enjoy the mess he'd stirred up between Tony and Nicole.

"Perhaps it's because you're so young, but let this be your first lesson," the snake said with great pleasure. "Self-interest always wins in the end."

"It wasn't self-interest," Cai denied. "You didn't sway Jake with your talk of promotions. It was the safety of his men that convinced him to take your deal."

Elliot unfolded his hands and used them to lever himself out of his chair. He came around and sat directly across from her on his desk. It put him much too close, but she met his cold eyes without flinching. "It was self-interest," he said coolly. "Although maybe a less obvious version. Your receptor wanted his men safe so that he could have peace of mind."

"You think that not wanting their deaths on his conscience makes him selfish?"

"Still defending him." Elliot shook his head sadly. "I bet you believe he'll return to save you. I assure you, he won't. Even if he did have some grandiose plan to rescue you, he'll be unable to implement it. My men will see to that."

"Maybe he will leave the Raft Cities without me," Cai agreed, although she didn't believe that for a minute. Somehow she managed to sound resigned and that helped the lie. "But he made the decision he had to make. Six men's lives versus one person's freedom. I'd make the same call in his shoes."

She sat quietly, afraid that if she tried to prevaricate any more, he'd see through her. The stakes were high; she couldn't lower their chances of escape by giving anything away.

"He won't be coming back for you," Elliot reiterated. "Once I have the connector probe removed from your pretty head"—he tapped her temple with two fingers and

Cai fought not to cringe from his touch—"your receptor will believe you dead. Or that the implant overloaded. And the UCE would never sanction a mission to rescue a useless anchor. You are a soldier, after all, and knew the risk involved with your job."

"My parents—"

"Are civilians, true. However, who is going to believe Captain Tucker—if he even says anything. He never saw them. And who would believe that I'm on the Raft Cities, one of the world's poorest places to live? If necessary, I'll have my PR team work overtime to dissuade anyone from listening to such a far-fetched story. They'll claim I've been ensconced on a private island estate for years, battling some difficult-to-cure disease. I held you at bay; I can hold off anything Tucker tries, too."

Cai didn't know if his words were true or not. She did know he'd said them to deliver another shock, to keep her off balance. Well, it wasn't going to work this time. Instead of becoming distressed, she stared at him with a bland expression.

As far as she could tell, it didn't bother him that his barb failed to draw blood. Then something about his satisfaction made her study him more closely. A few things occurred to her. One was that she'd been taking Marchand Elliot at face value, which was stupid. He was ruthless and supremely self-serving—though he didn't see it that way. The man honestly believed he was entitled to whatever he desired. Like a spoiled child, he wanted another child's plaything, and would lose interest once he had it. She was nothing but the latest toy.

He wasn't bored with her yet, but when Jake was out of the picture, it wouldn't take long. Which wasn't necessarily bad, but it did put a new perspective on things. She was first and foremost a tool.

But most important, she realized Jake and company didn't need to make it home alive to stop the missions to the Raft Cities. *My God.* Why had neither of them seen this before? She should have realized the instant Elliot proposed the deal that he wanted Jake dead. It was the easiest way to end their link permanently. When her partner made contact with his men, they would notify the army that Maguire was captured, the commander rescued, and that the team was ready for extraction.

Then Elliot could wait until the extraction transport was over international waters before shooting it down, and the UCE would be able to recover the bodies. The powers-that-be would verify that Maguire and Armstrong were aboard and have no need to send another team. The attack would likely be chalked up to the usual animosity between the UCE and the Raft Cities pirates. Since no one knew Elliot was here, this act of terrorism would carry no repercussions for him.

Firing on the transport had probably been part of Elliot's original plan—the one where she and Jake escaped, grabbed their quarry, and ran. That was something she should have guessed sooner, too.

Yes, the best way to ensure that Elliot's presence remained a secret was for him to kill Jake and anyone else who knew too much before they could pass along the info. It wouldn't be hard; there were many different weapons that could reach a target at sea, and he had the resources to purchase them.

Another thought occurred to her: when she wasn't found with the transport, the army would think she was dead too, that her body had been washed away with a current. This was a good way to ensure that there wouldn't be a rescue attempt. No one would be alive to say she wasn't on board, and the military had never been able to track the nanoprobes.

"Shall I arrange for your mother to join us for dinner tonight?" the bastard asked calmly.

Cai needed a second to mentally switch topics; then she said, "I want to see my father too."

"And you will. Perhaps tomorrow night."

She didn't argue. "Yes, I'd enjoy dining with my mother."

Elliot was being cautious, and that surprised her. With his arrogance and his brigade of mercenaries, she'd expected him to agree to her request. She'd underestimated him. Keeping one of her parents locked up at all times was smart. The man was aware that she could mess up his systems with her implant, or connect with a UCE computer and tell the army exactly what was happening. But as long as there was a risk to her mom and dad, he knew she wouldn't do anything.

Jake, have you finished making contact with your men?

Yes, he replied, and she knew he was wondering what she was up to, why she was asking.

Where are you now?

Headed out of the mansion, toward the rendezvous point.

You realize when you get on that transport, Elliot will have it shot down, don't you?

She felt his grimness. *No shit. You know, right, that I have no plans to leave here without you?*

Of course I do. That's why I sent you the info on the strength of Elliot's forces.

Sweetheart, about that search on your parents—

Keep your mind on what you're doing. I trust you, end of story. We can talk about this later. Now I'm going to create a diversion to siphon off as much manpower as I can. Be ready.

And she'd do her best to make sure it was big enough that Elliot was diverted too. She'd been thinking about how to stop the wreckers since being taken captive, and had come up with an idea. It might not work, but she wanted to try it on a test group without anyone present to sound the alarm if it was successful.

"I'll issue the invitation," Elliot said with that slick smile of his. He was talking about dinner, and she had a million other things on her mind.

"Perhaps I can speak with both of them beforehand?"

"Perhaps. We'll have to discuss what you'll give me in exchange."

Cai smiled faintly as she pretended to listen to the man's monologue, and she dipped back into his computer. This time she didn't get far before she found Nicole shadowing her, but she ignored the other anchor.

Wary of an overload, she plugged into a few UCE systems. A quick sweep pinpointed precisely where Jake was, and she set off some alarms far away from his position. Nicole began to turn them off, and Cai dived in farther, intent on completing her plan. She wouldn't let anyone stop her.

After a moment of indecisiveness, she bit her lip and merged herself with the computer, falling into it the way she had with ADOK. As her consciousness mingled with the system's, the other anchor was unable to counter what she did.

Although she hated to call more attention to her parents, Cai knew the surest way to involve her captor was to make it seem as if someone were trying to break them out. She discovered the defense on the door was as complicated as Nicole had claimed, so she left it alone. Instead she triggered a hall alarm and hoped that would be enough to convince the security team.

Elliot was still pontificating when his comm unit chimed. Cai's breathing eased when he moved away and back behind his desk to answer the summons. Her scheme was working, and she struggled not to smile when she heard the icy crack of his voice as he demanded a report from his security chief. He abruptly cut off the comm and hurried toward the door. Before he opened it, he commanded the ten wreckers in the room to guard her closely. He didn't pause for confirmation before striding out and away.

Cai waited a few minutes to make sure he wouldn't return before trying out her theory. It was a simple one. She could manipulate and control many different kinds of systems with her implant. The armor the wreckers wore was riddled with nanocomputers that enabled them to move the heavy parts. All she had to do was shut down those tiny computers and they'd become instant statues.

Nicole continued to monitor her. Cai could clearly feel her presence, but she didn't want the woman to know what was going on, so she used the system to oust her. It was easier than she'd thought, but then she and Elliot's monster had merged till they were almost one, and it was simple to send a shock wave of energy toward Nicole that the other anchor couldn't simply ride out.

Since Cai knew she had to freeze every mercenary in this room at the same time, she reached in all directions simultaneously. She felt Jake's confusion over what she was up to and closed the pathway. Any distraction, no matter how slight, would be too much when dealing with millions, maybe even billions, of itty-bitty computers.

The job overwhelmed her, and she felt her head swim from the sheer numbers involved. That soft rumble started, the one she'd felt the day her probes had gone down, and sweat broke out on her brow. *Oh, God. Oh, God.* She couldn't let this happen. If she overloaded now, Jake was dead. But she had to take out the wreckers. Had to.

TREKS came to her rescue. That was Elliot's megacomputer's name. As it added its power to hers, the rumbling in her head receded. The computer was sentient, she realized. Or damn close. The shock froze her and she nearly lost her focus. *Think about the ramifications later,* she told herself. She shook off her amazement and worked on shutting down every single wrecker nanocomputer.

None of the mercenaries in the room moved, but since they always remained still when they were on guard duty, this wasn't proof that her plan had worked. Cai stood up. No reaction. She walked to one of the wreckers and reached for his weapon. When none of them did anything, she smiled and tucked the neuron fryer into her waist-band. These guys weren't a threat to anyone until she turned their microcomputers back on.

Ten wreckers out of commission, she told Jake.

What the hell did you do? He sounded pissed off, and she rolled her eyes as she helped herself to a few more fryers. She slipped one in the holster built into her boot and positioned another against the small of her back. She kept the last one in her hand. A quick glance verified that it was set on stun and she left it there. Unconscious was good enough.

I used my implant to manipulate the microcomputers in their body armor. What? Did you think I fought each of them hand-to-hand and managed to overcome them?

Smart-ass. Not an endearment this time, but a complaint.

With a smile, she went to the door. A quick peek showed the hall was empty, and she strolled out of the room. Although she didn't run, afraid it would attract too much attention, she made tracks to Jake's location. She had to shut down the unit of mercenaries guarding him, then free her parents.

She kept to cover as much as possible. It would be faster to travel directly through the estate, but she couldn't let haste trip her up. She had to remain undetected.

Where is the rendezvous with the transport? Is the rest of the team going to make it? If they were on the other side of the Raft Cities, she didn't know how they'd arrive in time, and she and Jake couldn't exactly sit around and wait.

They'll be here, no problem.

Something in Jake's tone tipped her off. She asked, *Why are you so certain? And so irritated?*

Because they're only two rafts over.

And they were getting ready to disobey orders and come in here after us? she guessed. There was no other reason for the entire team to be so near, and it would explain his exasperation.

You got it.

The sound of voices drifted her way, and Cai froze. When it was clear they were growing closer, she quickly looked around, searching for somewhere to hide. There was a row of hedges not too far away and she dashed for them, then tried to quietly slip between two of the bushes. Her hands got scratched, but her long sleeves and pants protected her arms and legs.

She regulated her breathing, making sure it remained even and slow. As they came nearer, she discerned three distinct male voices. Guards. She heard their exhilaration, their enthusiasm, before she heard their words. They knew something was going on, and they were speculating on what it could be. And she heard something else. These men were looking forward to a fight.

They passed in front of her, one wrecker and two regular mercenaries. The excitement they felt for killing was foreign to her. During the time she'd been connected to Jake, he'd never reacted like this. He didn't spend a great deal of time thinking about the lives he'd taken—he couldn't—but neither did he like that part of his job. These three relished it. She found herself wondering if that was the difference between soldiers and soldiers for hire.

While she waited, she continued to monitor her recep's position. He hadn't stopped moving, and she wondered how much his escort knew. She sent him the question.

They know there's trouble at the house.

Do they know about the wreckers I immobilized?

Doubt it. They'd be reacting more strongly than this. You realize, don't you, that their comm gear is part of their body armor, and when you took down your guys' nanocomputers, you cut off their ability to transmit and receive, right?

Yeah, I know. But if someone enters that room and finds them, the element of surprise is gone.

When she judged that enough time had elapsed since the men had faded out of hearing, she carefully wriggled her way out of the hedges. A branch cut the back of her left hand, but she wiped the blood on her pants and continued toward her recep.

Give me your position, he demanded.

Cai sent the info to him and got another shock. As she accessed the UCE systems, she realized TREKS was still merged with her—and she wasn't the one who maintained the connection. No computer, sentient or not, should be able to do that.

Okay, when you get closer, come in stealthily. And if you can, stay hidden when you work on disabling their body armor. It'll be safer for all of us.

Got it. He was right. There was no telling how the mercenaries would react if they spotted her, and if they made a move to fire, Jake would try to stop them. The problem was, cover was becoming sparser. She picked up her pace, hoping to catch them before the grounds were entirely barren.

Nicole was attempting to regain access to TREKS, but Cai and the computer easily pushed her out again. Cai bit her lip. She hadn't thought *she and it,* but *they,* and that made her nervous. Just how deep-rooted in her mind was this system?

There wasn't time to worry before she closed the distance with Jake's escort. She slowed, creeping nearer as surreptitiously as possible. When she reached the last good piece of cover, she stopped. Taking a deep breath, she reached out for their microcomputers. And again, TREKS was there to help her. The wreckers went still so suddenly it was startling. Two fell to the ground, caught midstride and off balance.

Her recep was arming himself before she reached him. He looked up when she arrived and gave a short smile. "That's some trick, sweetheart."

He returned to his search of the mercenaries without saying anything else. Since he had at least three neuron fryers stashed somewhere on his body, she wasn't sure why he continued checking them out. Cai kept watch, her eyes scanning the grounds as she waited, but she couldn't help wondering how he'd become so grubby in the short time they'd been apart. Before she could ask, she felt his elation and swiveled to look at him.

Jake held up a knife and grinned hugely. "C'mon, let's go. It's too open here. Wish we could move my escort out of sight, but they're too freaking heavy to drag anywhere." When they were behind a bush, he hid his blade in the small of his back. "Okay, that's eighteen wreckers out of commission, right?"

Cai nodded. "Eighteen down, forty-four to go."

"Is there any chance someone could reactivate them?" He bent over to stuff a fryer in his boot.

"Nicole, maybe, but she'd be the only one."

He straightened and stared at her for a minute. Then, surprising the hell out of her, his arms went around her and he dragged her against him. She let herself lean into his body, her own arms going around his waist, and when she looked up at him, Jake kissed her. It was fast, hardly more than a buss, before he put her away and said, "Okay, we have to make that meeting with the mutineers. Can you locate them?"

She closed her eyes and concentrated. It wasn't easy to find people who didn't have some kind of device she could track, and when she factored in the energy from the estate's force field distorting the readings, it became even more difficult, but she could pick up body armor. Odds were that there would be wreckers with them if for no other reason than to handle Maguire and Armstrong; the commander was a Navy SEAL and it would take more than a couple of regular mercenaries or outlaws to contain him, and Maguire had been a fighter pilot in her own time. Cai located two different clusters of wreckers and passed the info to Jake.

"Figures," he muttered.

"What?"

"Elliot had his forces separate them—I'll bet on it."

"Them? Maguire and Commander Armstrong?"

"Yeah, it makes sense. He wants to make sure I don't have anything up my sleeve. This way, I have to continue to play the game if I want both of them. Even with the wreckers, he'd be a fool not to take some precautions—and splitting my objectives into two groups is the easiest and smartest."

"It makes it tougher for us, certainly."

"Much tougher." He frowned and stared into space for a few seconds as he thought something over. "Can you disable the force field surrounding the grounds? I want my team in."

"Probably, but it'll cause a whole new set of issues," she warned. No point in mentioning her own sense of déjà vu. The barrier around the grounds and the force field on the previous mission bore a strong resemblance to each other. She wasn't sure, precisely, what had overloaded her probes, but her second guess, after the ADOK system, was the force field.

"Yeah, I know, but I think those problems can be turned to our advantage. Elliot isn't beloved by the pirate lords here, and if the locals can gain unlimited access to his grounds, it may keep his security forces busy long enough for us to get the job done."

Cai nodded grimly. At least if she lost her probes on the attempt, Jake would be around to carry her out. "This will take a few minutes."

"Go ahead."

She closed her eyes again and reached out for the barrier. This time the noise in her head was a low-level roar, blocking everything else. She had to bite her lip to keep from gasping. TREKS brushed a question past her, wondering what she was doing. When it discovered the answer, the computer showed her an alternate method, one that would take her even deeper inside itself. Cai abandoned her way and plunged down the path she'd seen. The roar dissipated. The barrier fell.

"It's down," she said and reluctantly looked at Jake.

"Thanks. Now send a message to Gnat. Tell him to let the pirate lords know these shields are down, then to bring the team in and join the fun."

This took a couple of minutes too, and she felt her recep becoming more intense. Finally she relayed, "Gnat said you have a strange idea of fun."

With a short grin, Jake jerked his head to indicate they should get going. They moved fast. The traitorous pirates likely wouldn't hang around long if no one showed up at the exchange. Not when their leader would be worried this was some kind of setup and that maybe Elliot was working with the pirate lord being betrayed. Jake and Cai were already late, but since the split groups weren't yet together, not too late.

Jake didn't slow down till he neared the first crew. He and Cai stopped behind another hedgerow—one tall enough to throw some shade—and Cai saw that every member of the ragtag group had a blade strapped to his thigh. Elliot's security force must have scanned the men before they were allowed to enter the grounds and confiscated all their high-tech weapons. But why the hell had he let them keep their knives?

Cai frowned and studied the group, but she wasn't able to spot either of the two people they were assigned to bring home. At least one of them should be here. The four mercenaries with the pirates did stand out, though, and she knew they'd be a huge problem.

Can you shut down these wreckers and the ones accompanying the second crew? Jake asked.

Yes. She bit her lip, then added, *but if I do that, they'll be completely vulnerable and the pirates might kill them. You know there are seams in the armor. All they have to do is run a knife along the one at the throat and those men are dead.*

I know. Jake sounded perplexed. He looked at her, and

what she saw in his eyes told her he was aware of exactly what would happen. Then her concern dawned on him. *We've been together long enough for you to understand there are casualties in battle, and sweetheart, this is combat. It's them or us.*

She nodded slowly. He was right. If she didn't take the wreckers out of the equation, other people would die. Maybe Jake, maybe the team, maybe her. It wouldn't be easy to live with the knowledge that she was responsible for the deaths of these mercenaries, but she was at war. She'd do what she had to do.

Cai reached out with her probes and turned off their nanocomputers. *It's done.* She fought back queasiness.

He ran his fingers down her jaw. *Wait here.*

What are you doing? He was leaving her safe while he went out and met the outlaws alone? She didn't think so. Her hand squeezed the grip of the neuron fryer she held.

He put a hand on her shoulder. *I'm going to try to bluff them. You stay put and, if all hell breaks loose, contact Gnat.*

Before she could protest, he was gone. *Damn him.* He was going to get himself killed and she was going to have a front-row seat. Not following was one of the hardest things she'd ever done, but she knew that if she popped out behind him, chaos would ensue. There was no way she was going to be responsible for distracting Jake and giving the pirates an opening to attack.

She couldn't see him, not at first, and when he finally made an appearance, it was from a completely different direction from where she stood. Leave it to him to go to those kinds of lengths to protect her. Cai shook her head and double-checked to make sure her fryer was set on stun. She had to be ready.

A man separated himself and walked forward to meet Jake. As they talked, a group of pirates came up to join them. Those men obstructed her view and Cai shifted, trying to keep Jake in sight, but the throng was too thick.

Everything seemed to be going okay so far, though, and Cai allowed herself a deep breath. That was a mistake. In the next instant, men were yelling and rushing at her recep, knives drawn. *Crap.*

At least it wasn't blasters or neuron fryers, she thought as she sent the SOS to Gnat and gave their location. Instead of using his fryer, her honorable idiot of a beloved met his enemies with his own blade. He wasn't going to last long, not one against many. Crouching behind the bushes, she ran along the hedgerow to put herself within firing range. She hoped Jake could hold out until she could give him some help.

There was a break in the foliage and Cai peeked through. The first thing that caught her eye was the four wreckers on the ground. She knew they were dead and swallowed back her remorse; those men would have shown no mercy if the situation had been reversed. As her gaze moved on, she saw three pirates were down, but her partner was surrounded. She was close enough, barely, to risk a few shots. Bringing her left hand up to support her right, she aimed at the bastard who was trying to stab Jake in the back.

Bull's-eye! She dropped a couple more, and raiders turned and rushed her position behind the hedge. Since she wanted to get nearer to the bulk of the group anyway, she ran.

By the time she reached the next break, she could hear men thrashing in the bushes where she'd been a few minutes earlier. Her heart pounded faster as she saw that Jake's shirt was slashed and that the light material had blood on it. Now she was pissed.

Cai pulled her second weapon.

She wasn't as proficient left-handed, but there were enough pirates clumped together that she didn't need to be completely accurate. Stepping into the gap, she began firing.

A number of the men abandoned Jake and headed for her. She picked them off, both neuron fryers blazing away.

Something made her glance quickly behind her, and she

saw the other raiders trying to sneak up on her. She stepped back through the hedge to evade their assault and continued to move. How many of these damn mutineers were there? The ground seemed littered with men, either unconscious or injured, and they kept coming.

Shots joined hers. Cai zeroed in on where they originated, and she briefly identified Mango before he slipped out of view.

Enough of the pirates were engaged in battle now that the cluster had decreased enough to see between several of the men and spot a woman. Her hands appeared to be secured in front of her, but that didn't prevent her from fighting, kicking at the mutineers who guarded her.

Cai ran a quick comparison between the hostage and what she knew of Bree Maguire. Height appeared to be about right, as did the shoulder-length dark hair. It was impossible to see her eye color from this distance, not without enhancing equipment, but the bone structure seemed to match as well.

For the first time, the woman became real to Cai, became more than a tale. It made her hesitate. They supposedly wanted the same thing—the restoration of freedom, of democracy—it was only their methods of reaching the goal that differed. Someone shouted a battle cry, and she turned and saw more pirates fighting Jake.

Cai shook off her doubts and continued moving, shifting to get into a better position. When the outlaws ran, and they would, she didn't want them taking Maguire with them. Not when that meant she, Jake, and the team would have to pursue. If Maguire were unconscious, however, they'd leave her; Cai was sure of it.

The gap widened and she took the opportunity. With the fryer she had in her right hand, Cai carefully aimed. She fired. Time slowed to a crawl. Maguire went down.

Chapter Nineteen

There was a lull. It lasted only a few seconds; then a surge came and Cai realized the second crew of pirates had arrived. The battle noise returned—grunts, groans, yelling, and cursing. Something, some instinct, made her glance over to see the barrel of a weapon aimed her way.

Crap. The outlaws had finally taken the opportunity to pull the neuron fryers from the bodies of the wreckers, and it was a good bet that they didn't have the weapons set to stun. She hit the ground in time to avoid the shot, but she swore she felt the tracer's warmth as it sailed past her head. Still, that was impossible; the energy wave didn't emit heat.

Rolling to her feet, she tried to stay low and offer as small a target as possible while looking for cover. Jake? Her eyes searched the swarm of men till she found him. The crowd around him was both an advantage and a disadvantage. On the plus side, it offered the only protection he had against taking a shot from a neuron fryer. The disadvantage was that the mob was so close, he couldn't draw his own fryer and had to keep using the knife.

Carefully, so she wouldn't disturb his concentration, she updated him on the situation. It wasn't good. Even with the help from the Special Forces team, there were too many raiders for the eight of them to handle. Not only were these men fighting with the pent-up frustration of years of poverty, they were criminals battling for their very lives.

Those fryers have chips, Jake told her. *Can you disable them without affecting ours?*

I'll try. It wasn't a bad suggestion. The chips were what cued the gun to go off when the trigger was pulled.

Cai moved again, avoiding another pirate, and sent out a steady stream of blasts from both her weapons. She needed time to attempt what her recep wanted. When she thought she'd created a pocket, she tried to access the chip inside the weapons and discovered it was too simple to allow for manipulation. She could blast out every weapon in the vicinity, but couldn't pick and choose. *It's a no-go,* she told him.

No response, but Jake was busy. She didn't have time to count, not with everything going on around her, but there had to be more than half a dozen raiders with knives surrounding him.

The pirates who had the fryers were trying to flush out the Special Forces team, so Cai tried to attract more attention to herself. With the limited cover in the area, she didn't think it would take long before Jake's guys were pinned down.

They were definitely in trouble here.

She had to hit the dirt again and, lying on her belly, she set down some rapid-fire cover to give the team breathing room. But with so many opponents, she barely made a dent, and one of her guns was almost out of charge. Still shooting with her left hand, she swapped out the depleted fryer for one that was fully loaded.

Help came from an unexpected source.

A squad of wreckers descended on the melee. Most of the pirates abandoned fighting Cai and the Special Forces squad to meet the new threat, and the number of remaining opponents seemed more manageable. It looked like Jake had taken another slash with a knife, and Cai levered herself to her feet again, intending to help him.

She didn't make it far before she spotted someone headed toward the prone Maguire. His intensity and determination were clear even at this distance. With his unkempt appearance, she thought it was another outlaw at first, but then something in the way he moved reminded her of Jake. Agile, smooth, disciplined. Well trained.

She narrowed her eyes and took a closer look. It might be. Keeping her fryer trained on him, she crept forward for a better view. Yeah, she decided, it was him. Had to be.

Commander Armstrong.

His hands were secured in front of him like the woman's had been, but he'd managed to disarm one of the mutineers and acquire a weapon. Cai shook her head. These men in Special Operations were a breed apart, no doubt about it.

A raider charged her from the side. She pivoted and pulled her fryer's trigger. But when she glanced back, the commander had his weapon aimed at her. He gave her a wary look. The general had said they thought he'd been brainwashed, and to consider him a hostile. She couldn't afford to wait and find out if it was true.

Without hesitation, she shot him.

I think we're going to have to call you Deadeye, Jake noted dryly.

Keep your attention on your own fight, she reprimanded— but was pleased by the compliment. Smiling slightly, she decided she had better check on their prisoners.

She didn't get far before she was grabbed from behind.

It was a pirate, she could tell by the stench, and Cai was pissed. With a growl she dropped her chin to her chest, bent her knees, and snapped her head back as she straightened her legs. The head butt made her enemy curse, and before he could recover, she turned out of his hold and delivered a snap kick to his groin.

She pointed her gun at him, but waited to see whether or not she needed to shoot. As he fell to his knees, she relaxed. This one was out for a while—had to be, as hard as she'd kicked.

Everyone seemed to be ignoring her at the moment. The invading pirates were losing badly to the mercenaries, but she had no plans to disable these wreckers. Nearly all the Raft Cities scum had gone to help in the fight, but Cai kept her eyes open as she started toward Maguire again. It was Jake who waylaid her this time.

"Are you okay?" she asked, her eyes scanning him from head to toe. His shirt was sliced open on the arms and rib cage, and blood stained the fabric. There was another slash on the left thigh of his trousers, but no sign of bleeding there.

"They're only a couple of shallow scratches. Nothing that needs to be patched up immediately." He surveyed their surroundings, then the unconscious Banzai Maguire and Commander Armstrong. "We have to get out of here before those wreckers finish with the pirates and come after us."

Yeah, he was right about that, but she wasn't leaving the Raft Cities without her mom and dad. Cai raised her chin, but didn't get a chance to speak.

"Gnat, you and the team get Maguire and Armstrong to the transport," Jake ordered as he put his knife away.

His XO turned from a pirate he'd just dispatched. "What about you and the captain, Tuck?"

"We'll be right behind you. Cai and I have something else we need to take care of first."

Their gazes met, and she grinned at him. She knew how seriously he took his job. It meant a lot to her that he would willingly stay back to help, and that she didn't have to argue with him over her plans. She wouldn't be alone in this rescue.

"I don't like it," Gnat said.

"You don't have to like it. All you have to do is follow orders. Get them to that transport. If things get sticky, leave us." Jake held up a hand before any of the now-appearing team members could interrupt. "You can come back later, but the important thing is to complete the assignment."

"Yes, sir." Gnat's tone, and his use of the word *sir*, gave away his displeasure. "You heard the captain. Move."

"Gnat," Cai called, "warn the flight crew about the likelihood of a surprise long-range missile attack."

The man stared at her for a few seconds, then gave a short nod and turned away. She watched him issue orders, watched Maguire and the commander hoisted over Mango and Kazoo's shoulders, and watched the team beat a strategic retreat. Then she and Jake were on their own.

"C'mon, sweetheart, let's move. We've been here too long."

Her recep headed in the opposite direction from the clash. The raiders were getting the worst of it, but they continued to doggedly fight. Cai hesitated. It wasn't that she had any sympathy for these pirates—invading Elliot's home at the first opportunity, they were every bit as vile as the mercenaries—but it was a terrible mismatch.

I thought you wanted to rescue your parents?

Cai took one last peek and then hurried to catch up with him. The battle would have to settle itself without her.

When they were far enough away from the skirmish, they began to circle back toward the mansion. Neither of them spoke, not even through their link. She knew that the nearer they got to the house, the greater the risk, but though her nerves were pulled tight, she felt a zing of anticipation. Soon she was going to see her parents again, hold them, apologize to them. Bring them home. She had to believe.

Both she and Jake kept their weapons ready and paid careful attention to their surroundings as they made their way across the grounds. There was too much open space and it made her edgy. They couldn't get caught now, not when she was so close.

Jake stopped and Cai pulled up beside him. She studied the vast expanse of green in front of them and knew this had her recep worried. It concerned her as well. There were a few flower beds, but there was nothing else to use as concealment.

It'll take too much time to go around, Cai said.

Yeah. Time we don't have.

And doing that would only hide us for part of the distance anyway. Eventually we'd have to cross.

I know that too.

He didn't say any more, and she wondered what he was thinking. Was he trying to come up with an argument to persuade her to turn back? She wouldn't. If he didn't feel comfortable, he didn't have to go with her, but she wasn't running away.

I saw that.

What was he talking about? *Saw what?*

The way your chin went up. You don't have to brace yourself for an argument. I'm not going to fight you on this. But I do want to study the area before we walk through.

Cai inspected it too. It didn't look any better on closer examination. She scanned the grounds for security, but found no inteltronic devices they needed to bother with. It seemed as if Elliot had put his faith in the force field around the estate, his army of mercenaries, and the house systems.

She was more than ready to go when Jake gave the signal, but if she thought he'd been alert before, it was nothing compared to how aware he was as they crossed the lawn. Cai's senses felt heightened too, her hearing sharper, her vision keener.

Her adrenaline spiked when she heard sounds she associated with the rapid movement of troops. She and Jake shared a quick glance, then ran, dropping to their stomachs behind one of the flower beds. It was their only hope of remaining unnoticed and it wasn't much; the plants weren't tall and the two of them would be easy to see against the backdrop of grass. They lay shoulder-to-shoulder, weapons pointed in the direction the noise came from, and waited.

The mercenaries never looked their way; they were deploying too fast. She and her recep remained where they were even after the men were out of view.

Something weird is going on. Can you tap into Elliot's computer and find out what?

Since she and TREKS were still connected, it wasn't a problem, but the computer didn't handle communications and she had to engage another system. *More pirates have figured out that the barrier around this estate is down. From what I'm picking up, it appears six more crews have banded together and are attacking en masse.*

She felt Jake's smile rather than saw it. *Looks like Elliot's security force is going to be busy for a while. Let's go.*

They reached the gazebo behind the house without being challenged. As they stood in the shadows of the structure, Cai transmitted detail to Jake about the wing her parents were held in and what she knew about the alarms and other precautions. She saved the complicated defense on the door for last.

What about security on the windows? he asked.

When he had the data, he shook his head. *Shit, that figures. Reinforced composite glass with enough sensors to trigger if the wind blows. Looks like we take the door. How long will you need to get through it?*

Cai sighed. *A while. If it were only inteltronic or computer-based, it wouldn't be a problem, but it's a combination of the two, with a some low-tech explosive stuff added.*

You can't circumvent the booby trap by accessing one of the systems and going around it?

Maybe, but it could take me weeks to work out how, she admitted reluctantly. And if it weren't for her implant already speeding things up, it would take months and months to figure out.

Shit, he swore again, and ran his hand over the back of his neck while he considered. *Okay, you handle the stuff you do best, but leave the detonator to me—clear?*

Clear. She only hoped Jake's training in defusing explosives was extensive enough.

For a moment he studied her, maybe making sure she really was agreeing to his decision; then he motioned. *Let's go.*

Her heart pounded, both with fear and anticipation as they entered the house and crept along the hall. Jake took point. He was careful, checking everything out before moving them past a door or around a corner.

She'd expected a few wreckers to be patrolling the wing, but it was deserted. Delving into the comm links again, she verified her guess. The situation on the grounds had worsened, and Elliot's thugs were being overwhelmed by the attacking pirates. She sent this info to her recep, but it didn't change how he proceeded.

Despite his caution, they were taken by surprise. The house plans weren't on any of the systems—at least Cai hadn't found them—but she should have delved deeper. If she'd found the blueprints, then they would have known there were secret passages, and they might have been prepared when the wall six feet ahead of their position swung in unexpectedly. As it stood, they were caught with nowhere to hide.

Nicole and Tony looked every bit as startled to see them.

Both Tony and Jake had lightning-fast reflexes, though, and their weapons were up and aimed immediately. Cai was a half beat behind. She targeted Tony, who had his neuron fryer aimed her direction. Jake's weapon pointed at Nicole.

"Drop it," De Luca ordered.

Her recep didn't even twitch.

"I'll shoot her."

"No, you won't." She'd never heard Jake sound so dangerous before. "You know I'll fire a split second after you do."

"Your fryer is set for stun," the other man said.

"Is it?" Jake's smile was cold.

No one moved. It was as if they were playing a game of chicken that neither man was willing to lose. Impasse.

Cai was aware that time was an issue, and they couldn't stand here indefinitely. Not only did it increase the chances that they'd be discovered, but the UCE transport couldn't wait forever. Jake had given orders for them to leave if they had to, and with battles being waged across Elliot's raft as the raiders fought to loot it, things wouldn't take long to reach that point.

A light mental nudge caught her attention. Though she kept most of her attention on the other couple, she investigated the summons. What she found left her flabbergasted. It was TREKS, warning her that Nicole was trying to get around the system block Cai had thrown by using the Monster, ADOK.

It made her wonder how smart TREKS was; that it recognized Nicole, knew that Cai wanted to keep the woman out and that she'd want to know about any attempted incursion. Then there were the questions of how it knew what was going on in a UCE machine and why it had chosen to side with her rather than Nicole. This was the other anchor's home system; if it were possible for a computer to form an allegiance, Cai would have guessed TREKS would stick with its regular rider. Questions about its sentience rose once more in her mind. Could her affinity for computers have made a positive impression on TREKS?

When the nudge came again, more urgently this time, she put her curiosity aside and moved to intercept the blonde. Cai didn't understand what Nicole hoped to accomplish, since most of the ADOK systems were good only for intelligence, but she was going to do whatever she could to foil her plan.

The idea of entering ADOK while merged with TREKS worried her, but resolutely, Cai accessed the system. She paused, waiting for a sign that her probes couldn't take the strain, but nothing happened. A bit more confident, she ghosted through the computer looking for Nicole. The blonde didn't stay in one place, though; she kept flitting around, and Cai found herself continually a step behind as she gave chase.

It didn't make sense. Yeah, these monster computers were amazing and could do a lot of things, but there was nothing that would end a standoff like this, so why bother? Cai stopped. There had to be a purpose, and she needed to think about it.

Overload.

That was Nicole's scheme. She was trying to impel Cai's probes to go down. Thinking back, she realized the woman had been there the day her implants had crashed, that she'd witnessed the beginning stages of it. Like Cai, Nicole had attributed the overload to ADOK, and was trying to lure her in deep enough for a repeat. She refused to play the game.

Cai pulled out of the system.

"No," she said, staring hard at the other anchor.

"It was worth an attempt," the blonde said. "It's of no consequence that it didn't work. We know that you can't afford to wait here long."

"And we know that you can't waste time either," Cai shot back. "Elliot's little empire is crumbling as we speak. Even the wreckers can't hold out forever against hundreds, maybe thousands of furious pirates. I'd bet that they know you're part of the man's top echelon, and they'll be gunning for you. How would you like to *work* for a pirate lord, Nicole? Like you do for Elliot? If they don't kill you first, of course."

The only sign that her words had hit their intended mark was the shadow that swept through the other woman's eyes. It was there and gone quickly, but Cai didn't miss it. Although she hadn't said it aloud, both of them knew the harsh reality a captive female would face here.

"You'd be in the same predicament," Nicole said.

"No, I wouldn't. Jake and I were taken prisoner very publicly, so the pirates know we're not working with your boss. That puts me in a completely separate category. Then there's the fact that I'm not so different from the women on the Raft Cities. My brown hair and brown eyes are commonplace, but a blue-eyed blonde . . . Well, they don't get that here every day."

Nicole's reaction was only slightly more noticeable this time, but Cai knew her points were valid, logical, and that she'd tipped the scales a bit in her favor. She wasn't comfortable using the very real threat of rape against the other woman, but she couldn't afford to be nice right now.

Not when time was short and lives were on the line.

Damn, sweetheart, you went right for the jugular, Jake said.

Not quite. Not yet. But she would. Cai knew exactly where to strike the deepest blow. Quietly, she said, "Do you think they'll keep your recep alive? He's not important to them, and he's been associated with Elliot's security team. The pirates *hate* Elliot and his mercenaries. You can see that."

Nicole shifted her weight. "Tony is too valuable," she insisted, but the false bravado behind the statement was apparent.

"No, he isn't. They don't know what you can do as a team, and even if they did, would they care? If they have you to provide intel over a comm unit to their ships, that would be good enough." She shrugged. "Tony is superfluous."

There was no sign that this found its mark, but the anchor's silence was telling. The other Quandem might be having problems, but the bond remained between them. If it didn't, De Luca might have taken his chances with Jake's weapon, and the man certainly wouldn't be trying to get his anchor out of this mansion before the pirates swarmed inside. Cai had already known the blonde would do anything to protect him.

They're discussing the situation, Cai said. *Any idea what alternatives they're debating?*

The options are limited. Jake kept his attention on the couple facing them. *We continue the standoff, that's one. Two, they try to run—but they know we can shoot them easily if they do that. Or three, this guy can call my bluff and fire at you. But if he tries, he's freaking dead. I'm guessing he knows that.*

Our options are every bit as limited.

De Luca must be aware of that. He's very well trained, Cai, so don't underestimate him. I wouldn't be surprised to find out he was UCE military at some point, in one of the elite units.

Special Forces?

Jake gave it some thought. *Not army,* he said at last. *He's not that much older than me, so if we hadn't met in person, I would have at least heard the name. But army isn't the only branch, and Special Operations isn't the sole select group. Don't forget the Rangers or the recon units.*

True, but she'd always thought of Jake as the best of the best. She switched topics. *So what's our plan?*

Our plan is to stay alive, to get out of here with your parents and make it to the transport before it leaves.

Which Cai took to mean they'd be improvising.

Nicole and Tony were still quiet, but the other man's attention didn't waver. She studied him in light of what Jake had said and decided she could see him in Special Operations. He had the intensity; there was no mistaking that.

"I can offer you a deal," the blond anchor said.

"What kind of deal?" Jake asked. His voice was hard.

Now Nicole did look nervous. "I can give you the way around the security on the Randolphs' door. Without it, you'll have to work in stages. Make one mistake and the device will go off. It's big enough to take down the entire wing."

Cai fought her excitement. She had to study this without emotion clouding her judgment. Would Nicole have spent the time necessary to puzzle through the door security? It was obvious that her mom and dad were important to Elliot; the woman could have decided to learn how to untangle the bomb when she'd tried to make the deal earlier. Or she could be suckering them into getting blown up.

The anchor met Cai's gaze without flinching, but that didn't mean she was being honest.

"And in exchange you want?"

"The same thing as before. Safe passage back to the UCE."

"With immunity," Tony added.

Jake shook his head. "Cut the bullshit, De Luca. You're familiar enough with the military to know what I can deliver and what I can't. Immunity falls in the second category."

The man's lips twisted slightly, and Cai guessed that condition had been tacked on in an effort to throw them off the truth of their desperation. "We'll settle for the trip back home then," he said.

"I'm supposed to believe that's all you want?" Jake asked. "I didn't believe it before, and I don't now."

He had a point, Cai thought. The path around the door security was worth a lot, and a simple transport ride back to Fort Powell was hardly of equal value. Especially since army officials would haul the couple off for questioning and might arrest them.

"It *is* all we want," Nicole said to Cai. "I offered you an even better deal before, so you know how badly we want to leave."

Cai didn't like how the woman appealed to her. That put a tick in the minus column. If she were on the level, why not address Jake? He was the one with the power to say yes or no. On the other hand, Nicole had tried to make a similar bargain earlier, and Cai believed that she'd been truthful. Then there was the upheaval going on outside; that was worth at least ten points for the plus column. Cai wouldn't want to be in Nicole's place when the pirates fought their way inside.

She scrutinized the other Quandem a few seconds longer before deciding they were legit. *I believe them,* she said, but had little hope that Jake would act on her say-so. He hadn't trusted her discernment before, and she didn't think he would now either.

He said nothing for a long moment. "Instead of giving us the secret to the door, you'll be with us, and Nicole will be the one who goes through. If you agree to that, then we have a deal. If not . . ." Jake shrugged.

Cai tried her best not to look shocked. He was going along with this? On her recommendation? She bit her bottom lip to keep from saying anything, and waited.

"Agreed," Tony said.

They ran into another sticking point when the recep refused to give up his weapons. Jake didn't insist, and that stunned Cai again. Of course, it made the rest of the trip to the area where her parents were held more tense because they had to keep watch over Nicole and Tony. It would be too easy to find the tables turned, and Cai and Jake weren't taking any chances.

Cai had to battle to keep from crying when they reached

the door. Her parents were on the other side. It had been a long, lonely six years. No one to confide in, no one to hold her. Then Jake's arm slipped around her waist and she realized that wasn't entirely true. She hadn't been able to tell him much because of her lie, but she hadn't been completely alone either.

Still, there were times, even at twenty-one, when she'd just wanted her mom. Or her dad. No one, not even the man she was in love with, could fill their shoes.

"How long will this take?" Jake asked.

"A few minutes. It's a complicated procedure," Nicole said.

Will you know if she's messing with us?

Yes, I think so. She's right about it being complicated, though, and she'll have to do it slowly to make sure it's right.

"Go ahead," he ordered.

Although TREKS wasn't connected to the security system, Cai used it to monitor Nicole's progress. Cai liked the cautious, methodical approach she was able to sense, and she liked how Tony stayed in the background yet reinforced his partner. That kind of support suggested their bond remained undestroyed despite the strain caused by Elliot.

Perspiration covered Nicole's brow, and it was De Luca who gently wiped it away. Cai was sweating herself and knew it was nerves. One slip and everyone, including her parents, was dead. She wished she could stop thinking about that.

At the halfway mark, a loud bang made them freeze. The noise came again, then became steady, regular.

"They're trying to break into the house," Tony said gravely.

"Then your anchor had better hurry," Jake shot back.

If she hadn't been so tense, Cai would have laughed. God, she loved him. He'd hang in till the bitter end for her, and a man with that kind of loyalty didn't come along every day.

Cai debated. She could help. Maybe. If she didn't overload her probes in the attempt. It wouldn't be easy and would require her to handle an incredible amount of power, but it was the best way to keep the pirates at bay. A few minutes, that was all she'd have to hold the security for. She could do anything for a few minutes, right?

Since she was already merged with TREKS, she used it to call energy from the systems at her disposal——one hundred and fifty-four if you didn't count Elliot's. She took them in chunks of twenty, not wanting to flood herself, and directed the power through her probe and into the walls, doors, and windows of the house. With two groups of systems, she was able to create a light force field and make it harder to gain entry.

What the hell are you doing? Jake demanded, but she ignored him. She had to concentrate.

She pulled another block of twenty and added them to the mix, then another. That rumble started again, the one she associated with frying her probes. Cai stopped and worked to smooth out the flow. Jake was there; she could feel him. He couldn't do anything, not with his connector implant, but his presence calmed her and solidified her resolve. The shakiness went away and she brought another block online.

Another rumble, another pause to acclimate. She was hyperaware of Nicole's progress and knew the woman was going much slower now than before. But then she was at the trickiest part of the procedure.

Cai brought the last group of systems up. Her vision began to tunnel. *Crap.* She couldn't go down. Not now. Then it occurred to her that she didn't have to bear the burden alone. She tapped into Jake, using him to double her capacity; then she opened herself completely to Elliot's machine. She'd never done this before, never trusted she'd emerge whole if she allowed full assimilation.

TREKS was fascinating. She nearly became sidetracked by her desire to explore more fully, but she remembered her purpose and allowed the system to share the energy. Her eyesight returned to normal, the roar inside her head quieting.

She'd mastered the monster by joining it, and Cai knew she'd never have to worry about overloading again.

The pirates were blocked out, but even with the help, she couldn't funnel energy indefinitely. Unlike computers that were built to function with these massive amounts of power, her body would grow fatigued in a matter of minutes.

Hurry, she thought as Nicole continued to work the door, but she didn't say it aloud. Her knees sagged and Jake's arm went around her once more, keeping her steady. She felt her command falter and fought to hang on. *Hurry,* she urged again.

The door buzzed, then clicked. Cai stopped funneling energy immediately and took a deep breath. She had to have enough strength left to get to the transport.

Are you okay, sweetheart? Jake asked.

Yeah. And she was. Both probes were up and running. She was tired, but she'd recover. The door opened then, and her parents stood looking into the hall, taking in the scene. When their eyes met, Cai smiled shakily, a thousand emotions welling up inside her. Yeah, she was fine.

She dashed forward but pulled up short of throwing herself into her parents' open arms. For a second she drank in the details. Mom smelled of vanilla—Cai caught a small whiff—and Dad's T-shirt was faded and looked wonderfully soft, same as it always had. When he turned to share a glance with her mom, Cai noticed he wore his hair shorter than she'd ever seen it, but still he had enough left for a nubby ponytail at his nape. She took another step forward, but stopped again.

"Dad, I'm sorry." Her voice came out thickly, and it shook. "I didn't mean what I said before you disappeared, I swear."

"We know that, baby."

He started to reach for her, but Cai shook her head and turned to her mom. Taking a deep breath, she spoke in the language of her ancient Vietnamese ancestors "Con xin lỗi mẹ."

"Oh, sweetie," her mom said, choked up. "You don't have to apologize; we know your heart."

Tears tracked down her mother's cheeks, and when she opened her arms again, Cai didn't hesitate. Less than two steps closed the distance and she was enveloped in a warm hug. As they clung to each other, she felt her dad's strong embrace surround both of them, and she couldn't contain her own tears any longer.

So long. It had been so long. "I love you."

Her throat was so tight, what she'd said was barely recognizable, but it didn't matter. She knew they understood before her dad said, "We love you, too."

And with those words, with such easy forgiveness, acceptance, and love, the emptiness inside her was finally filled. After six endless years, she'd found home again.

Chapter Twenty

Jake watched the three-way hug and swallowed hard. Cai's parents were holding on to her tightly and crying. His anchor was crying too. He couldn't see her face, but he felt it. Every now and then the good guys won, and he was glad this was one of those times.

The banging noises came to an abrupt halt.

"They're in," De Luca said, his voice low.

Jake nodded. Although he hated to interrupt the reunion—God knew the family was entitled to it—he had no choice. They couldn't get caught by the pirates. "Cai, we need to go."

No reaction. He didn't think she heard him. Keeping the other Quandem in his sights, Jake went to her and ran his free hand down the length of her braid. His tone was urgent when he said, "Sweetheart, we have to move. Now."

That penetrated. She straightened and took a step away, breaking the embrace. A trembling hand rose to wipe at her cheeks. Jake rubbed her back below her hair and addressed her parents. "Sir, ma'am, do you need to bring anything with you?"

Her father walked away from the door, and Jake bit back a curse. *Shit.* The last thing they needed was to waste time while her folks packed. He was pleasantly surprised, though, when the man returned in seconds.

"Everything we need is here," he said, holding up a small bag. "We gathered our things when we first saw our daughter."

Jake nodded, unable to speak. He found it amazing that they had such incredible faith in Cai. They'd seen her through a holounit and knew she'd free them. There didn't seem to be a question in their minds whether she'd succeed.

"It'll be safer to go through the secret passages," De Luca said. Jake raised an eyebrow. "Yes, you'll have to trust us to guide you," the man continued. "But believe me, you can. With these pirates taking over everything, I'd have to be a fool to betray you."

"Or a very loyal member of Elliot's entourage."

The man's eyes hardened. "I have no allegiance to Elliot. He's an employer and nothing more."

De Luca did have reason to dislike his boss. The man had coerced his way into sleeping with Nicole. Jake went with his gut. "Okay, lead the way."

The other couple went first, Jake followed; then it was Cai's parents, with Cai pulling up the rear. He'd prefer to have her in another position, but she was the only person he trusted at his back. She had the skills necessary for the job, he knew that, but damn, he hated having her at risk.

Despite being hidden, the secret passages were clean and well lit. The group traversed them easily and reached an outdoor exit in minutes. That was where the good news ended. From the monitoring system, Jake saw the pirates had completely overrun the grounds. "Is there another way out? One likely to have fewer people around?"

Shaking his head, De Luca said, "I doubt it. This was the area I'd targeted as being the least congested."

Jake studied the scene but didn't like the odds. Even if

the number of foes was cut in half, there would be too many men to get past. There were only six of them. Cai's parents were doctors, so it was unlikely that they had any training in melee. That left four, and looking at Nicole, he doubted she'd ever held a weapon. So they were down to three, and he wasn't sure how much he trusted De Luca, which meant it was him and Cai.

"Would a diversion help?" his anchor asked quietly.

"It would have to be something big enough to draw off all these pirates. Why, do you have something in mind?"

"I do," she said aloud, then switched to their link. *What if I made Elliot appear on the other side of the house? Wouldn't they charge over there to get him?*

Probably, but how are you going to manage that?

There are holos of the man in his system. I could project one through the units on the outside of the building.

Yes, the chaos might disguise the translucency of the image. . . . He didn't feel certain of that, though. In the bright light of day, it would be almost impossible to hide the faults.

I think I can make it more solid with a boost, but I've never tried before. Still, we have to do something, and if this doesn't work, we can think up plan B.

Are you going to be able to do this? Remember, I felt how tired you were while you were keeping up the security.

I'm okay, I promise.

If Cai was all right, they might as well give it a shot. He had to trust her judgment. *Go ahead.*

He felt her tapping energy, but kept his eyes on what was going on outside. If this worked, they'd have to move fast; the pirates wouldn't be fooled for long.

"De Luca," he said softly, not wanting to distract Cai. "Does your anchor have any combat training?" He wasn't surprised to see the other man shake his head. "Okay, mine does. We'll form a triangle. You get the front; Cai and I will flank you. We'll put Nicole and the Randolphs in the center so they'll have maximum protection. Do you know where the transport landed?"

"Yeah, once we get off the grounds it won't be far, but you'd better check to make sure they're still there."

Jake nodded. If he knew Gnat, he'd keep that flight crew from taking off until the last possible moment—but that might have passed. "Let me have your handheld," he said. De Luca handed it over without comment. Jake didn't speak, but quickly used an encrypted channel to contact his warrant officer and apprise him of the situation. "They're there, but won't be able to stay much longer," he said, pocketing the unit.

While he waited for his anchor to do her job, he briefed her parents on what he expected from them. "Ma'am, sir, when we exit, I want you to stay between me and your daughter. Will you be able run if you have to?"

He saw Mrs. Randolph's chin go up and had to smother a smile. Now he knew where Cai got that gesture from. "We won't slow you down," she said resolutely.

"No offense meant, ma'am, but you've been in captivity for six years. I don't know what kind of exercise you've had."

Mr. Randolph took his wife's hand and said, "Because of our imprisonment, we began a program to ensure we were in good shape—in case of a situation just like this. I promise you, we'll be able to run and keep up with the group."

"Thank you, sir." He looked past them to Cai and asked, "You about ready with that diversion? We've got to roll."

"I'm ready."

Cai strengthened their connection, and he felt an incredible surge of power as she created the illusion. Jake set his feet and did what he could to steady her mentally. He didn't know what had happened earlier, but there had been a change. Cai had gained a confidence she hadn't had before. That was something he planned to ask her about later.

A roar went up outside and became louder as it carried closer to their side of the house. The holomonitor showed the pirates running, weapons brandished above their heads, as they yelled their battle cries. Everyone, it seemed, wanted to be the one to kill Marchand Elliot. The few remaining mercenaries went in pursuit of the outlaws. In no time, the yard was deserted.

"Let's go," Jake ordered, as his anchor released the systems. "You okay, sweetheart?"

"I'm fine. It wasn't as much as earlier." Although she spoke cryptically, he knew she referred to the amount of energy.

They didn't run across the lawn, but they did move fast. The ground was littered with bodies, pirates, wreckers, and regular mercenaries. It must have been a hell of a fight.

When they reached the edge of the estate, Jake looked around and got his bearings. The area was mostly empty, but as they saw the UCE transport, that changed. There was a group of outlaws, maybe twenty of them, exchanging fire with his team. He knew that wouldn't last. Reinforcements had to be on the way. His men were in their protective vests and had donned their comm gear. Jake pulled the unit he'd taken from De Luca and alerted them that they were present and trying to get aboard.

Tactics changed as the team worked to open a safe path for them. Jake passed the other recep a second weapon. He had to trust the man now; there was no choice. "I want you shooting with both fryers. You too, Cai." She nodded and drew another one. Jake turned to the three remaining people. "Stay behind us and run directly to the boarding ramp. Don't hesitate; don't wait for us. Get on. We'll come in behind you. Got it?"

When he'd received acknowledgments from them, he let Gnat know what they were going to do and then pulled another neuron fryer from his cache of weapons. "Let's go."

The sudden addition of firepower from a different direction seemed to cause momentary confusion. It lasted long enough for them to reach the transport. And just as he'd known would happen, Nicole and Cai's parents hesitated. "Get on," he ordered. "Now!" They laid down a steady barrage, but it wouldn't work long, and he wanted the civilians out of the way ASAP.

They got on and he breathed a little easier. "You're next, Cai, and don't argue with me."

"I wouldn't dream of it," she shot back before obeying.

"Okay, De Luca, your turn." The engines had been running, but the pitch increased, and he knew the flight crew was ready.

He and his team had been through similar situations dozens of times before, so once everyone else was out of the way, they handled the boarding process with almost choreographed precision. Jake and Gnat were the last on, closing the ramp behind them and securing the door. "Go!" he ordered.

They were scrambling into seats and fastening harnesses as the transport made its vertical lift. He winced as the engines shrieked, but trusted the flight crew to get them out of there in one piece. The ship's guns fired steadily, keeping the pirates back, but despite that, he felt a slight jolt as they took a hit. He didn't breathe easier till they reached altitude and were off.

Jake searched for Cai, and found her sitting beside her parents. None of them looked the worse for wear. His men appeared to be okay too, as did the other Quandem. His eyes swept the interior of the transport until he located Maguire and the commander secured side by side at the back. Both remained unconscious, but he guessed the team would be safely back at Fort Powell and in the bar celebrating a successful conclusion to the op before those two woke up.

Gnat nodded toward De Luca and Nicole and asked,

"What's the deal with them?" Although the pair sat next to each other, they weren't talking, and the rift between them was plain to see.

Letting out a sigh, Jake explained the agreement he'd made, then added, "I want you to assign someone to keep an eye on them. The man is armed, I don't know about the woman, but we can't afford to trust them. Put someone on Maguire and Armstrong too. It's unlikely they'll wake up, but better to be safe."

Gnat didn't have to speak. A couple of gestures and the assignments were given. Gator and Kazoo drew the Quandem, and Inch got the prisoners. With those duties taken care of, Jake was able to relax. The transport reached cruising level and the ride evened out. Harnesses were unsnapped as his men shifted into more advantageous positions.

"Good thing you came up with them," Gnat said, indicating Maguire and the commander. "None of us found jack shit on the rafts we were checking. No one knew anything, no one had seen anything."

"Yeah." His eyes went to his anchor again. Damn, she was beautiful. "Apparently they weren't out on the public rafts, but had help from one of the big-time pirate lords."

"We never would have located them then, not if they were on a pirate lord's home ground."

"Probably not."

"Now, Tuck." His warrant officer's tone drew his attention away from Cai. "What the hell are those people doing with your woman?" The man's social polish hadn't improved after a few days on the Raft Cities.

"They're her parents."

His XO nodded. "I figured that out on my own. Captain Randolph looks a lot like her mother. What I was asking was, how did you pick them up? The Raft Cities aren't a vacation destination or anything."

"It's a long story. Why don't you wait for the debriefing so I only have to tell it once."

Jake didn't stay around for an answer. He unfastened his harness and headed for the tiny galley on the port side of the transport. There wouldn't be much, but he needed some water. He walked past Cai, but she was so busy talking to her parents that she didn't look up.

He knew things would change between them now. For years, he'd been able to reach for her anytime, anywhere. He'd been spoiled and had taken her presence for granted, no question about it. The fact that he'd thought she was a computer wasn't an excuse. From now on, though, he'd have to consider whether she was busy—whether she was doing something with her parents, or someone else, and didn't want to chat with him.

Maybe part of their relationship, her accessibility when he wasn't on a mission, her willingness to talk with him for hours about anything, was based on her loneliness. Instead of opening the chilling unit, he leaned his hips against the counter and closed his eyes. Now that she had her mom and dad, would she need him as anything except her recep?

Cai checked to make sure her parents' harnesses were securely fastened, then frantically scanned the cabin. She didn't relax until she saw Jake was aboard and that he didn't appear to have picked up any new injuries. Relieved, she dropped into the seat next to her mom and belted herself in.

After all this time, she had her parents back. She stared at them, trying to absorb the changes that had taken place over the years. They both looked older, but then she'd gotten older too. She saw her dad's lips move and knew he was talking, but with the loud booms from the ship's guns and the whine of the engines as the transport went vertical, she couldn't make out what he said. She shook her head and yelled, "What?"

He spoke again and she thought he was shouting now, but while she could hear his voice, the words were indistinct. She shook her head once more and held out both hands in a helpless gesture. Her dad nodded and subsided.

The sound from the engines concerned her. They didn't need a mechanical failure, not now, and if they went down, they were finished. The memory of the bodies she'd seen on their arrival on Malé flashed through her mind, and the thought of the men being mutilated and put on public display sickened her. She decided not to borrow trouble.

There were a million questions she wanted to ask her parents, a million things she wanted to share. She gripped her mom's hand tightly, reassuring herself that she was there, and scrutinized their faces once more. They'd forgiven her so easily, but she should have known they would. Their love for her had always been endless.

The transport lurched, and Cai realized it had been hit—not with a big weapon, but it reminded her that she was on a mission and she couldn't sit and smile sappily at her parents. She needed to do her job. She had to know what was going on at the estate and if a missile threat continued to exist.

She started to delve into TREKS to find out what was happening back at Casa Elliot, but the computer blocked her. A second attempt met with an even more urgent push by the system. In fact, TREKS began pulling away from the merge, putting space between them rapidly. Cai let her mind separate, not fighting to hold the connection, but she was confused.

The UCE transport reached altitude and began moving forward. She was thankful when the shriek mellowed into a normal hum, allowing conversation, but she barely noticed. She was busy trying to figure out what was going on with the supercomputer.

She didn't come up with any answers, but when the break was nearly complete, she felt something. Gripping her mom's hand more firmly, she rode out the reverberations jolting through her head.

"Are you all right?" The concern in her mom's voice was clear.

Her voice failed, so Cai nodded. She was, but only because the system had been almost completely disconnected from her when it had been destroyed. If she'd been fully immersed . . . Well, she didn't want to think about that.

There was no doubt TREKS had known something was wrong and it had done what it could to protect her. Cai had no answers, only speculation. It could have been a self-destruct mechanism buried inside the computer, or maybe one of Elliot's employees had orders not to let the system fall into enemy hands. The third option was that the pirates had demolished it in a fit of rage.

"Cai Margarete Randolph, you talk to me right now or I'm going to yell for a medkit, do you understand me?"

"Mom, I'm fine." Cai put aside her sense of loss. "You doctors," she teased, "always looking for a billable hour."

Her mom gazed pointedly at her, then down to their hands, and Cai relaxed her grasp. She hadn't realized how strongly she'd been clinging as she'd withstood the waves. "Sorry," she apologized, and laced her fingers in her lap.

Her parents shared a look that spoke volumes, but they didn't ask any questions. Instead her dad said easily, "You can't blame us, baby. We haven't had office hours in years."

She smiled, relieved that they weren't going to launch the parental inquisition. Yet. Before they could change their minds, she said, "I knew Elliot had you, but no one would believe me. I'm sorry it took me so long to find you."

"Everything happens for a reason," her dad said. "We had unlimited resources at our disposal for six years. Do you know how much we were able to accomplish with no interruptions?"

Cai laughed. That was her dad, always looking on the bright side. His unfailing optimism had made her insane at times, but she was so happy to see it again that tears filled her eyes. "God, I missed both of you so much," she barely choked out.

"We missed you too," her mom said thickly. There was a short pause; then she scolded, "What were you thinking to come to the Raft Cities? Do you know how dangerous that place is?"

"I had to get you out."

"You should have hired someone," Dad chided gently. "Or let these men do it. They look tough enough to handle themselves."

"Where did you learn to use a gun like that?" Mom chimed in.

"I'm an Army officer, Mom. I'm expected to know how to handle weapons." Her parents shared another glance. *Uh-oh.* This was news she should have broken more carefully, but she'd forgotten their views on the military and how the UCE used it.

"Sweetie, how did you wind up in the army?"

Cai wasn't fooled by the calm voice. Her mom wasn't happy. And they didn't know yet how old she'd been when she'd received her gold second-lieutenant's bar. That info would send them through the roof. She couldn't keep it from them, but this might not be the best time or place to fill them in.

"I was recruited. They had a systems project they wanted me to work on." That was kind of true. The transport hit cruising altitude and she heard the click of harnesses being unlatched. "Maybe we can discuss this in more depth later. In private."

"We *will* talk, Cai."

She didn't doubt it, not when her mom used that tone.

They might not approve, but she knew they'd come around. Her parents had always stood behind her even when they disagreed with her choices. Besides, it wasn't like the army would let her go, not with the expensive nanoprobes in her brain—and she didn't want to leave anyway. Not only did Jake need her, but where else would she have access to such incredibly powerful computers?

A thought suddenly occurred to her. "You're both okay, right?" Why hadn't she asked this question immediately? "Elliot didn't mistreat you?"

Their hesitation made her cringe. "Not physically," her dad said at last. "He did like psychological games, however."

That could be worse, could leave wounds that were difficult to heal. Cai bit her lip and leaned forward to study her parents. They both had closed expressions, and she knew they wouldn't say anything more. Reluctantly, she tabled her questions. Once they were back home, she'd give them time to get their feet under them, then see what she needed to do.

"Relax, baby; we're fine. Our biggest fear was that he'd get his hands on you. Do you have any idea how crazy it made us to be locked up once we knew you were under his nose?"

"I can guess," Cai said. She watched Jake stand and make his way toward her before looking back at her parents. "That's why you sent me to the academy—to protect me from Elliot. I figured that out after you disappeared." Cai got a good look at Jake's face when he neared and she tensed. He appeared weary. Her hope that he planned to join her didn't last long. He kept walking and disappeared into the galley.

The sound of a throat being cleared made her tear her eyes away from the back of the transport. "Would you like to tell us about that young man?" her mother asked dryly.

"No, not now," Cai said. Then she excused herself to follow Jake.

The fatigue she'd seen etching his features concerned her, and she needed to make sure he was all right. Her worry increased when she saw he had his eyes shut. She paused in the entry to the galley, then stepped inside and said, "Hi."

His gaze found her. "Hey, sweetheart. Are you okay?"

"I was going to ask you that question."

"I'm fine." She made a show of moving her attention to the side, where he'd been sliced, and he grimaced. "I told you, they're just scratches. When you knife fight, you have to expect to be cut. That's part of it."

"Yeah? Well, let me check out your *scratches*, cowboy." The galley was small, so it took only one more step to put her directly in front of him. She didn't have to remove his shirt to see the damage; she merely separated the slits. His arm didn't look bad. Although the cut was nearly four inches long, it was as shallow as he claimed. She reached for his side next. Same thing. Crouching down, she examined his leg, but the blade hadn't drawn blood. With a relieved sigh, she straightened.

"Satisfied?" he asked with irritating smugness.

"I was a few hours ago," she said suggestively. That wiped the smirk off his face and heated his gaze.

"Don't tease." The warning was clear.

"It's only teasing if I don't intend to follow through."

Their positions were reversed so fast, the half spin nearly left Cai dizzy. He pinned her against the counter he'd been leaning on, and she felt the tension of his muscles. His hands rested on the ledge to either side of her hips, and wrapping her arms around his waist, she smiled up at him. Now was the right time, she was certain. It took all her courage, more than she'd dreamed, but she said softly, "I love you, Jake."

If she weren't so anxious, she would have laughed over his dazed expression. When his face became unreadable, she bit her bottom lip. This wasn't a good sign. She pulled her arms back and wrapped them around her own waist.

"Sweetheart, adrenaline has a way of making everything seem more than it is. It's been a hard few days, a dangerous few days, and while you might think what you feel is real, it isn't. A week from now, you'll be wondering why you said this."

He was giving her an out. If she were smart, she'd take it, since it was clear he didn't feel the same way. But that would be gutless. She might go down in flames, but at least she'd be able to look at herself in the mirror and know she wasn't a coward. "It's not the situation. To be honest, I fell in love with you years ago, long before we ever met in person. But you don't have to worry. I won't make a pest of myself or bring this up again. What we had in the Raft Cities will stay there. We'll be able to work together, I promise."

Cai tried to push his arm aside so she could escape and lick her wounds in private, but he tightened his grip on the counter and wouldn't let go. She made herself meet his eyes.

His stare was so long and intense, bravery nearly deserted her. She still couldn't read anything from him, but at least she didn't see pity. That would have killed her. She hugged herself harder and hoped his scrutiny would end before she broke down and did something stupid.

"Are you sure?" Jake asked, his voice so guttural she barely understood what he said.

"Honestly, you don't have to worry that I'll—"

He covered her mouth with his, cutting off her assurances that she wouldn't do anything to make him uncomfortable. At first she didn't respond; then she decided, *What the hell*. If this was their last kiss, she wanted to enjoy it. By the time he raised his head, she was the one who felt dazed.

"Are you sure?" he demanded again.

Another chance to save face, but she wouldn't take this one either. "Yes, I'm sure," she said, her conviction coming through in those few words.

She got another kiss hot enough to scorch her neural implants. By the time Jake stopped, she didn't care if there were a dozen people on the other side of the wall. If he wanted to hoist her on the counter and have his way with her, she'd be more than happy to accommodate him.

"If you have any doubts, you'd better speak up now," he said. Cai could see how tightly he gripped the ledge behind her by the tautness of the muscles in his forearms. "You tell me you're sure one more time and I'm not letting you go."

"What?" Obviously the heat they'd generated had destroyed brain cells. He wasn't making sense.

"You heard me."

She huffed out a loud sigh and lifted her chin. "How many more times do you want me to say that I'm sure?" She paused to rein in her anger. It didn't help. "I love you, Jake Tucker, but right now you're really pissing me off."

He smiled suddenly. "Damn, Cai, you really know how to turn a guy's head with all your sweet talk."

Now she was more confused than ever, and insecurity returned. "Don't make fun of me, okay? Not about this."

That sobered him. Jake reached for her hands, unwinding them from her waist, and kept hold of her. "I'm not making fun of you, I swear." He gave her a squeeze and took a deep breath. "This isn't easy for me. I don't let people close, not really; you know that. But I thought you were a computer, so you were safe." His lips quirked up ruefully. "Only it turns out you're this beautiful woman who's kept me off balance since the minute you faced me down in Hell. Not safe at all."

It was hard not to say anything, but Cai bit her bottom lip and waited. She didn't want him to stop talking, and he might if she interrupted. He wasn't understating it when he said this was hard for him; she was sure it was. He was so contained.

"I did figure out some stuff fast, like the fact that I trusted you despite the omission. Other things took me longer."

Now he looked even more uncomfortable, and Cai found herself firming her grip on his hands, going from receiving support to giving it. What he'd said presented an interesting insight. He hadn't needed to develop any kind of emotional relationship with other people because he'd always had her for that. *Safe,* he'd called it. And it had been. A computer wouldn't expect anything from him; a human would.

When the silence dragged out, she took a chance and prompted him. "What other things?"

He tensed further, but he did answer. "Like, that I wanted more than friendship. I can't tell you how many times I started to kiss you or reach for you and had to remind myself you were my anchor, that I had to keep my hands to myself."

Physical stuff. This wasn't what she'd been hoping to hear.

"It took me even longer to figure out that what I felt was more than desire." He took a deep breath. "It wasn't until this afternoon while we were sitting in the office and I thought you might not forgive me that the truth finally hit. It answered a lot of questions. Why I've spent so much time talking with you over the years. Why, as soon as we met, I wanted to touch you, hold you. And, yeah, why making love with you was more powerful than anything I'd experienced before."

He freed his hands and cupped her face. "I'm in love with you too, Cai. Looking back, it happened years ago for me as well." She opened her mouth, but he shook his head. "I gave you a chance to run. Now it's too late, and you're stuck with me. But I warn you, it won't be easy to be involved with someone in Special Forces."

"That's why you kept giving me opportunities to recant what I said?" He nodded. "You're forgetting that I know what your job is like. I probably know better than anyone who hasn't been on the teams themselves. For five years I've been connected to you through training exercises, missions that went smoothly, ops that went to hell like the one before this, and everything in between. If I haven't run already, I'm not going to now."

Jake's grin was slow and easy. "That's true. You have been through it all with me. I had to be sure, though." His smile dimmed. "My next promotion should take me out of the field, except with the implant . . ." He let the thought trail off, but she knew what he was going to say.

"Except with the implant, the army may decide you're too valuable to pull and they'll have you continue as you are."

"Instead of three more years, it could be ten, even fifteen. Think you could handle being married to a man who might be gone more than he's home?" he asked nonchalantly.

Cai blinked. She wasn't fooled by the tone, not the way his fingers had tightened against her scalp, but she couldn't speak immediately. "You want to marry me?" she finally managed, her hands coming up to rest on his forearms.

"I want you tied to me in every way possible. Like I said before, you're stuck with me for good, so you may as well agree."

"Yeah, I can handle it—but what about our age difference? You've brought that up more than a few times."

"I also said that it's not the years; it's the miles. And you've gained a lot of experience on this operation. I'm not worried about a small gap. But if you have concerns over—"

"Jake"—she couldn't stop a slight smile—"I've never had

any concerns about it; five years is nothing. I would like a real proposal, though. Do you think you can manage that?"

"For you, yeah." He leaned closer. "Sweetheart, I know you can do better than me, but I love you. Will you marry me?"

That was her recep, straightforward and to the point. She could be every bit as direct. "Yes, I will. And there is no one better than you. I love you, Jake, for always."

The kiss was long, slow, leisurely, and he ended it much too soon. His hands went to her shoulders and he put her away from him. Although they were on opposite sides of the galley, it was small enough that only a couple of feet separated them. He stood staring at her, but he didn't say anything, and Cai was confused.

"I need to look at you," he explained. "I need to see you're safe. Too much happened today."

That, she could understand. There had been a couple of times she'd been concerned she was going to lose him, and Cai took the opportunity to check him out too. The scratches would be treated when they landed at Fort Powell, so she didn't worry over infection from unsanitary pirate knives. Other than those wounds, he appeared uninjured. *Thank God.*

She studied the rest of him. His clothes were streaked with dirt and blood, not all of it his. When she took in the stubble on his face that he hadn't had time to remove today and his hair falling onto his forehead, she had to admit that he looked almost as disreputable as the outlaws.

While she did enjoy watching Jake, she began getting restive after a couple of minutes. Her mind started to whirl, and she realized there was one question that bothered her. "What do you think happened to Elliot?" she asked quietly. "Did he escape, or was he killed?"

He shrugged. "Things fell apart fast today."

"So you think he's dead? That the pirates found him?"

She took a step forward, anxious over his answer. Her parents had just been rescued; she didn't want to worry about losing them again. And if that snake wanted those nanites bad enough . . .

With obvious reluctance, her recep shook his head. "No, I think he got away. The man might be an arrogant son of a bitch, but he's cunning. My guess is that he had at least half a dozen contingency plans in place so he could escape in a worst-case scenario. If I had to bet, I'd say he was off the Raft Cities before we ran into the other Quandem."

That was what she'd been afraid he would say. She gave the garnet stone on her ring a quick rub for reassurance. "So my parents are still at risk after all this?"

"I don't know." His expression became even graver. "Odds are they'll be safe. It looked like most, if not all, of Elliot's illegal activities were based on the Raft Cities. He lost a lot of assets and manpower today. It'll take him years to bring his operation back online, and even then it's unlikely ever to return to its former strength."

"You're right." The man had spent a long time building his criminal empire, and it would be difficult to re-create no matter how much money his legitimate concerns raked in. She took a deep breath and shoved the fear away. For today, at least, she'd simply enjoy having her mom and dad back. She'd think about the rest tomorrow.

Jake closed the remaining distance between them and pulled her back into his arms. "Don't worry so much. You're not in this alone anymore, sweetheart, I promise."

"I'm not alone," she said, the wonder she felt at that idea in her words. God, she'd been fighting solo for so long she'd forgotten there was anything else, but she had Jake now. Really had him. Not only as someone to talk to, but as someone who would help and encourage her through the difficult things in life. There was no way for her to explain to him what it meant to her, but she wanted him to know, so she sent it along their link. His arms tightened around her.

"Damn, Cai, I wish I'd known. I'd have been there for you."

She could see he was kicking himself, and she quickly said, "You were with me when I needed you most, and you'll be with me from now on. That's what's important."

His blue eyes were blazing with so many strong emotions, she wasn't able to read them all, but she easily picked out love. Tugging his head down to hers, she kissed him, wanting to show him how deep her feelings for him went. It didn't take long before they were on the edge of control. Jake pressed her into the counter, and she started thinking about how the height would be exactly right for the two of them to—

"Sir. Ma'am."

Jake broke off abruptly but didn't pull away. "What?" he growled, turning his head to glare at Gnat.

"The captain's parents are wondering about her. And before you give me shit about bad timing, Tuck, you should know that if it wasn't me, it was going to be Mom and Dad. I thought you'd both prefer me interrupting whatever was going on in here."

Cai took a deep breath and looked to her right. The XO's broad shoulders filled the doorway, his muscular arms folded across his chest, and his expression amused. Instead of becoming embarrassed, she had to fight the sappy grin that wanted to emerge. She was just so damn happy.

"Thanks, Gnat," she said, when she had the smile controlled. Her parents had always been protective, and it wouldn't have been the most propitious way to introduce them to the man she was going to marry.

"You're welcome, Captain." He waited a few beats. "Tuck, you could stand to learn some manners from your woman."

"Let me get this straight," her recep said, stepping back from her. "*You* think *I* need lessons in manners? The man who suggested to General Yardley's mother that her disposition would improve if she had a good f—shag?"

"Just goes to show how bad your deportment is." Gnat's grin split his face. "And I was right about the general's mother." He walked away before Cai could ask.

"You've got to tell me that story. Soon," she said.

"Yeah, it's a good one." He sighed and gave her a hopeful look. "I don't suppose we can stay in here, huh?"

"It won't be that bad. Besides, I'll protect you." Cai took his hand. "Come on, Jake. I want you to meet my mom and dad."

Epilogue

Cai wished the mission would just end. She tried not to be so impatient, but she couldn't help it. Her heel tapped against the footrest of the chair, an outward sign of her antsiness.

Three hours. What the hell was he doing?

She was worried. This was a long time for him to shut her out. Debriefings rarely lasted for such an extended period, not for an op like this one. Her eyes slid to the quire resting at her elbow and she squinted to decipher her writing. She should have let Jake make the notes. He could print legibly.

The guest list for their wedding seemed to be growing exponentially: Jake's team, associates of her parents, and officers who needed to be invited for political or career considerations. Their small, intimate ceremony was becoming a show of near-epic proportion.

Things had been a whirlwind since the transport landed at Fort Powell. Her parents had stayed with her only one night before going home. It hadn't been enough time, but they had to unravel the red tape surrounding their return from the dead. The UCE with its layers of bureaucracy was making it more difficult than it should be. Cai sighed and slumped back in her seat. At least she'd inherited everything and had held on to it for them so they had their house and their belongings.

Reluctantly she smiled as the first official meeting between her mom, dad, and Jake came to mind. Her poor recep had been so painfully courteous and polite as he'd tried to make a favorable impression.

On the other hand, her parents had been faintly challenging, suspicious of the warrior with their daughter. They'd heard him call her *sweetheart* several times during their rescue and had gone into watchdog mode. Mentioning the engagement had made them even more vigilant, but she was sure they'd come around. The only thing they wanted, after all, was for her to be happy.

She checked the time, but only ten minutes had passed. Cai sighed again. "Come on, Jake," she murmured.

While she waited, she turned on one of her screens, propped her feet up on the console, and flashed through some decorating ideas. Their quarters weren't going to be only a place to live; she was determined that the two of them were going to have a real home. She wanted something warm, something welcoming, something that encouraged relaxation and ease—especially when Jake came in wound up from a mission. There were so many different options, though, that her head was spinning in no time.

The comm unit chimed, and with a frown she reached out with her probe. Though it was a relief to be distracted from color schemes and accent pieces, she didn't feel like talking.

"Captain, did you do something to disengage your visual mode?" Yardley's voice boomed out at her. "This is the second time I've contacted you and received nothing on-screen."

"Sorry, sir. Let me see if I can get it working." Cai lowered her feet to the floor and tried to wipe the grin off her face. The general would have his suspicions confirmed if she weren't serious. When she had her expression under control, she activated the visual interface. "There must be some glitch," she said soberly. "I'll fix it after we're finished, sir."

And she would. It shouldn't take too long to set up her unit to automatically send an image if anyone from the general's office contacted her, yet remain inactive for everyone else. She hated the intrusion into her home and wasn't about to allow it.

Cai met the general's glare impassively until he shook his head and asked, "Is Tucker there?"

"No, sir."

Yardley glanced away for a second, then said, "I'm leaving for a meeting in ten minutes, so you'll have to pass the information along to him. We caught the officers who drugged his extraction team. They're still being questioned, so we don't have a lot of details yet, but the evidence is solid."

She blinked, stunned by how quickly they'd been found. "Are these the people responsible for the deaths of Jake's men?"

"We're not sure, but if not, we'll have those names by the time the interrogation ends. That, I promise you."

This should relieve Jake, at least a bit. He'd been anxious about going off on a mission and leaving her unprotected. Her recep had issued so many instructions on how to stay safe while he was away that she'd been ready to shove him bodily out the door. It wasn't that she didn't appreciate his concern—she knew it came from love—but she wasn't an idiot.

"Have they confessed? Are they tied to the Shadow—"

"I'm not at liberty to say more, Captain, but I thought Tucker deserved to know that we're making progress locating those guilty of setting up his team."

"Thank you, sir. I know he'll welcome the news. I don't suppose this means the level of danger has gone down, does it?"

"No, Randolph, I'm sorry. Both you and Tucker should still be careful." There was a murmur she couldn't make out; then the general said, "I have to leave. If I feel there's anything else either of you needs to know, I'll be in touch."

Once the viewer was off, Cai sighed and leaned back. Damn, she wanted Jake out of harm's way, but Captain Maguire's arrest had made the world situation more precarious. There had been uprisings in protest and vows to free her no matter the cost.

Cai was aware that the woman was being held at Fort Powell, but didn't know exactly where and she didn't know where Commander Armstrong was either. She could find out, it would only take a little hacking, but she'd opted to remain ignorant. It was tempting to take a quick peek, but if anyone found out, she'd be at risk. And if she were in danger, Jake's protectiveness would have him right there with her. Still, if she were careful enough, no one would know she'd ever been in the files.

Slouching farther in her chair, she put her feet back on the console. There was one thing she had kept up on. Nicole and Tony were being detained by the army. The debate raged on about what to do with them, but Cai suspected they'd be drafted into the Quandem Project. Tony had been a marine in a reconnaissance unit, and with his experience he could easily be used. If they could trust him.

Her lips twitched. She couldn't help but wonder what Nicole's reaction would be to military training. The woman was so polished that Cai couldn't visualize her on the obstacle course. And firing a weapon? She laughed quietly.

The sound of her door opening wiped the smile off her face, and she scrambled to her feet to face the threat head-on.

"Jake Tucker," she complained mildly as she crossed the

room. "You know you need to warn me before you walk in. I'm not used to living with you yet."

"Sorry, sweetheart." He pulled her into his arms, kissed her long and slow, and then held her. "We could put your adrenaline surge to good use, though."

Cai tipped her head back and grinned. "I'm counting on that, cowboy." The smile disappeared. "But first I have to tell you something." She repeated what General Yardley had said.

Jake's hold tightened. She read his turmoil and rubbed his nape, trying to offer comfort. "My men deserve justice."

"They'll get it. The UCE wants the traitors as much as you do." Maybe even more, although she didn't share that thought. Her recep needed redress for the deaths; President Beauchamp and his cronies were becoming desperate to hang on to power.

She felt him take a deep breath and start to lock down his emotions. He called it compartmentalizing, and Cai knew this topic of conversation was finished for now. He'd be better off talking things through, but he was improving about sharing the bad stuff with her. One small step at a time, she reminded herself. Neither she nor Jake was going to change overnight.

"Why did you block me through the debriefing?" she asked softly after he'd been quiet for a while. "You never have before. And why did it last so long?"

He kissed her again. "I blocked you," he explained when he lifted his head, "because you were giving me a hard-on. I know, I know," he said quickly when she opened her mouth to protest, "you weren't doing anything. Didn't matter. All I could think about every time our minds brushed was taking you to bed."

"And the three-hour-plus debriefing?"

That earned her a grimace and a reluctant admission. "It wasn't only debriefing." She let the silence stretch until he felt compelled to explain. "I had my first session with a counselor about my nightmares."

"Jake?" He couldn't have surprised her more.

"I won't chance hurting you," he said intently. "And if that means spilling my guts to a f—freaking stranger, then I'll do it. I still break out in a cold sweat when I remember waking up and finding my hand at your throat."

She lightly stroked the back of his neck once more. "I love you."

That worked. The tension left his body. "I love you too, Cai. The feeling, it's so enormous, it scares me sometimes."

"Me too," she agreed, but she'd lost interest in talking. Her mind had moved to more lascivious thoughts, and she sent them to his recep. She felt Jake growing hard against her, and the two days without him suddenly seemed like an eternity. When he picked her up and headed for the bedroom, she smiled. He put her on the bed and covered her with his body.

You know, she told him, *you worried about this Special Forces thing for nothing. About being gone all the time.*

I did?

Yeah, think of all the great welcome-home sex we'll get to have.

He gave her a slow, wolfish grin, and then he set out to prove how good it could be.